THE FAMILY MAN

DCI JOHN DRAKE
BOOK 1

M. R. ARMITAGE

zb
zenarch books

For my parents,
Richard and Rosemary

PROLOGUE
OCTOBER 1998

The Man hunkered down against the base of the oak tree, its huge trunk straddling the border between the substantial garden and the forest beyond. It was a position from which he had observed his subject many times for the weeks and months leading up to this moment. A rudimentary wire fence was all that stood between him and his 'Purpose.'

Amidst the intensity of the night's storm, he watched, tasting the rain on his lips while it pelted his waxed raincoat. The tree's branches and a few shrubs afforded him only the most basic cover. But the Man didn't pay the weather much mind. Instead, he patiently maintained his vigil, eyes narrowing only a fraction more while he looked out into the darkness beyond. The pattering of raindrops on wax was simply another instrument in the cacophony of wind, rain and distant thunder.

Absently, he worked the knuckles on each hand, each joint returning a loud click while he traced the familiar floor plan of the Georgian house out in his mind's eye. He recalled every detail, no matter how small: the ostentatious living rooms, the fireplaces, the grand dining room that looked out onto the garden beyond, the shutters at every window, closed now, barring one upstairs in the master bedroom, which gaped like an open wound. He recalled the photos and trinket boxes arranged on the woman's dresser, the toys in the children's rooms, even the old network of servants' bells which ran through the house like veins. To the rear, a large, decked balcony protruded from the master bedroom. This feature had served as his point of entry these past few months, thanks in part to a trellis trailing up its side, a thick rambling rose threading its way through every nook and cranny.

A flash of lightning peeled across the sky, lighting up the property and gifting him a fleeting glimpse of what lay ahead. If the occupants had been peering out, he would have been visible, if only for a second.

But they did not look out. They did not see him.

A huge rumble of thunder followed sooner than he expected, causing him to flinch despite himself. He growled, irritated at his lack of composure. He knew he needed to be in control for what he was about to do.

Another light followed, but this one was different. This time, it was exactly what he wanted, the glow in the bedroom contrasting starkly with the darkness.

The Man's eyes locked on to these first signs of life. His hands trembled slightly while he reached for the binoculars at his side. He trained them on the light, wiping away drops from the lenses to ensure nothing obscured his vision. As he watched for the first signs of movement, his tongue worked the point of a canine.

Moments later, the young mother, whose delicate features had drawn his attention all those months ago, came into view. Her figure was framed by the window, the pose reminiscent of the many photographs he'd taken. He placed her in her early thirties, her days spent alone caring for her two offspring while the husband devoted his to work, away for weeks at a time. But she'd not been alone, not really. The Man had been there, studying her, night after night.

He leered at her while she brushed her waist-length brown hair. Judging by the photos on her dresser, she'd worn it at that length since her late teens. He liked that.

Lightning tore across the sky once more, the light flashing on the lenses of his binoculars and blinding him. Again, had the woman been paying attention, she could have seen the reflected glint of light. But she did not. He chuckled to himself while he watched her, bemused at the continued display of ignorance.

It pleased him to see his woman was not alone. Her husband, a dark-haired man in his forties, towered over her as he came up behind the mere slip of a girl. He wrapped his arms around her, nuzzling her neck while they laughed and joked.

Soon after, as if on cue from a stage manager, the couple's little girl entered the scene and started tugging at her father's trouser leg. Their youngest also made an appearance, a boy, no older than three, pushing at his sister while they vied for their father's attention.

'Excellent...' the Man murmured, a wicked smile forming while he stowed away the binoculars, his time in the shadows finally at an end.

The father paced over to the window and closed the shutters. His family was off-limits, if only for a few minutes more.

1

SEPTEMBER 2018

Detective Chief Inspector John Drake opened the window in his study, allowing an autumnal morning breeze to flow in. He hoped it would go some way to removing the stuffy atmosphere that had settled in the room since he'd been away. He closed his eyes and breathed in the cool air, feeling a semblance of calm he hadn't felt for several months.

It was good to be home. Home to his family, his wife Rebecca and daughter Eva, for the last sixteen years. Home to happy memories, but also to many uncomfortable ones, brought about by his work and agonised over in his corner of the house. Even so, being among familiar surroundings comforted him and largely outweighed the more unpleasant memories it conjured.

The room itself was small but functional, and packed to the rafters with journals and books dealing in psychology and criminology, while copies of case files in old manilla folders sat in more or less orderly piles on the floor. He kept the photos locked away, for the sake of his family. But he couldn't keep them locked out of his mind, no matter how hard he tried. The acts of depravity were forever seared into his consciousness.

Moving back from the window, he knocked a pile of print-outs with his foot, just managing to steady them before they keeled over. He spent a moment carefully rebalancing them before stepping around. There was a comfort to be had in his organised chaos.

He stood amidst the quiet of the room, running his fingers over the corner of the desk and tracing a series of smeared paths in the dust that had gathered in his absence.

When they'd moved in all those years ago, he'd ensured the desk had been placed to look out towards Barndon Forest. The way in which the oak, chestnut and birch trees swayed in the breeze soothed his mind and provided a natural barrier between him and Barndon village – a place he actively despised these days. Though technically the house had a Barndon address due to its location on the county lines of Oxfordshire and Berkshire, Drake had chosen never to venture into Barndon outside of work necessities. The quiet village had left a sour taste in his mouth from a case long ago, and he preferred not to frequent the place unless he had to.

Drake shook the thoughts of Barndon from his mind before sitting down with a satisfied sigh in his old green Chesterfield desk chair. He leant back, causing the chair to emit a familiar pained creak. He noted the looseness of the frame and made a mental note to get it fixed; the same mental note he had made many times before. In all fairness to the chair, he was not the svelte young man he was when he bought it all those years ago, but nor was he out of shape. One sergeant had referred to it as 'dad bod'. He took it as a compliment.

He picked up the silver-framed family photograph on his desk and smiled. It was one of his favourite photos of the family together. His smile turned to a frown at the face of his younger self smiling back. Time had not been kind to him in the way it had been to the rest of his family. Becca still looked as radiant as the day the photo had been taken; she'd always stood out from the crowd with her shoulder-length black hair and subtle grey-blue eyes. Her beaming smile still had the ability to take his breath away.

Drake, on the other hand, had been close to entering middle age when it was taken, already looking a few years beyond that hurdle, if truth be told. The photo presented a powerfully-built man with a pale complexion and deep-set blue eyes, his short brown hair greying at the temples of his slightly hawkish face. Coupled with the frown lines and unshaven face, he thought the touch of grey gave him a wise appearance. But his smile for the camera belied the horrors he had witnessed in the preceding years.

He'd developed a more haggard appearance since then; a stereotype of a detective, his eyes were sunken, the frown lines deeper and the hair considerably greyer. The stress of the last few months without his family had robbed his skin of what little colour it had held, giving him a faint but discernible pallor.

Drake's smile returned as he looked at his daughter, Eva. Aged two at the time, she sat on his knee with a cheeky look in her deep-brown eyes, the one physical attribute she had inherited from him rather than Becca. A mop of untamed black hair tickled the younger John Drake's nose. Those were happy times.

A lot had changed in twelve years.

* * *

Since his last argument with Becca, his enforced time apart from his family had driven him to the brink of depression. The doubts, the concerns and the hindsight; all had eaten away at him when he was alone at night in his sparse bedsit in Putney, London, without his work to distract him. What if he hadn't gone into the station that one evening after they'd argued? What if he'd just picked Eva up from school on one of the many times he said he would?

So many examples, so many 'what ifs' that served only to increase his guilt. The irony was that it had been the work which kept him going during this period. He'd done what he did best and thrown himself into his caseload.

His role as Detective Chief Inspector in the SMT, the Specialist Murder Team, allowed him to take a desk at whatever station made sense for his current case. It meant he'd been primarily working out of Wandsworth police station during this period. Not that he'd been working his usual run of cases, anyway; his boss, Detective Chief Superintendent Laura Miller, had seen to that when he confided in her about his family troubles. Lumping him into doing some regular detective work had been a kindness in some ways. Not so much in others.

Recent months had seen him working on a straightforward dockland gang murder and the inevitable reprisal resulting from it. He'd even been able to follow up that particular treat with a case back near Barndon. But still, he'd respected Becca's wishes and kept his distance.

Then one evening, she'd rung out of the blue.

'John.'

'Becca, are you all right? Is Eva all right?' He'd longed for her call, but its suddenness worried him.

'Yes, yes, we're fine. Eva is fine. Don't worry.'

'Okay,' he said, the relief clear in his voice.

'It's just that... Eva misses you. *I* miss you; I miss us.'

'Becca, I—'

'John, just come back. We need to try. There's no point in keeping this artificial distance any longer. What good is it doing? We need to focus on us and how we move forward as a family. We need to make this work.'

Could he do it? He still spent every waking hour working his current caseload, despite everything. But if he could somehow find a balance between his family and his work...

'Okay. I'll get my things together and be over tomorrow.'

'Can you come now?'

The first test. He realised that this was a point where he had to do something demonstrable. Offer *something*. He pursed his lips. 'Give me a couple of hours to collect my things and settle up with the landlord.'

'You're not at work?'

'No – no, I've finished for the day,' he lied. He was sitting at his desk, a case file open in front of him. He hated himself for it.

'Great, Eva will be so happy to see you.'

'Me too ... both of you.'

'Don't be too late.'

'I won't. I'll be a couple of hours. I love you.'

'See you soon.'

Drake would have been a lousy detective if he hadn't noted the lack of reciprocation.

He'd closed the case file after ending the call. Sitting in silence in his corner of the office, he'd acknowledged to himself that things had to change. His work couldn't be the all-consuming whole it had been, or there would be no second chance. Becca would not stand for it, would not *accept* it again. But there was always that pull, that adrenaline rush upon receiving a call which kept pulling him back in, compelling him.

* * *

He'd hurried back to the flat, shoving his clothes and other items into a single duffel bag and his battered leather briefcase. The landlord had been understanding of the short notice and had even left an open invitation to him returning.

'You know, should your circumstances change.'

It wouldn't come to that, Drake swore to himself. He'd seen the back of that place. At least, he hoped he had.

When he'd pulled up in front of his home a few hours later, he'd taken the conscious decision to ring the doorbell rather than use the key. Eva had answered, greeting him with a huge smile and an enormous hug. Becca had maintained a neutral distance by the stair banister, her hand held up in greeting.

Serious talking would be required, but that evening, they had put that aside and concentrated on being a family. When it was time to go to bed, Drake had gone to sleep in the spare room without question.

'John? Are you okay up there? Are you coming down for breakfast?' Becca called up to him the following morning.

'I'll be down in just a minute.' Drake set down the picture and got up from the chair with a creak.

He surveyed the room one last time.

This time, it would be different. *He'd* be different.

2

The car crunched over the pothole, causing a grimacing Ben Whitman to take a nervous glance at his wife in the passenger's seat. When he saw the impact hadn't woken Andrea, the sudden knot in his chest released as he breathed out quietly. She was still as serene as when she'd first fallen asleep, her long black hair affording her some cushioning against the seatbelt.

He was ashamed; his wife shouldn't be having this effect on him. He was just surprised that she had fallen asleep on the journey, let alone not woken up at all on the long drive down to Barndon, such was her mood that morning.

Best not to dwell on it. He drummed the steering wheel lightly with his fingers while keeping the car at a steady pace. Cars inched past in the next lane and flew past in the third as they made their way down the motorway. There was no rush, and he was happy to take his time. However, the incident that morning had caused Ben to be on edge. On more than one occasion, he had even braced for impact upon seeing a pothole or bump.

Ben let out a sigh and muttered to himself. 'Come on, man. Pull yourself together.'

He knew he shouldn't be so sensitive; this was the reality of their relationship now, there was nothing out of the ordinary.

Or was there?

She *had* been very skittish of late, and more than a little on edge. Her long-standing issues more apparent, more profound. She seemed... well... *different*. There was no other way to say it.

According to Andrea, her troubles had been an infrequent presence since she was a teenager. But since they'd met, and in particular since they got married and had Cari, the headaches and "episodes" had become more frequent and more intense.

Since then, numerous doctors' visits had resulted in diagnoses of mental health disorders ranging from bipolar to schizophrenia, with sporadic attempts to manage the symptoms through medication. But both Ben and Andrea had been reluctant to explore matters further, fearing the possibility of her being institutionalised, a worry her mother had apparently shared when Andrea was growing up. In any event, the medication she had been prescribed only seemed to make her symptoms worse.

Ben always feared the early telltale signs of confusion. Andrea wouldn't understand who she was, losing her connection to Ben and their daughter. She would think strangers were in her home and seem to become a different person.

Ultimately, these symptoms would escalate into full-blown episode territory that would force her to become bedridden for days at a time, her headaches almost crippling in their ferocity. He'd been witness to her writhing in bed from the pain, her fingers gripping the bed in such intense agony that it was a miracle they didn't snap.

Her silent episodes were even worse; in these, she was effectively catatonic, staring into space, her eyes non-responsive. Ben panicked that she was gone, that she'd never return to him. At least with the more obvious pain she suffered, he knew she was still *there*, however selfish that made him feel.

His eyes dropped in shame at the thought.

He knew their unwillingness to push for more conclusive tests could be interpreted as dangerous by some. But they were terrified at the prospect of her being poked and prodded for eternity in some hospital somewhere, medicated to her eyeballs. After all, she could still go months without an episode. That meant there was still hope, right?

Ben was struggling with his own feelings of guilt and resentment, but he knew his emotions had to be put to one side. Andrea was his wife, and a wonderful mother to Cari. For her daughter's sake, she always tried to hide what she was going through and have a smile on her face. He figured she was probably overcompensating because of her terrible upbringing, but who could blame her? From what she'd told him, her long-deceased mother had abused her and treated her with utter contempt.

Ben's eyes widened as yet another pothole – deeper this time – came up out of nowhere on the passenger's side. There was no opportunity to avoid it, and the tyre crunched in deep.

'Uh... mmm?' came the sound from the passenger's seat.

He winced.

3

Ben watched as Andrea roused from her nap. She unfurled from the comfort of the seatbelt and stretched like a contented cat. Her elbows clicked as she stretched her arms, her brown woollen jumper sliding down to reveal her thin, bony wrists. Deep, intelligent brown eyes peered out from beneath her nest of hair. A red mark was present on her face when she turned to him, her hair not having quite shielded her from the strap after all.

'Hey,' she said, sleep heavy in her voice. She followed up the greeting with a loud, gaping yawn. The sight and sound caused Ben to mirror her yawn, along with their unusually quiet teenage daughter in the backseat.

'Thanks for that,' he said, laughing, blinking away the wetness that had gathered at the corners of his eyes. 'How we doing?'

She peered over at him. 'I could ask you the same thing. How long was I out for?'

'A few hours... most of the journey, in fact. Looks like you needed it though. We're only a few miles out, according to the satnav.'

'Woo-hoo!' A sarcastic cheer sprung up from the backseat.

'All right, young lady. That's enough of that, thank you.' Andrea frowned.

'Sorry.' Cari replied, not sounding particularly apologetic.

'So, I missed most of the motorway?' Andrea turned her attention back to Ben. 'Perhaps I need to sleep in cars more often. Maybe I'll get a full night's rest for once.' She smiled, amused at the discovery.

Ben reciprocated, then focused back on the road. 'So, how *are* you feeling? I thought for a minute there we might have had to delay the journey awhile.' Inside, he was willing for a positive response, begging for it.

'Seriously, I'm fine. It was just a momentary thing – you know how it is. I'm excited. This is a new beginning for all of us. New house, new town, new people.' She looked over at him again. 'New school, new beginnings. Everything's new. Let's focus on that and focus on me later, okay?'

He felt the tightness within him release a little. She was right. This was a new beginning for all of them; for Andrea, for him, and definitely for Cari.

His heart dropped when he thought of his little girl. He couldn't help but dwell on the things that must have happened to her away from his protective gaze. The incidents that he'd not been able to shield her from. Things that must have occurred while he'd been sat behind a desk or in a meeting room, some inconsequential meeting playing out before him or on a computer screen, all while his daughter needed his help. It had left him with a feeling of vulnerability and failure.

But it was a reality – school had been tough for Cari, and was one of the primary reasons for their impending move. His beautiful daughter's Turkish and English heritage had been enough to attract attention from the bullies at her secondary school. Despite her hard-nosed exterior, their behaviour had clearly affected her, but his and Andrea's concerns had been brushed off with comments about "kids being kids".

It was a strange stance for a school to take in this day and age, though Ben supposed Cari did call attention to herself, simply by being different. She wasn't keen on "mainstream" music, as she called it. She didn't conform to social norms in how she dressed. Typical of the usual stereotypes for young teenagers, he'd figured. Irrespective of the issues and despite her naysayers, Ben and Andrea were proud of their daughter for not conforming. Quite the little anarchist.

Ben smiled. 'Okay, well... if you're sure, then I'm happy.'

'Good.'

Cari emerged between the two front seats of the car, a mass of black hair pointing in his direction. One earphone blared out indecipherable white noise as it dangled over her black t-shirt. Her hair was like her mum's, as were her dark brown eyes. He'd always been secretly disappointed about her lack of resemblance to him, other than her lighter skin tone, but she was a beautiful girl and that made him proud. And much to his dismay, she had also recently discovered makeup. He didn't want to lose his little girl.

'Cari, come on, put your seatbelt back on.'

Cari ignored him and poked his shoulder, a look of concern on her face. 'Dad, will we have Wi-Fi? I want to be able to talk to my friends properly. I don't have much credit left on my phone.'

'Yes, don't worry about it. It'll be up in a few days,' he replied, keeping his attention on the road.

'A few days!' She looked crestfallen beneath her hair.

'Yes, you'll just have to use the landline until then.'

'The landline! This isn't the nineties. It's not the same!'

'Well, that's how it is, Cari. I'm not sure what more I can say on the matter.'

'Hmph!' She dropped back into her seat with a thump and crossed her arms.

'Do we at least have TV?'

Ben's eyes rolled.

'Yes, Cari, we have TV.'

This appeared to satisfy Cari. She went quiet, and they sat in silence for a time.

At the junction, Ben took the road signposted to 'Barndon', while Andrea started humming to herself. Ben couldn't make out a particular tune, but she sounded restful, content even. The edgy feelings from earlier had almost melted away.

He allowed himself to feel happy.

'When do you start work again? It's a bit later than I thought, right?' Andrea asked, breaking the relative silence and jolting him out of autopilot.

'Yes, a whole week. So, we should look at sorting out the furniture and the like before then. Maybe even some wallpaper stripping or painting – and not the kind you're used to doing with an easel,' he said with a wink. 'I know you like to be settled. The removals lorry should be with us within an hour or so, meaning we can get cracking whenever we fancy, if you're feeling up to it?'

'I'll be fine. Don't worry, honey. It must have just been a build-up of nerves before we got going.'

'Okay.'

He sighed at the thought of work as they drove through a neighbouring village. He didn't want to go back to his day job; a programme manager in an IT Telecoms company hadn't been where he'd wanted or expected to be spending most of his waking hours. The move to Barndon had meant little more than working at a new office. He had negotiated several days a week where he could work from home, but the fresh start Andrea spoke of didn't *quite* apply for him in the same way. Ben didn't relish the thought of journeying back up north occasionally. The prospect of a cheap hotel coupled with cheap food and bugger all company expenses was hardly inviting.

Mostly, though, it was the thought of leaving Andrea and Cari alone that gave him an uneasy feeling. The idea of them knocking around in that house without him for days at a time worried him. Perhaps when everyone had settled, he'd look for another job.

The satnav chimed. *In 100 yards, take the next left.*

'Nearly there,' Ben said.

'Great.' Andrea smiled, putting her hand on Ben's leg and giving it a squeeze.

He returned a half-hearted smile, his chest tightening again. The squeeze had been much harder than necessary.

4

'Mum!' Eva shouted from the living room.

'Yes?' Becca answered from the kitchen, her voice the definition of calm. She rolled her eyes and smiled at Drake before continuing with the dishes. He reciprocated and continued drying a breakfast bowl, both waiting in anticipation of Eva's usual question.

Drying duties had always fallen to him. Becca didn't trust him to get everything perfectly clean. He chose not to point out the grease spot he could see on the wet plate awaiting him on the dryer.

Eva stomped past the doorway. 'Have you seen my school bag anywhere?'

'It's where you left it ... by the stairs.'

The sounds of rummaging in a distant cupboard came thick and fast, followed soon after by more stomping. His daughter was working her way through every conceivable location, barring the obvious.

'I can assure you, it's not!'

'Well, I saw it right there a moment ago, so unless I'm imagining things, you'd better take a look.'

The teenager stormed into the hallway towards the stairs where her bag lay, the main zip compartment half open with the heel of a shoe sticking out. It was a sorry-looking thing, the start of a tear in the corner near the shoulder strap, likely created from the months of misuse and casual abandonment it had been subjected to since replacing the last one.

Eva's black hair hung in her eyes as she bent down to retrieve the bag.

'Thanks,' she said, the sentiment unconvincing, though Drake thought he noticed a slight hint of remorse at her previous surliness. It was another typical school day with Eva, and he'd missed it terribly. The few weeks since his return had followed a familiar pattern, but he'd cherished every second.

'Have you made sure you have everything you need in there for today?' Becca said, the implication clear as day.

'Yes, Mum.'

'Even your PE kit?'

'Shit.'

'Eva! You know not to use those words in this house.'

'But—'

Becca raised an eyebrow. '*Eva*—'

'Yes, Mum. I'm sorry, okay?'

The whirlwind left the hallway, dragging her bag with her to the back room where the clothes horse stood, her PE kit ready and waiting. Drake and Becca had toyed with the idea of not doing these things for her one day to see what would happen, and thought better of it. They valued their sanity.

Becca dried her hands, took an exaggerated deep breath, and closed her eyes for a moment. Exhaling, she made her way over to the hallway just before Eva returned. Drake followed.

'That's everything, right?' Becca asked.

'I think so.'

'Well, last chance before your dad needs to set off. You still want a lift?'

Eva screwed up her face and attempted to recall what her day required of her. 'Yep! Got it all. And of course, I do.'

Drake laughed. 'Such a daddy's girl.'

'You know it.' Eva smiled.

He pulled on his woollen charcoal trench coat and picked up his old briefcase, while Eva hefted her school bag on to her shoulders. His wife unlatched the door, arching her arm for their daughter to go under.

The sound of birds chirping and the rustling of the nearby trees greeted them, a cool breeze following close behind. The sun shone golden on the well-tended front garden; the small maple tree they'd planted in the centre over a decade ago was shedding its leaves, a semi-orderly pile appearing beneath it.

Drake gave Becca's shoulder a gentle squeeze and kissed her temple. 'Thank you for breakfast.'

She gave him a sideways glance before finally saying the words he'd wanted to hear for months. 'Love you,' she whispered. His heart nearly leapt out of his chest.

Eva was already halfway down the path leading to the gate before she stopped in her tracks and turned. 'Love you, Mum,' she called back towards the house.

Becca raised her hand in send-off.

'Come on, you.' He swung the briefcase in Eva's direction, motioning her onward down the last few steps of the path while he followed close behind.

* * *

It wasn't often that Drake drove to London. The train and underground had been his usual routine before the forced separation. He'd often used peak-time and rush-hour as a reason for staying late so he could avoid "the rush". But since returning home, he'd taken to driving when he expected to get away a little earlier. This seemed to be happening more often than not these days, since they had moved him off the big cases his team had been working on. This "distancing" was not typically done for so long, but DCS Miller still appeared keen on giving him a little slack because of his situation.

The pair of them had made a good team over the years; firstly as peers, then Miller had become his commanding officer once they'd moved to SMT. She'd opted on keeping Drake on an even keel rather than applying unnecessary pressure while he got himself sorted. He'd noted the concern and loyalty expressed and appreciated it a lot, though he knew SMT could ill-afford to lose his experience in the long term. He would look to return the gesture in future should the need arise.

Drake tapped the steering wheel while they sat in the usual school-run traffic. Leaves had fallen from the trees that lined the street, amassing on the pavements and roadside. Young children attending the nearby primary school were running along, kicking at them and bunching them up in their hands, causing chaos in the crowds from the ensuing flurries. The parents who had braved the weather on foot kept a distance, frowning at their children dirtying themselves before they'd even reached the school gates.

'Dad, are you on any big cases at the moment?' Eva asked. 'Going to catch any big bad guys today?'

'Not today. And even if I was, I couldn't discuss that with you,' Drake replied, turning down the radio. 'You know that. My job is not a pleasant one, and I'd prefer to keep you from it.'

'I'm not a kid!' she retorted. 'I know you keep crime scene photos and stuff locked away in your study.'

'Eva ...' Drake hesitated. He didn't want to get into an argument just before school, not with the traffic indicating they'd be sitting there for some time. 'It's because I don't want to scare or worry you. Some things I see and deal with are not meant for anyone of any age to see – I don't even let your mum in on many of the details. It's because I care for you, not because I like being secretive or keeping things from you.'

She seemed placated, at least for the time being.

They sat in silence while Drake navigated the traffic as best he could. For all the progress they were making, he could probably have pulled over and walked, but he knew Eva wouldn't want her dad escorting her to the gate.

'I suppose that's that, then,' she said suddenly. 'I'm sorry, Dad.' Feeling this was an unsatisfactory conclusion, Drake offered an olive branch.

'All I can say is, since I've been back, I've focused on the "gentler" side of the job more,' he told her. 'Paperwork and such like – you've liked me picking you up from school sometimes, right? That's one of the things I couldn't do in these big cases. I want to be straight with you when I can, Eva. You know I do my best to speak to you as an adult, don't you?'

'Yes, Dad.'

'You'll always be my little girl though,' he said, smirking and ruffling her hair with his bear-like hands.

'Dad!' She swatted at him while wriggling in the car seat.

'Okay, okay.'

He spotted a car pulling away by the gate and he jumped into the space before anyone else got a chance.

'Here we are. Have a good day, little lady.'

'You too.'

She opened the door, and with that she was gone, vanishing into the throng.

5

Come on, Andrea. You can do this, I murmured, though the words may have been out loud. Ben said I had a habit of talking to myself. But I can't say I'd noticed it much before now.

I shivered as I walked. He'd warned me to wrap up warm, as the forecast was for bad weather. But I'd only remembered his saying so – and that I was supposed to be doing some food shopping – after I had been wandering in the opposite direction for a good while. I'd since borne the brunt of a light rain shower too, for my sins – without a coat, of course.

Arriving at a steep set of tree-lined steps, I looked up toward their summit, the throbbing in the back of my skull getting progressively worse. The blustery wind whipped damp hair across my face as I stood staring at the sky, overcast and miserable amidst the tunnel of trees. The sun struggled to push through the oppressive clouds, and it gave me a strong feeling of claustrophobia, the ominous outlook reflecting my unease since we'd moved into our new home.

Shaking free of the moment, I gripped the railing, and willed myself up the muddied steps. Each one took more effort than it should have, and I felt an irrational sense of relief when I reached the top. The oppressive claustrophobia left me instantly at the sight of the swathe of parkland opening out ahead. A winding gravel path carved its way through a batch of trees and foliage, and the hilly grassland rolled off into a steep incline to my left, giving way to the views I had come to see. The wind gusted again, this time bringing a light spray of rain drops. I winced at the thought of more rain.

I began making my way along the path, feeling the pounding of my heart with each step amidst the crunch of stones underfoot. *It won't be much longer. Just a little more and you'll be at the spot she always talked about. Views of the village, the forest and the sweeping hillsides she so loved, just like she described all those times. It'll be like she's there with you. Like she's by your side after so many years apart. It's why you wanted to move here, right?*

A couple came into sight, their brightly-coloured waterproofs contrasting sharply with the greenery, a small dog trailing at their heels, off its lead.

I shuddered at the sight, immediately becoming self-conscious of how ill-prepared for the weather I was. I didn't want to be looked at. Judged. Beads of sweat began to form on my forehead and between my shoulder blades.

I took a deep breath. *Come on, keep it together. Keep going. Head up. Look forwards. Look normal.* Fresh air, stretch the legs, all the usual reasons any sane person would have, that's why I was there. But the familiar sense of regret was seeping into my bones. I'd imagined it would be a good idea to escape from the house for half an hour. What was I thinking?

I knew I wasn't quite "with it", not these last few days. My old friend - the dull ache - had taken root soon after arriving in

Barndon and was proving stubborn. My pretence of being *fine* was becoming harder to maintain. To be honest, I struggled to remember a time when it wasn't there, gnawing away at me like a ghoul with a fresh bone in the dark recesses of my mind.

On those rare occasions when it had subsided, it was never gone for long. It was just biding its time, like it always did, seemingly choosing to wait until I was most content; until I was feeling better, feeling happy. But lately it felt as though I was losing the war with myself, not just another battle. I knew that somehow I had to muster more strength. It was the only way. I had to keep going. If not for myself, then for my family's sake.

Positive thoughts breed positive actions. That's what the psychologist had said that time.

'I will get better. I *will*.'

The couple looked over at me as they walked by, a confused look passing between them. This time I'd definitely said it out loud.

Breathe. Embarrassed, I quickened my pace, rounding the corner and ducking under a particularly overgrown set of tree branches before I spotted what I'd come here for. It was the park bench my mother had spoken of, it had to be.

A surge of warmth bloomed in my head following the sight, and the throbbing dissipated as though washed away. I sped up again, leaving the path to navigate the few meters of grass over to the spot where she'd once sat. She'd said it had been her favourite place to relax and forget the day's work. To leave her past and just sit. To take in the landscape and forgo her place in the world, imagine herself in different times, in different circumstances. I always wondered what she'd meant by that.

The bench wasn't much to look at. There was an indentation where a commemoration plate must have once been fixed, and though the wood wasn't rotten, it wasn't recent or particularly clean. Old graffiti was carved into a few of the back slats and some empty food wrappers littered the slab of concrete the bench was bolted to. But it was where my mother had been all the same.

Scouting around for other people and spotting no one, I took a seat and looked out over the view. Seeing it as she would have seen it all those years ago before she'd had me, before her life had changed forever. Perhaps she hadn't been so hateful back then? So angry at the world?

The village church tower poked through the wooded area at the base of the deep slope and a few rows of houses and quaint shops stretched into the distance, giving way to more forest beneath the muddied sky. I could see why she liked the view, it did have an oddly meditative quality to it with the trees swaying slowly, almost hypnotically. Tears formed in my eyes as I imagined her sitting there in solitude.

I couldn't say how long I'd sat there when a drop – sweat or rain, I wasn't sure – caught my attention as it hung from the tip of a stray hair. I studied it, my vision blurring as I focused. I thought I saw an image of me shouting or screaming in its teardrop-shaped perfection before it spilled to the ground. At the same time, a shudder ran down my spine, seemingly out of nowhere, as though someone had just walked on my grave. I wrapped myself in my arms, forcibly trying to stop another shudder and fighting a new-found urge to run home. The church bell tolled, its mournful sound further adding to my irrational sense of dread. *No, she'd want me to stay here. This is our place now. I need to stay.*

The throb in my head returned. My skull felt as though it was on the verge of bursting. Something felt wrong. Indescribably wrong. I gripped my head in my hands, leaning forward into my knees, trying to make myself small.

No-no-no, not now. Please. This shouldn't be happening, not here. I don't understand. Being here was supposed to help.

I felt a hand clasp my shoulder. I looked over to see who it was and all the feelings of panic fell away from me.

6

Ben took his time walking to the shop on his lunch break. He was pleased to be out of the house and in the fresh air, even if it was overcast and miserable with the sun struggling to break through the dense cloud. He stuffed his hands in his coat pockets, pulling it in around him as the wind picked up. It was colder than it should be for October, and the trees lining the fenced path were already changing colour. Scatterings of damp leaves lay in his path, trodden-in and mucky.

He'd asked Andrea to venture out for milk that morning while he worked, but when he'd gone downstairs to the fridge, she'd not done it and she was nowhere to be found. This was a new tendency of hers, to wander off for a few hours, her mind elsewhere. He knew he should have been keeping an eye on what they had in the kitchen too, but work had been distracting of late. At the very least, he'd been keeping his eye on her latest medication; she'd been taking them consistently from what he could see.

He continued to worry as he walked. Was he asking too much of her? But surely creeping around on eggshells and treating her with kid gloves wouldn't do any of them any good in the long run?

He soon regretted his slower pace when the wind blew another gust, and a few drops of rain peppered his face. Taking Mother Nature's hint, he picked up the pace as he neared the local shop, the *Barndon General Store*. The place had served as a lifeline for their meals since they'd moved, neither of them having had either the time or the inclination to wander further out to the supermarkets near Oxford.

That's what you get for going for a village like this over a town or city, eh? Always been a sucker for a bit of greenery.

Ben turned the corner and saw the shop ahead. A sad-looking sign above the entrance boasted about having served Barndon for the last fifty years. The sign's thick black lettering had begun to peel away from the white backing board.

The owners were the Jackson family. Alan Jackson, who seemed prone to over-sharing, had told Ben that he and his wife had intended to pass it on to their son, Adam. But Adam – understandably, in Ben's opinion – hadn't taken to the idea of staying put and had moved down to Cornwall, leaving his parents to figure out their next steps.

Ben had joked to Andrea that this could be their next adventure, much to her consternation. She sometimes took him a little *too* literally, Ben thought. Though, admittedly, there had been some sort of twisted hope on his part. Anything to get him out of working in IT.

The shop's old bunting hung limp over the store's limestone exterior as Ben approached. He crunched over the gravel parking spaces out front and opened the door, the shrill tinkle of the shops' brass bell greeting him.

On second thoughts, I better get a few more things together while I'm here, can't just live off milk, after all.

Ben picked up one of the small shopping baskets provided next to the door. He'd only just started browsing through the meagre offerings when Alan Jackson came out from the back.

'Ah! Mr Whitman, good to see you again.'

'Hello Alan, and please, it's Ben,' he said. 'You know there's no need to be so formal with me.'

Alan Jackson was in his early sixties, a timid man with short grey hair cropped on the sides and very little on top. He sported a pair of thin metal-framed glasses, not unlike Harry Potter, and a neat moustache. Ben suspected him of having spent far too long with a pair of nail scissors in front of the bathroom mirror, trimming it just so. The man was tall, standing around six feet tall when he wasn't hunching over in the meek, awkward manner he tended towards. Ben considered himself fairly easy-going, but he had little time for Alan; the man certainly wasn't someone he wanted to spend his lunch hour with his unending small talk and strangely snide comments.

'Okay ..."Ben", what can I get for you today?' Alan cocked his head and gave a watery, forced-looking smile.

'No need to trouble yourself, thanks. I only want a few things.'

'Oh... okay. If you're sure?'

'I'm sure. Thank you.' Ben focused on a solitary pizza in the chiller cabinet.

He quickly finished shopping and took his basket to the counter. Alan hadn't spotted he was ready, so Ben let out a short, sharp cough to signal to him. The man flinched and looked up from the shelf he was tending, before scuttling round to operate the till.

Ben unloaded his few items on to the counter, not wanting to make eye contact with Alan and start any small talk. He questioned a few of the new purchases he'd picked at random – a pineapple? – but all he wanted was to get going.

The shop bell sounded.

'Ah, bugger!' Ben murmured, his voice louder than he'd intended as he finished unpacking.

'Is there a problem, son?', a coarse voice behind him asked.

Ben craned his head to look at the owner of the voice. 'Just realised I didn't bring a damn bag with me.'

The man looked to be in his mid-to-late fifties, but his advancing years didn't seem to have got the better of him. He was broad-shouldered and tall. And with the way he sounded and the clothes he was wearing – a chequered shirt, light blue and white, coupled with beige chinos – he had to be a farmer of some sort. His hair was grey and short, and a similar beard framed his craggy face. Brown eyes peered out from beneath his brow, and the way he stood gave him an air of authority. *If I looked half as fit at his age, I'd be pretty happy,* Ben thought.

'Why would you go and do that, eh? That's madness, son,' he said, in seeming amusement, although he wasn't smiling. The man's voice had a strange twang from the little he'd heard, the accent a mix of west country farmer and London cockney. He'd learned since their move that it was pretty typical of people who'd lived in Oxfordshire for generations.

'Welcome, Mr Barrow,' Alan interrupted. 'And how are you today?'

'Just need the usual when you can, please, Alan,' the man replied, ignoring Alan's pleasantries.

'Of course.' Alan turned his attention back to Ben. 'I'll just be a moment collecting Mr Barrow's items from out back. I guess you need to figure out what you'll be able to take, seeing as we don't give out bags anymore. We sold out of those fancy ones too.

Silly government decision if you ask me, but that's the policy now, I'm afraid.'

'Okay, thanks,' Ben sighed in frustration. Work, or his worry for Andrea, was making him absent-minded. Or was it both?

He sensed the Barrow man come up behind him, almost close enough for him to feel his breath on his neck. Ben shuffled forwards before turning full profile to face him, his back now pressed up against the shop counter.

'You the husband?'

'I'm sorry?'

'The husband, you know ... the new family that's moved to my village. News gets round in places like these.'

'His' village? Please.

'Oh, I see. Yes, that's us, sorry, I mean, "me". Been a few weeks now, nigh on a month.'

There was something about him that made Ben feel off-kilter and foolish.

The man known as Mr Barrow didn't answer before Alan came back out with a box of produce.

'Here you go, Samuel,' Alan said. He handed the box to the man, who took it under one arm. 'Happy to serve. How's Ann and your boy, Jonah, doing?'

'It's good, Alan, we're good. Life is peachy.'

He sounded like he wanted to get away. Small talk with the local shopkeeper was seemingly not high on his list of priorities.

That makes two of us.

The man turned back to Ben and put his free hand on Ben's shoulder with a firm grip.

'Say... how about this? Since you're now a local boy, how about I give you a lift back with your shopping? I'll even stretch to giving you a bag, eh? Let me show you how we treat our own here in Barndon,' he said, a smile fixed on his face.

With an offer like that, and seeing the threat of rain now kicking up a notch through the shop window, Ben could hardly refuse.

7

Ben rushed to stow away his shopping on the rear passenger seat of the huge black Land Rover before the rain soaked him. He closed the passenger door just in time before Samuel Barrow started the ignition and reversed out, his arm outstretched behind Ben's headrest.

He felt uncomfortable being in a total stranger's car, and it wasn't helped by the fact it was *pristine*. No crumbs or errant strands of hair. Not at all like their family car. It even smelled new. But he supposed he couldn't turn down the man's offer for no good reason, what with the weather the way it was.

He looked at his watch; only twenty minutes to get back and in front of his laptop, ready for his first meeting of the afternoon. He was starving, but it looked like lunch would have to wait.

'So, what's your name, son?' the man asked, his voice startling Ben for a second.

'Oh, sorry. I'm Ben.'

'Name's Samuel Barrow. My friends call me Sam. Perhaps one day, I'll let you call me that, eh?' he said, winking at him.

If he'd worn a Stetson, Ben imagined he would have tipped it in his direction, not just gifted him a wink.

'And you... you're a Whitman, right?'

Ben nodded. 'How did you—'

Samuel chuckled. 'I told you, news travels fast round here. I already knew your name. But it's only manners, ain't it?'

'Do you know where we live too?' Ben said, sounding more accusatory than he intended to.

'Of course. Not been round them parts in a long while, but it's not really out of the way for my journey. So, only common courtesy for me to offer you a ride.'

'Thank you again, Samuel.'

Ben noticed that Samuel's enunciation seemed to slip the more relaxed and talkative he got, becoming more of a drawl.

They drove in silence for a moment, the sound of the windscreen wipers keeping a metronomic beat.

'That name "Barrow" sounds familiar,' Ben remarked.

'Ha! Well, you'd be right. We're kind of the "original" family around here.' He paused for effect and failed to get the reaction he expected. He continued: 'Us Barrows go back generations. We own the estate on the edge of town. Acres upon acres of farm-land, a royal pain in the arse if all we were doing was farming. But we've diversified. You know how farming can be otherwise, I'm sure. Long days and shit to show for it. That's not what I want, not for my family while I'm in charge, not now and not for the future. Family is all we've got. Without that, we're nothing.'

Samuel paused for breath while he turned out of a junction and continued in the direction of Reeds' Lane, towards Ben's home.

'It's just Ann, Jonah and I up there now. We keep it small... keep it tight. But we have a lot of people working for us. We make sure the cogs are turning and the money's coming in.'

'Oh, right...' Ben said, mustering a weak reply.

Not long to go now, just a minute or two out, and I'll be back.

'So, what made you decide this little village was for you?' Samuel asked as the car stopped at a set of roadworks. Two men in hi-vis were digging up the road in a small JCB, while another worked the traffic lights, boredom etched on his face.

'Well, we felt we needed a change. I fancied a bit of country-side living while still being close to places like Oxford and London. And my wife, Andrea, she wanted to come here. Her mum was here for a time and always spoke highly of it.'

There was a sudden jolt as Samuel pulled away, the traffic lights having changed.

'So, yeah,' Ben continued. 'We figured a change of scenery would do us good, and Barndon stood out.'

'Interesting, so there are some familial roots here. That's what I like to hear.' For some reason, Samuel laughed as he said it.

After a few more awkward minutes, they entered Reeds Lane. It was a beautiful outlier of Barndon itself. A regiment of old oak trees lined the field opposite the houses, creating a half-arch over the lane. Andrea had said it looked like a golden canopy above them, but Ben didn't have her level of imagination and romanticism.

'Lovely house, this,' Samuel observed as the building came into view.

He was right, Ben thought; it *was* a lovely house. It stood detached from the rest, with a not inconsiderable distance between them and their neighbours. The distance provided some much-needed privacy, and also spared the neighbours from Cari's questionable music taste.

It was a Georgian house. A grand hallway with a mosaic floor paved the way to the large reception rooms, kitchen and lounge. There were four bedrooms, of which they used two. The others were used as a study for Ben's work and a box room, the latter literally taking on that name for the moment, being full to the brim with boxes from the move. He was still undecided about what to do with it, though Ben suspected it would become a small art studio for Andrea eventually.

'How's it coming along with the move? All settled?'

'Yes, I think we're getting there slowly. We're going to look to do it up as we go rather than in one fell swoop. It's just my wife, Andrea, who isn't working right now, and our daughter Cari and I, so it's going to be a while until we get more money together.'

'I see, I see. Maybe I could throw some work her way, eh?'

'Thanks for the offer. I'll let her know.' Ben smiled politely, knowing it would not be the best of ideas.

Samuel pulled in next to the fence, the car coming to an abrupt halt.

'Well, then, here we are.'

'Thank you very much for the lift.' Ben undid his seatbelt before collecting his shopping and pulling on the door handle. Sticking around for more chat was not high on his list of priorities.

'No problem, son,' Samuel looked over at him, one hand resting on the steering wheel.

He wished he didn't insist on calling him 'Son.'

'Hope you're done decorating soon.' He chuckled, finding himself amusing once again.

'Thanks. Maybe Andrea and I will see you around sometime.'

'Yeeep.'

He drove away, an obnoxious honk of his horn signalling his departure, while Ben hurried inside.

8

'Boss.' Drake raised his hand in greeting to DCS Laura Miller, taking a swig of the coffee he'd picked up from a stall near their Putney headquarters in London. Their nondescript offices, which were home to several specialist divisions besides theirs, were relatively near the New Scotland Yard building in Westminster. But they were also just far enough away to feel like they were not being constantly spied upon by the hierarchy.

Miller was leaning against the corner of a corridor as she cast an eye over a report. A young detective, looking decidedly nervous, awaited her response at a safe distance.

The sound of phones and chatter permeated the prefab open-plan office. Files were piled high on desks, and stark strip lighting hung overhead, highlighting the grey carpet tiles which had worn thin long ago. The air conditioning ceiling units were smoke stained; smoking was still allowed throughout the office space when it was installed years before, such was the age of the system. It served as an ugly reminder of the budgetary constraints of the police force and their special unit, in particular. The only positive he could muster was that the office was on the top floor, offering an ample view of the city and the Thames.

Miller was Drake's height, six foot two inches, and at fifty-eight, a few years older than him. She had steely blue eyes and long mousy grey hair, currently tied back. She let it down outside of work, which had the effect of making her appear less stern. Her impressive height had given her the awful nickname 'GM,' or 'Giant Miller,' over the years. She never liked it when she was working up the ranks, but even when she heard the nickname after having made DCS, she still allowed it.

Her face spoke of her intelligence and experience. Miller had a tendency to look at people as though peering directly into their soul. It had unnerved many a suspect over the years, making them doubt themselves and feel like she'd questioned them without her having uttered a word.

Today, though, she looked tired; subdued even. Circles lay dark under her eyes, and her usually immaculate uniform was creased.

'Morning, Drake.' She didn't look up from the report. 'How are you doing on wrapping up the latest Thames floater?'

Drake winced at the term. Frequently used for victims of death by drowning, or bodies disposed of in the water, it was an efficient, if callous description, though he knew Miller meant no disrespect to the victim by it.

The "floater" Drake had been working on was a Jane Doe, now known to be Lisa Beresford, born and bred in Hackney. Her body had washed up on the edge of the Thames, just down from Putney Bridge. On first inspection, he'd thought she may have been the victim of foul play because of the fresh wounds to her arms; large, diagonal slashes that made him wince. But once the post-mortem results were in, her death had been deemed to be suicide, specifically death-by-drowning. Due to the angle and pressure of the kitchen knife used to make the cuts on her body, they appeared to have been self-inflicted in the hours prior to the incident. Her body also carried layers of older scarring, covering her arms and legs, which had been amassed over several years. Drake had realised in dismay that she'd likely self-harmed since her early teens.

Drake was thankful that she hadn't been in the water for more than a few hours. It meant she had little opportunity to be disturbed by boat propellers or the Thames' sea life, something he'd seen before with bodies exposed to the indiscriminate waters for longer periods.

He'd contacted witnesses who'd called in regarding her erratic behaviour on Putney Bridge; CCTV had shown her climbing the walls of the bridge, tiptoeing along as if walking a tightrope, rather than a three-foot-wide solid stone wall. Then she dropped in. No ceremony, no hesitation. She'd just turned and walked off straight off the edge. Later, the lab work had revealed a high level of MDMA in her bloodstream. Lisa had only been seventeen years old, just three years older than his daughter.

Cases like these made Drake realise how innocuous acts and moments in people's lives could shape them and set them on a certain path. The dead girl had made him even more determined to ensure he was always there for his daughter, now and for the future. He was determined Eva would always feel she could talk to him and not hide her feelings.

However, that morning's car journey played on his mind. He wanted them to be open and honest with each other. But what good would it achieve telling a teenager about the kind of cases he was working on, however much detail he left out? Some boundaries needed setting, surely?

He realised Miller was still waiting for an answer. 'Good. It's ... good,' he said, the words ringing hollow in his ears. A young girl had died, the system having failed her, as it did countless others like her. 'I should have it all wrapped up by midday.'

'Excellent,' Miller said, looking up. If she thought it was "excellent", her expression certainly didn't show it. 'John, I know I'm not using you to your full ability with these cases, but you're doing good work, regardless. Keep it up. I'm around in my office today should you feel you're ready to step up again, or if you need to talk further.'

She turned her attention to the young DC still awaiting her response, and nodded a curt approval.

'Thanks, Laura.' Drake moved to walk away, but Miller called him back. 'Actually, I *do* need to speak to you in a few hours. 11:00 please, my office.'

* * *

Tap, tap.

'Enter.' Miller answered through the door. She didn't look up when Drake stepped in. 'One moment, please.'

Closing the door behind him, he remained standing. He didn't need to, such was their friendship, but the mutual respect was there, and he took opportunities such as this to show it rather than just sitting himself down uninvited.

Her office was one of the few overlooking the Thames; not a huge space, but enough to generate the necessary sense of seniority over the main office in which she presided. Boats idled along the river against a backdrop of tall office blocks and cranes working. The weather had taken a stormy turn, the clouds overcast and oppressive.

Despite the relative grandeur of the office, it was piled high with files of all kinds. Photographs of his boss with various ranking officials hung on the walls; in some, Miller wore one of her rare smiles, but the majority showed her habitual serious expression.

She motioned for him to sit. Drake did so, undoing his suit jacket to make himself more comfortable.

'I—'

Tap, tap.

'Ah, DS Wilkinson,' she said in confirmation. 'Enter.' The door opened and in stepped the mystery Detective Sergeant.

'DCS Miller,' DS Wilkinson said with a tense smile as she entered.

Drake stood up in greeting. The DS' eyes lit up when she saw him, betraying a hint of recognition. He vaguely recognised her from the office, but didn't think she could have been around long. She must be a recent addition to the prefab's luxury.

The woman appeared to be in her early thirties, her skin a deep black, her eyes light brown. She sported a wavy blonde pixie cut on top, her hair graded tightly on the sides, and wore plain clothes rather than a uniform; a dark purple turtleneck with a black suit jacket and black trousers. He and Miller towered over her. She must have been around five foot eight at a push. Not short, but not quite their level.

The young woman had a smile that could brighten up a room; an asset for a police officer considering the grim subjects they dealt with. He recalled that the few times he'd seen and heard her in the office, it was typical for laughter to be involved. But now Wilkinson appeared nervous, like someone stepping into the headmaster's office expecting detention. To be fair, though, his boss had that effect on most people.

Miller motioned for her to sit, and Drake followed suit.

'Detective Chief Inspector John Drake, this is Detective Sergeant Ellie Wilkinson. I'm assuming you haven't met. At least not officially?'

'No, ma'am,' came the joint reply.

'Excellent. Well, Drake, you're looking at your new colleague. She has just transferred to CID, and more to the point, our Specialist Murder Team, from the local Response unit. You're to guide her and bring her up to speed on how things work round here.' Miller stared intently at him while she gave him the news. 'By all accounts, DS Wilkinson is an excellent student, and in particular, she's handy with technology. Something I know you're not too keen on.'

'Now wait a moment—' Drake started, but his new recruit jumped in.

'Yes, ma'am,' she smiled. 'Thank you, ma'am.'

'On the other hand, Drake, DS Wilkinson has had little experience in dealing with crimes of a more *final* nature. So, this is where I feel you two are well suited,' Miller continued. 'Please bring her up to speed on the case we talked about earlier – I know it's not typical of what we do, but it should serve for now. Run through labs, photos, etc.'

Miller turned to Wilkinson. 'Don't hesitate to ask DCI Drake any questions you may have. He's one of our top men, and this is a prime opportunity for you to learn from the best on something ... uncomplicated. Do not waste it.'

'Yes, ma'am.' Wilkinson's earlier nervousness had returned, her hands twisting below the desk.

'Ma'am, may we speak in private?' Drake requested.

'Of course. DS Wilkinson, please wait outside,'

Miller stood, and Drake did likewise. The sergeant looked surprised for a moment, but followed suit. 'Yes, ma'am.' She extended her hands in thanks. 'Thank you for your time and for the opportunity.'

Miller gave her a firm handshake. 'We'll speak again soon.'

The new addition left the room, closing the door carefully behind her, and Drake took a deep breath.

'Laura, really? You've got me on babysitting duty now? I know you're trying your best to keep me busy. But please, do it with cases. Not this.'

Drake did his best to control his temper. He knew this wasn't the time to let rip, but it was tempting to use this as an excuse to let out all the frustration he had been feeling these past months. Biting his tongue, he paced the space in front of her desk instead. This was not what he did. He led teams, he didn't manage one on one – and certainly not with a relative rookie.

'I understand your frustration, John. Really, I do,' Miller told him. 'But what do you expect? It's been a few months now. I know things have been hard for you with your family. I understand that, and I've made allowances. This is the next thing I have for you. It's this, or I put you back front and centre. What's it to be?'

Drake felt played. Was she trying to push him back out there, to work him into a corner and force his hand? She knew he wanted back in. But he couldn't. *Shouldn't.* Still, he knew he needed to choose his words carefully. He was going to be on thin ice if he kicked back much more. 'So, how long are you expecting this to play out for?'

Miller sighed and scratched her cheek. 'A few weeks, maybe a month or more. She's bright. Let's see what comes up.' There was a finality in her expression that told him it wasn't up for debate.

'Okay, fine.'

Her work mobile buzzed on the desk, a text message.

'Thank you for your understanding,' she replied, glancing at the notification. 'Now, I need to make a phone call. If there is nothing else?'

'No, ma'am.'

'Thank you, John. I'll see you soon.'

She picked up her mobile from her desk and stood, dialling the number with a few taps. Miller greeted the person on the other end of the call, looking out over the river as Drake closed the door behind him.

9

A hand shot into the space in front of Drake as he finished closing the door to Miller's office.

'I'm looking forward to working with you, sir,' DS Wilkinson said with a smile. Drake turned and shook her hand with a firm grip. He knew this wasn't her fault. He shouldn't take it out on her. 'Thank you.'

'I've heard a lot about you from the guys, both here and in Response.'

'All good, I hope.' He motioned for them to walk, and she fell in line with him.

'Yes. I've seen your solve rate is second to none. You've been on some very high-profile cases over the years. Some of them sounded truly shocking,' she blurted out.

'They were. But – and please remember this – there are real people behind these cases. Victims. It's not glamorous. If you're of that mindset, I'm not going to be keeping you around for long, regardless of the efforts you've put in to get a move here.'

Drake winced to himself, realising he might have come on a little strong. His words sounding like the rantings of a bitter old man. 'Should I call you Wilkinson, or do you prefer Ellie, or something else?'

'Just call me Ellie. Wilkinson is a bit of a mouthful.' Clearly, she'd chosen to ignore his earlier comment.

'Okay, Ellie it is.' He continued the journey back to his desk, Ellie following close behind.

'And you?' she asked, looking at him.

'Drake. Just Drake is fine.'

His irritation flared again as he came upon DC Bowen sitting in his seat, talking to a colleague. Drake nodded at him to move and he did, but only to the seat next to Drake's.

'Not that one. DS Wilkinson has that one from now on,' Drake growled, his agitation in no way diminished. He knew he'd need to keep it in check with his new understudy.

Bowen looked sheepish as he moved on. 'Apologies, sir.'

Drake noticed Ellie scrutinising the chaos of desk. He could guess what she was thinking. He knew his desk screamed "preoccupied workaholic" more than most as evidenced by the fact that, apart from a lone photograph of his wife and daughter, the entire space was covered in paperwork. Hastily written phone numbers, other notes, some remnants of old ones (pins still attached to ripped remains in some instances) littered the blue fabric pin board, while an impressive tower of used vending machine coffee cups teetered in the corner. The adjacent desk was a mess of dust and paper. Elastic bands and cables for connecting a laptop and telephone lay strewn across its surface in a tangled mess.

'I'll bring my things over later, and probably clear this shit to somewhere far, far away from here.' She scrunched her nose as she picked up an old coffee soaked post-it with her fingertips.

Drake smiled, calming slightly as he sat down. He agreed. It *was* a bit of a shithole.

Ellie seemed pleased she'd got a friendly reaction out of him. She took a seat and leant in his direction.

'So, are you able to give this case the once over with me right now, or do you want me to come back in a while?' she asked.

Before he could respond, he had a sudden, desperate feeling of wanting to go home and get away from it all. He felt trapped. The thoughts were completely alien to him.

Christ, what's the matter with me? He took a deep breath, doing his best to shake off the thought. 'No, no. Now is fine. Let's crack on and see what your initial thoughts are. Here's what we've got.'

He rifled through the pile of papers in his leather briefcase and pulled the case file for Lisa Beresford.

Drake noticed Ellie judging his preference of paper over using his laptop, which remained shut on his desk, but he chose not to explain. 'Right. This was the situation.'

* * *

By mid-afternoon, Ellie was digesting what her new boss had told her. The sun had decided to venture out for a short stint before sundown and was casting a hazy glow into the office, causing many to pull down blinds to shut out the beams shining in their eyes or creating screen glare. She hadn't moved from where she'd perched since entering Drake's domain.

The case, though simple, was fascinating.

Her new boss was scrupulous in his detail. He could have shot through it all without much care, but he didn't; even though it might be small fry in the grand scheme of things, he took care to treat the victim as a person, not an object or a number. Ellie liked that. This man seemed to be proper police. Old school. If she was given the chance, she felt there was a lot she could learn from him.

She noticed that Drake seemed to appreciate the care she was taking, too. She'd made sure she had taken copious notes throughout his run-through, and had done her best to ask sensible questions. He'd appeared pleased she'd picked up on the manner of the marks on the victims' arms and had hypothesised the same outcome as the post-mortem report.

Time went on and she held tight to her rule; make no assumptions, and no jumping ahead, at least not out loud. She could already see he could be a little testy. It was clear her appearance at the meeting with Miller had set him on edge.

They were just wrapping up when the faint buzz of a mobile phone started. Drake looked around, his head darting left and right, unable to spot the source. Then, realising he'd buried the mobile under a pile of paper, he rifled through and soon found the phone just as Ellie was going to help.

DCS Miller. 'Drake,' he answered.

'John, come to my office right away.'

'Is everything okay?' He frowned. His boss sounded tense.

'No, it's not. You're going to want to see this.' She hesitated. 'John, the Man is back.'

'The Man? What do you mean? What man?'

'The Family Man.'

Drake threw the phone on his desk with a clatter and ran to Miller's office, leaving a confused-looking Ellie and an office chair spinning in his wake.

10

'Hello? Anybody home?' Ben called out as he made his way along the hallway from his office space.

He was relieved it was the end of the day and he could close the door on the study and his work. It had dragged way too much for his liking. He called out again. Still no answer and no signs of life, either.

She must be asleep. I swear I heard her come in earlier.

He scratched at his stomach and frowned. Andrea had been sleeping more, a lot more. Ben couldn't decide what was worse, her sleeping more than usual or less. He was finding it hard to keep track. And despite the house move and her newfound passion for walks, Andrea's episodes were becoming more severe of late.

That was why, for the past few weeks, when he had to be on site in the local office, he'd been ensuring he arrived home before Cari got back from school. He didn't want a repeat of her coming home to find her mother behind the sofa, screaming at her to get out of the house because there was 'something' upstairs, or Cari finding her mum on the floor of her bedroom one evening, huddled in a corner and screaming that a man was dead in the master bedroom.

Secretly, he'd found it even more draining since their move. It was draining always having to be the one on an even keel, the responsible one. The good guy. Draining being the one that couldn't get agitated or lose his cool when she spiralled. Ben sighed. He shouldn't even be thinking like that. He had to try harder; for his daughter's sake, if not his wife's. They'd find her the right medication soon enough, the one that would set her on an even keel for the rest of her days. He knew they would. They *had* to.

Ben took off his slippers and crept downstairs, not wanting to wake her with the sound of his footsteps. He peered into the dining room next to the stairs.

The room was twice the size of their old living room, and they hadn't even had a dining room at their old place. The shutters and window were open, letting in the last remnants of the afternoon sun, now that the rain from earlier had abated and the clouds cleared.

A breeze wafted in, the tablecloth moving gently at its touch. Ben could smell the remnants of rain in soil. Boxes of crockery sat still unopened in the corner against the waist-high wood panelling. But unless she was in a box, there was no obvious sign of Andrea, so he wandered across the hall to the lounge.

Sure enough, there she was, curled up asleep on the sofa, a light frown on her otherwise peaceful-looking face. She had her hiking shoes on, fresh mud caked on them.

He grimaced at the mud on the carpet and sofa, but rationalised that they were on the long list of items to be replaced at some stage, so he wouldn't pull her up on it.

Andrea must have felt his presence, because she started

fidgeting before slowly opening her eyes. 'Oh, Ben. How long have you been standing there?'

'How are you feeling?' he asked, ignoring the question. He reached down and tucked some stray hairs behind her ear, waiting – and wishing – for a positive response.

'I'm feeling good, thank you. Sorry, I realised I was supposed to go to the shop to get the milk you asked for when I'd been walking for ages already. I'm sorry. Figured I needed a walk to clear this brain of mine.' The tone of her voice and repeated apologies made it sound like a bigger deal than it was. He shook his head.

'That's okay. I grabbed it earlier, along with some other bits. But we'll still need a proper shop at some point. That place left me a little wanting.'

She forced a weak smile. 'Great.'

'You sure you're okay? You look a little pale.'

He didn't feel completely convinced by her responses. Even before the move, he'd had the nagging suspicion that she had been hiding things from him, perhaps out of a fear of worrying him. But if she didn't tell him, what could he do to help? He didn't want to smother her.

'Ben, yes... please, I'm fine.' She sat up, still groggy from sleep. At least, he hoped it was just from that.

She smiled at him. 'I dreamt about Mum again. But this time … this time she was happy.'

That was a relief, he supposed, but her comment still made him uneasy. When Andrea dreamt of her mother, there was *never* a positive outcome. Her mother committed suicide in front of her when she was eighteen, after putting Andrea through years of mental and physical abuse.

'That's great. Maybe it's a sign? Perhaps we did the right thing in moving to Barndon? You wanted to be closer to where she lived before you, after all.'

'Yeah, maybe,' she said hesitantly. 'She told me to be careful, though.'

'Careful?' He frowned. 'Careful of what?'

'I don't know. I can't remember now.'

'Okay,' he said. He hoped that wasn't as ominous as it sounded.

'But it's something, right?' She looked up at him, her face lit up. 'Even thinking back to it now, I feel positive, like a weight has lifted. Perhaps I won't have that other dream of her again.'

'Let's hope so. I feel so powerless when you have those dreams.'

'Anyway, how about we go to the pub for dinner this evening? We could do with getting out and about, and you'd love a pint, I'm sure.'

'Sounds great,' he said, stuffing his hands in his pockets. 'But are you sure that's a good idea? I don't want to put you under any pressure.'

'I'm sure. Come on, it'll be nice. Cari will like it too.' She stood up from the sofa and wrapped her arms around him, a sleepy smile on her face. 'Come on, what d'you say?'

There she was, there was his Andrea. 'Well, okay! Let's go around seven – give Cari a chance to do some homework, and then we'll make a move.'

'Great.'

'Speaking of work, I just remembered I need to print off a few bits, then I'll be back down,' he said, motioning towards the door. But before he could release himself, she pulled him towards her and kissed him hard.

'What was that for?' he asked, surprised. Something about her seemed off.

'Oh, nothing, just ... you know.'

'Well, I'm not going to say no to more of that.'

'Oh, really?' she whispered in his ear. Her hand moved to his crotch.

'Andrea ...'

She carried on kissing him, running her hands through his hair. He put his hands on her hips and nudged her in the sofa's direction.

'Mr Whitman ...'

'Yes, m'lady?' he said with a small chuckle, forgetting his concern immediately.

'Carry on.'

'Yes,' he whispered, his breathing becoming heavier by the second.

* * *

Flopping down on the sofa, I looked over Ben's shoulder towards the corner of the room. There was something drawing me to it, an urge. Something exciting, but also strangely calming somehow.

Ben continued to paw at me, pulling my jumper over my head as I did my best to make the right noises, my mind not entirely present while I tried to understand the feeling. I squeezed my eyes shut, helping him fumble with the rest of my clothes, before taking another look over his shoulder towards the corner of the room.

I smiled.

My mother smiled back.

11

The blinds in Miller's office billowed and clattered with the sudden gust of air as the door was flung open, juddering against the wall.

'What do you mean "he's back"?' Drake shouted.

The office hushed as people turned to see what was going on. A solitary ring tone in the background rang out, resonating awkwardly in the sudden silence.

'John, calm down,' Miller said, in a vain attempt to placate him.

Drake knew his face was a deep crimson; he could feel the veins straining on his temples and forehead, the mixture of fear and rage boiling over for all to see. He grabbed the door and slammed it shut behind him.

'Shit!' He ran his hands through his hair and moved for the blinds, angling them closed. With nothing more to see or hear, the volume of the main office ramped back up to its usual level.

'You can't mean what I think you mean. Tell me everything you know. I ... I need to understand. What the hell's going on?' He folded his arms, barely containing himself.

Miller's eyes fixed on his, her hands clasping the edge of her desk while she considered where to start.

'A few hours after our meeting this morning, I received a call from the DCS for the West Yorkshire Constabulary, regarding their Keighley station,' she told Drake. 'Early this afternoon, the local Response unit received a call from a housekeeper who works in a village called Haworth. The woman had entered the property of the family she worked for, the Cartwrights, to find the whole family dead in their dining room. Or so she thought.' Miller paused, giving him a resigned look. 'But we both know the actual outcome, don't we?'

Drake shuddered. This could not be happening. It wasn't possible. It *literally* was not possible.

Miller continued: 'Upon attending the scene, the officers –,' Miller looked at her notes, 'one PC Robert Melford and one PC Sarah Billing, met the housekeeper outside the property. She was unwilling to go back inside. She'd told them she had relocked the door, just in case, so no one could go in or – perhaps she thought – leave. She handed the house key over. She was very distressed.'

Drake ran his hands up and down his face, dragging the skin, his stubble making an audible crackling sound against his fingers. He could guess what was coming next.

'The two PCs entered the property. They could see no sign of forced entry at the front door, and there was no answer to the usual announcements. Nothing was out of place in the hallway apart from a blood spatter on the wall next to the house's alarm system.' Miller paused, hesitating for a moment. 'Upon entering the dining room, they found a family of four: One adult male, and one adult female. The little boys were at the table, as were the parents. The children were blindfolded and their throats had been slit.'

Drake's eyes widened in shock at Miller's description.

'They were bound to the chairs by their bodies and fore-heads,' Miller continued. 'The bindings for the parents were the same as the children, only their heads were left free. The mother—'

Drake broke in, his voice carefully dispassionate as he recounted the words he knew off by heart. He couldn't believe he was repeating this scenario again. 'The mother was kept alive and made to bear witness to what the Man exacted on her family. She will have witnessed the killings of her children, then the mutila-tion and death of her husband. Made to watch his hands being removed and tongue forcibly cut out while still alive. Then, made to watch the Man disembowel him and slit his throat in front of her, for good measure.' Drake let his words sink in. 'That's correct, isn't it?'

He hadn't needed to ask the question. Miller's grimace told he'd been only too accurate.

'Yes,' she confirmed.

Drake's hands gripped the back of the chair. 'God damn it. God *damn* it!' His knuckles turned white, his throat tightening as he gripped the chair with all his strength.

Miller pursed her lips. She knew what this meant for him. And for her, too.

He peered at her. 'Was the symbol there?'

'Yes.'

'Where was it this time?'

'Carved into the dining room wall.'

'God *fucking* damn it.'

* * *

Twenty years earlier, during an unusually wet October in 1998, the then DS Drake and a soon-to-be-promoted DS Miller had worked together on a series of murders in the small village of Barndon. The case was to be their first together in the recently formed SMT.

Drake had soon discovered "murders" had been too slight a description for what he'd had to deal with. The term 'serial killing' felt more appropriate, but even that felt inadequate to describe the Family Man murders. They were *the* worst Drake had seen or investigated in his entire time on the police force.

In total, there had been four separate incidents, four separate unrelated families. Eleven people had been butchered over the course of a year. Eleven innocent people: seven young boys and girls, some as young as *three* years old. Four adult men; all fathers. Four mothers left alive to bear permanent psychological scars and trauma.

There was nothing linking them on a substantive level. The only commonality came from the level of affluence that afforded them the large homes in which the crimes took place. And, of course, that the victims were young families.

Families destroyed in a matter of hours, just like that. All sat at dining tables, all bound, the children with their throats slit. Fathers mutilated and disembowelled. Mothers made to watch the brutality meted out to their loved ones. Consigned to living with what they saw, what they *endured*, for the rest of their lives. The nature of the selection of the victims, together with the symbol found at each scene, led to the police and the media referring to the killer as 'The Family Man'; a fitting moniker, if a little ridiculous, considering.

Drake and Miller had worked tirelessly over that year, working every angle they could come up with, no matter how far-fetched. Scores of people were canvassed and interviewed. Nothing came up.

No suspects were linked to the murders. There appeared to be nothing driving his actions. No evidence that might have given them a fighting chance. It had scared Drake then, and it still did now.

The "Man" had been an intelligent sociopath; and a sadistic one, at that. The removal of the hands and tongue implied rage, but was it directed at the victims, or the idealism of the victims' family unit? The way he'd placed the offerings he'd severed on the table must have some implication, surely? Some ritual somewhere in the world to give reason to the methods used?

All these questions still remained unanswered.

There was no traceable motive, and the nature of the killings meant there'd probably be no informants, no snitches with information or leads to follow up.

The Man was meticulous in his preparation; thorough. Drake maintained he had to have stalked his victims in the preceding weeks and months. He'd even theorised that The Man gained entry and stole keys, making copies before replacing them.

Nothing linked the locations of the families; no locations were frequented by them all, and no services worked for the same families. All the incidents occurred in and around Barndon, Oxford and Reading in a rough thirty-mile radius, an area similar in size to London.

By mid-1999, there seemed to be no end in sight to the killings. The months rolled on into July, and a fourth family had just been butchered. The team was running on empty. But one day, out of the blue, Drake's team had received a tip via the hotline which had been set up; a man was confessing to the crimes, detailing specifics that only the police knew.

The address he provided was that of a local Barndon man by the name of Stan or Stanley Lawton. Drake and Miller had rushed to the address, but Stan, armed with a shotgun, had apparently had second thoughts about turning himself in.

A chase had ensued, ending with Drake and Miller cornering him in a fenced off section of Barndon Forest. After a fraught encounter, Stan had shot himself at point blank range, having once again confessed to the murders. No more killings occurred. The case was closed, and Drake and Miller thought they'd seen the last of the Family Man.

They thought wrong.

12

'John?' Miller said. Her frown had gone, replaced by a look of concern for her friend and colleague. 'John?'

The words echoed around Drake, but didn't quite register. They'd caught the bastard and he'd died, Drake had seen it with his own eyes. The case was closed. How could this be happening? How could *He* be back?

The Family Man murders had been the biggest, ugliest case of his career, and the biggest drain for him *and* for Becca. He couldn't think straight. He couldn't get sucked back in, not now. He just couldn't. It had to be some sick copycat. How could it be anything else?

'Huh?' Drake said. 'Sorry, you were saying?'

'I was saying, I understand your reaction. I was there. I went through it all too.' She cocked her head and studied him. 'Do you need a minute?'

'No... no. I'll be okay. It's just a ... a *shock*. How the hell could this be happening again?' He released his grip on the chair and sat down, returning Miller's gaze.

'I know. I felt the same when I heard the news. Though I had the luxury of hearing it alone in my office,' Miller said. 'And I didn't call you in immediately. I needed some time to myself.'

He sat silent again for a few moments, digesting the news. 'So, what's the plan? What're you going to do?'

'Well, West Yorkshire raised this to me because of my involvement on the original case, the *striking* similarities, and the fact it sits within our team's remit. I'm going up there in the next few hours, when it will officially become our case. They're extending any help that we may need – and we *will* need it, John. Our resources are stretched seriously thin.'

'Have the press been notified?'

Drake cringed as he remembered the shitstorm that had occurred after each incident twenty years ago; he and Becca being hounded on a daily basis, and the press attempting to sneak into hospital rooms. He dreaded the thought of what it would be like now, with social media, the dark corners of the internet, the leaks.

'Yes, but they're not aware of the details. The official line is "unexplained." In the meantime, reporters are being unofficially fed the line that it was a burglary gone wrong. It should buy us some time and breathing space. But not much,' Miller said, concern etched on her face.

'Mmm,' Drake concurred. 'You know it won't be long, though. The housekeeper, her family or the victim's families will be contacted. They won't hold out for any substantial length of time. She saw what she saw.'

'Agreed, but by all accounts, the housekeeper didn't stick around to look at the finer details. She didn't realise the wife was still alive, for example. And the wife herself, well, she isn't in any fit state for talking to anyone, let alone the press.'

'A small mercy for her, at least, and most definitely for us. She won't respond well to the hounding. The housekeeper, on the other hand ...'

Miller nodded. They sat in silence for a while longer, processing what these killings could indicate and how they could even be happening.

Drake saw Miller's expression change, and he knew what was coming. He hoped she didn't want to do it, hoped she knew she shouldn't. But he knew she had to ask.

'John ... do you want the case?'

Silence, before he shook his head. 'I'm sorry, Laura. I can't. You know what this would do to me and my family.'

'Okay.' Miller scratched the back of her neck. She must have known that would be his answer, but Drake knew she'd still hoped for a different response.

He'd been the bedrock of the original case. Yes, she had worked it with him, but as a newly promoted Detective Inspector. It hadn't helped that their superiors had been next to useless throughout, but it was *him* the case had consumed.

It had been him regularly sleeping on the office sofa throughout that year, sitting bleary-eyed in the office, day after day; analysing and re-analysing crime scene photos, witness statements, lab work reports, following up leads and documenting anything and everything at all hours of the day. Rightly or wrongly, Miller had left it to him. He'd had to make sure another victim would not be down to him, not on his watch.

Drake realised that the "Family Man" murders had been responsible for the first real chink in his family's armour. That small weakness had worked its way in, and then it had grown, leading to his current situation at home.

This new case might prove to be the final straw.

* * *

Drake sat quietly, his mind racing, while Miller tapped away on her laptop. But unlike the typing, his thoughts wouldn't end anytime soon. He knew his response had been the right one for him and for his family; he knew it. He couldn't go back to what it had been like, working that case. It would break him. It would break *them*.

But I could still get updates? I could provide insight while working on my other cases. That would be okay, wouldn't it?

'Laura?'

'Yes?' She looked up from her laptop.

'When you get there, let me know what you find. I feel I should help in some way, even if it's from a distance.'

'John, is that a good idea?'

'Please. Let me help.' Drake attempted a smile. They both knew that it would be very hard to stop him from becoming involved, despite his assurances of "distance". Miller *knew* it would be a bad idea, and she was running with it anyway. But then, wasn't he just sitting back and allowing it to happen?

'Okay. Let's see how it goes when I get there.'

'Thanks.' Drake got up and made his way to the door.

'John?'

'Yes, Boss?' He turned, his hand resting on the door handle.

'Go home. Be with your family, that's an order.'

He didn't respond, closing the door behind him.

13

Drake pulled in to the parking space at the roadside outside his home. He could see light escaping around the edges of the curtains at Eva's bedroom window and the front reception room.

He turned off the ignition, sighing as the car went silent, the occasional ping of the cooling engine breaking through. He knew he'd have to talk to Becca about what had happened, and he could already picture her reaction.

Drake took a deep breath, inhaling through his nose and exhaling through his mouth. He repeated the exercise three times, still maintaining his grip on the steering wheel. A family therapist had recommended the technique many years ago, and at the time, it had helped to calm his thoughts and focus his mind. Tonight, however, his mind was refusing to slow down. During his drive home, he'd been unable to stop thinking back to the old case, the memories flooding back in one overpowering, brutal wave. He could *smell* the blood, taste its copper tang. Recall the stink of death like dust in his nostrils.

Drake rubbed at his face, as though trying to physically wash away the thoughts and feelings. He needed to force some good humour and warmth back in to himself before he faced his family.

He glanced at the briefcase lying on the passenger seat. Inside were the notes he'd put together regarding the Haworth crime scene before he'd taken Miller's order seriously and gone home. He snatched it up and got out of the car, fighting the buffeting wind while he wrestled with the rusted latch of the old wrought-iron gate. He made his way up the pathway, the apprehension growing with every step. The trees swaying in shadow around him.

'Becca? Eva? You home?' Drake called, entering the warm glow of his home. It was a habit more than anything, he knew they were in. Despite the day's events, it felt good to be back.

'Hi honey, you going to close that door or what?' Becca rubbed her arms, her bare feet padding on the tiles. She greeted him with a kiss as he closed the front door.

Becca looked beautiful in a mustard-coloured cable knit jumper and dark grey jeans, Drake thought. It was rare for her to wear socks or slippers in the house. He loved her quirks.

He put his arms around her. 'How was your day?'

'Busy ... isolated, but busy. You know how it is when working from home.'

'You didn't get stuck on another day of conference calls, did you?' He cocked his head to one side. 'You know those can fry your brain, right?'

'Very funny. My brain is in one – extremely – intelligent piece, thank you. My sanity, however ... phew! Different day, same old corporate crap. You know how it is.'

Thankfully, he didn't. Drake didn't know how anyone could work in a corporate environment, but he respected her patience and level-headedness. He wouldn't have been able to bite his tongue if he'd had to work with some of the colleagues she'd described over the years.

'Doesn't sound good, love. But don't worry. Big, bad detective Drake is here to save you,' he said in a gruff voice, curling his arms and stomping the ground, doing his best King Kong impression – and failing miserably, judging by Becca's reaction.

'Wow... erm, don't ever do that again,' she laughed, and Drake flushed in faint embarrassment at his cheesy attempt to cheer her up.

'All right, all right. I promise.' He looked over Becca's shoulder. 'Where's Eva?'

He wanted to be close to them right now. Miller's news had dredged up too many old feelings and reopened too many old wounds. He wanted to press home the feelings of love he had for his family. To forget again, if only for a moment.

'Are you okay?' Becca studied him. 'You've got that *look*.'

'What look? I'm fine. Don't worry.' Drake leant back against the front door. He was sure his body language hadn't given anything away, but Becca could read him like a book.

'The look that tells me something's weighing on your mind. Nine times out of ten, it's work. You're going to have to tell me sometime, you know.' She looked as though she was trying her best not to frown. 'We agreed, no more secrets. *Especially* regarding work.'

'Okay, okay. I promise I'll tell you later, but not before dinner with Eva.'

Becca didn't press him any further, though she was clearly worried. She knew better than to push him, particularly when he didn't dismiss her concerns outright. But would she really want to hear what he had to say?

'Sounds good,' she said, not sounding as though she meant it.

'Eva's in her bedroom. I'll be in the kitchen cooking up a storm like I do every *single night*. And it won't be long, so try to drag her down, will you? You know you don't pay me enough, right?'

'All right, I can take a hint. I'll cook soon,' he said, knowing he'd promised this exact thing on many occasions. 'I'll check in on her. I'm looking forward to dinner, but don't disappoint me or there will be hell to pay.'

'Is that a promise?' She smiled in return and wandered back towards the kitchen.

'You betcha.'

* * *

Tap, tap.

No answer.

'Eva, you there? Can I come in?' Drake said through the door.

He expected his daughter would be in her usual position, her daily ritual after school and homework; sat on her bed, listening to music while messing around on social media on her phone. Drake could hear The Smiths' *How Soon is Now?* reverberating softly through the door.

At least she has good taste, he thought, though he wondered if this might be the ushering in of the dreaded depressive teenager phase.

'Okay, if that's how you want to play it,' Drake murmured.

He moved in for the kill, crouching down and opening the door a crack. He gave her a fair warning by sticking his arm through the doorway and waving his hand in the room. When there wasn't any noise, he opened it further and moved in while remaining close to the ground. Sure enough, she was on her bed, looking down at her phone.

Her room was pretty typical of that of a teenage girl – music posters and photos of her and her friends plastered the walls, a small desk holding her laptop next to her bed. The desk lamp and phone emitting the only glow into the otherwise dark room.

Eva was still looking down at her phone as he tapped her on the head.

Gotcha!

'Dad!' she said with a start. 'Jeez, don't scare me like that.'

'Sorry, couldn't resist after you didn't answer when I knocked on your door, *and* called your name too.' He stood up and turned down the music before setting himself back down on the edge of her bed, wincing as it creaked. He really was getting paranoid. It *was* him causing everything to creak in this damn house.

'You weren't around to pick me up today after school,' she accused, getting straight to the point, her face a picture of disappointment yet again.

'I know, I'm sorry. I was called into my bosses' office to discuss something. I couldn't leave.'

'A likely story. You were out duffing up bad guys, weren't you?'

He sighed. 'No, Eva, I don't do that. Come on.'

'I'm only joking, Dad. Man, *someone's* sensitive this evening.'

Shit. Is it that obvious? 'Sorry love, long day. How was school?' he asked, fiddling with the edge of a green schoolbook on her bed.

'Subtle change of subject, Dad. I like it.' She was teasing him, but he saw a look of concern flash across her face. 'School was pretty good, I guess. Tasha was funny, lessons were boring. The usual crap, really. Watched stupid YouTube clips at lunch.'

'Wow, back in my day we had to actually, you know, *talk* to each other at lunch.'

'Yes, Dad. but back in your day you used wax tablets for writing, and finally learning the times table when you were eighteen was seen as an achievement.'

'Thanks for that. When did my daughter become such a comedian? You've cut me to my very core with your acerbic wit.'

'What does "acerbic" mean?'

'Never mind,' he groaned with a roll of his eyes and head, exaggerating to the point he almost flopped his whole body off the edge of the bed.

She laughed. 'Dad, you're awful.'

'Eva! John!' Becca called up to them. 'Are you coming down for dinner?'

'Best get down there. She's had a crap day.'

'Oh, really?' *Weird. That's not the impression I got.*

'Yep,' she said, non-committal, 'coming, Mum!'

They got up and made their way downstairs while Morrissey continued to lament in the background.

* * *

Drake put the dinner plate back in the cupboard and picked up the next one while he continued his drying duty. Becca focused on washing a saucepan, the suds creating a cloudscape in the sink to such an extent it engulfed the remaining pots and plates.

It was good to spend time with them both while they were unaware of what was dragging down his thoughts. He didn't want their behaviour to change because of the circumstances. He didn't want them to change, period. To see him in a different light; to second guess him. But that's what would happen as soon as he told them. Once the cat was out of the bag, they would start to worry, casting their minds back to other cases where he *had* let things get to him.

He was thankful that Eva wasn't around when the Family Man first made an appearance. The case had such a significant an effect on him and Becca in the first year of their relationship, they'd even questioned whether it was right to bring a child into their life. Or to be more specific, *his* life... *his* career.

'You okay there? You've gone distant,' Becca said.

Drake came back to the present and realised he'd been drying the plate to within an inch of its life. 'Yes, sorry. Lost in thought for a moment there, wasn't I?'

'So, now are you going to tell me what's on your mind?' she asked, emptying the washing-up bowl and resting it on the sideboard to dry. The plughole gurgled as she folded her arms across her chest.

Drake sighed. This would not end well.

'Okay.' He put away the last plate and hung up the tea towel. Taking her hand, he led her into the lounge to sit on the sofa. Eva was back upstairs, the distant rumble of music still making itself known.

'No, I don't want to sit. Just tell me what's going on.' Becca said, letting go of his hand. She was biting her lip and already looked on edge, as though she was preparing to soak up the bad news, and he hadn't even said anything yet. It never ceased to amaze him how well Becca understood him. She knew it wasn't just any old work issue he had on his mind. She knew it was something; something big.

'Okay. But before I do, please try to trust me and believe me when I say I'm not, I repeat, *not* going to be directly involved in what I'm going to tell you.' He looked her in the eyes, trying to convince her of something he didn't fully believe himself.

'John, you're scaring me now. What is it?'

He hesitated, before looking her in her eyes. 'It ... it's "Him".'

'What do you mean, *him*?'

'The Family Man. There's been another incident.'

'What! How? That man died. You *saw* him die, John.' Her face began turning a deep shade of red, her anger rising. 'You told me he was dead. That it was over.'

She collapsed on to the sofa and looked at him in despair, disbelief etched on her face. Drake sat next to her, willing her to look at him, but she continued staring at the carpet.

'Becca, it was. I mean, I thought it was...'

'Then what the hell?' She was fighting back tears, whether of anger or sadness, he couldn't tell. 'How is he alive? How is he still out there?'

'We got a call today. There was an incident in Haworth up in Yorkshire – where we went on a break that time, remember? Unfortunately, it has all the hallmarks of being a Family Man killing. Miller spoke to the DCS there.'

She didn't say anything. 'Becca, Miller's on her way to the scene,' Drake went on. 'Right now, we have no idea if it's a copycat, or if we have been duped somehow.'

His voice caught in his throat. They'd bottled up the raw emotion of twenty years ago, sealed it in a container and locked it away. But now the seal was broken, the pieces lying shattered on the floor.

'Becca... Miller asked me if I wanted to lead the case,' he told her. He reached over and cupped her clenched fists in his hands. 'I said no.'

'What? Why did you do that?' she snapped, pulling away from his grip.

Why is she asking that? I thought she'd be pleased. 'What do you mean, why?' He did his best to sound calm, but Becca was confusing him. Drake knew was close to losing his cool.

'Why would you say no to the return of the biggest case of

your career?' Becca demanded. 'Are you trying to show solidarity with Eva and me? Is that it?'

'Yes. Becca. I don't understand—'

'I don't believe you,' she said simply. 'I'm trying not to sound harsh, but I think maybe that's what you *think* you're doing. And we appreciate the sentiment. We do. But I think you're in denial – once you've got over the initial shock, you'll be back on the case. I know you too well. You won't be able to help yourself.'

'I did it for us, Becca. You know what this case means, and I don't want to put you – and now Eva – through it. I won't do that to you again, I swear.'

Becca took a deep breath and held it in. A slight hint of a sob gave her away. 'I know what it means. I'm just finding it hard to take this in. I want to believe you, but I'm not sure I can. I'm sorry.'

Drake nodded. 'You and me both, Becca. But I really am trying here – Miller's calling me later to go over the details when she's had a chance to look over the scene. She'll be able to confirm whether it is actually a copycat. There are specifics that were not made public, that only the killer and we know. If these are present ...' *If those are present, then all hell will break loose.*

As soon as he mentioned Miller contacting him, Becca stared at him in disbelief. 'You just said you weren't getting involved.'

'I'm not. I'm only trying to help with the confirmation. As I said, I won't be getting directly involved.'

'John—'

'Becca, I—'

Drake's phone blared, scattering his thoughts. It reverberated on the coffee table, the screen displaying *DCS Miller*.

Neither of them spoke. The mobile continued, the sound growing more insistent and more obnoxious by the second.

'You know I've got to answer that.'

'Well, you'd better answer it then, hadn't you, *DCI John Drake*,' Becca hissed.

He grimaced at the words before reaching for the phone. He answered. And with Miller's reply, Drake's world fell apart.

14

The Barndon Arms was a family-run pub at the centre of the village. It had been under the Randall family's ownership for generations, likely since the founding of the village itself. Like most villages in England, it was very much the beating heart of the community. A village green sat across from the pub, ringed with a white chain-link fence. The fence was low level and Ben could imagine the locals, having had one too many drinks, tripping over it on many an occasion as they made their way home.

The pub's owner, Michael Randall, had answered when Ben called to book dinner, and he'd sounded distinctly put out. Randall wouldn't be getting any awards for customer service anytime soon, but the pub was ideal for Ben, about a five-minute drive away from their new home. He enjoyed the close-knit feel of the place, and if it had been summer, he might even have been able to persuade his family to walk there. Stranger things had happened.

He slowed to a crawl as he looked for a parking space. The building, which was spread over two floors, loomed over them, odd shadows dancing across the large limestone walls lit up by the exterior lighting.

Ben spotted what appeared to be the last space and pulled into it. While he'd been driving and off in his own world, Andrea and Cari chatted about a story in Yorkshire that had made the news. Ben hadn't tuned into what they were talking about other than overhearing the talk of several deaths.

'Right. All set, guys?' Ben asked, unbuckling his seatbelt and looking over his shoulder at Cari in the back passenger's seat.

'Yeah, I'm still not that hungry though, Dad. Do we have to be here long?'

'Come on, Cari, you've got to eat something. You don't want to be as skinny as me, I can assure you,' Andrea said, rubbing her stomach. Ben winced at the flash of her hip bone pressing against her skin.

'We won't be hours and hours, don't worry. Though your mother and I have worked up an appetite today,' he said, winking at Andrea. He received a hard, back-handed slap to the chest and a stern look from his wife in response.

'What do you mean?'

'Well, work for me, and Mum went for a walk earlier.' He coughed guiltily as he tried to get out of the hole that he'd dug for himself. 'Anyway, let's get going. Quicker we order, the quicker you can get back to your room and develop some more of that teenage angst you've got going on.'

Ben opened the knotted wooden door to the pub. The sound of cutlery on plates and good-natured chatter flooded out to greet them. He motioned Andrea and Cari through and followed in close behind.

Before them stood the bar, filled with locals on bar stools with gaggles of men and women surrounding them, either queuing or engaged in conversation. A few lads, who looked to be in their early twenties, wore hi-vis jackets. Others wore overalls, or the typical farm worker uniform of chinos or jeans and a shirt. Waxed coats hung off the back of stools. Some men looked to have custom pint glasses and mugs in their well-worn hands. Brass taps lined the bar and all manner of spirits were spread over the shelves behind.

Much to Ben's relief, it hadn't turned into a scene from a film where everyone turned around to see who had entered their domain, the place falling silent because the new family in town made an appearance. Instead, the locals carried on as though they weren't there at all.

Ben soon spied the restaurant seating area located past a tight corridor. The worn floorboards creaked as they made their way through the crowd and past the old, dusty ornaments on the walls.

'That looks like ours,' he said, ducking under a low wooden beam. The chunky oak table sat nestled in the corner beneath a painting of a fox-hunting scene. The dogs were foaming at the mouth, and the horsemen weren't far behind, judging by the crazed looks on their faces.

Ben sat down, landing with a thump on the bench set against the wall that made up two seats. It was lower than he'd been expecting, and Cari let out a sharp laugh.

'What?' Ben said, bemused, holding up his hands.

'Been putting on the pounds, eh, Dad?'

'What can I say, I like my food!'

'Evidently.'

'Wow.' Ben looked over at Andrea. 'Are you going to let her dish it out like that?'

'Well, you *have* got a little "something, something" going on there, honey,' Andrea said, settling in across from him. She made a show of pointing at his slight paunch.

'Wow, you too? I'm speechless. I give up.' He put up his arms with a look of mock resignation, knowing he wouldn't win this fight.

Soon after the outright attack on his physique, Ben left the table to get the pint that Andrea had promised him. He got the barmaid's attention, and it wasn't long before he had the old-style tankard in his grip. He stood for a moment, supping on the ale.

The place reminded him of when he and Andrea had met fifteen years ago, in a pub not dissimilar to this one, on the outskirts of Leeds.

He'd stopped off after work and Andrea had been with friends. He'd turned and bumped into her, almost spilling his drink. She looked like she was just about to admonish him, but she met his gaze and something stopped her. She said later she knew then that there was something there. Ben teased her about the old "spark" cliche, but she said it was just his blue eyes and mop of brown hair that sold her to him on the spot.

So, a spark then! He remembered them arguing in jest about that for hours. It was almost tragic how stereotypical the encounter was.

Within a year, she was pregnant with Cari and they had moved in together. Her "issues" were much less regular back in those days, and he didn't even witness a minor episode until seven months into their relationship. It was before her pregnancy, and by then he was completely committed and hadn't batted an eyelid. Instead, he'd done his best to show compassion and support.

Now, with a few more years under his belt, Ben wasn't so sure. He wasn't regretting things, but life had certainly taken him down an unexpected path.

15

I washed my hands at the sink in the pub bathroom and studied my reflection in the old brass framed mirror. Decades of grime had tarnished it, and the corners of the glass were cloudy. Somewhere, a tap or pipe dripped. It was already driving me to distraction.

I looked thin, almost gaunt. It was obvious I hadn't been sleeping well, and the effects were presenting themselves, dark bags slung heavy under my eyes.

I know I need to sleep and look after myself better, but it's so hard. She won't let me.

I splashed cold water on my face and wiped it off with the sleeve of my top as best I could. Anything to avoid using the rather mildewy-looking towels provided. What kind of pub toilet used cotton hand towels, anyway?

'Tough day?' A quiet voice piped up from behind, the words slightly masked by the loud flushing sound from a cubicle.

I turned to see a small woman in her mid-to-late-fifties staring at me from a cubicle. Her hair was tied back in a greying blonde bun, and her skin looked weathered and taut beneath her floral blouse. She seemed overly thin, by the look of her tight, worn denim jeans. The flush from the toilet cubicle emitted a loud gurgling sound before finally tailing off behind her.

'Yes, something like that,' I said, not wanting to commit to a conversation with a stranger in a grotty bathroom. Another one of my headaches was making itself known. I didn't want someone new exacerbating my pain if I was to continue hiding how I'd been feeling from Ben and Cari. I didn't want to worry them, not so soon after moving. It was supposed to have solved my problems, after all. Not made them worse.

'Ah, sorry to hear that, love. Say, you're that new family, aren't you?' The woman moved to the adjacent sink and looked in the mirror. She pushed at her cheeks with her fingertips.

'Yes, we moved in a few weeks ago. I guess news must travel fast round here,' I replied, looking across at the woman.

'Oh, not really. I think your man had a lift from my husband earlier today. Samuel's his name.'

I felt momentary relief that there was some common ground, even if it was just a simple association.

'Ah! Yes, Ben mentioned. It was ever so kind of him.' I forced a smile while my temple continued pulsing.

'Indeed, dear,' the woman said, looking down at the floor. I noticed her hands clenched tightly at her sides. It made me feel uneasy; in fact, the whole situation seemed strange. I couldn't quite put a finger on why, but there was a funny air about her.

'I'm Andrea,' I offered. Anything to cut through the moment's awkward silence.

'Ann. Ann Barrow,' she said, turning the tap on. The tap gave out a pathetic dribble, causing her to huff at it and turn it off again.

There was another awkward silence. I didn't know what to say, and Ann wasn't offering anything. 'Well...' I said, backing off towards the door to the bar. 'Nice to meet you, Ann. I'd best get back to my family. We've just ordered food and they'll be wondering whether I've got lost.'

'Okay, dear. I'm sure we'll see each other again.'

'I'm sure we will.' I gave a polite smile, and made a swift exit.

Ann didn't make any move to follow.

* * *

'Hey there, darling,' came an unfamiliar coarse voice, a silent 'g' on the word 'darling'.

Christ's sake, was this what it was going to be like everywhere I go round here? And what was this? Cowboy roleplay time?

I turned to greet someone who could only have been Samuel Barrow, waiting for his "darling" wife. The man had his head tilted and his hand held out in front of him. I met his gaze, and he frowned, if only for a second.

'Hello.' I gave another of my polite smiles, and shook his hand, killing the smile before it became a rictus one. The blood pumped around my skull, and the sensation was wearing me down. 'I'm sorry. Do I know you?'

'Yes – well, your husband does. I'm Sam. Samuel Barrow.'

'Lovely to meet you, Sam.' My heartbeat was racing, fogginess creeping in at the corners of my vision. I tried to blink it away, hoping he wouldn't notice. 'But I'm sorry, I've got to get back to my family – your wife and I spent some time chatting in the bathroom just now, and they'll be wondering where I've got to.'

'No problem, this won't take a minute,' he chuckled, leaning his elbow against the side of the bar. 'As I mentioned to your husband, I have a proposition for you.'

'Oh?' That piqued my attention. What could he possibly have

to offer a complete stranger? I hoped it wasn't something awkward that I'd have to wriggle out of.

'Yes, little lady.'

'Okay.' I rubbed my temple irritably as I waited for him to get to the point.

'I hope I'm not imposing, but how would you like some work?'

'Oh. What kind of work was it you had in mind?'

'Well, you know... a little of this and that,' he drawled. 'Firstly, please tell me if it's not for you. But Ann and I, well, we were looking for a new assistant for the day-to-day upkeep of the house. You see, the place has grown over the years and we're so busy with the business these days that we don't want it to go to ruin.'

'You mean a cleaner?' I crossed my arms, feeling a little belit-tled by the offer. It irritated me that someone who didn't even know me would assume I'd want that sort of job. Not all people of Turkish heritage were cleaners or low-level workers. But I suppose he wasn't to know my mum had been one.

'No, no!' He held up his hands in defence. 'I didn't mean to cause offence. It's true there is an element of that, but it's more of a clerical and housekeeper sort of role.'

'I see. Well, can I speak with my husband and let you know? Would that be okay?'

I supposed it might not be so bad. Maybe it would do me some good to get out and about and occupy myself a bit more.

'Yes, of course. You take your time. I thought I'd give you the first refusal either way. You're a local gal now, and I want to keep the workforce that way too. Let me know when you've had a chance to discuss it and come to a decision. Here, let me jot down my number.'

Samuel took out a small notepad and jot down his number

with an expensive-looking ballpoint pen. He tore off the note and handed it to me just as Ann came out of the toilets.

'What's this, Sam? I leave you alone for five minutes and you're handing out your number to the new woman in town?' There was a snide tone in her voice, at odds with the timid woman I'd met before.

Samuel cut her an angry glare. 'I was just giving her my details. As you know, we have that assistant role that's come up recently, and I figured we should offer her some work. If she was in need, that is.'

'I see.' Ann seemed to remember herself and shrunk back.

'Okay, well...,' I hesitated, feeling awkward. 'Thank you both. I need to be going back to my family now.' I didn't fancy getting involved in what looked like shaping up to be a domestic.

I made my way back to the table, looking at the piece of paper I'd received. Samuel's number was written in a surprisingly ornate-looking hand.

Maybe things were looking up, after all.

16

Ben was mid-conversation with Cari about some French horror film she was far too young to have watched, when his wife returned from a very long trip to the bathroom.

'Hey, where were you? You okay? We were starting to think you'd escaped out the bathroom window.' There was a tinge of concern in his voice. The thought had genuinely crossed his mind.

Cari shuffled in again to let Andrea through, hitting her knee on the table leg in the process. 'Ow, fuck!'

Ben stifled a laugh. 'Come on, Cari – not in public, please. You know you shouldn't be swearing like that.'

'Ah, come on, it *fricking* hurt, Dad.' She emphasised the point by rubbing her knee, her bottom lip poking out while she concentrated on tending to it.

'Yes, Cari.' Ben turned his attention back to Andrea. 'So, what's up?'

'Oh, nothing. I just made a friend on the long, *long* trip to the bathroom and back.'

'Nice. That's good to hear that you're making friends.

Speaking to people besides us ... particularly besides this one.' He nodded in Cari's direction and got poked in the hand with a fork in response. 'So, who did you meet?'

'Ann Barrow. She was in the toilets – glamorous, eh? And your best bud, Sam Barrow.'

'Schmoozing with the elite now, eh, Mum?' Cari said, nudging her with her elbow. 'Remember us when you're big and famous, please.' Before adding with a whisper and a wink: 'I want your money.'

'It wasn't like that, Cari,' Andrea snapped.

'Chill Mum, I was only joking.'

'Sorry,' Andrea said. 'It's just that he offered me a job up at their house, as a housekeeper of sorts. Apparently, there would be some office work too.'

She looked genuinely excited. Ben frowned at her. 'Really? Just like that? Do you think you're up to it right now?'

'What, so you don't think I'm able to work? I'm an invalid, is that it?' Andrea said, raising her voice and glaring at him.

'Whoa, whoa, steady. I wasn't saying that,' Ben said, shrinking back from her look.

'Yeah, well, it sounded like it. Just because I've ... I've not been well recently,' she said quietly. 'It doesn't mean I can't try to bring in some money.'

Ben nodded. He hadn't meant to coddle her, but she *wasn't* well. *It couldn't be a good move, could it?*

'Good for you, Mum. I think it's a great idea.' Cari leant her head on Andrea's shoulder and gave her arm a squeeze. 'It will do you good. I'm proud of you.'

It's not been you trying to keep her together though, has it, Cari? Ben thought. *You haven't been the one doing his best to stop her losing it.*

Shit, what was he thinking? That was his daughter.

'Okay, let's not get ahead of ourselves,' Andrea said. 'I've not accepted it yet, I was just excited. Weirdly, I don't go accepting things without discussing it with my husband first to see what he thinks. But it seems that's pretty clear now.'

She folded her arms and leant back in her chair. Ben wasn't sure what to say, and her comment hung in the air.

'Two ham and egg, and one Caesar salad?' A young barmaid interrupted the awkward silence, and Ben nodded, forcing a smile.

'Yes, that's us. The salad's for my daughter.'

The barmaid handed them their plates. The eggs looked greasy, and the ham looked like it had seen better days. 'Enjoy,' she said, her own smile a little forced.

I'll try. I'll really try, Ben thought, as he skewered the meat.

17

Becca had been upstairs in their bedroom since storming off after Drake had answered Miller's call. It had been a brief conversation, but a devastating one.

He knew from their earlier discussions that it was more than likely these murders would turn out to be a Family Man case. But he'd clung to the hope that maybe, just *maybe,* it was a mistake. Maybe there was some other sick bastard out there who'd decided to butcher a family as a one off, getting his kicks from something he'd read online. The details were everywhere, after all, having been covered in a slew of articles and documentaries. Drake had always refused to take part when contacted, keen not to glorify the murders or rake over the details again. For his own sanity, if nothing else.

To his dismay, however, Miller had confirmed the case bore every hallmark of a classic Family Man killing. It was as though the Family Man had just carried on from where he left off twenty years prior.

Since Becca had stormed off, Drake had remained sat on the sofa with his head in his hands. He wasn't sure how long he'd been there, but the grandfather clock he'd inherited from his father, an ornate, hand-carved beast of a clock, had just chimed eight, which meant he'd been stewing alone for a good hour.

Drake was just about to seek her out when he heard her feet on the stairs, and she came back into the room.

'Becca ... I'm sorry. I had to tell you. I didn't want to keep anything from you,' he blurted, genuine concern etched on his face.

She didn't reply. Instead, she padded over to an armchair that faced the sofa, a big brown leather number that had seen better days. She had been crying upstairs, her eyes red rimmed and puffy. She didn't appear upset any longer, but she had a strange look about her Drake couldn't put his finger on.

'Becca, you've got to talk to me. Are we okay? Please say we are.'

'Go.' Her voice was barely a whisper.

'Huh?'

'I said... *go.*'

'I know what you said,' he replied. 'But what do you mean, "go"? You want me to leave again, is that it?' He did his best to remain calm. 'If that's the case, I think we need to talk this through rationally, because I've not done anything wrong. I said I wouldn't take the case, and I meant it.'

His mind was all over the place, like a dog that had lost its owner. Were these just empty words coming out of his mouth? He couldn't lose them. He couldn't mess things up again. Christ, he'd not even taken the damn case.

'No, John, I mean go to Haworth. Go to Yorkshire. Do what you're meant to do. Solve this damn case once and for all, so we can all be fucking done with it,' she snarled at him. 'Maybe then, you can think about what you value more – us, or your job.'

'What! No! I'm not leaving you and Eva.' He didn't understand. She *wanted* him to work the case? Why the sudden turnaround?

'Yes, you are. Seriously, I'm not having you in this house for the next however bloody long, with that distant look on your face. I'm not having a huge "what if" hanging over us for the rest of our days. Listen to me – I'm giving you free rein, one last time. Then you're going to have to make a choice.'

'Becca, I ... I don't know what to say.'

He could be gone for a long time, they both knew that. She was right, though – it would be a constant in his mind until it was over, and she and Eva didn't deserve that.

'You can come back to the house when you're back in the area,' she said, her voice catching. 'I don't want this to hurt Eva. I want her to still see and hear from her dad.'

'Becca, I've not said I'll do this yet. I certainly haven't agreed to the what, why and how of it all.'

'You don't have a choice,' Becca told him. 'This is no time for you to take some noble stance. Please, just take what I'm offering and go.'

This was a new side to her. Becca was usually one for internalising her anger, but this was out in the open and raw. Her fists were clenched, her eyes blank and brimming with tears that threatened to run down her cheeks.

Giving him this "opportunity" was hurting her, but she was doing it for them – one last attempt at salvaging what they had. He thought about what she said about him having to make a choice, after it was all over. Could he leave his job? He didn't want to even think about that right now.

But maybe it wouldn't come to that. He immediately regretted the thought. *For God's sake, man. Can't you see, this is your last chance?*

He sat dumbfounded for a time, before he finally nodded. 'Okay.'

'Okay, what?' Drake knew she needed him to confirm he was going to take the case. The thing that exemplified everything she hated about his job.

'Okay. I'll do it.'

Her eyes narrowed. 'Good. Now, say goodbye to Eva.'

'*Now*? It's eight o'clock in the evening.'

'You want this case?' Becca's words were laced with a venom he'd rarely heard from her. 'Then you better get fucking started.' She got up and stormed from the room. He heard her put on shoes and a coat, followed by the sound of the front door opening, then slamming shut.

Drake took a deep breath and sat amidst the silence. His body shook from the bouncing of his knee while he tried to process what had just happened.

He would do this case right if it killed him.

* * *

'Eva?' He knocked on her door. No music was coming from her room now, so she should be able to hear him.

'Come in.' Her reply was muted by the door.

He opened it to find her peering through the curtains and out of the window into the darkness. The room felt stuffy to him, enclosed. He didn't want to say goodbye to his daughter like this.

'Where's Mum going?'

'We had a bit of a fight. She just needs some time to herself.'

'Again? I thought you guys were better now,' Eva said, before correcting herself. 'No, that's harsh on Mum – I thought *you* were better. What did you do?'

'It's a case that's come up, Eva.'

92

'It's always a case, Dad. When are you going to learn?'

Her comment took Drake by surprise. Eva had been doing a lot of growing up these last few months, it seemed. And now, he'd be missing it all over again.

'It's a big case. It's *the* case, the one we've spoken about before. The Family Man case.'

'Huh? But, that guy... you said he'd died? How's that work?'

'He did. But there's been another similar incident up in Yorkshire – you might have heard about it on the news today? I'm going up there to find out what's going on.'

'What, so you're going right now? This evening?' She couldn't stifle her surprise.

'Yes.'

Her eyes started welling up. 'So, you're really leaving us again?'

'Yes, but not for long, I promise. Mum and I have agreed that this will be the last time. Then I'll be back for good.'

'Bullshit, Dad. Why do you keep doing this to her ... doing this to *me*? You didn't see what she was like when you weren't around. She was so sad.'

'I know. I just... I have to do this.'

'I hope you know the cost then,' her voice trembled. 'You're a fucking arsehole.'

'Eva, don't say that.'

'You are. And you're going to be one until you're back. I don't care.' With those last few words, she started crying, the tears rolling down her face.

He moved to console her, but she pushed at him. 'Leave me alone.'

'Eva, please.' He backed towards the doorway. 'Please don't leave it like this.'

'No, Dad, I want you to go ... *Now.*'

'I'm sorry, Eva. I truly am. I hope you know that,' Drake said, backing out of the room.

'Fuck you,' She screamed, slamming the door in his face. He heard a muffled metallic noise followed by a *click*.

'Eva!' He tried the handle, but it wouldn't budge. He could hear her crying inside as he pressed his forehead up against the door.

'Eva, I'm sorry. Please believe me. I'll be back soon. Things will be all right.'

His voice was cracking. He stepped back and ran his hand through his hair, continuing to stare at the closed door. Was this really worth the pain he was putting them through?

It had to be, Drake told himself. The emotional cost was too high a price otherwise. He went to the master bedroom and packed a change of clothes before stopping by his study to collect his briefcase. Before going downstairs, he dialled Miller's number, the phone screen shining brightly in the darkness of the room.

'John, what is it?' Her voice was a distorted echo, perhaps because of a poor signal. He could hear chatter in the background, and it sounded like she was still at the crime scene.

'I'm coming to Haworth. I'm taking the case. Make sure they don't remove the bodies... Shit, make sure they don't move *anything* until I'm there.'

'Wait, what—'

Drake hung up.

18

'DS Wilkinson.' Ellie answered her phone, attempting to balance it between her shoulder and ear while she muted the television. Her husband groaned and her four-year-old daughter mimicked him.

'Ellie, it's Drake.'

Drake? What could he want at this time of night? She hadn't seen him since he'd gone to Miller's office. By the time she'd returned to his desk to check in a few hours later, he and his briefcase were long gone.

She'd heard from her colleagues about the drama at the entrance to Miller's office. It sounded like Miller and Drake had kept a tight lid on everything thereafter, though. She hadn't been able to get any further information out of anyone.

'Sir, what can I do for you?' Is everything okay?'

'Ellie, I need your address. I'm coming by to pick you up immediately.'

She frowned and gave him her address, the television's silent glow casting deep shadows on her face.

'Sir – Drake – what do you mean? What's going on?'

'A case has come up. A *big* case. You want to be part of the investigating team, you need to be ready by the time I arrive. Be ready in twenty.'

'I ... okay. How many days we talking?'

'One? Two? I don't know. Just pack something.'

'On it,' she said and provided her address. 'Can you—'

Drake had hung up. 'Arsehole,' Ellie muttered.

'Everything okay?' Len asked, a concerned look on his kind, angular face.

'Yeah ... I mean, I guess so. That was the DCI I was telling you about. Drake. He wants me to pack up some things and go somewhere for a few days.'

'Sounds exciting. When're you going?'

She shrugged. 'In the next twenty minutes, apparently.'

'What!'

'Yeah, I know – I'm sorry, babe. You going to be all right with that little troublemaker over there for a day or two?' she said, sticking her tongue out at her daughter, Bella.

'Of course.'

His initial surprise had disappeared once he knew it was work-related. That's why she loved the man. In the five years they'd been together, three happily married, Len had always been there for her. He understood the nature of the job from the night shifts she'd worked in Response, and this was just a few days, after all. A walk in the park.

'Thanks.' She kissed them both on the forehead, giving Bella a long hug before running upstairs.

19

Ellie busied herself with adjusting the passenger seat, wincing as Drake slammed the boot of the car. The sound left her in no doubt that her new boss was in a bad mood.

He seemed to have made good time getting to her place in Harrow, northwest London. She wasn't sure where he lived, but it couldn't have been far. Or perhaps he'd broken a few speeding laws on the way over?

Drake's car was a black Audi. It had a few years on it, and judging by the numbers on the dash, quite a few miles on the clock, too. She always thought these models looked like they were owned by drug dealers, particularly when they came with tinted windows like these. She wouldn't be saying that to Drake, though, that's for sure. He didn't seem to be one for jokes, and certainly not this evening.

The torrential rain had started the moment she stepped outside, and promptly soaked her as she walked down the path. The sound of the raindrops pelting the top of the car perfectly encapsulated the mood of the evening, and Ellie hoped it wasn't nature's way of warning her of what was to come.

She was still adjusting her seat when Drake opened the door. The sound of the rain increased for a second before he closed it and turned on the ignition. He sat motionless, seemingly deep in thought, and Ellie wondered what was up with him. The man looked drawn and a little sad.

Drake seemed to recall what he wanted to do, and started with setting the destination on the satnav in the centre console. Ellie watched him enter a postcode she didn't recognise, before the screen presented directions to a place called Haworth in Yorkshire.

We're going to Yorkshire at this time of night? What the hell? She made more of a show of looking at the screen before confronting Drake. 'So... Yorkshire?'

'Yes. Haworth, to be precise.' He put the car in gear and pulled away from the curb, offering no further elaboration. The wipers started working hard to keep the screen clear, punctuating the silence.

She vaguely recalled catching on the news that there'd been several unexplained deaths in Yorkshire that afternoon. Maybe that was it? But the press hadn't mentioned murder from what she could remember.

And what did that have to do with their team? They didn't get involved in non-suspicious deaths. Their team worked cases that weren't on the straight and narrow; they'd come in and take over from the existing police force when it was clear it wasn't a run-of-the-mill murder enquiry.

The opportunity to be part of something that was radically different to her days on the beat was what had excited Ellie from the start. The SMT were small in number, but the team was proving essential these days, as CID was being stretched ever thinner with the day-to-day grind. *So, that means there must be more to this Yorkshire incident than was fed to the press?*

'Is this related to what's on the news right now?' she asked, twisting in the passenger seat to look at him.

Drake didn't make eye contact, maintaining his focus on the road. His lips were pressed into a tight grimace, and she could tell this was going to be hard work.

'Ellie...' A traffic light cast a red glow on his face, highlighting his angular cheek bones as he glanced briefly at her.

'I can see you're keen to understand what's going on, and why I've dragged you away at this time of night for a fun-filled four hour drive up north,' he said. 'It's understandable. But please, can you cut down on the questions and the enthusiasm for a bit?' He kept his attention trained on the road ahead. 'I need time to process things, and driving is usually when I do that. I need to think. I'll answer your questions in a while.'

His directness cut her like a knife. Sure, he outranked her and was much older, but she'd worked damned hard to get into the team, away from Response and into something that meant more to her. He should respect that, but his tone made her feel like a child.

Maybe he's upset about something else, she thought. *Maybe it wasn't work-related?*

She sat back in her seat, with a resigned look. 'Okay, sir.'

'Please, it's Drake.' He headed for the M25 Eastbound. 'You don't need to be so formal with me.'

'Sir ... Drake, I'm sorry. It's just ... I've only just joined SMT. This may not be new to you, but it's new to me and it's exciting. I understand your request and I'll leave you to it for now. But you *will* need to tell me what's going on before we get there. Please.'

'I'll tell you soon, don't worry. Maybe get some sleep.'

Ellie took the hint and fell silent. But she couldn't relax, her mind jumping to all kinds of conclusions. *There has to be some-*

thing 'off' about the scene, she realised. *This is something big. It has to be.*

Her mind was working overtime, the thoughts spinning round in her head, but it wasn't long before her body took Drake's advice. Soon she was sleeping to the sound of the engine's hum, her face illuminated by the streetlights as each one flew by.

20

They were halfway up the M1 motorway, having just passed junction 28; almost halfway to the crime scene, and it was approaching midnight. Drake wasn't tired, though. The anticipation was making him delve into the recesses of his mind to recall the minutiae of the Family Man cases.

He wondered what he'd find when he entered the house; how it would make him feel when he entered the kill room and saw those familiar sights again, the ones he'd locked away so long ago. He knew he felt conflicted right now. That was one thing he was sure of.

There was the familiar feeling of excitement, of *adventure,* and that repulsed him. People had died; and not just died. Someone had murdered them brutally. Children too. And Becca had pushed him to take this case. He couldn't let her down. He felt an incredible amount of love for her, but it was mixed with pain. He knew what he was about to put her and his daughter through, if the "Man" was truly back.

And was bringing Ellie in on this case a good idea? It would take her in at the deep end, maybe damage her too, in the end. Did she have a family? She hadn't said, and he realised he hadn't asked. If so, he'd have to use his experience to help her.

He realised he needed to put in the effort to make this team work. They would be spending a lot of time together, so he shouldn't be snapping and making things difficult for the sake of it. The last thing they needed was to rub each other up the wrong way. This case was going to be a struggle, and he needed her to be on point, with no distractions.

Holding the information at arm's reach wasn't helping, he conceded. So, he supposed now was as good a time as any.

* * *

'So...' Drake said.

Ellie woke with a start and put her hand to her face. It came back wet. She'd been dribbling in her sleep. She rubbed it away, hoping he hadn't noticed. *Shit, of course he noticed,* she thought, *it's frickin' DCI Drake.*

She saw it was darker now they were outside of the city and driving up the backbone of the country. Only the odd motorway lamppost was lit, as many had been turned off to save on energy.

'Wah ...?' Her mouth was dry as she tried to form a sentence. 'How long was I out for?'

'Only about an hour or so. Don't worry, you'll be grateful for it soon enough.'

'Now you've really got me worried. Are you going to tell me or keep me in suspense for even longer?' She tried to inject a little humour into the car's stifled atmosphere, hoping it wouldn't fall flat again.

'To be honest, with this case, you *will* be worried,' Drake told her. 'Worried that this person is out there and that he might repeat what happened today. It will eat at you,' he warned.

'Okay. So, tell me what's going on.'

'Fine.' He paused. 'Are you familiar with the Family Man case?'

'Family Man? You're playing with me, right?'

She frowned as she realised he wasn't joking. Of course, she knew who the Family Man was. *Everyone* knew about the Family Man. She'd only been at secondary school a month when she'd first heard about it. It had been the talk of the school for the best part of a year, and covered extensively on the national news.

The murderer had taken on an almost boogie-man level of notoriety at the time. It got to the point where her parents had even argued about getting a burglar alarm fitted after the third incident. Her dad had thought it was stupid, and he'd argued there was no point. The Family Man seemed to only pick large, posh houses full of affluent white people, not black families living in terraces in Hackney.

From what she had read, he'd killed himself before they could question him, so what did Yorkshire have to do with a twenty-year-old case? There had never been any activity that far north either, from what she could remember.

'Yes, I'm aware of it. It was a case I read up on when I was in training. Are you saying something happened up in Yorkshire, something related to that case?' Her eyes widened in surprise. 'Like, seriously? How is that possible?'

'Yes.'

'But that's insane. He's dead.'

'I certainly hope he is. But we may have a copycat on our hands,' Drake said. 'A family, the Cartwrights, died this afternoon – all except the wife, of course. Miller's up there now and has confirmed it for me. She says the scene looks as though he never stopped.' The last few words were said through gritted teeth.

Ellie winced. That went some way to explaining his behaviour today. By all accounts, Drake had lived and breathed that case, only to have the answers he desperately sought torn from him, when the psycho killed himself. To have it come up again had to take a heavy toll. 'Are the bodies still in situ?'

'I've asked that they don't move anything until I've – we've – looked over the crime scene, which is why we're making our way there now. You're going to be privy to your first murder investigation of this calibre – one of *the* most heinous kinds at that. It's not just the brutality of the father's death, but the children's too. It's a hard one to stomach. I wasn't a father at the time, and I found it challenging enough. Now, I've got a teenage daughter. I don't know if you've got kids?'

Ellie was quiet for a moment. She tried not to think about what she would do if it had happened to her beautiful little girl. 'I have a daughter, too. She's just turned four years old.' She caught herself smiling and stopped.

'Then you understand it will be difficult to work the scene,' Drake said. 'Have you had to deal with anything involving children in your Response days?'

'My fair share in terms of domestic abuse, or minor accidents. But I've been fortunate to miss any involving DOAs of children in my time.'

'The victims, in this case, are two boys aged ten and four.'

'No!'

'I know.'

Ellie looked aghast. She couldn't prevent her mind filling with images of her daughter's beaming face looking back at her. Bella's first day at preschool; taking her home from the hospital when she'd given birth three weeks premature. She was so tiny. How could anyone do that to a child, and *repeatedly*? Those kids must have been so scared. And the parents, it didn't bear thinking about. *Shit*.

Ellie fought to gather herself as they drove in silence. They were only a couple of hours out from Haworth, from the victims, when Drake spoke.

'I brought along some of my case notes from the previous murders. They're on the back seat if you want to go over some of them.'

She leaned into the back, reaching for the set of case files, bound with a sturdy rubber band. The files were bulging with paper, and Ellie guessed the computer-based information Drake had on the case would be lacking, if not altogether non-existent.

'Thanks. And don't worry about the kids. I can do it, Drake,' she said. 'You can count on me.'

'Okay. But know that I won't judge you if you need a time out. These things affect people in different and unexpected ways. Particularly when it's your first one.'

'Thank you, si—' She winced at the realisation that she'd almost made another naming error, but Drake let it slide.

She was about to open the files when she stopped. 'Actually, I don't think you need to tell me more right now. I'll leave these for now, too – I've read about the case before, and I think I should try to come at it with a reasonably fresh pair of eyes. Perhaps I'll see things others won't.'

'Might be a good idea.' Drake sounded appreciative. 'It's a little raw for me just now, frankly, and you may be right.'

'Here's hoping.' She yawned and burrowed down a little into the leather seat. 'If you don't mind, I may try to sleep a little more before we get there.'

'Be my guest. We're just coming up to Sheffield, so you should get an hour.'

'Satnav says two hours—'

'Maybe, but I'm getting impatient.'

She felt the car accelerate and his face took on a determined look. *Fair enough,* she thought. *Better get to it, then.* Before long, she was back asleep. Bella was in her thoughts again, but her little girl wasn't smiling this time.

21

Ben woke to the feeling of pressure on his chest. Coming to, he looked down to see Andrea's head resting on his stomach, just in time for the evening's events to come flooding back in an unwelcome blur. The pub, the well-intentioned job offer, the small domestic that had followed. It had all led to a rather strained dinner.

He'd done his best to bring the mood back up a notch or two by talking to Cari about her music, and her aspirations to follow in her mother's footsteps. Andrea had been an artist so it had the desired effect of bringing Andrea back into the conversation, and her mood had lightened a little thereafter. Enough for her to lie on him this evening, at least.

The television was silent now, though, the screen blank; Andrea had shifted onto him from the other end of the sofa. Cari must have switched off the set and gone to bed. Ben assumed she'd snuck off so they could spend some time together. Despite appearances, his daughter was more thoughtful than he could have imagined.

The job offer worried him, though. Andrea hadn't had a

"proper" job for a good few years. They'd felt it best to have her focused on her paintings. That way, she had an outlet that didn't involve crowds and the typical social pressures associated with an office. They concluded it might even help ease her episodes.

He wondered how she would manage on a large farming estate. He supposed it *might* be okay; she would be in the main house and offices with the Barrow family, rather than amidst dangerous farm machinery. Her mum had been a cleaner, so maybe when she heard the role had involved an element of that sort of work, she'd felt some sort of draw. Though he imagined the thought of her cleaning also agitated her.

He looked down and studied his wife for a moment, her breathing slow and measured while he stroked her hair. Ben's mind wandered to another of the worries on his already burgeoning pile. Despite her positivity about it, lately Andrea had been speaking about her mother a lot.

He could imagine the time spent in this new house was making her fixate on Miray, who'd once lived in the same village. Maybe that's why Andrea had been seeing her more in her dreams. Ben suspected those dreams were likely more nightmarish than she'd let on, and what she'd said earlier had unsettled him. But maybe he was worrying too much. Perhaps the move was just making her sentimental?

Not that she had anything to be sentimental about; from what Andrea had disclosed, Miray wouldn't have won any awards for mother of the year. She'd abused Andrea physically from a young age, beating her when she wasn't home from school on time or when she didn't answer her questions the way Miray wanted. She was never far from a slap or a bruise, and Andrea said it was akin to having a child for a mother; one that wanted all the attention and would play up when she didn't get it, however unreasonable the situation.

The older Andrea got, the more the abuse became mental rather than physical. Miray had continued locking her in her bedroom, screaming and crying when she didn't like Andrea's behaviour. Her mother implied that she wasn't a good daughter if she wanted to spend time with the few friends she was allowed, and insisted she was the daughter she never wanted, anyway. Andrea's birth had been unplanned, and her father had never been in the picture.

Regardless of the continued abuse, her mother's suicide had been the traumatic event which Ben believed acted as some sort of catalyst for Andrea's present mental health troubles. She had never gone into detail about the circumstances of her mother's death, beyond the shocking sight of her mother slitting her own throat in front of her.

Apparently, there hadn't even been an argument preceding it. It was highly disturbing and sad; he couldn't even begin to imagine seeing something like that and Andrea, of all people, certainly didn't deserve to be left with that after what the woman had put her through.

There was so much unanswered, so much mystery. What had happened for Miray to have behaved in such a way? The topic had been an extremely sensitive subject since, and Ben had never pushed the matter, certainly not during these last few years. He wanted a simple life for her and Cari.

Let the past be the past.

After a few more moments of dozing, Ben braved waking his wife. He began rubbing her side to stir her awake.

'I think it's time we got to bed,' he said, nudging her. 'Andrea?'

'Hmmm, okay.' She dragged herself to her feet and gave an enormous yawn.

Ben felt the warmth fade from his stomach. He should try to make her happy, he supposed, even if what he was about to say went against his better judgement. 'Andrea, if you still want to do it, I think you should take the job. It sounds like it would make you happy. And if you're happy, I'm happy.'

Surprise swept across her face. 'You do? Seriously? Thank you!' She let out a squeal and pumped her fists with excitement, the sleepiness gone. 'Did I ever tell you how much I love you, Ben Whitman?'

She jumped into his lap and put her arms around him.

'Oooff!' He huffed as he took her weight. 'No, but you're going to, many times over.' He wrapped his arms around her and smiled.

'Oh, I can do more than that.' With that, she cajoled him upstairs and closed the bedroom door.

22

It was not long after one in the morning when Drake pulled into a parking space off a main road, behind an old white van with *Clean me* written on the mud-splattered rear door.

Never gets old, he thought. The sight reminded him he was guilty of doodling such witty comments too when he was younger. Switching the ignition off, he let out a yawn and rubbed at his tired eyes. He felt like he'd been driving for days.

Ellie yawned next to him. She'd woken up about ten minutes prior to their arrival. Her demeanour had changed in the last few miles of their journey; the scratching of her leg and the absent picking of an errant thread on her trousers giving away her restlessness. It amused Drake that he wasn't the only one with a behavioural tic; in his case, he knew, he rubbed at the stubble on his cheek when thinking or agitated.

Drake took a sip from the Starbucks coffee he'd picked up at the last service station before coming off the M1. It was tepid now, but it would do. Ellie's coffee sat untouched. She said she was hyped up enough not to need the coffee, and anyway, what if she needed to piss at the crime scene? She couldn't do it.

He'd surprised himself by producing a grim chuckle; maybe they were going to get on, after all. He still couldn't believe that just twelve hours ago he'd been winding down a standard case – a non-SMT case at that – and now he was going to be back leading the biggest case he'd ever had. The world was a heartless bastard sometimes.

'You all set?' he asked, undoing his seatbelt and reaching behind to the backseat for his coat.

'Got to be, haven't I? No backing out now. Plus, you've driven me four hours away from my family. What else can I do?' She shrugged, trying to lighten the mood again.

'Yep, that's true.'

'No, seriously. Let's do this. Got to do it for the family, if nothing else. Got to catch the sick bastard – the sooner, the better.'

Drake opened the car door, stepped out, and stretched. His arse ached; he was getting old, and driving long distances wasn't for him anymore, but at least the rain hadn't followed them up north. *Every cloud* ..., he thought.

He'd forgotten how quiet it could be up here. The street seemed eerily silent. No lights shone from the windows of the terraced houses, nothing permeated out the edges of closed curtains. A fox yelped in the distance.

Drake looked up as he stretched before pulling his coat tighter around him. The crescent moon and the stars shone brightly. He'd always enjoyed being away from the South. Less light pollution. Maybe someday they could move further north and give Eva a more "country" upbringing and lifestyle. He realised that was a pipe dream, though; he kept forgetting she was already fourteen. There weren't many more years in which to make that sort of move, and he knew she wouldn't be happy leaving her friends now, let alone in a few years.

'I've never been to Yorkshire before,' Ellie remarked. 'It's so quiet here. I know it's nighttime, but there seems to be a distinct energy about the place.'

'It's a fantastic area. You'll like it. You won't have time to see much of it though, sorry to say.'

'Yeah,' she replied, her eyes dropping. 'I know.'

'Let's go.'

* * *

The crime scene was only a five-minute walk. Drake had figured it was better to park further away to garner less attention from neighbours, plus he'd needed to stretch his legs. Now he was here, he was feeling apprehensive. He hoped no one had tipped off the local news reporters, or they would spot him up here by accident. He was nearly as well known as the Family Man because of the coverage. Miller, by contrast, got lucky and avoided most of the attention, despite being the new Detective Inspector on the case.

Drake was still busy gathering his thoughts when they turned the corner and spotted the police cars towards the end of a long country lane. Large, gated properties lined the streets. The long-established trees that lined the lane had shed for winter, leaving a sinister moonlit red trail towards the house.

Two police cars and a SOCO (Scene of Crime Officers) van stood parked on the road and muddied grass verges outside. Drake praised the almighty that his fears seemed to be unfounded; the press was nowhere to be seen, and the initial throng of police that would have attended had died down. The bland statements they'd issued to the press must have done the trick.

The dark oak gates were open, but police tape barred entry. Two uniformed PCs were leaning against the wall that surrounded the property.

They stepped forward at Drake and Ellie's approach.

'This is a crime scene—'

'I'm DCI Drake, and this is DS Wilkinson. DCS Miller is expecting us.' Drake said, as he and Ellie pulled out their ID. He never had liked his photo. Too tired-looking as always.

'Sorry, sir, apologies.'

The first PC couldn't have been any older than twenty-two, but was built like a rugby player. Something akin to a 'brick shit house' would have been Miller's description back in the day, the PC's body all muscle and shoulders. 'It's a horror show in there, by all accounts, sir. I've not been inside myself, but that's what everyone says, other than that weird SOCO lead guy.'

'Even the pathologist was a little green around the gills,' the second PC added stiffly.

She appeared to be in her late thirties or early forties, her hat pulled down so far over her face it was hard to make out her eyes.

'I'd recommend you don't go in there either, at least not before they remove the bodies,' said Drake, his expression serious. 'It's something that will stay with you for a very long time if you do.'

'Yes, sir. Appreciate the advice, sir.' She brought the tape up for them to step under.

Ellie ducked sideways under it, and Drake followed suit, feeling like a crab as he did so.

The officers made their way back to their positions against the wall. 'Good luck in there. Hope you catch the bastard soon – we don't get this sort of stuff round here. It's not the seventies. We don't want another Ripper on our hands.'

Drake looked round, taking in the details of the property. It was, as Miller had said on the phone, a prime example of a Family Man hunting ground.

A sandy-coloured shingle formed the driveway, twisting

round the side of the house to a generous parking area and garage. The house itself was a Georgian red brick, with grand, white-framed bay windows. White and pink climbing roses trailed up and around the right-hand window, ending over the front door. At the front of the house, a stone porch would shield any visitors from the rain.

Even at night, it was picturesque. Drake could imagine the family living there, could almost see the children playing through the windows, bathed in the warm glow of the house, all smiles.

'Quite the place they've got here,' Ellie noted. 'Puts my little terrace to shame.'

'*Had*,' He corrected, arching an eyebrow at her. 'And it didn't do them much good. You're safer in your house than you are in somewhere like this – you won't have people creeping around your grounds the same way they can in these types of places.'

'That's a nice thought. Thanks for that.'

Drake shrugged as he looked over the front door, which was ajar to allow the teams in and out. Each time previously, there had been no obvious signs of entry from the front. The Family Man never broke in. It was as though he walked in off the street with a key. As though he owned the place.

He looked up, noting a small black CCTV camera above the door. He'd need to check on the footage from that. Times had moved on since the last victims twenty years ago. Sophisticated home security set-ups were a lot more prevalent now. But Drake was surprised; with this family's obvious wealth, they could have got one of those doorbells with the camera in it. Perhaps their man hadn't thought about the cameras, but it wasn't like he'd be ringing the doorbell either. Drake whipped out his notepad and pen and jotted down the CCTV details anyway.

'You ready, Ellie?' he asked.

'As ready as I'll ever be.' She took a breath, her expression set.

There were some shoe coverings to the side of the door. While he slipped them on over his shoes, Ellie struggled a little with hers, and ended up putting a hand on Drake for balance.

'Okay, let's do this,' Drake said, and opened the door.

The hallway was generous, with elaborate cornicing outlining the ceiling space and an expensive-looking crystal chandelier. A set of stairs were to the right-hand side of the hallway, framed by an ornate banister. An intricately-patterned mosaic floor of black and cream Georgian tiles led through to the back of the property.

Ellie glanced at the isolated room to her right; probably some sort of snug, Drake supposed. He went into the room on the other side, his shoe coverings rustling as they met the plush carpet. A TV room or maybe the lounge, he assumed, judging by the huge television and speaker system dominating the room. Sofas and armchairs encircled it at one end and there was a window seat in the bay window with some toys scattered around. A bright red plastic toy tractor and a green train set had been left unattended.

The dead family smiled back at him from the photos adorning the mantelpiece above the large fireplace. They were all blonde, the Swedish father having given his children their Scandinavian looks, although his own hair had since whitened.

'John, you made it.' Miller's voice came from off to the side at the entrance to the lounge. She was still wearing her uniform from earlier in the day, but it appeared slightly more dishevelled, unbuttoned at the front and showing her shirt. She looked even more tired than this morning, as though the evening had drained her remaining reserves.

That'll be me soon enough, Drake thought. 'I did. Are they still here?'

He didn't want to engage too much in conversation, needing to focus on his inspection.

'Through the back to the left. It's a large kitchen with a short corridor leading off to the even larger dining room – you can't miss it. SOCO and the pathologist are done with their preliminary inspection and photos. At my request, they won't move the family, or anything else, until you've finished.'

She turned her attention to Ellie, who'd followed in after her. 'DS Wilkinson, I'm glad you could come at such short notice. Have you read about today or what happened previously, at all?'

'Yes, ma'am,' Ellie said, her voice grim.

'Excellent, please try to not let what you see get to you. I understand that you have a young family at home.' Drake knew Miller sometimes struggled in her dealings with her female colleagues, and expressions of compassion didn't come easily to her, but she was clearly trying here.

Ellie nodded. 'Thank you, ma'am. I'll do my best.'

'John, I'll be out front getting some air if you need me.'

'I expect I'll be doing the same soon enough,' he told Miller, following her and Ellie out into the hallway. There appeared to be nothing out of the ordinary at the front of the property.

Miller pulled the door closed behind her as she went outside, the sound echoing in the hallway.

'Ellie, glad to see you didn't rush on into the kill room, and took the time to look over the rooms preceding it,' Drake said. 'It's best to get acclimatised to the place before going in, as you might miss elements if you were to look later.' He was beginning to think they might be more alike than he'd thought.

'Figured I should take my time if I'm arriving after the fact,' she agreed. 'As you say, might miss something if your head's foggy from reviewing the scene. In Response, we didn't always get that luxury though.'

'I can imagine. I went straight to CID, so never had the pleasure.'

'It takes a certain type.' She cocked an eyebrow in his direction.

'I'm sure it does. Right, before we go through to the back, what do you make of this?' Drake pointed to the small blood spatter by the small alarm panel. The controls looked dead, and there was no digital display showing a status of any kind. The alarm system's power had been cut or disabled somehow. Most of the blood had dried in place at the point of impact, but some spots had trickled down the wall.

'Looks as though someone tried to raise the alarm before being attacked? I'm assuming it's one of the adults because of the height, and likely a forehead and nose impacted against the wall due to the amount of blood,' she said. 'Unless they were stabbed clean through from their shoulder front to back, or vice versa? But that wouldn't fit the Family Man MO and there's no blood elsewhere. There's never any damage above and beyond the main focal points, such as the hands and throats.'

'Good, Ellie. Good.'

Her eyes lit up at the encouraging words, but Drake was concerned. He'd never seen any signs of struggle – certainly not blood – beyond the crime scene proper before. Why hadn't it been cleaned up? The killer was usually fastidious, so this was new.

Did it show the Family Man was rusty? Or maybe was he rushed – caught by surprise, perhaps. Did this point to a copycat rather than the 'original'? That's what this seemed to imply; it would make more sense, and there was no evidence to the contrary just yet. He hoped to God it was some inexperienced copycat.

With Ellie following, he walked into the kitchen, the polished dark wood flooring making his steps reverberate around the room. A SOCO stood with their back to them, leaning against the white granite kitchen island, tapping away on what Drake hoped was their work phone. This wasn't the place for personal conversations. The officer was kitted out in the standard white overalls, along with latex gloves and a mask.

The SOCO must have heard them enter and turned in greeting. 'Ah! DCI Drake?'

'Yes.'

'Graham Reynolds. They're just through there.' He pointed with a gloved hand to the door arch in the corner of the kitchen. 'If you could keep to the floor plates we've placed around the scene, we'd appreciate it. There's... well, there's a fair amount of "mess" on the floor, if you catch my drift.'

The man winced saying the word 'mess'. But there was an element of excitement in his voice which didn't match the facial expression.

'We're just waiting on you now, so please let me know when you're done and we can get the bodies over to the lab.'

'We'll do our best.'

'Here are some gloves. And please, put on the masks and overalls provided. They're on the side just there.' He leant over the island and handed over a couple of pairs of blue latex gloves.

Drake took the gloves and started wrestling with them. He hated the things; his hands were already clammy and he knew the gloves would make them worse. Ellie seemed to have no issues, snapping hers on with quick, smooth movements.

'Before we go in, anything of note we need to be made aware of in the kitchen?'

'No, there were the usual knives, utensils, etc. in the drawers and knife block. Unused, at least for tonight's purpose. And there weren't any further signs of struggle like there were by the alarm panel.'

'Not even blood on the floor? Unusual. Seemed quite the impact out there,' Ellie jerked her head towards the hallway.

'Nope, nothing.'

'Okay, thanks.' Ellie nodded, apparently satisfied, but Drake got the impression she was crossing something off a mental checklist.

'I'm just going to make a call so the bodies can be collected, now that you're here. I expect you'll be done by the time they arrive, yes? If you need me, I'll be out in the hallway.'

Reynolds dialled a number on his phone and skirted past them, his overalls making a swishing sound.

Drake picked up a set of overalls between two fingers and sighed. It wasn't like the old days where he could just saunter in, although the advances in forensics certainly made his job easier in the grand scheme of things. He passed a set to Ellie, and they put them on in silence, rustling like a pair of bin liners while they did so. He pulled the mask over his mouth before shutting his eyes and taking a deep breath.

Time to look in and see what had changed in the past twenty years.

23

Drake stepped on to a strategically placed access plate upon entering the dining room. The plates ensured there would be minimal disturbance to the room while the SOCOs carried out their work.

He surveyed the room from the entrance, his heart sinking as his pulse speeded up at the sight which met his eyes. His stomach roiled, making him fight the urge to gag as the stink of death hit. Before him was the scene he'd been both dreading and needing to see since the news in Miller's office that afternoon.

A grand, dark oak dining table dominated the sage green dining room, complete with matching old-fashioned high-back chairs. It immediately brought to mind images of a medieval banquet table or themed restaurant.

Beyond, a set of floor-to-ceiling patio doors provided a view out to the garden. The moonlit sky cast an eerie glow onto the lawn beyond. The patio doors and garden fencing were the only thing separating them from the deep wooded area and the elements. Drake imagined the killer watched the family from those woods when he was staking out the house.

Four of the imposing chairs flanked the table, with a further two at either end. Three of the chairs were occupied. The fourth, at the end of the table furthest from Drake, was upended and empty on the floor.

Blood had drenched the tablecloth. There had been significant arterial spray across its expanse from each of the three occupied seats, dyeing the otherwise pristine white cloth a deep crimson. The fabric had dried, but the room's stark lighting gave its surface a disturbingly wet sheen.

Drake could see the seated profile of the younger boy, Matthew. The eldest, Tomas, was seated to Matthew's right, next to where his mother would have been. Their bodies, still confined by their bindings, had slumped slightly forwards. Unlike their parents, they had been strapped in place at their heads and across their chests, with their blindfolds still in place. The father, Mikel, was opposite Tomas.

Drake heard a sharp intake of breath behind him.

'Bloody hell,' Ellie whispered.

Drake turned to see her holding her hand to her mouth despite the mask. Her eyes were wide with shock, taking it all in.

'Je-sus fucking... *Christ*.'

He ignored her and moved closer to the boys, giving her space to step into the room. She started coughing and making a gagging sound before regaining her composure, muttering to herself as she stepped on to the raised plate to his left.

Not used to the smell, Drake thought. He couldn't make out what else she was saying, but she sounded annoyed at herself. He moved onto the next stepping plate and turned his attention back to the father.

The man's stunted arms hung lifeless at his sides, his severed hands placed before him on the table. Blood had oozed darkly from his butchered hands back towards his lifeless body. Between the man's hands, Drake could see a lump of flesh had been placed. He assumed it was a portion of the father's tongue, a standard practice for the killer.

He studied the man's ruined face. His jaw had been hacked into from behind, the corners of his mouth slit further back to enable better access. The cavity itself was a pulped mess, his chest covered in a torrent of blood from his tongue and, later, his throat. Drake noted a scrape on his forehead and nose besides the significant bruising. Presumably the husband had encountered the killer in the hallway.

Drake moved on to the left side of the room, next to Ellie, who appeared to have regained her composure.

From this angle, he could see that the father had been gutted, much like the original crimes. His intestines and viscera collected in a slimy heap on the floor in front of the chair. Drake had thought the smell of death in the room was thick and foul before, but this close up, the stench was even more potent. His mask was all but useless in staving it off, and he pressed the back of his hand to his nose in a futile attempt to override the stink with the smell of latex.

From his new vantage point, he could see the boys' throats had been cut, but they appeared otherwise unmolested. He was selfishly glad that they had been blindfolded. He didn't think he could bear to see them looking at him. Accusing him.

'Why did you let this happen to me? To my family? Why didn't you stop this?'

He pulled his gaze away, made himself focus. Details provided by the survivors of past cases had suggested there was a sinister routine the killer followed. The Family Man's preferred method was to first maim the father, rendering him powerless. He would then slaughter the children in front of them, followed by the irrevocable act of disembowelling the father and slitting his throat, all of this while the mother was made to watch.

If either parent passed out, the killer either waited or found ways to revive them before continuing. They were threatened with death if they closed their eyes, not through words – the Man never spoke – but through actions such as a knife pressed under an eye socket or held to the throat. Once her family had been taken from her, the mother was left tied up in position at the head of the table. The Man would then carve his symbol before leaving the property as stealthily as he had entered it.

Drake guessed, judging by the position of her chair, that this woman had fallen in her bid to get free of her bonds.

'I wasn't expecting it to be quite so—'

'Vicious?' Drake offered.

'I think callous is the word I was looking for.' Ellie moved to the next plate to peer at the fallen chair, before turning her attention back to the father.

'Why do you say that?'

'The way he subjected the father to such horrific abuse. And in front of his children, too – his wife must have been terrified. What he did with the man's mouth... that must have taken time. He *worked* at it despite the noise and resistance the father must have made and despite his family's pleas and cries. It didn't bother him.'

'Yes.' Drake didn't want to entertain the finer points regarding the technique for cutting and cracking open a man's mouth to get at his tongue right now. It wasn't new to him. In these last few moments, he felt as though the twenty preceding years had only been a few hours earlier. As though he had been fast forwarded to this point and just moved on to the next scene.

He wondered if that was why he felt so numb to what was before him. He should feel *something*, surely? It concerned him to think he was returning to the matter-of-fact attitude he'd taken on all too easily with the latter scenes he'd witnessed. He hoped not. That kind of attitude could dull your wits if you weren't careful.

He surveyed the room for one of the key details from the earlier crimes, a futile hope building in his belly. That hope turned to ash when he spotted the symbol. He hurried back to the stepping plate farthest from the mother's chair, skirting past Ellie.

The Man's symbol peered out at them, carved into the wall directly opposite where the mother would have been sitting, beyond the foot of the table.

Traces of blood were apparent in the crude channels of the carving and the plaster dust scattered on the floor. The Family Man would always carry out the carving after the killings. Drake assumed it was to show he was watching the mother and to gloat, or to exert some kind of dominance or ownership.

Drake's team hadn't understood the significance of the symbol until the third Family Man case. Not sinister in itself, it was Nordic in origin, a little-used glyph meaning 'Family.' Back in 1998, with the internet still in its infancy, they had needed a contact from the police in Norway to explain its meaning; the circles represented children, the centre line and upper half points represented the father, and the lower outer triangle, the mother.

The symbol had been present at all the crime scenes. And

from the second scene onwards, insignificant items from the previous one would also turn up with the symbol carved into them. Items such as hairbrushes, watches, and even a key fob. He hadn't heard from Miller or Reynolds whether any such items had been found yet, but he couldn't imagine that would be the case. *That would be impossible. It was twenty years ago, and Stan was dead.*

'Wow, so that's His symbol?' Ellie had come over for a closer look. 'I couldn't remember seeing it in the file I'd looked at years back.'

'Yes, it's another of the ritualistic elements at every scene. We kept it back from the press. It's a sort of calling card. As if the act itself wasn't enough. It's like he's mocking them – mocking us.'

'We should check in with Reynolds and Miller regarding whether there are any items left elsewhere.' She frowned. 'Remind me, was there anything left at the first crime scene? I mean, he wouldn't have taken something from somewhere else, as it was his first, would he?'

'You're right. But that's one of the other details we kept from the press. It's how we thought we had our man with Stan as he mentioned it in his letter to prove his involvement.'

'What was?'

'It was a sort of rudimentary construction, using twigs. You know, sort of pagan-esque. It was in the shape of the Family Man symbol, complete with little circles hanging from thin lengths of grass. He left it resting on the top of the entrails of the first father. The source of the materials could have been anywhere, but we suspected it had to be Barndon Forest, as the village was where the first murder took place. Stan Lawton worked on a farm in Barndon, so it seemed to fit.'

'He liked homecrafts then. Pleasant.' she remarked grimly.

'Something like that. But he didn't repeat it for the subsequent scenes. No one knows why, other than the assumed lack of materials prior to the first family, I suppose. Second family onwards, he took up carving some of their personal effects instead.'

While he'd been talking about the carvings, Drake had noticed Ellie was avoiding looking at the children.

'Ellie, you sure you're okay?'

'Yes, why?'

'You seem to be keeping your distance from the boys.'

'I'm working up to it. I'll be all right, Drake. 'It ... it's just so messed up though, you know?', she blurted out. 'How he could do this to a family, to those poor children? I don't want to imagine it. How do you keep yourself from doing that? Imagining it, I mean?'

'You don't. It stays with you.' Drake lifted his hand to rub his face before pulling it away, realising he was still wearing a mask. 'It's always stayed with me. But it *does* get better. I used to see my daughter when I looked at the victims, or them when I looked at her. But that fades with time. A long time, mind.'

'I hope so. It needs to.'

'So, whilst we're on the subject.' He took a few steps back round towards the boy's stepping plates and motioned for her to join him. 'What do you make of it?'

'Drake—'

'Come on, I need you on this. You need to distance yourself.'

Ellie groaned and made her way over to him before leaning down and tentatively peering up at the youngest.

'His neck ...' She cleared her throat before composing herself and starting again. 'His throat has been cut. But... hang on, it doesn't look like it was a precise, one-action motion like the others I've read about – after all, we know him for his clinical way of working, don't we? This looks like it took two or three attempts till he got what he wanted.'

She sounded excited now, looking up at Drake as she continued speaking. 'That's new, isn't it? Even at the first scene, he was quick, as though he was slaughtering animals.'

'Let me see.' Drake processed what she was telling him. Could this be it? Could this be what proved it was a separate person?

Ellie stepped back, and he leaned in, gently tipping the boy's head back. *She's right,* he thought, *this is different.*

There were three slashes in total. When he examined the extremities of the ugly red cuts, the first two didn't seem deep enough.

'You're right,' Drake confirmed. 'We should raise this with the team when they perform the post-mortems, then we'll get a clearer picture.'

'I did good?'

'You did great. But come on now, don't seek approval – this isn't school, Ellie.' He met her gaze with a stern look, but her eyes still lit up a little.

Drake moved over to the next plate, squeezing between the two boys to better inspect the eldest boys' injuries from both sides. This boy, too, seemed to have had several relatively superficial cuts before the fatal one. He wondered what it could mean. Was it more frenzied, more uncertain, or even some sort of inexperience that had caused these wounds? It was something to ponder once he got the lab report.

'The bindings are different too,' Ellie noted. 'And the blindfolds.'

'The bindings might be down to the passage of time or availability,' Drake pointed out. 'Natural rope might not have been as readily available this time, so he went for the nylon kind. Who knows?'

'Yes, probably for the bindings. But The Man always used towels for blindfolds, right, sourced from the family bathroom or whatever? These are cotton sheets. That might be significant. We should check in with the team and take a look, see if the bedrooms have been disturbed. Otherwise, they might have been brought in ... like, pre-prepared, right?'

'Hmmm, good thinking, Ellie.' Drake was becoming more hopeful that this was some sort of copycat. What they'd had seen so far must be readily available on the internet somehow. It had to be. But his mind kept returning to the symbol. That wasn't common knowledge.

'Boss,' Ellie said, interrupting Drake's thoughts. 'Actually, if you consider the boys' injuries, and then take another look at the dad ... does it seem like maybe that had taken more effort than it should have done too?'

Drake made his way over to the other side of the room, one plate returning a loud creak as he went.

Christ's sake, not you too, he groaned to himself.

He rooted around in his pocket for his phone before taking it out and enabling the torch function. Leaning forwards, he used his phone to illuminate the father's face.

Ellie grimaced at the brightened facial injuries.

'What do you see?'

'You could be right.' He squinted at the injury detail, carefully positioning the man's face in order to expose the left side to the torchlight. 'I'm no expert on the process of tongue extraction – particularly under duress – but he does seem to have made a meal out of this.'

Drake paused, squinting a little more. 'There are all sorts of superficial cuts and gashes here – now, that wasn't unusual for the original Family Man, you understand. The victim wasn't willingly going to let him do what he did, but this seems less... *confident* somehow.'

'Another one for the lab, then?'

'Yes.'

While he had the light available, Drake pointed it at the mess at the base of the chair. Being in such a close proximity to the man, he caught a strong smell of shit at the wrong moment and felt bile rise in his throat.

He took a moment to compose himself, squeezing his eyes closed before opening them with a few frenzied blinks and causing them to water a little. Composed again, he turned his focus back to the task at hand and leant down further, grunting at the awkward angle. He needed to be sure. If he had to stake out a short-lived career as a contortionist while doing so, so be it.

He was relieved to see nothing had been left on the man's innards for them to find. No twigs, nothing. Another wave of relief spread over him. He knew he should trust SOCO, but he had to see things for himself. This tendency of his had caused friction with colleagues in the past, but Drake had a feeling he should make time to attend all these post-mortems.

'See anything?' Ellie asked.

'No.'

'You sure? Maybe you should go back down there again.' When he rolled his eyes, she shrugged. 'Come on, it's not often I'll get to see DCI Drake twisting and turning like that.'

'*Ellie...*' he warned.

'Sorry.'

Drake shuffled past the father's chair, knocking into a sideboard. A candlestick wobbled but stayed put, and he made a mental note to breathe in on the way back.

He knelt to look at the mother's upended chair. At first inspection, nothing looked out of the ordinary. He took his phone out again and flashed the light on the chair. There were slight abrasions on the arms, which he expected from the rope used to tie her up. The strands were left discarded in situ on the floor after the attending PCs had freed her from her restraints. Otherwise, there was nothing crying out to him.

'Okay, I think we're done here for now.' Drake stood and scribbled a few extra notes on his notepad. 'What say you, Sergeant?'

'I think I've had my fill,' she agreed, taking a last look around the room, looking above the boy's heads. 'I might come back later when the bodies are gone. Take the room in without the... *ambience.*'

Drake nodded in agreement as he made his way back, breathing in while he passed the father and creaked along the plates to the entrance.

Ellie let him out first before following close behind.

They didn't look back.

24

Miller was secreting a cigarette in a small metal container, having just extinguished it on the lid, when Drake and Ellie emerged from the house, stripped of their overalls. He'd bumped into Reynolds on the way out, letting him know they were done, and had used the opportunity to hand them over.

His boss rarely smoked now, not like she'd done in the old days. Drake thought she looked a little more relaxed since leaving the house, but she looked even more drawn, as though her last energy reserves had finally been sapped. The potent smell of cigarette smoke coming off of her made his nose itch.

'Ellie, could you give us a minute, please?' Drake requested. He wanted to speak to Miller in private about what he saw, but he also wanted to check in with her as a friend.

'Sir, ma'am.' Ellie nodded and wandered off to the side of the house to look at the grounds and garage area.

'Laura, don't you think you should call it a night soon? You look knackered.'

'You're not looking too great yourself, John, but thanks for the concern.' She shrugged, avoiding the question. 'So, what did you make of it in there?' Miller said, studying him with one of her trademark stares. Though he had nothing to hide, of course.

'Pretty bloody awful, to be honest,' Drake said. 'It's just like it was back then. I'm almost *numb* to it again. It didn't feel new – even after all this time. I'm still struggling with the idea that someone's come out of the woodwork and done this. But it can't be the same guy. It just can't. None of this makes any sense.'

He looked around. The rugby-playing PC had moved in front of the gate and away from his position of leaning against the wall, Drake noticed. Keeping up appearances for the DCS, no doubt.

'Much the same as me, then.' She moved to one side to let Reynolds pass. 'I felt more emotional when that old dickhead of a DCS, Sanderson, left the police force than when I was coming up and seeing this mess this evening. Perhaps it's grief? I'm finding it hard to get my head around it all again.'

Drake managed a weak chuckle. *That DCS was a dick, though. Particularly to me.* But Sanderson moving on had allowed for Miller to take her next step up the career ladder.

To the sound of a revving engine, the two PCs removed the police tape to allow a nondescript van access for the removal of the victims. Drake always found it a sobering sight, this removing the last remnants of life from a house that must have been full of laughter and love just a day ago.

'Seriously though, you think it's a copycat too, right?' he asked, turning his attention back to Miller.

'At the moment, I do, yes. I'm sure you noticed that the knife attacks appeared somewhat more frenzied than the previous cases.'

'Yes, Ellie picked up on that. She's sharp.'

'Good,' Miller said, sounding distracted. 'They took away the wife not long after the cavalry showed up. She's at a hospital close to the station. I think you and Wilkinson should speak to her as soon as you can, tomorrow morning, no later. We need to be on this, John – she wasn't in a fit state for questioning when I got here.'

'Okay, Boss, will do.'

Drake rubbed his hands together against the chill, and looked at his watch. 2:30 a.m., way past his bedtime. He was going to feel like shit in the morning. The late nights weren't as easy as they used to be.

'Oh, and Laura ...' he recalled the crime scene. 'I was going to ask Reynolds, but I'll ask you too. Did you find any additional items, things that might have been from the fourth family? No effigy or other items have been removed as evidence? Nothing to show a new cycle starting?'

'No, I would have told you. You know that.'

'Sorry, getting twitchy in my old age,' he said. 'Once the grey sets in, so does the edginess ... Okay, I'm making that up. Clearly, I'm bloody tired. You're right.'

Miller nodded, her face expressionless as ever. 'You taking to DS Wilkinson? I understand she can be—'

'Enthusiastic? Inappropriate when faced with difficult situations?'

'No, keen was the word I was thinking of. I can see she's got you agitated.' Miller gave him a faintly amused look.

'No, she's okay, really. She's good police. Doesn't seem to be one of those fast-rising bullshitters that seem to get about the office like a rash these days.'

'I hope I'm not part of that collective.'

'Laura, no, that's not what I meant.'

'I'm fucking with you, John.'

'Oh ... I'll shut up, then,' he said, stuffing his hands in his pockets.

They both went silent while Reynolds and his aide wheeled through two trollies, a set of thick black body bags on board.

'Sorry, coming through,' Reynolds warned. The trollies bobbled and crunched on the shingle, kicking up a few stones before hitting the porch paving. He coughed behind his mask and continued through, propping the front door with a doorstop.

'Anyway,' Drake went on. 'One other thing –were there any sheets missing from upstairs, or was there evidence of the upstairs rooms having been searched for white sheets? The blindfolds were sheets this time, rather than the usual bathroom towels.'

'No.' Her eyebrow arched inquisitively. That was a look he hadn't seen for a while. Miller was always the one that caught those kinds of observations.

Ellie did good, he thought. 'Hmmm, okay. He always used to use what was available at the house. Presumably less to carry. That's something new too, then.'

'Though with the number of white sheets sold ...' She paused, thinking. 'It's pretty ... no, it's *extremely* unlikely that will lead anywhere. But yes, get the lab to check those over.'

'Will do.' Drake was worried; this had all the makings of not being a one off. 'What's going to happen in terms of press control? This is going to get out at some point, if it hasn't already. And I'm not sure we can present this as anything other than a copycat Family Man killing.'

'We've spoken to the housekeeper, and she's made assurances it won't be coming from her anytime soon. I think I trust her,' Miller said. 'She's of an age where I can imagine she'd keep it to herself. But you never know with these sorts of things.' She sighed. 'You and I know that the less scrupulous sections of the press might offer money if they suspect anything, and then she could cave. And you know from personal experience that this can come from within too.'

He did. Back when Drake was a DI and still had some semblance of colour to his hair, he had been leading a nasty case involving multiple homicides.

The killer had warned via a payphone that if anything hit the press about the nature of the deaths, he would kill again. Unbeknown to Drake, the press had an informant, a young DC. He'd told a reporter all about the killer's sadism towards young homosexual men. As a result, the next day a red top had been shouting about the sexual nature of the crimes. Two more people had died, this time women, a supposed consequence of the leak. It was never proven, but the man they caught said it resulted directly from those stories. He'd never harmed women before, after all. Hard to trust a killer, but Drake was inclined to believe him, and had been anti-press ever since.

'Well, do the best you can. We want to keep this quiet for as long as possible. No need to stir up the hornets' nest and have every nutter and misfit calling up claiming they're "The Family Man" if we can help it.'

'It can work in our favour, though,' Miller pointed out. 'Having you and me in the spotlight last time led to Stan Lawton contacting us. I don't think he would have been in touch so soon otherwise. He must have felt we were on to him.'

He supposed she was trying to see the positives. It was an admirable attempt, but he wasn't convinced. 'Maybe, but things have moved on since then.'

A rattling metallic sound came from deep in the house, and the trolleys appeared in the hallway. The first body was making its way out, Reynolds pushing it with care. The SOCO moved past with his cargo, which must have been the youngest boy, Matthew. The bag wasn't even half full. A wheel caught in the stones when the trolley met the driveway, causing Reynolds a moment of consternation, but he got it going again.

The next body was accompanied by Reynolds' assistant, a woman who looked to be in her mid-forties, short in stature, with brown hair tucked into the hood of the overalls. Smudges of blood tainted her gloves and front.

Her subject was larger, and Drake assumed it was the body of the eldest, Tomas. He was relieved she didn't have the same difficulty that Reynolds had with the driveway and she made it over to the van without issue. They decanted the victims and came back with one trolley again, this time for the father.

While this had been going on, with Drake keeping a respectful distance, Miller had retired to look at her work phone. Ellie was still off in the background, also on her phone, probably informing her family where she was. Drake realised he wasn't sure if she even had a husband. She hadn't mentioned one when speaking about her daughter. He sighed. He should know who he's working with better than this.

'I think I'll come back here after questioning the mother in hospital. Will you be here tomorrow, Laura?'

She looked up from her phone, her mind coming back to attention. 'Sorry?'

'Will you be here in the morning? What are your plans?'

'No, I'll be bringing everyone up to speed in this area, so they'll be on the lookout for anything suspicious,' she stated. 'As you know, I've got extremely limited resources at the moment to deploy. And to put it bluntly, we've been caught with our trousers down on this one. DCI Collins has commandeered a lot of our resources leading a case in Bristol, and DCI Nielsen stole pretty much everyone else for the case involving those dismembered remains that keep turning up.'

She pinched her brow between two fingers. 'But luckily for you, now that you're the designated Senior Investigating Officer, I've managed to get another detective to run the background work you'll need, pulling up old files, etc. He's going to be working the other cases too, unlike you and DS Wilkinson, so use him wisely.'

Drake turned his nose up. 'Greedy bastards. So, who is my leftover then?'

'Bradfield. That's all I have for you, and he'll be desk-based.'

He nodded his approval. 'Competent, easy-going, a mate... sounds good to me, no problem.'

DS David Bradfield wasn't a careerist, which pleased Drake to no end. He was also coming to the end of his tenure, not having pushed for Detective Inspector or even for early retirement, which was surprising. He was pretty much winding down, so wasn't the fastest worker these days, but Drake felt okay about it. At least it meant he could work at his own pace, mostly, and he wouldn't have two detectives breathing down his neck. Ellie was quite enough.

'I wasn't asking for your approval,' Miller told him. 'This is who you're getting. Be happy you even got him.'

'Oh, I am. He won't piss me off,' Drake remarked. 'Where's he based these days? I've not seen or spoken to him in a long while.'

'He's back in Barndon with his wife – not far from you, in fact. Apparently, he'd had enough of London life and since Barndon station covers more than just Barndon, it made sense.'

She looked like she was growing impatient. Same old Miller, never one for long conversations. It must have rubbed off on him these last few years. He was getting short with people, too. 'Okay, I'll get in touch with him tomorrow.'

'Good, see that you do.'

'Right.' He pulled his coat around him. 'I think I'll look to finding a place to crash for a few hours.'

'No need. I took the liberty of organising it while you were in the dining room. Here,' Miller said, texting him the address of a local hotel.

'Oh, that's ... *unusually* kind of you, Boss.'

'Don't go spreading it around.'

'I won't.' He smirked. He took whatever humour he could from their conversations.

'Right, I'm going to make a move in a minute, once they've finished with the bodies. I'll speak to you soon. I need to make a call.' He nodded, and she turned away from him, greeting someone soon after placing the phone to her ear.

Drake walked over to Ellie. She had her hands stuffed in her coat pockets. It was cold enough now that their breath was producing misty clouds whenever they exhaled. She was looking as tired as he felt.

'You two done?'

'Yes.'

'I didn't want to bother you, but I believe I've found our suspect's entry point,' she said. She wasn't betraying any emotion, which Drake thought was unusual for her.

She pointed to the side of the house. 'It looks like he climbed that trellis and used part of a drainpipe to access one of the house's few original latched windows, judging by the others I've looked at.'

'Unusual – we've only spotted a few minor signs of entry in the past. Miller said that there were no signs of disturbance upstairs, no sheets were taken.'

'Interesting.' She frowned at the potential implications.

'The lab will provide more information on those,' Drake told her. 'But as Miller said, it's unlikely we'll get a lead on that unless he somehow left his DNA for us to match against Stan. Then again, who knows with this new suspect? Maybe he was sloppy and we'll find something?'

She shrugged. 'We can but hope.'

Drake walked over to where Ellie had indicated, and saw the trellis and iron drainpipe. The window at the top was still ajar, the light shining out with a few moths making a nuisance around the glass.

He took his phone out and cast the torch over the lower end of the trellis. Sure enough, there were signs that someone had climbed it; scuffed vines and a broken section where it must have been brittle from the exposure to the elements. Nothing jumped out at him or seemed to provide enough of a sample, and there were no partial footmarks that he could see them being able to extract, just scuffs.

Drake looked back towards the front of the house. Ellie had left him to inspect alone and was still standing where he'd left her, looking up at the moon. On his way back, he saw the father's body in transit to the van. He felt glad to be at a distance; being downwind of the smell of death again was not high on his to-do list.

'I don't know how SOCO and pathologists do it. Having to deal with the dead like that. Moving the father must have been awful. All those... parts.'

Drake didn't respond, his mind distracted by thoughts of his wife and daughter. He made a mental note to get in touch with them the following morning. He hoped Becca would answer her phone and not shut him out. He needed to keep the communication going, keep the lines open. No radio silence for days on end this time.

This time it will be different, he vowed. *That will have to be my mantra until this case is over.*

Drake watched while Reynolds closed the doors of the van and spoke with the driver.

'So, what're your plans, Chief?' Ellie asked, gazing up at the night sky again.

He frowned at the nickname, choosing not to bring attention to it. 'I think we should make a move. We've got a busy day tomorrow.'

'What's next? The wife?'

'Yes, we need to talk to her. She likely won't be able to speak about the details too well. Severely traumatised like the others, I expect, but whatever we can get might be of use. For example, if he was a particularly short, then we'd know immediately that the ghost of The Family Man hasn't risen to kill again. Stan Lawton was six foot, and each of the survivors confirmed someone of that stature.'

'Sounds good. I'd suggest we come back here after, if we still have daylight, unless there's something else we should do before?' she said, kicking at the shingle to reveal the dirt beneath. 'What do you think?'

'Sounds about right.' Drake nodded. 'We've also got a little help assigned to us as of tomorrow – DS Bradfield. Know him?'

'No, not had the pleasure. Have you worked with him before?'

'A few times through the years. Good guy. He'll do any background work we might need. But go easy on him, he's got other cases on the go, too.' He imagined the torrent of questions the man might get over the coming days if he wasn't careful.

Ellie smiled. 'I can take a hint,' she promised.

25

Andrea gasped. 'What was that?'

'Huh...? What... sorry?' Ben said, his mind bogged down in a fog of sleep.

'Didn't you hear that?' she whispered, holding his upper arm in a vice-like grip. 'There was a noise.'

'I'm sure it was just a bird, or an owl, or something. We live in the countryside now. Go back to sleep,' he groaned. He squeezed her hand before reaching over to rub her arm.

'But it sounded like it was coming from the box room. Are you *sure* you didn't hear it?'

Andrea stopped holding on to him. In the darkness, he could see her slowly pushing herself up, as though fearful that whatever had disturbed her would hear her movements.

The moon peeked through the clouds and the curtains for a moment, casting a shard of moonlight onto the bed and making her eyes shine in the darkness.

I better nip this in the bud. Ben had dealt with things like this before. Andrea had moments where she was convinced there were things in the house, moments of paranoia. He supposed it was understandable, given the new surroundings.

'Andrea, you're just getting used to the house. There will be all sorts of weird and wonderful noises that we're not used to here. Wildlife, old pipes, even tractors – though probably not at this time of night.' He tried to make light of the situation as he sat up in bed too, taking a lot less care with making noise.

'Ben, take me seriously, please.'

'Okay, okay. I'll check it out. Then, can we *please* go back to sleep?'

'Yes, I would like that.'

'Okay,' he said, squeezing her hand once again. 'I'll be right back.'

He pulled back the covers and gave her a peck on the cheek before clambering to his feet. *I didn't hear anything. Must be a fox.*

Ben yawned as he ambled round the bed frame to the door, which they always kept ajar.

'Be careful!' Andrea whispered when he put his hand on the handle.

'Don't worry.'

He kept the lights off so he'd not wake Cari; he didn't want *two* Whitman women wide awake. His eyes slowly adjusted to the darkness, aided a little by the moonlight as he opened the door and stuck his head out. Exaggerating his head movements, he scouted out the corridor, making Andrea hiss her disapproval at him.

All clear on the western front, now time for the box room. The apparent source of all evil.

He crept across the corridor, the window at the end of the hallway closeted in darkness with the new curtain he had put up at Andrea's request. The door was closed, just as it had been when they went to sleep.

Nothing out of the ordinary so far.

As soon as the thought entered his head, he heard muttering coming from their bedroom. It sounded like his wife was whispering to someone.

'Andrea, what're you saying?'

'Huh?'

'What did you just say?'

'Nothing, you're imagining things!' she hissed.

'Okay, okay.'

He definitely hadn't imagined it. Refocusing on the task at hand, Ben gripped the door handle, his heartbeat increasing.

Oh, come on, pussy! There'll be nothing there.

Ben readied himself, took a deep breath, and opened the door. He was greeted with the silence of a room empty of anything other than piles of boxes and Andrea's paintings, stacked high against the walls on both sides.

He sighed. He was vaguely disappointed, which he found both amusing and strange considering those feelings stemmed from there *not* being an axe murderer in the room, ready to cleave his head in two.

Ben walked over to the small window at the far side of the room, and looked out into the darkness. The road to the house and the trees looked exactly as they should, nothing out of the ordinary.

'Honey,' he called out. 'There's nothing—'

Crash!

'Holy shit!' he shouted. He bounded sideways, losing his balance before grabbing on to the side of the curtainless window frame to steady himself.

A box had fallen down, and various items had spilled out,

ones they'd decided were worth packing, but apparently not worth the effort of unpacking: Cari's sports day trophy from when she was seven, some of Ben's old DVDs and such like. He must have brushed the box when he'd made his way to the window. *Idiot*.

'Ben! Ben! Are you okay?'

He regained his composure just before she ran into the room, her arm above her head, brandishing a slipper, her eyes wild.

'I'm fine, I'm fine. It was just a box.' He caught his breath and rubbed his arm, which he'd scraped on the wall. 'You're not going to hit me with that thing, are you?' He held back a chuckle as he pointed at the slipper.

'Piss off, Ben! I thought you were being attacked!'

'Thank God you were here to save me with that thing.' He was struggling to keep a straight face.

'Ben!'

'Okay, okay, *sorry*. But as you can see, there's nothing here. You must have been dreaming, or it was an animal like I said before,' he said. He walked over to her and set the weaponised slipper down on a box before catching her hands in his.

'Dad! What's going on?' Cari called out from her room.

'It's nothing, Cari.' Ben said. 'I just walked into something when going to the toilet. Go back to sleep.'

'Uh ... okay. Thanks for waking me up! Really appreciate that.'

'I know what I heard, Ben,' Andrea ignored Cari's continued complaining and looked up at him, a serious expression on her face.

'Are you sure? It's not like ... in your head?' He winced to himself, regretting the words as soon as they spilled from his mouth.

Her face soured. 'How could you say that? I'm doing so well.

Don't make it out to be in my head. Just don't. You know that's not fair.'

'I'm sorry, I shouldn't have said that. It was insensitive of me. Look, as a peace offering, I'll check the rest of the house for you. How about that? Go back to bed.'

'Thank you,' she said, padding back to the bedroom.

Ben checked over the rest of the house, and found nothing out of the ordinary; all the locks were in place and all the curtains were drawn, exactly as they'd been when he'd done the rounds earlier. He finished his inspection and turned off the lights at the back of the house before going back upstairs.

The flick of the switch also hid the brief glimmer of light from the binocular lenses in the undergrowth.

The shadow grunted in amusement.

26

Drake crept towards the muffled sound coming from the room ahead. There was light framing the door in the darkness. Whatever it was, it sounded like it was in distress.

'Miller? Ellie? You there?' he called out tentatively.

His voice echoed around the house, but there was no reply.

Drake continued to make his way forward, edging closer to the door. The sounds became more panicked as he drew near.

A light shone above him and he felt something wet on his hands.

He looked down to see a pool of blood was forming on the floor before him. He looked at his hands and saw them running red.

'What the—'

A hand seized his mouth and put a knife to his throat.

Drake woke with a gasp. He clutched at his throat in panic, turning like a whippet to take on whatever had grabbed hold of him. There was nothing but the headboard of the bed.

Jesus Christ! It was just a dream. A bloody awful, harmless dream.

By the looks of things, he'd not had the most restful of nights. The sheets were damp, and half of the duvet lay on the hotel room floor, the rest hanging on for dear life beside him.

Drake collected himself, letting out an exasperated sigh as he cast a miserable eye over his surroundings. The morning light was creeping in through the hastily drawn curtains, showing him a spartan but clean room. A mass-produced watercolour of a beach-side scene hung on the wall next to a cheap flatscreen television, and a kettle accompanied by the usual hot beverage-related bits and pieces sat on a tray; otherwise, there was nothing to distinguish the modest hotel room from countless others of its type.

A sudden overwhelming feeling of missing his family came over him. Something that would have felt alien to him until recently.

He wasn't used to these feelings when in the middle of a case. He'd normally throw himself in at the deep end, and Becca and Eva would crop up sometimes when he washed back ashore, whether it be on the phone, or via text. But even then, he'd keep them both at arm's length.

It felt unreal that he was on this case with the ominous 'blessing' of his wife. But he seriously doubted he was using the term correctly. Drake looked at the time: 6:30 a.m. Just shy of three hours' sleep. *No rest for the wicked.*

Once he was dressed, he decided he would give Becca a call. He took out his mobile, pausing while he summoned up the courage to dial her number. The background image of Eva and his wife popped up on the screen as it rang.

When Becca answered, she didn't sound enamoured with him calling her. He guessed that was to be expected with how things had been left yesterday.

'Becca, it's me. I thought I'd call you and check in, see how you're doing this morning after last night. I'm worried about you.'

'You sure it's you? Are you all right? I'm not speaking to an imposter, am I?' There was a snide tone to her voice which Drake didn't appreciate, but he took it. He'd earned the reaction and worse over the years. He stifled an ill-timed yawn.

'Very funny. Yes, it's me. Big, bad John. I told you, this time it'll be different. Christ, I sound like an alcoholic – I just want to ensure that you and Eva are with me every step of the way, where possible.'

'Thank you.' That response didn't fill him with confidence, either. *I'm trying, aren't I?*

'So, how are you both? When I left yesterday, Eva was not...' He hesitated, trying to find the right word, '... happy with me. Has she calmed down?'

'She's a teenager, and a teenager who feels let down by her father. She'll pull through. You've got to give her time – and the more you're around, the more it will put her at ease. That goes for me too.'

He looked out the window of the second floor, admiring the glorious view of the car park and wishing he was home. 'Fair enough. I'll do the best I can.'

'Okay.' She sighed. 'Anyway, is that all? I've got to get going with breakfast for her ladyship and for myself, for that matter.'

'Yes, okay. As I say, I was just checking in. Hope you have a good day, and I'll call you when I can. I love y—'

'Okay, good luck,' she said and hung up.

Ouch. He stared at his phone while the screen faded to black. *Went as well as it could have done, I suppose.*

* * *

'Drake! Hey!' Ellie waved at him as he entered the breakfast area. It was fairly busy, with several tables each occupied by only one customer. Standard working week for the corporate world, he supposed; lonely dinners, lonely breakfasts.

'Over here!' she repeated, as though he'd not seen her. He wasn't sure why she had to gesticulate so much.

'All right, all right,' he murmured, not returning her wave while he made his way over to her. She stood up to greet him. She wore a green cashmere jumper and black trousers; a different outfit to yesterday's, unlike him. He'd forgotten to pack any more shirts, such was his rush after the arguments with his family. He hoped she didn't point it out.

'Christ, someone's excitable this morning.' He frowned. 'I take it you're a morning person, then?' He took off his coat and hung it on the back of his chair, and left his briefcase by his side.

'Whatever gave you that idea? I hate mornings. Usually means corralling a small child to eat and a grown man to do the same.'

'Ah, so you do have a fella, then. I realised I didn't ask much about you yesterday,' he said. He sounded somewhat apologetic, which surprised him. Must be warming to her a little.

'Yep, Mr Len Wilkinson, we've been together for five years now. He's handsome, he works in management in the Finance sector and he's how I like my coffee in the morning.'

Drake batted away a small pang of jealousy at their happy relationship, but her last comment amused him. 'Christ again! *Airplane* quotes at this time of the morning. Aren't you a little young for that film? It's well before your time.'

'No one is too young for that film. It's brilliant. Besides, Len and I are film geeks.'

'Oh, I'm not disagreeing with you. Just surprised.' He laughed, despite himself. 'But that's great. I'm fond of a good film, too.'

'You know, that's the first time you've properly laughed in my presence. I've either worn you down or you've not slept well,' she said.

'I'd say it's probably the latter. Need a bit more sleep at my age.'

'You're not that old, Chief.'

'Thanks, I'll take that. Though, to be fair, you are very wearing.'

'Hey!' she said, feigning upset.

'And what's with calling me "Chief"? A little American, don't you think?'

She shrugged. 'I guess, but I like to mix things up a little.'

'Hmm, fine. Something different, I suppose. Just don't overdo it, all right?'

They ordered their breakfast while they discussed the case and the evidence, or lack of. The difference in neck wounds, the different bindings and blindfolds, the lack of any symbolic items at all; these were all points to note, but it didn't necessarily give them anything to work with. They were lacking hard evidence and motive. There were bodies. There were symbol carvings. But he had nothing more concrete than he'd had in the past.

It was as though the murderer came in, killed, then left the room and vanished. That was what had been so difficult for the investigation the first-time round. They'd suspected it could have been someone with an agricultural background because of the twig symbology, and the way the victims were killed, like animals brought in on a truck and ushered to their fate beneath the knife.

They'd found one footprint at the second killing, indicating a man who wore large boots, but even that was circumstantial, as anyone could have left it. Stan Lawton had fitted their extremely basic profile of the killer, and he'd confessed. Then he'd died.

Despite the suicide, Drake had to face the stark reality that

Stan was on their doorstep in Barndon, and neither he nor Miller had had the faintest clue. It was unsettling and humiliating. This time, he was worried that, as with Stan, he and Ellie were up against a killer who had a talent for not leaving anything behind that could be traced back to him. Even with how far modern technology had progressed, this was going to be a problem.

It troubled him how it was all following the same worryingly familiar pattern so far. He was positive he'd hear the same story from the mother: the killer had worn black gloves; black overalls, a black mask and hat combination or balaclava of some sort. He didn't speak. There were no fibres, no hair. He never removed his gloves. There would be nothing she could give them.

Even in the previous cases, the discovery of his ethnicity was down to two survivors seeing his eyelids when he blinked and a modicum of white skin around the eyeholes one time.

He desperately hoped his pessimism was unfounded, that Robyn Cartwright gave them something to go on. He needed something. *Anything*.

27

Drake's car rolled into the hospital car park. The fact he hadn't had to sit in traffic for an hour to even get a space pleased him no end. He'd had his fair share of that when his dad had been ill; he estimated he must have spent days of his life in interminable stationary traffic during the months he'd visited. Hospitals and hospital car parks never failed to bring down his mood, and he already knew the forthcoming interview with the Cartwright wife would be a grim one. To top it off, the day was overcast and miserable; the clouds were slung low and oppressive, an almost literal weight bearing down on him.

The chat with Ellie over breakfast had lifted his spirits a little, energising him like a partially inflated balloon. But since they'd started their journey, that energy had been in gradual decline, the balloon pissing out what little air it had collected.

'So, Robyn Cartwright – they discovered her on the floor of the dining room, right? She wasn't sitting in place when the housekeeper found her?' Ellie mentally checked her facts as Drake finished manoeuvring the car.

'She'd fallen when trying to break free of her bonds. That's according to Miller's account, which she double-checked directly with the attending officers later. The housekeeper assumed that Robyn Cartwright was dead too, and understandably hadn't stuck around to confirm. Mrs Cartwright had knocked herself unconscious from hitting her head on the floor. She didn't react well to being touched when they brought her back to her feet, probably assuming the Man was back to finish the job.'

'Rough. Imagine coming in for work, thinking it's a normal day and coming across a scene like that... A normal old lady. She must have shat herself.'

'Maybe *don't* phrase it like that when we speak to her in future, and certainly not with Robyn Cartwright.' He frowned; Ellie really had a way with words. Perhaps she was just getting it out of her system? He hoped that was it, anyway.

'Noted. Sorry, I know I have a tendency to be a little blunt or inappropriate. It *is* endearing to my friends, at least.' She looked apologetic as she opened the car door.

Drake huffed and got out of the car, closing his eyes for a moment at the feeling of the rain peppering his face. They hunched up and made their way towards the hospital entrance.

Grim-faced families, hospital workers and ambulance crews combined to make the reception area a bustling hive as they approached. Sheltering just inside the entrance, they orientated themselves to where they needed to go.

The hospital was too busy, and it was already irritating him. He ran his hand through his hair, and it came back slick from the rain. He wiped it on his damp coat, which did little to dry his hand. 'God's sake,' he muttered to himself.

'You all right?'

'Yeah, let's just find the room and get this over with,' he grumbled, wiping his trouser leg instead. A feeling of unease was spreading through him.

* * *

They found the floor where Robyn Cartwright was being monitored. Drake saw a nurse walking in their direction after leaving a room and stopped her. She had a kind oval-shaped face and long blonde hair tied up elaborately. There was a certain air of world weariness about her, however, that suggested she was finishing a shift.

'We're here to speak with a Mrs Robyn Cartwright. Is she able to take questions now?' Drake asked, showing his identification.

'Nurse Tyler,' she said. 'Yes, she is. But please, be very gentle with her – she's barely said a word, and hasn't eaten. We need to ensure she doesn't withdraw into herself for much longer. I'll be joining you, and if I feel things are going too far, I will have to ask you to leave.'

'Fair enough, I understand. I've dealt with victims in similar situations in the past,' he said. He didn't want to diminish the impact of the mother's situation, but he *was* used to conducting interviews in very similar circumstances.

'Okay, if you'd just follow me.'

The room which held Robyn Cartwright was poorly lit and cast in a hazy grey half-light. The blinds were down part way, shielding the woman from the clouds, but they couldn't hide the room's grim sterility.

Robyn was sitting up in the hospital bed. She was dressed in a plain white gown with her knees drawn into her chest, her arms wrapped tight around her legs. She had blonde shoulder-length hair, and an angry-looking contusion to her left temple, presumably where she had fallen and hit her head when trying to free herself from the chair.

Her wrists were red and sore from her bindings, one graze half-hidden beneath her hospital bracelet. Otherwise, she seemed unharmed physically. However, her mental condition was a different story. Her nails looked like she had been picking or biting at them continuously; dried blood ringed many of her cuticles, while her eyes were glazed over, her lip quivering as she ran through some silent thoughts.

She didn't acknowledge their presence in the room, nor stir when Nurse Tyler refilled her glass. The woman only flinched at the sound of the water jug being placed on the tabletop.

Drake stood to her right, his hands at his sides. He was doing his best to look non-threatening or demanding. However, answers were needed, and needed fast. He couldn't spend hours coaxing a response, and he imagined she wouldn't want that, either. Drake expected she wanted the man who murdered her family dead, preferably at her hands, and the sooner, the better. He knew he would.

'Mrs Cartwright, I'm Detective Chief Inspector John Drake, and this is Detective Sergeant Ellie Wilkinson,' he said softly, moving in towards the side of her bed so she would have to look at him. 'We were hoping we could speak to you about the incident last night at your home?' He cringed at his voice, unimpressed with his take on a gentle tone.

'Incident?' she murmured, not looking at him.

'Yes, last night.'

She was silent as she let her knees go. She turned on her side and lay down with her back to him. This would not be easy.

'Mrs Cartwright. Can you speak to us? Anything you say could be of great importance in helping us find the man who did this to you – to your family.'

'Mike l...' she stammered.

'Yes, your husband. Would you be able to tell us what happened before he... before they were killed?'

'Tomas...' She sniffed. 'Little Matthew. He was so-so-so...

small.' Her body started shuddering, as though wracked with violent sobs, but she didn't make a sound.

'Mrs Cartwright?'

'My boys—' she murmured.

'Yes, Mrs Cartwright ... Robyn ... your boys. Help us help your boys ... and your husband. Help us find the man who did this.'

He moved to the side of the room Robyn Cartwright was facing. Her eyes were red-rimmed as tears broke free and ran down her face but still, she didn't engage directly with him.

He felt a knot of frustration building deep within his chest; the familiar feeling from twenty years ago was worming its way back to the surface. While he knew it wasn't her fault, and the situation was incredibly challenging, what good was this to either of them if she didn't help or offer any insight?

The more information she could give; if there was anything more that she could provide, that perhaps was *different* to the previous scenes; that would be enough. He was human, after all, and a father. He didn't want her to relive every single detail. But he was expecting something from her responses that he could use, not this.

'I'm sorry, DCI Drake. This doesn't seem to be doing her or you any good. You may have to think about coming back another time,' the nurse whispered, putting a hand on his arm. He felt a slight pull.

'I'm sorry too,' he said, trying his best not to snap. 'But I'm going to have to press her a little further. We can't leave it like this – more people's lives could be at stake.' He looked the nurse in the eye and he felt his frustration bubbling closer to the surface as she frowned at him. He wanted this man caught, but he didn't want to cause Robyn further distress, either.

Ellie stared pointedly at Drake and shrugged. Maybe he

should let her try, Robyn was obviously closing down on his tried and tested approach. She shrugged again, very slightly, and Drake stood aside to let her make her own move.

'Robyn,' Ellie said gently. She moved in front of Drake and crouched down to the woman's eye level. She reached for Robyn's hand, but she withdrew it as though she'd been scalded.

'Robyn, my name is Ellie. We've been assigned to your case, and we're here to bring to justice whoever did this to you and your family. Please. Anything you can tell us will help. Anything... anything you can remember, anything at all. Please.'

Barely a whisper, Robyn finally spoke. 'Anything?'

'Yes. Anything.'

Without warning, the woman tore off the covers of the bed, sat up and started screaming. 'Well, how about the fact he was fucking *filming* it all? He filmed himself butchering my family. Cutting my boy's throats. *Gutting* my husband. *He. Had. A. Fucking. Camera!*'

28

Ben woke to the sound of excited chatter in the hallway. It was Andrea.

Why was she so worked up at this time of the morning? Particularly after last night.

He sat up in bed and scratched his head, his eyes taking their time to acclimatise to the halogen bulb glaring down at him. The bedroom was still bare since the move and in need of some attention, much the same as the rest of the house.

He knew he needed to get on it, but his work of late hadn't let up. Working from home on and off felt like it made him busier and less flexible rather than the other way round. He couldn't just pop over to someone's desk for a quick chat or to get an answer to a question. Instead, he ended up stuck on a myriad of interminably boring phone calls and video conferences. He hoped Andrea didn't feel like she was getting the same attention this bare room was.

'Okay...okay...' he heard through the door.

Who could she be calling at – shit? What was the time?

He looked at the clock. It had just gone 9:03 a.m.

'Crap!' he said, remembering he had a call at half nine. Last night's events must have tired him out more than he thought.

He jumped out of bed and headed for a quick shower.

* * *

Showered and dressed, he made his way downstairs to find Andrea in the kitchen. She was humming some random tune to herself while she fiddled at the kitchen island, spreading a thick layer of butter on the bread she had toasted. The smell of toast and fried food was making him hungry.

She'd been busy for him too. A fried breakfast sat waiting for him; eggs, sunny side up, streaky bacon and baked beans. Her cooking usually indicated her mental health was in a good place, though she appeared a little more amped up than usual.

'Morning, you,' she said, greeting him with a smile. 'How are you today?'

'Sleepy. You kept me up last night, and I'm not just talking about the event with the boxes,' he said, winking at her and grinning.

'All my fault, was it? I don't think so,' she said, reciprocating the wink.

He sat down on a stool opposite her and grabbed a slice of the toast she had just prepared.

'Hey!'

'Snooze, you lose, right?' He took a large bite out of the toast before offering it back to her.

'Well, you're the one that slept in. Wait... you're not late for a meeting, are you?' she asked, looking at the kitchen clock and waving away the half-eaten toast.

He put it down, grabbed some cutlery and started on his

breakfast. 'Nah, got just under ten minutes before the first one. Then back-to-back for the morning.'

He remembered he'd heard her talking earlier. 'Who were you talking to just now, before I got in the shower?' he asked, wolfing down the last of the fried egg.

'Oh, I thought I'd show I was genuinely interested and call up Mr Barrow about the job.'

'Wow, you are keen,' he said. 'But that's good. Shows him you're serious about it. Are you sure it's what you want?'

'Yes. Honestly, please don't worry.'

She didn't sound annoyed, more slightly exasperated and playful. He was pleased.

'He just asked a few straightforward questions and seemed happy with my responses. I think it'll be great and it'll keep me out from under your feet when you work from home.'

'You don't get in the way,' he protested. 'Don't think that.'

Though she was right to a degree; he was more distracted when she was around. In fact, he'd been distracted more often than not these last few weeks. He was worried about her. He couldn't imagine he'd ever stop worrying, not now. *Hopefully, this job might go some way to stopping it.*

Wishful thinking, and he knew it. 'So, when do you start? He has agreed to it, right? He hadn't just committed to something because he was drunk?' he teased, poking her with the business end of his fork.

'Of course he's agreed.'

'Awesome, so come on. When's the big day?'

'This afternoon, if I want. It will give me a couple of days, then I'll have the weekend as a break before starting a full week next week. He said it wouldn't be flat out every day, so as long as I do what's needed, I won't have to work nine to five. I can make my own hours within reason.'

'Wow, that's *quick*,' Ben said. He saw her face fall, and hurried to turn on the positivity tap and recover some ground. 'I mean, that's great. So, are you excited? I'm not sure I can tell if you are or not.'

'Oh, shush you.'

She threw a tea towel in his face, resulting in him biting down on the tea towel and baked beans before his brain could compute what was going on.

'Nice,' he said through the tea towel, pulling it off to discover baked bean juice all round his face as she laughed.

It was good to hear her laughing again, Ben realised. He continued with the remnants of his breakfast, and she browsed what looked like the news on her phone while he ate.

'How awful it must be for that poor woman,' she said, her voice tinged with sympathy.

'What woman?'

'This woman in Yorkshire. Did you not listen to me and Cari in the car last night?'

'Sorry,' he said, lost as to what she was talking about.

'This woman's family was murdered, and she survived – supposedly a burglary gone awry. Who could do such a thing?'

'Man, that's awful.'

'Yeah, like, who gets up and thinks, "Oh I'm just going to kill a load of people today,". It just doesn't make much sense.'

'Sorry, hun – that's the world we live in these days. People have access to all sorts of messed up shit on the internet, I guess. Gives them ideas, supports their crazy theories. I know I work in IT, but I kind of miss the days when we didn't have social media and all that stuff. Things were... simpler. You know?'

'Yeah, I guess. I didn't get into any of that for a long time. My mother couldn't afford to give me the latest technology, laptops, mobiles, and all that jazz. Nor would she have allowed it, anyway.'

'Probably a good thing. Anyway, babe, I've got to get on the laptop now before I get usurped by that dickhead in my team. Pray for me.'

'I will,' she said, putting the tea cloth on her head and pretending to pray like Mother Teresa.

'Nice one. You've got baked beans in your hair now,' he said, laughing.

'Damn it!' She pulled the tea towel off her head in disgust and discarded it in on the kitchen counter. He laughed again as he left the room to retreat to the office.

Closing the door upstairs, he could have sworn he heard further talking in the kitchen.

He shrugged. *Probably nothing.*

29

By the time the nurse had ushered them out of the room, Robyn had been hyperventilating and wild-eyed, the tears streaming down her face.

Drake had been shaken by the depth of her anger following her revelation about the filming. He hadn't seen someone behave in such a way for a long time, not even with the Family Man's other victims. The camera element had tipped her over the edge, their questioning shattering her fragile mental state.

'Camera? What camera? Where was it? Was he operating it?' he'd asked, wanting to grab her shoulders to keep her flailing arms down. He'd never heard of the Man behaving this way before, filming his atrocities.

'Yes, a camera,' she'd shrieked. 'What more can I say? He set it down and killed my children. He re-attached it to his chest on some kind of clip whenever he felt like it. I don't know why. Why don't you fucking watch it!'

'Robyn, Robyn, listen to me,' Drake had said, crouching down and looking into her eyes. 'Was there anyone else with him? Was he alone? Was he tall? Short?'

She had stopped screaming at that point, her anger displaced a little by his torrent of questions. But her crying had grown more intense as he made her focus on her family's murderer.

'It was just him. He was male – I could just sort of *tell*. Like, how he carried himself. I didn't see anyone else. He was, I don't know ... I guess, the same height as my husband. Sort of.'

'Did he tell you anything?'

'No, he didn't bloody say *anything*,' she yelled.

'Robyn, try to stay calm. You're doing great. What you're telling us is great.' Ellie had chimed in. Looking at Drake, she'd been excited. Her eyes had sparked at the revelations. She was still excited afterwards.

He'd continued with her. 'When did you first encounter him?'

'I went upstairs to ... to... check on the children. And I was in the bedroom and...' She'd developed difficulties in speaking through her breathing spasms. 'Then, I felt something on my face and the next thing I knew, I ... I was in that *room*.' She wailed again. 'My little boys! Who would do such a thing? Why!' She screamed into her pillow, and Drake knew they were losing her.

'Robyn... please, was there anything else? Anything at all?' Drake had begged.

She hadn't responded. She'd just continued sobbing into the pillow.

'Right,' said the nurse, who'd remonstrated to little effect behind them throughout the outbursts. 'Both of you. I'm sorry, but I'm going to have to ask you to leave. If you need her again, please call first.'

* * *

165

Drake and Ellie travelled back down to the ground floor in silence. Not wanting to talk through the encounter in the corridor or elevator within earshot of anyone. Ellie spotted a quaint cafe that would do the job. It was nigh on empty and someone soon served them. He chose not to dwell on the price.

'Drake, this is huge,' Ellie said excitedly as they sat down at a corner table.

Drake took a swig of his coffee. It burnt the roof of his mouth, but it helped steady him after that shit show.

'I know, Ellie. You don't need to tell me. But what can we do with this? Really? We know he's filmed this one crime that we know of, but no recording has been recovered, nor do we have the video camera. I guess this rules out that it's somehow the original killer. There were no recordings back then, and no cameras that anyone said they saw. So, Stan Lawton is still in the frame for that one. Thank God for small mercies.'

'But this could mean it might get put up online somewhere? This sort of killer ... They don't just film it to keep it to them-selves, do they? Not these days.' She took a sip of her peppermint tea, her expression distant, as though she was thinking out loud.

Drake gave a slight nod. 'You could be right. But it could be days, weeks ... *years,* even, before that would make its way into the public domain. So, for now, that's not something to rely on. I expect he's probably just filmed it for his own sick gratification. That's what usually happens in my experience.'

Ellie pursed her lips. 'Even so, it might show that this person could commit another crime and build a collection.'

'Ellie, let's not get ahead of ourselves here. There's nothing to say that this isn't just one isolated incident.'

'But we should assume that's not the case – that's the way we should be approaching this, isn't it?'

'Yes, I suppose so.' Drake gripped the table and leant back in his chair. 'Damn it, I'm just hoping it's true, that it *is* a one off. Let's call it old case baggage.'

'Understandable, Chief.' She nodded.

'Anyway, you have a think for a bit. I'm going to make a call to Bradfield and check in with him, see if he can rustle up any more details for us,' Drake said. He stood up, leaving his coffee to cool down so it wouldn't be mimicking lava by the time he returned.

'Sure.'

Drake wandered into the newsagent's outlet next to the cafe. This section of the hospital was calmer than the reception area from earlier, and he was grateful for that. He was getting increasingly fed up with large gatherings of people as he got older. He milled through the rows of magazines and books, the headlines and titles all merging into one. While he waited for Bradfield to pick up, he could hear a cash register working and someone being given change in the background.

'DS Bradfield?' the man answered absently.

'Dave, it's Drake. I hear you've had the onerous task of working with me bestowed upon your lofty shoulders. I feel I must apologise.'

'Ha, you're quite right, my good man. How goes it?' Dave sounded cheerful, like a man who knows he isn't long for the job. Drake felt a pang of jealousy. What had got into him? He used to feel sorry for the man, soon to be finishing work, having to find hobbies and do *stuff*.

'Difficult is the word I would use, difficult. Appears someone has got a hard on for being a copycat Family Man killer,' he said, scrubbing his stubble with his free hand.

'Not ideal. As we've said all these years, there are some sick bastards in this world. We just have to get them one at a time. They're like weeds though, eh?'

'Got that right. This one's like bloody Japanese knotweed.'

'Nightmare. So, anyway ... What have you got for me?'

'I was hoping you could do some more background on the Cartwright family. What their business was, what dealings they had. Do a pass across the old case files, data and reports we produced all those years ago.'

Drake poked through some books while he talked. Nothing caught his eye. 'We'll do some of the legwork up here with the housekeeper and known associates. If you find any others we should speak to, let me know. Also, when you're done with them, bring out all the old files, evidence, etc. I'll swing by when we get back from Yorkshire and get back into it proper. I don't want to rely on just memory for this. I've got a recruit eager to make a good impression.'

'Okay, got it, Boss, nothing too hardcore to do. I like it. So, a shiny recruit, eh? What's she like?'

'Excitable, keen, young. Basically, what we used to be.'

'Ha, don't we know it?'

'Sadly,' Drake said, a tinge of regret seeping into his consciousness.

'Okay, I'll get on with that,' Bradfield said. 'Let me know when you're back and I'll ensure it's all ready for you.' Drake heard him swallow something, and he scrunched up his nose in distaste. 'Great, thanks, mate.'

'Good luck!' And with that, he was gone.

Drake sighed and wandered back to the cafe.

* * *

By the time Drake re-joined Ellie, she'd polished off the rest of her tea and was on the phone. It sounded as though she talking to her husband, her voice pitched as though she was reassuring him she wouldn't be in Yorkshire for too much longer. Drake realised it was how he used to sound with Becca. All reassurances and promises, soon to be broken or forgotten.

He felt odd, hearing the flip side for a change and realising that it never sounded convincing. No wonder Becca was so apathetic when he told her it would be different this time. Did he mean it, or were those just empty words? He was finding it hard to tell.

Ellie hung up soon after his return.

'Everything okay in paradise?'

'Yeah, all good. Just wanted to make sure Len wasn't being torn asunder by the little monster,' she said, giving him her full attention.

'Is she as "enthusiastic" as her mother?'

'More so, and hey, I'm not that enthusiastic. I just want to do right by the families. There's a difference. Anyway, enthusiasm isn't a bad thing ... is it?'

'No, you're right. I guess I'm just not used to it these days. I work with many people who seem—'

'Worn out?' she offered.

'No, I'd say world weary.'

She pouted. 'That's sad.'

'That's the world we inhabit, Ellie. It gets to you eventually.'

'Well, maybe I'll be the exception.'

He gulped down the last of his coffee and stood up. 'Maybe. I'll check in with you a year from now and see what you think then.'

'I look forward to it,' she said, uncowed by his negativity.

He huffed an acknowledgement and headed for the exit. 'Right, let's get back to the kill room.'

30

It was just after midday when they arrived at the same parking spot they'd used the previous evening. Drake still preferred the walk to get himself straight rather than turning up right outside the scene.

As they approached the house, Drake saw that the area was busier than it had been the previous night, but it was still hardly teeming with people. He spotted one local news van, and the SOCO van was back, as well as a police car. For that, he was grateful.

He didn't see the either of the officers from the previous night anywhere, so he assumed they'd been relieved for the day rotation. The news van, *Keighley News,* emblazoned on the side, appeared a little battered; rusted wheel arches, dilapidated paint job and no hiding a dent in the front passenger side, either. *Local news, cheap van,* he surmised.

Drake rounded the side and almost walked into a man who was sitting on the tailgate and eating a sandwich, his legs stretched out in front of him. The man didn't react when he saw him, or more accurately, his shoes. He looked like a cameraman, or some other backroom staff. A bald spot glared back at Drake while the man continued to chow down on his lunch.

'If you're looking for the reporter, she's poking around the perimeter,' he said, not looking up as he spoke through a mouthful of food.

'I'm not, thanks.'

'Oh.'

The cameraman looked up, mayonnaise dribbling down his chin as Drake walked off with Ellie.

* * *

Drake greeted the new PCs. They appeared more strait-laced than the night shift, and they pulled up the tape to let him and Ellie under with only a modicum of small talk.

Even in daylight, the house bore an ominous look. The open door awaited them like the mouth of a cave, and the skies still hadn't cleared from the morning's sullen showing. If anything, it would be just as dark in the back of the house as it had been after midnight.

A strong breeze made the trees move in greeting; what leaves remained rustled and cracked in protest. Some toppled and bobbled along the shingle ahead, with many having retreated to the periphery of the driveway. Drake saw no sign of Miller, and he realised he hadn't received a call from her to check in.

Need to get on that sooner rather than later, he thought. See *what she thinks of a video camera having been part of the crime.*

The man from last night, SOCO Reynolds, was in the hallway when they stepped inside. He looked up, this time removing his mask in greeting. He had a wide mouth and thin lips. Drake preferred him with the mask on.

'DCI Drake. DS Wilkinson. How are you both today? I hope our finest hotel treated you well?'

'Oh yes, smashing. Loved everything about it,' Drake remarked.

'That's what I like to hear,' Reynolds replied. He sensed the man didn't deal in sarcasm and took his words at face value. Through his years of service, Drake found that forensics and related lines of work seemed to attract that type of person.

'So,' Reynolds went on, appearing a little jittery, 'back for another round? I've nothing more of note to bring to your attention since last night, I'm afraid.'

'We have a few questions ourselves, actually, if you don't mind.'

'Sure, fire away.' Reynolds looked round as though he had somewhere else he wanted to be.

Ellie moved on into the kitchen while Drake continued with Reynolds.

'Firstly, we've learnt the suspect filmed the crime. He had one of those cameras you can attach to yourself via a mount or clip of some kind.'

'Really? Sick bastard, though quite clever when you think about it,' Reynolds said, his face bunched up in disgust. 'Well, there's nothing from last night to suggest it being filmed, but I guess there wouldn't be based on what I've read from the other, similar cases. A tidy guy. No loose ends...' Reynolds surmised. He arched his eyebrows as he thought of a question: 'I'm assuming you spoke to the wife to get that information? Did she give any more details?'

'Just that he set it down at points. Must have been trying to get the best angles.'

'Sadly, that's not going to provide us with much to go on.'

'No, I thought not,' Drake sighed. He glanced toward the

front door. 'The other thing was, I noticed there's CCTV at the entrance to the house, and there's an alarm panel that looks to have been disabled. Was it like that at the time of the attending officers and yourself, or was it disabled later? To stop a silent alarm, maybe?'

'Someone had already disabled it when they got there. I can show you where the cable was cut outside, if you like? Seems the family were lax, not having a system that sounded when power was lost, and no backup either. Money doesn't buy sense, it seems.' He shrugged. 'There was nothing on the remaining recording leading up to the incident, either. I checked. The system appears to have been knocked out a few hours prior to the evening's events, so it's certainly premeditated.'

'Yeah, I'd expect so with a murder like this. The person who did this wouldn't have just happened upon the property – and no, seeing the cut won't be necessary. I assumed as much, but you don't ask, you don't get. I would like any recordings, though, regardless. Please, can you send it on to a DS Bradfield in SMT when you can, and copy me in too?'

'Right.'

Drake turned to make his way to the kitchen before remembering he had one last question.

'Oh, and you've got my number if anything crops up?'

'Yes, DCS Miller passed it on yesterday for me and my guys.'

'Good. Thanks for your help,' Drake ended the conversation quickly, so that he could check over the room again. He felt like a kid, not wanting to share.

* * *

Drake soon found Ellie leaning down by the chair once occupied by the father, Mikel Cartwright. She seemed to be lost in thought, staring at the spot where his entrails had been. The father had been a Swedish IT professional for a software development company, who'd moved to England at a young age. His parents had adopted an English surname, thought he'd kept their heritage alive in naming his son, Tomas.

Well, at least he had done until now, Drake thought. Mikel's heirs had been completely wiped out over the course of one evening.

The room itself looked little better in the cold light of day. Much like Robyn Cartwright's hospital room, the light only seemed to bring more shadows with it. The tablecloth hadn't been removed yet, either, and somehow its staining and that of the flooring seemed more pronounced without the bodies in situ.

A dark, ugly muddiness despoiled the tastefully decorated room. The candlestick holders showed up more of the fancy detailing that the halogens of the night hadn't brought out. They were exquisite copper work, just the slightest amount of wax having tarnished them, suggesting they were more for show than anything else.

Drake, realising he'd not got another pair, pulled out the gloves of the previous evening from his coat pocket and donned them again. He instantly regretted his decision when he pulled them on. The material made his skin crawl, like putting on a t-shirt that was still damp from a workout. Still, at least there wasn't a need to wear any damn overalls now, with most of the work now completed, but he made sure not to touch anything to risk any potential cross-contamination from the previous evening's inspection all the same.

'Anything?' he enquired.

Ellie almost bumped her head on the table when she got up to respond.

'No, nothing that I can see. I thought I'd check the floor area and underneath the table, see if anything had been secreted up there, but no, sadly not. Clean as a whistle. Well, you know, apart from all the blood and stuff.'

'Disappointing.'

'Quite,' she said, in agreement. 'I thought that coming back again would jog something or make it appear different, but the only difference seems to be the lack of dead people blocking the view.'

'I know, very inconsiderate of them.'

'Totally, I mean—' she stopped herself. 'Hang on, that was sarcasm, wasn't it? I was doing it again, wasn't I? God's sake...'

He smiled. 'Least you're aware now.'

'All right, I'll learn. I promise.'

They continued inspecting the room. Ellie opened the patio door before closing it again, realising the wind was too strong, as Drake started to remonstrate with her.

Shortly after that, something caught Drake's attention. On the sideboard, next to an ornate lamp with a base composed of stylised brass antlers, sat a carved wooden bowl. The family appeared to use it as a dumping ground for knickknacks, miscellaneous junk, coins, receipts and such like.

'Ellie, have you looked through that?' he asked, pointing behind her. She turned, gave him an enquiring look.

'No, I assumed a SOCO would have.'

'Whoa, hang on there, you know what they say about "assumption", right?'

'No? But I'm sure you're going to tell me.'

'Assumption is the mother of all fuck ups. Assume and you make an ASS out of U and ME. Need I go on?'

'All right, all right. I get it. I'll check the damn bowl,' she said, rolling her eyes while she fished a pen out of her pocket.

Drake did the same and joined her in pushing through the

assorted junk with their stationery. It contained a supermarket receipt, a pound coin, a comb in a plastic wrapper that must have been the present from a Christmas cracker one year (along with the accompanying atrocious joke), and another receipt, apparently from a newsagent, dated 2017. The family clearly hadn't sorted through it very often. But moving the receipt to one side, he saw something that immediately made his heart skip a beat.

'Oh shit, you've got to be kidding me. No... no-no-no.'

Drake's eyes narrowed while he tried to manipulate the object with his pen, his heartbeat ramping up.

'Drake? What? What is it?'

He hooked his pen in and lifted the object for him to get a better look.

It was a single earring. An enamel drop hoop, with a swirling gold and grey-brown metallic colouring.

'Oh ... Shit,' She gasped, her hand covering her mouth.

'Yes, "Oh, shit", indeed.'

The earring dangled from his pen, and with it, the symbol of The Family Man. The symbol was carved finely, just enough that a glancing look may have missed it completely.

'This just means it's him following the same pattern though, right? If we go upstairs, we'll find the other one there in her dresser or something,' she suggested.

'No, not going to happen, I'm afraid,' he said, anger bubbling up inside him, his heart now pounding in his skull.

'This earring... it's the one that the Burgess mother reported missing in the fourth and final case in 1999.'

31

An earring from twenty years ago, from the Burgess murders; the fourth and, until that moment, final family.

Drake still couldn't believe it as he sat in stunned silence in his car. He didn't *want* to believe it. What he'd thought was happening was completely upended, like a card table in an old western bar fight, and now he needed to put the pieces back together. Reconstruct. Rearrange. With this evidence, it couldn't be a copycat, could it?

Stan Lawton didn't have any family, so it couldn't be a passing of the torch – a man proudly passing his killing tendencies on to his son. But, how did this guy get hold of the earring? Did it mean that Stan Lawton was an accomplice, or did he take the fall for someone else? It didn't make sense to Drake. Going to prison for someone else, maybe. But killing yourself? That seemed too far-fetched.

Drake was shaking his head as Ellie spoke to him. Her words passed through him, background noise to the internal voice that was raging at him.

How could you be so blind? So goddamn stupid? You must

have been so desperate to get the case closed, anything, or anyone, was acceptable. You just happily took Stan to be the killer. He must have been, because *he told us he was*. Idiot.

It took all his willpower to stop himself from pounding the side of his head. It wouldn't knock any sense into him, not now.

'Drake?' A look of concern flashed on Ellie's face before her expression reverted to something more professional.

'Drake? John?'

'Huh? Sorry, what were you saying?'

The rain had started up again, continuing its beat on the roof, the wipers the only other sound punctuating the space while they laboured at removing the deluge from the windscreen.

'I was saying, what do you think we should do now?'

They had gone straight to Reynolds on the discovery of the earring.

The man photographed and bagged it immediately. Drake had pressed upon the strangely unperturbed SOCO the importance of doing another sweep of the property in no uncertain terms. He *may* have shouted. But, despite the extensive second search, they hadn't turned up anything else. Ellie and he had taken part themselves, searching through drawers and the dresser in the master bedroom. Nothing was apparent. Reynolds had sworn blind that the earring hadn't been there before. He claimed he'd gone over the bowl himself in the hours after the murders.

This might imply that the killer had returned after the fact, after they had been in the house. That was insane. It would have been beyond risky for him to have returned so soon after. It didn't seem to fit with the profile. But then, Drake thought, what did he know? It was looking more and more like the man he'd assumed to be the Family Man killer was just some crazy man in a grave-yard somewhere.

Drake followed up on the search with a call to Miller. She'd sounded distant while he told her the news.

'Christ,' had been her only reaction as he filled her in on their discovery, before stating that they may need to break it to the local and national press.

'That way, people could be more vigilant,' she'd reasoned.

Vigilant, maybe. But then the phone lines would be clogged up with families concerned for their kids, people from all walks of life proclaiming they'd seen someone suspicious, or seeing it as an opportunity to settle a score with a neighbour or something equally petty. The depths that Joe Public could plumb didn't surprise Drake anymore.

He'd said all this to Miller, who she'd try, but couldn't promise anything. It *would* get out. It troubled Drake that she didn't show more concern. It was her case too, wasn't it? Surely she must be angry that they'd wasted all these years? Another family had been butchered because of their ineptitude.

They were culpable. It was on them.

'I think we need to continue with our enquiries,' Drake said. 'Speak with the housekeeper and neighbours while we await the outcome of the post-mortems and a detailed inspection of the earring.'

'But, isn't there more we could do?'

'Such as?' he snapped.

'I don't know,' Ellie said. She seemed taken aback, deflated by the lack of eureka moments and their lack of direction.

'Exactly. Welcome to my world, circa 1998. We have no clues, just a damn repeat of an MO. And in all likelihood, I got the wrong man and a fucking serial killer has been on the loose for twenty years. *Twenty. Years.*' He could feel his anger burning a hole in his chest.

'But there has been nothing else from him until yesterday?'

'That we know of,' Drake told her. 'He could have just got bored, or felt that he needed to switch things up to keep us on the back foot. It's very rare that a serial killer just stops. They have a compulsion – a compulsion which typically only gets stronger and escalates further, becoming more and more out of control. That's how they usually get caught. They get reckless.'

'Chief, don't say that. You did what you could with what you had. You couldn't have known.'

'Wrong, Ellie. I should have known. It's my *job* to know.'

Drake went silent and stared out the car window. The stone-hewn terraces stared back at him, climbing higher up the steep incline of the hill before them, only chimneys to be seen in the distance. Stone walls glistened from the pelting rain. Puddles overflowed from the pavement, running down the hill in steady streams, the muddy water roiling as it washed down the drains.

'Well, let's take this one step at a time. Review what the circumstances are.' She pulled a small notepad out.

'Ellie, is now the time?'

'Time's what we have, right?' she said, frowning at his reluctance. 'Now's as good a time as any.'

'Let's do this after the housekeeper. My head is spinning.'

'Come on, Drake. You can't let this get to you, not now.'

'I'm not. Seriously,' he said, a stony look on his face. 'Let's do the housekeeper, then we'll see where we stand.' He focused on the satnav, entering the housekeeper's postcode.

Ellie looked dejected. 'Okay, you're the boss.'

She stowed away the pen and notepad in the car door, saying

nothing while he pulled away from the pavement. They drove up the hill, battling the gradient and traffic, towards the outskirts of Haworth. The outlook of row after row of terraced houses lined the view beneath them like teeth, jagged and dangerous.

* * *

Drake pulled up to a small-holding, off to the side of a rough dirt track. They'd swerved into the track in the nick of time, having just spotted it a few yards off the main country lane.

The little farmhouse sat on a small incline, built to follow the slope. On a sunny day, it would have been charming, but the rain had dulled its rough stonework, giving it a grey muted appearance rather than the picturesque look it might have offered in better weather.

They parked outside before hurrying up the steps to the postbox red front door. Drake wanted to get out of the rain as soon as possible. Ellie took hold of the large cast iron door knocker and gave it an aggressive whack.

A light came on near the entrance, and Drake saw a small shape through the stained-glass panel to the right side of the door.

The door opened with a comical, ominous creak – Drake half expected Lurch from the *Addams Family* to answer – and a woman in her late seventies peered out from the half-light. Under normal circumstances, Drake thought, she'd be a kind, approachable sort of woman. But now she looked downtrodden, as though a malaise had taken a hold of her spirit. He supposed the wanton murder of a family could do that to a person.

'Mrs Jenkins?' Ellie asked her.

'Yes? May I help you?' Her voice was muted, nervous, a Yorkshire accent coming through.

'This is DCI Drake and I'm DS Wilkinson. May we come in?'

They brought out their identification to reassure her.

The old lady had to put on her reading glasses before being satisfied enough to let them in and away from the downpour. By then, Drake was almost soaked through, which wasn't helping his mood. Ellie seemed impervious to the effects of the rain and wandered in, a professional smile locked firmly in place.

The house was silent, a well-worn patterned carpet underfoot, and a tidy though old-fashioned decor greeted them. Small oil paintings of country life peppered the walls, only an old grandfather clock with the steady tick of its brass pendulum permeating the quiet. It reminded Drake of his father's clock from back home. His mind flicked to the last time he heard that clock, the evening of his arguments with Becca and Eva, before he forced himself back to the present. He didn't want to bring his mood down further.

'Would you like some tea?' Mrs Jenkins offered. She seemed happy to see them now. There was a brighter edge to her tone and her face had more colour to it too. She probably didn't get too many guests. He contemplated how difficult it must have been for her to discover the horrific scene, particularly as she was so isolated otherwise.

'Yes, please,' they said, almost in unison, making them all smile.

'Very good, well … just a moment.' With a small pant of exertion, she went through to the kitchen. 'It's nice to have visitors, despite the occasion,' she went on. 'I don't see many people since my husband passed and I have no family nearby, not anymore.' The detail tinged her soft accent with sadness.

Drake and Ellie sat in silence to the tick of the clock for a few minutes. He could hear the tinkle of teaspoons on cups and the mechanical *click* as the kettle finished boiling. He was looking forward to a proper Yorkshire brew. None of that hospital stuff – it's why he'd opted for coffee back then.

Mrs Jenkins returned with a tea tray decked out with a teapot, cups and digestive biscuits. She had a stoop, and Drake felt an urge to help her with the tray, but he knew she wouldn't thank him for it if he did.

He looked over the tray when she set it down. *This is exactly what I needed,* he thought.

'Thank you. Looks lovely,' he said after she poured the tea. The cups were steaming and not milky either. Strong, how he liked it, no sugar. She hadn't asked how he wanted it, she'd just gone for it. His kind of lady.

'I don't know where to begin. Such an awful tragedy, awful,' she said, with no prompting. Drake judged her to be a talker.

'Mrs Jenkins—'

'Call me Audrey.'

'Audrey, how about we start from the beginning?'

'From the morning when I arrived?'

'Yes, please. What did you do? What did you see? Was there anything out of the ordinary when you arrived?'

'Yes, there was. I made my usual journey – I still drive at my age, don't you know – and I usually park on their driveway, through the gate and to the side, so as to not be in the way if the Cartwrights came back.' She paused to take a large gulp of tea. 'But this time, their cars were still there. Even Mr Cartwright's car. There's been a few times where Mrs Cartwright has been there because of the children being sick or what have you. But this time, both were there. So, I parked outside of the gate on the road so as not to get in the way should they need to get out.'

'So, you were immediately wary? Concerned?' Drake asked, hands clasped.

'No, not really. Families are families. Things come up, don't they? I certainly didn't expect to see what I did inside.'

'Of course not. It must have been awful,' Ellie chimed in. She set her cup back down on the tray.

'Oh, it was, dear. It truly was ... I don't even want to think about it now. Those poor children. Poor *bairns*, poor Robyn. What will she do now?'

'Sorry, so—' Drake tried to get them back on track. 'So, you parked outside? There was nothing different leading up to the front door?'

'No, there was nothing, nothing to see. I hope they catch—'

Drake interrupted her. He didn't want to seem impatient, but this could be a long conversation if they weren't careful.

'Sorry, Audrey. So, when you went into the house, what happened?'

'Well, the door was partially open, which was strange. It's never open – they're quite safety conscious, with the young lad Matthew in the house.'

'We were told that the door was closed when you arrived, and you opened it as normal?'

'No, no, that's not right, I'm sorry, I must have been in a muddle yesterday morning. It was quite a shock, as you can expect.'

She took another long sup of her tea and put the cup back on the saucer. Drake saw her hand was shaking. 'I definitely only locked the door behind me when I rushed back out,' she said, her voice firm.

That confirmed to Drake that the killer must have entered through the window and exited via the front door. He must have been in a hurry, otherwise why not pull the door closed?

'Okay, so you entered the house. Then what?'

'I called out, "Hello? Mr Cartwright? Mrs Cartwright? Are

you home?" I didn't want to surprise them, you see. And obviously I got no reply.' She wasn't looking comfortable now, the memories of what she saw obviously front and centre in her mind. Her lower lip was trembling and her eyes were on the verge of tears.

'I went through to the back via the kitchen, thinking I could see if they were in the garden.' She took out a handkerchief and dabbed at her face. 'I entered the dining room, and, oh, I had the most awful fright. There they were. All bloody and ... oh, it doesn't bear thinking about. Do I have to describe it? Please?'

'No, no, you don't have to, Audrey.'

Mrs Jenkins gave Ellie a small smile of appreciation.

'So, what did you do then?'

'Oh, I got out of there as fast as I could. They... well, they didn't look *alive*, you see. I was scared. I felt so ashamed afterwards. Knowing that Mrs Cartwright was actually still with us. I could have comforted her. I...I...' She looked down at her knees, and used her handkerchief again.

'It's okay, you weren't to know. You did the right thing, Audrey.' Drake squeezed her hand. It felt cold and small in his.

'I locked the door after me. I wasn't sure if whoever did this was still there or not, because I thought I heard a bang upstairs. But I can't be sure.'

'Wait. You heard something?' Drake said, setting his empty cup back down.

She nodded. 'I think it was a bang, sort of like... I don't know, perhaps a drawer shutting or a cupboard door. Something like that.'

Ellie looked at Drake, her eyes widening. He nodded at her.

'You're positive?' Drake asked. 'It was upstairs? Did it *feel* like someone was there still? Anything else? Anything, I don't know...

Maybe like someone running or walking on the stones outside at any point?'

The killer must have still been in the house when she entered. That sound could have been a dresser or a drawer being shut.

Maybe he was looking for his next set of keepsakes before making his exit? He must have exited earlier, then come back through the window again after he saw her car, perhaps. What was he doing back at the house again?

'No, it was silent after that. I was so scared,' Mrs Jenkins went on. 'I locked the front door and went to my car as fast as I could, and used the central locking before calling the police. They were very good. They were there within ten minutes. I felt terrible.'

'You didn't see anyone come out from the gate entrance?'

'No, no one.'

'Nothing else you can recall?'

'No, that was it. I'm sorry I can't be of more use,' she said, and finished off the last of her tea.

'Don't be sorry, Mrs Jenkins. This will help us more than you realise,' Drake said with a smile, and he put his hand on top of hers again. She was still cold. He hoped she would move on from this soon. It wouldn't do for her to dwell, not at her age.

They sat with her for a while longer, both having another cup of tea before leaving. Drake felt it was the least he could do. As he left the house, he looked up. The skies hadn't brightened any since they'd been inside.

Mrs Jenkins, looking more diminutive than ever, waved them off before returning to the dark recesses of her house.

32

Drake suggested they stop for a late lunch at a cafe he'd visited once before. He'd been to the place with his family on a short-lived hiking session in the dales. Eva hadn't lasted long, having picked up a stomach bug almost immediately. They'd ended up spending most of the time in their rented cottage, nursing her back to health before retreating down south.

The cafe was near the Brontë sisters' family home, their parsonage now a museum. It was next to the cemetery, and even had its own murder of crows keeping a watchful eye over the cemetery inhabitants. He heard them squawking in the distance on their approach to their lunch spot.

It was a welcoming little shop, set before the steep inclines of the Yorkshire hills. The main street itself was on a sharp gradient and paved with centuries old cobble stones. Several people were still milling around after lunch, getting themselves ready before setting off on hikes and cycling excursions. Brightly coloured bicycles rested against the stone walls. He was happy to see the place hadn't changed since he'd last visited.

Despite the activity outside, it was surprisingly quiet inside.

They grabbed a table in the corner. Only a smattering of people remained in the cafe, the remnants of their lunch still to be cleared. They weren't too close, so Drake and Ellie could discuss the case with little fear of being overheard. His press paranoia was reaching a steady burn.

They chose their food, and Drake ordered at the counter before sitting back down. 'Right, so, where to begin?' he said, clasping his hands together and leaning on the table.

'Indeed.' Ellie whipped out her notepad and pen. 'Let's run through the salient points, and we can try to understand what this means for Stan Lawton?'

'Okay, sure.'

'The killings here in Yorkshire,' Ellie began. 'They're in the same vein as the original murders, right? So we don't need to go over that again. But we have some differences – new elements have revealed themselves since we talked to Robyn Cartwright, Audrey Jenkins, and after revisiting the scene today.'

'Go on.' Drake folded his arms and leant back, trying his best not to look defensive. He was getting more and more aware of his body language around her for some reason, and he didn't want to come across as guarded or irritable.

'This "new" Family Man killer used a video camera to film the crime. Why, if it is the original killer, has he started using one now?' she mused, tapping her pen against her cheek. 'We know he may have been rushed or perhaps just forgetful, as evidenced by leaving the front door unlocked. This presumption of rushing is backed up by the fact he *may* have returned to the scene of the crime later that day, at least based on Audrey's statement. Perhaps to gather up additional items? Again, he *may* have come back yet again after our first visit to plant the earring from the Burgess murders, for all we know.'

She was ticking things off out loud and on her notepad as she went. 'Sheets, bindings, and CCTV we've already worked through, waiting for further info from the relevant team. But none of that is looking promising, if we're being honest. Though that earring may already have been in place the whole time, for all we know? It could be down to lax work by the police up here – and by us to be honest, because we didn't look either.'

Her shoulders sagged, as though she thought she was going to get a critical review for her work. 'So, despite what you said, Drake, we *may* have more than we thought we did.'

'Yes, and no.' The arrival of their food interrupted him for a moment. The waitress set out two steaming bowls of spicy beef goulash with fresh bread rolls, and his stomach growled at the sight of the food.

'Let's leave this to cool for a moment,' he suggested, and unfolding a napkin and placing it on his lap. Drake continued his previous train of thought.

'Since arriving at Mrs Jenkins's, I've been thinking – we genuinely have nothing more to go on than what we did twenty years ago from an evidential perspective. Now, I know you may disagree.' He paused as Ellie scrunched her face. 'But from what I can see, it's all the same place settings, all the usual quirks, despite a few behavioural differences from potentially being rushed. Yes, he could have just been out of practice. But what we *do* have to go on is the fact that it destroys our belief in Stan Lawton's guilt. That means we need to go back to ground zero on that particular thought process.'

'How do you mean, Chief?' Ellie asked, arching an eyebrow.

'Don't get me wrong, Stan Lawton isn't completely out of the picture. He knew things that only the killer knew. But him being dead and all, it's a little hard to pin this Cartwright scene on him.' He smiled, ripping off a piece of bread and buttering it.

'So, the way I see it, we need to go back and speak with the people that knew him. I still live relatively near Barndon, and I know he worked for the Barrow family for many years. He also had friendly dealings with the local pub, and its landlord, in particular. Stan was a Barndon man through and through.'

He paused, picking at his bread roll. 'He wasn't universally liked, either. As far as I know, all the usual suspects from twenty years ago are still living there, and I definitely want to check in on them again. The Barrow family still maintain their seat at the "high table," so to speak, and are easy to get access to. You'll soon see why – shifty, all of them. So, perhaps ...' He balled his fists together, agitated at the thought of what was coming, what might have been right under his nose all along. 'Perhaps this means The Family Man – the *real* one – is still a Barndon man, after all.'

33

The mother let out a gut-wrenching scream, struggling at her bindings while her daughter's life ebbed away in front of her. The yellow tablecloth turning a deep crimson as the material absorbed the spray.

A mother's scream for her child. High-pitched, raw and agonising.

It went on for several *glorious* seconds, her voice becoming hoarse, before a series of heart-wrenching sobs overcame her, the sounds muffled by the gag around her mouth. Her teeth clenched over it, her face a ruddy red and her eyes straining. Tears were streaming down her cheeks, mixing with the sweat of her fear, a mother's agony wrought plainly for all to see.

For *him* to see. For *his* hungry eyes to drink in.

He moved on to the next child, the boy's brown hair bunched in his fist, the boy's head held in place by the restraint.

He was crying. The annoying, whining cry of a six-year-old. A pathetic little cry for his dead sister. For himself too, knowing what was coming next, and for his mother's pain.

The Man brought the knife to the boy's throat and—

<< Pause >>

The image stood still, the boy's demise frozen in time while the mother's eyes remained wide and unblinking amidst the horror of it all.

He soaked it all in.

This ... *this* had always been one of his favourite moments.

A sigh of contentment spewed forth from his lips as he leant back in his chair, his hands forming a knot behind his head. The monitor cast a pale glow across his skin, the images from the monitor reflecting in his eyes.

His heart pounded.

The eyes, it was all in the eyes. How the eyes, *her* eyes, could convey so many emotions at once had always astonished and pleased him in equal measure.

There was pleading. There was love. There was pain. There was anguish. There was even something he interpreted as *sympathy*.

The father was off to the side, slumped over, looking to have passed out from shock, a loss of blood, or even both.

He cared not.

The father's hands were in pride of place on the table, along with his tongue. The sight always made him chuckle. It was just ... well, *pathetic*. He was background noise, if that.

To him, it was all about the mother's suffering. It always had been. He could rewatch *that* for hours. The hours passing by in a blur of utter joy and pleasure.

He had always enjoyed looking back over past works. He knew the visual quality of the first four wasn't quite up there with his most recent one, but the quality of the subject. *Wow!* It was a sight to behold.

The single slice; savage.

That flourishes at the end of each; magnificent.

The camera's technical quality and through a window, however...

He tutted to himself and sighed.

That didn't help matters, particularly with the first one and the rain. That had spoilt his viewing, somewhat. The technology wasn't there back then though, he rationalised, not like now, not with wearable tech and the visual fidelity that came with it nowadays.

But he had been pleased with his recent scene, however. *That* was next level. That was what he would strive for, henceforth.

Let's compromise here...

He weighed the first scene up in his mind while he picked at his nails.

That *had* been the first of the families. And that *was* a learning curve.

That *was* twenty years ago.

Improvements had been made, and they were all beautiful to behold in their own way.

Again ... And again ... And again.

He smiled.

This one, though, the third recording, it was his personal favourite. The mother was a beauty. She clearly *loved* her children. *Loved* her husband. *Loved* her life.

He felt himself getting hard. He considered undoing his trousers and enjoying himself to her. Showing her what it meant to him. But he'd done that before, and the ambience wasn't right tonight. He'd leave that for another time. He had other pressing things to do right now, at this moment.

He sat deep in thought. The minutes ticking by.

He leant forward, typing a few commands on the computer. Hesitating, he clasped his hands and put his fingers to his lips, contemplating what he was about to do.

Should he? Could he be so bold now?

He felt it was his duty. He shouldn't be so selfish.

No. He shook his head. But ... *should* he?

He sat for what seemed like an eternity, then reclined back in the chair and stretched forth one hand.

No, he couldn't be selfish. He wouldn't stand for it a moment longer.

The decision was made. People needed to see.

All of them.

He moved the cursor to the large button marked *Upload*.

Click.

He smiled and let out a large, satisfied sigh.

34

Cari Whitman was downstairs at the breakfast table answering a text on her phone when her mum entered the room. She looked tired, and put out, like she hadn't been sleeping well. She hoped that wasn't down to her medication, or that she had started struggling again. Cari hated seeing her mum deteriorate during one of her episodes.

'Morning, my little *bebek*. Did you sleep well?' Andrea said, pushing a plate of toast in Cari's direction.

It always creeps me out when she calls me that. I'm not a "Baby," Cari thought.

Her mother sat down to eat breakfast opposite her. Cari realised she'd not spoken to her mum much since she'd been working at the farm with the Barrows. She was sleeping even more than usual. The activity seemed to knock her out.

'Mum, *please*. Stop calling me that. I barely speak Turkish and I'm not a baby, either,' she said, biting into her slice of toast with a look of indignation.

'You'll always be my *bebek*. Don't think otherwise,' Andrea said, locking her eyes on her.

Why's she staring at me like that?

'Are you looking forward to work today?' Cari asked, keen to move on from the strange atmosphere. The look on her mother's face was giving her the creeps.

'I am! It will be good to do a proper stretch, rather than just those few bits last week,' she said, holding her nose before squeaking out the last few words. 'Though the smell of shit is pretty strong up there.'

Cari laughed and smiled with her. Her mum always looked so much better when she smiled, something that was rare lately. She tried to shake the thought from her mind, not wanting to think about her mum's future, not now.

They sat in silence while they ate. Cari noticed her mum begin staring off into the distance; as though she had zoned out, her shoulders drooping.

'Mum? Are you feeling okay?'

'Yes, why do you ask?'

'You kind of glazed over for a moment there,' Cari said, raising her eyebrows, concern on her face.

'Oh, *shut up!*'

Cari recoiled from her outburst. *What was that? She never snaps like that at me.*

'You know ... just thinking of what needs doing today,' Andrea said nonchalantly, picking at a cuticle. None of the previous moment's rage was apparent anymore, as though it had never happened.

'Mum, stop, you'll make your fingers bleed.'

Andrea ignored her and carried on. Cari knew her mum did this when she wasn't being honest. She'd done a lot of growing up since she'd started helping her dad out with her care.

She tried starting a conversation again. 'Cool, well, I'm so proud of you for working. You seem more relaxed – well, besides now, maybe.'

Andrea smiled. 'Oh, I *am*. Thank you. Come here.'

'What?'

'Come here.' she repeated, sounding more like a command than a request as she waved Cari over.

'Er, okay.' Cari walked over to Andrea's side of the breakfast bar and gave her a hug. She felt so thin beneath her fingers.

Her mother squeezed her tighter. 'I love you, Cari. Don't you forget that.'

Cari noticed her mum looking over her shoulder like there was something or someone in the room.

'I love you too, Mum.' Cari backed away from the hug and made a move for the door. 'Mum, is it okay if Eva – Eva Drake – comes over this evening? We were just going to listen to music, maybe watch a film.'

Andrea cocked her head to one side. 'Of course, honey. It's nice you're making new friends. You've mentioned her before. I'm sorry I didn't see her last time. I was just so tired.'

She shrugged. 'It's only Eva. I don't have any other friends.'

'It'll come. You'll be the most popular girl at school, you'll see.'

'I don't want that.'

'Don't say that. Of course, you do.'

'No, Mum. That's not "me," you know that.' She felt disappointed her mother didn't understand that it was just something she didn't want.

'Well, whatever makes you happy, I suppose.'

'Okay,' Cari smiled. 'I'll just say bye to Dad and then I'll go to school. Thanks for the toast.' She waggled the rest in front of her mum before walking out and thundering up the stairs.

* * *

Ben was replying to an email when he heard his daughter enter his office.

'Dad?'

'Yes, Cari? Morning, how are you?' Ben said, glancing back over his shoulder from the small desk. The sunlight was causing a strong glare on his laptop screen.

'It's Mum. She ... she's being strange again. Scatty... jittery, weirdly angry, you know?'

'I know, honey. We'll ride it out. She'll be fine,' Ben said absentmindedly before turning his attention back to his laptop. He continued replying to a work email.

Workshops, really? Do we need to have a workshop? Can't we just agree to something with a thirty-minute meeting? Why does it have to be half a day with half the office... jeez!

'Dad ... seriously, do you think so? I mean, she's been quite up and down lately.'

'I know, Cari,' he said. 'I do, truly, but you know what we agreed – no more doctors for a while. We don't want her to be messed around again, do we? She just acts up sometimes, you know that.'

He turned away from the laptop and spun round on the office chair, giving her his full attention. She was growing up fast. Too fast. His daughter was like a mini adult in the way she talked, and in her emotions. He guessed she had to be with their current situation. He was proud of her and sad for her at the same time. Cari shouldn't have to deal with this at her age.

'Dad, you know that's not it. I think she might need help, like different medication again or something?'

'Cari...' He gently took hold of her arms, trying to reassure her. 'Cari, we agreed ... You and I, remember? We'd see how it went. What's got you so spooked?'

'I caught her looking at something when she force-hugged me just now. Like she was acknowledging someone who wasn't there. It was weird.'

'It's nothing to be worried about. I'm sure you misinterpreted what you saw.'

Even as he said the words, Ben thought back to the times he'd heard Andrea talking to no one. He didn't want to worry Cari, but he didn't know what to do. He couldn't admit defeat, not yet. This was supposed to be their new beginning; new area, fresh start and all that. Andrea was working. She even *liked it*, by all accounts. Maybe he should stop by sometime, bring her a gift. Check out the place.

'Okay,' Cari said doubtfully. 'But the other night when I brought Eva over ... she thought she was weird, too. She asked if mum was all right. That's not a good sign, a stranger thinking that, is it? And just now, mum couldn't even remember *seeing* her, and she was at the table with us for a good half hour.'

'She *wasn't* all right that night, though? That's why I got her away as soon as I could. You know that.'

'I know. I know Eva won't spread it around either. But I think I might stop bringing her round if mum's not well again. Just in case.'

'Do what you think is best, honey. And please, if you see or hear anything that doesn't seem right, you come and tell me, okay? We can do this together.'

'Okay, Dad, if you're sure,' Cari said, a note of sadness in her voice.

'Want to hug it out?' he asked. He held out his arms, beckoning her over. 'Come on, hug it out with your old man.'

'Dad! No, not really. I've had one weird one this morning. Don't fancy another right now.'

'Hey!'

'Sorry.' She laughed. 'I better get going. I'll be late for school.'

'Love you, Cari.'

'I know, Dad.' She said gave him a small smile, and went out. He heard her running down the stairs at a rate of knots, followed by the sound of a door slamming.

'I hope you know what you're doing, Ben Whitman,' he muttered to himself. He turned his attention back to his work laptop and the email.

Fecking workshop. He sighed.

35

Drake woke to find an empty void in the bed where Becca should have been. He placed a searching hand in the space and felt a pang of relief. It was still warm; she hadn't been gone long.

He felt pleased to be back home with the two most important people in his life. The pair had been surprised, too, to see him show up on the doorstep out of the blue. He'd wanted to surprise them, to not have them beholden to a date and time. And perhaps selfishly, for him not to be held to one, either. He'd enjoyed their reactions.

There had been nothing of note in Yorkshire since the interviews with Robyn Cartwright and Mrs Jenkins. The follow-up interviews with neighbours turned up nothing. The houses were far enough removed from each other that 'neighbour' was perhaps too strong a word. But either way, the other residents had seen no suspicious vehicles or people in the vicinity. All in all, it was a typical crime scene in keeping with all the other incidents the Family Man had been involved in. No sightings, no suspects, no leads. Nothing. It was proving hard to handle.

Drake still desperately hoped that this Family Man incident

was a one off. Maybe he was just getting one final killing out of his system after years of storing it up? But that was wishful, even stupid thinking. There *would* be another, Drake could feel it in his bones.

And he had evidence that pointed to the likelihood of more killings too, now that Robyn Cartwright had confirmed items were missing from the house: another earring, a small gold ring bequeathed from her late grandmother, and a hairbrush had been taken. The removing of a hairbrush and earring had been done before, so if the Family Man turned up again, it seemed possible he'd go for a bit of metalwork with the ring, just to mix things up a little and keep him entertained. As though the Man hadn't been entertained enough already.

Drake hoped he'd have a bit of time before that theory was proved or disproved. The past cases had all been a few months apart, and they'd taken place in neighbouring towns or cities near Barndon, namely Oxford and Reading, before the killer had returned to Barndon once more. Haworth was conspicuous in how far from the others it was. Perhaps the Man had moved away in the last twenty years?

Either way, Drake figured staying in Yorkshire had no benefit to anyone right now, particularly with the post-mortem having been inexplicably delayed due to the continued staffing issues. The pathologist assured them they would receive the report as soon as humanly possible. The situation left them with having gleaned what information they could, and this way he could be with his family and still be in touching distance of Miller and Bradfield, and some of the sorry wretches he'd be revisiting for the case in due course.

Ellie, too, was close by, and being her superior, he'd felt duty bound to ensure she wasn't away longer than was needed. The old Drake wouldn't have dreamt of it; he would have stayed, making repeat visits to everyone in the neighbourhood, and he would have pushed his colleagues to similar states of breaking point. There had been complaints in the past about it. Complaints that had been handled and swept away.

Drake lay in bed and started thinking about the day ahead. He'd got a meeting with Samuel and Ann Barrow of Barndon farm (or Barrow farm, depending on who you spoke to) who'd both been away with work over the weekend.

He wasn't looking forward to that session very much. They were a strange bunch. He'd always suspected them of wrong-doing; not involving murder, just plain old dodgy deals, backhanders and threats. Old school. It would go some way to explain the rapid expansion of their enterprise in recent years.

Before that, he had the grim task of speaking with the owner of the Barndon Arms, Michael Randall. The man was a pathetic excuse for a human being, a knuckle-dragging cretin with a strong dislike for women, or 'whores', as he preferred to call them. He'd been a prime suspect at the time of the original killings, but as with everything else in the case, Drake had hit a dead end, as it had been impossible to physically place him at the scenes. However, Drake's instincts made him feel there was something there, something he couldn't put his finger on. It would be interesting to see and hear Ellie's take on the man.

'Dad!' he heard Eva call from downstairs.

'Yes, honey?' he bellowed back.

'Breakfast! Get your arse down here!'

She's getting quite the mouth on her, he thought. It was sort of endearing. He mustered up the effort to get himself out of bed, dragging himself up with a series of tired grunts before grabbing his dressing gown. *I'm getting too old for this shit,* he thought.

He made his way downstairs, stopping in his tracks as he

caught some of a BBC News bulletin blaring from the living room.

'*...the mother of the murdered children and husband is recuperating in hospital. It appears the Family Man, the serial killer from twenty years ago, who supposedly died, has struck again—*'

'Oh shit, it's out there.' Drake rubbed his face. The act of hearing it on television brought on a strange feeling of reality and revulsion, and the last sentence hit him particularly hard. How could he have known?

'It is indeed,' Becca said. She padded through from the lounge, her eyes following him as he lumbered down the stairs.

'Have they shown me or mentioned me at all? That's the last thing I want. People bothering me, bothering *us*, the way it was last time—'

'Not that I've seen, but give it time. I'm sure we'll get a few people knocking on the door wanting a damn comment,' she said. 'Social media is doing its thing as we speak.'

She pulled her phone out and showed him that the Family Man was 'trending'.

'Hopefully Miller will get an official statement out there and they'll leave us to it.'

She cast him a doubtful look. 'Wishful thinking, don't you think?'

'Yeah, probably. Just got to be vigilant for Eva, and not give out anything but the usual responses.' He shrugged. He felt defeated already, and the day hadn't even started. 'Anyway, breakfast!'

* * *

Breakfast was a muted affair. Drake had turned the TV off to avoid getting too many prompts for Family Man questions from

Eva, and he didn't want to get more pissed off than he already was. He'd seen the reporters had been badgering Mrs Jenkins at her home that morning, too, and the footage showed them harassing her while she walked to her car.

The car she was still driving. He smiled at the memory of her telling him proudly about it.

She'd been good enough to bat them away, but soon she'd have to give them something so they'd leave her alone. In the meantime, her face was full of fury and she'd told them where to stick it in her blunt Yorkshire way.

Damn press. Sooner we catch that prick, the better.

'John, will you be able to give Eva a lift to school this morning?' Becca asked, looking intently at her work phone at the table.

Eva looked up with expectant eyes.

'I'm sorry, love... kiddo... I can't. I've got a few interviews to carry out,' he said. He could feel the mood in the room drop straight after the words left his mouth. He turned to Eva. 'But I could see about grabbing you later on. How about that?'

'Well, one out of two isn't so bad. Can't complain, I suppose. You're getting there, Dad!' She stuck her tongue out at him and giving him a sarcastic thumbs up.

'I am trying.'

'We know ... You're very *trying*,' she retorted.

He sighed. 'These plays on words never get old, you know?'

'I know.' She smirked. 'Though, just remembered, I think I was supposed to be seeing Cari at hers after school. Is that okay? Could you maybe pick me up from there later?'

Becca didn't join in the conversation, continuing to do whatever she was doing on her phone.

'Sure, that's nice that you've made a new friend,' Drake said. 'She's new too, isn't she? To the area, I mean – that's good of you to make her feel welcome.'

'Yeah, she's fun. She's a bit different from my other friends, and I like it,' Eva said through a mouthful of cereal. 'Though her mum's a little strange. I think she might have some kind of... mental health issues or something.'

'Oh? Like what?' Drake frowned, not liking the idea of having his daughter with someone who may be mentally unstable. Then he immediately felt guilty about being so judgemental.

'Dad! Don't give me that look – she's just a bit forgetful and spaced out, from what I've seen,' Eva said, rolling her eyes at him while she polished off the last of her cereal.

'Okay, well, text me the address and a time later. I'll see what I can do. May want to check this woman out for myself. Or maybe your mother might have to, if something comes up.'

She winked at him. 'Okey dokey.'

Becca gave him a thumbs up and a grunt of confirmation, seemingly still intent on her work phone. Drake wasn't sure if she was giving him the silent treatment, or whether it was just a work thing, but he didn't want to press it, not in front of Eva. She'd had enough ups and downs with them of late.

Eva had left the table and was in her usual rush upstairs getting her school things together, while he watched Becca continue tapping away on her phone.

'Are we okay?' he asked outright, breaking the silence.

She put the phone down, the screen fading to black, and smiled at him. 'Yes... yes, I think so. Do you think so?'

'I hope so. But I've two incentives now, eh? Catch the killer to save people's lives and save my marriage.' He said, perhaps a little more bluntly than intended.

She flinched. 'No, John, that's not the kind of pressure I want on you. We're not going anywhere. I'm just ... urgh, ignore me, okay?'

'Becca, I want you to be happy. What will make you happy?'

Drake said, cocking his head to one side. She didn't respond, her eyes deep in thought.

'If I solve this case, do you still want me to think about my job?' He pressed. 'My future as a detective?'

'No ... no, I don't think I do. I've had time to think since then. I think it's all about the here and now. This damn Family Man shit.' She paused and took a sip of her coffee. 'I think it's the reason you've been so crazed with all the cases you've had since. Like you've had a monkey on your back, or whatever the expression is. You definitely didn't seem so... overzealous with work prior to that case, not that I'd known you very long.'

'I see.' Drake thought over what she was saying. 'Well ... I guess I can see what you mean. It's hard for me,' he said, resting his arms on the table. 'This case feels like a second chance at so many things. Getting the bastard, saving our relationship, then perhaps moving on from those sorts of cases. Maybe even moving on from SMT. As you say, maybe it never left me. I mean ... it never left me in terms of what I'd seen, but I guess I didn't realise how much it had been – and still is – affecting me.'

'This is all getting very deep, isn't it?' Becca said with a chuckle. She smiled and lifted her coffee mug again.

Drake laughed, but deep down, he still felt the same. He had to solve the Family Man killings, once and for all. For all their sakes.

36

Drake growled at the sun blinding him while he drove, and pulled down the sun visor in the car. Despite it having been miserable up north, he found he was missing the overcast weather now that the sun had ventured out. The brighter weather seemed at odds with the task at hand.

'So, what's the deal with this guy? Why have you singled him out for a round with us?' Ellie asked. Since he'd picked her up, she'd been quiet for much of the journey, which was unlike her. He was getting used to her good nature and, despite his initial grumbles, he had enjoyed having her around. He hoped it wasn't a result of him dragging her away from her family for the few days they'd been in Haworth.

'Ah, Michael Randall, he's a peach. He was my prime suspect after the first killings – the Taylor family murders. And here's my three reasons why,' he said, holding out a fist to her while he drove, counting out the reasons with his fingers. 'First, he never had a concrete alibi for the first murder twenty years back, and weak ones for the rest. Second, he has a history of violent behaviour, predominantly towards women. And third, I have a strong dislike for him, even more so than the Barrows, who we'll also be paying a visit to today. There's something there I can't quite put my finger on. I haven't seen him for a few years, and perhaps he's changed his ways, but I sincerely doubt it.'

He paused, seeing Ellie thinking. She was just about to speak when he pipped her to it while taking a left-turn down a narrow-terraced street. 'Now, I know you're going to ask about the alibi situation. He literally had none. He was at home whilst his family were away for the first one.'

'And you couldn't find anything that would stick, right?'

'Right.'

She frowned. 'What about the other murders?'

'He was in the general vicinity of *all* of them.'

'What?' she said, a look of incredulity on her face.

'I know.' Drake sighed heavily.

'But, how?'

'He's the landlord for the Barndon Arms. He goes round the local area, visiting breweries and such like, so he was near the Reading and Oxford murders. He argued it was a coincidence. And to be fair, he's not far wrong – you can't just go pointing fingers at people because of perceived coincidence, and we lacked a motive and that crucial thing called evidence. Believe me, I would have loved for it to be him. He's scum. But he's innocent scum until we can find something on him.'

Ellie sighed. 'Nightmare.'

'You're not wrong.'

'But, with the first one, if he runs this pub and his family weren't on hand, then how did no one see him if he was at home the entire time?'

'There was a full contingent of staff on at the time, and he said he'd had an early night. No television on, no phone calls, nothing. Not a soul went upstairs to see him. He didn't come down to see to the staff, nothing like that. No one heard *anything*. When his wife, son and daughter returned from visiting a relative the following day, he was in bed.'

'Hmmm, that just seems very convenient, doesn't it?'

'I know.'

'You said he was violent?'

'Yes, he's done time for abusing his long-suffering wife, Sarah. It's why I went after him the first-time round. There's not many people in Barndon as it is – particularly not of the violent kind. And there's only so many people you can suspect of killing around these parts before having to cast the net wider,' he said with a sardonic smile. 'I've been told that neighbours have called the police numerous times. They've heard him lash out at his children, too. The guy has a serious temper.'

'His wife's still with him?'

'Yes, I believe so.'

'Urgh.'

'Can't get involved in that.' Drake gripped the steering wheel and grimaced. 'She's never raised a formal grievance. He only did time finally for beating her because he did it in front of her sister when he was drunk. The sister took a beating too, and she would not put up with it, unlike the wife.'

'Good. Men like that make me sick.'

'You and me both, but have to keep a cool head. You'll be seeing him in a few minutes.'

Ellie frowned. 'I'll try my best.'

The pub had only been open a matter of minutes when they arrived, yet Drake could make out one or two drinkers inside already. An elderly window cleaner was in the middle of sudsing the windows. Thick foam dripped off the windowsills and pooled on the paving slabs while he worked. Drake noted he seemed to be moving gingerly.

'Morning,' he said at Drake and Ellie's approach.

Ellie's face didn't change, and she didn't respond to the man's greeting, leaving Drake to break the silence.

The information about Randall must have really touched a nerve, Drake thought.

'Morning to you, too. Though not much of that left, eh?'

The man smiled a warm, toothy smile. Lengths of white hair curled out from under his peak cap and round his ears. 'I s'pose not. Still a good hour to go, though.'

'Is Michael Randall inside? Do you know?'

'He should be, and he better be. I need paying once I've done these,' he said with a wry laugh. A flicker of a frown crossed the man's face when Ellie stormed inside, leaving Drake to thank the man and follow her in.

A muscular man with short blonde hair in his late twenties was standing at the bar, methodically wiping over the surfaces with a rag in his enormous hands.

'Is Michael Randall in?' Ellie asked.

'Dad? Yeah, he's about. What's going on?' The man continued working the bar, before looking up and flinching when he made eye contact with Ellie.

'Police business.'

Drake caught up behind her and nodded in greeting to the man.

'Paul, isn't it?'

'Yes, who are you?' He looked away, his eyes flitting anywhere but their faces.

'Paul – just get your dad down for us please, or take us through to him?'

'There'll be no need for that,' came a voice, accompanied by the tinkling of a belt buckle.

Michael Randall emerged from the area signposted for the

men's toilets. He leered at Ellie, making a show of zipping up his jeans in front of them. Despite his grubby appearance, he still looked fit for someone in their early fifties. Someone who could easily scale the side of a property in Yorkshire, for instance.

Randall had always been the surly sort, but in the years since Drake had last seen him, he'd developed a ruddy complexion and lost most of his blonde hair. He wore a stained white shirt with one too many buttons undone, revealing his pallid skin, white chest hair, and a cheap silver chain. Faded tattoos of questionable quality adorned his forearms. The weathered skin of his right arm bore an inscription encased in a dubious-looking heart shape, the wobbly black scrawl reading *Sarah, Paul and Jessica*.

'Mike, it's been a while.'

'Who're – ah, it's you. Drake, wasn't it? And it's Michael, or Randall. You ain't no friend of mine that can go calling me Mike.' Randall stood back, nonchalantly scratching at his arm with a dirty-looking hand.

'Fine ... *Michael*. Is there somewhere we can talk?'

'I ain't talking to you, pigs. Particularly no black pig whores,' he said, sneering in Ellie's direction. She held firm with the same stern expression. Drake's eyes narrowed at the man's reprehensible behaviour, while also being impressed by how she wasn't rising to it and because of that he chose not to either. But he knew she'd want to take a pop at him for his hate speech – Drake certainly did – but that wouldn't help matters.

'Michael, you can't go calling my colleague that. Let's not go make this a big deal, please. Can we go upstairs?'

'What are you? Deaf? *I said* I ain't talking to you. Now fuck off and get out of my pub.'

'Randall,' Ellie said in a flat tone before Drake had a chance to reply, 'if you choose not to speak with us now, we can make a very big show of taking you down the station. Do you want that spreading around the village? Or do you mind taking five minutes out of your busy schedule to speak with us?'

'Fuck's sake.' Michael's face turned an ugly shade of red. 'You've got some whores with a smart mouth now, eh, Detective Drake? You going to let her talk to me like that?'

'Dad... you can't call people that, please!' Paul pleaded.

Randall shot his son a look. 'And you can shut your mouth too, ya little shit.'

Visibly cowed, Paul looked down at the bar as though a funeral procession was passing.

'What's it going to be then, Mr Randall?', Drake asked.

The man growled at Drake and slapped the top of the bar with an open hand. 'Fine. If talking to you means you'll sod off, then let's get it over with.' He stomped over to a table in a far corner to the right of the bar. Randall made a show of pulling his sagging jeans up as he moved past an old regular with a drooping white moustache, who was watching them from his perch by the entrance.

Paul Randall winced and mouthed a timid 'Sorry' from behind the bar to no one in particular, while they followed his father through.

The table he'd chosen was situated next to an old soot-stained fireplace adorned with all sorts of brass fire-tending paraphernalia. Drake was pleased to see there were no sharp pokers or other such instruments nearby.

'Out with it then,' Randall said. His small, flinty grey eyes bored into them as they took their seats.

'We'd like to speak with you regarding your whereabouts on the evening of Wednesday 24th October,' Ellie began.

'The 24th, last week, you say? Hmm...' He made a show of thinking before continuing. 'I was attending some brewery meeting about a new ale we're going to be stocking. Went to sample it. Yeah, that's what I was doing. What's this about?' he said, sitting back and crossing his arms.

Drake looked at Ellie from the corner of his eye before returning his gaze to Randall. Same old story.

'Where was this brewery?' Ellie continued.

'*You* first. What's this about?'

'Answer the question please, Mr Randall.'

'No.'

'This isn't going anywhere. Let's take him down to the station,' Ellie said, making a show of standing up and staring at Drake.

Randall's eyes widened. 'Whoa, *steady* on now. Let's not be so hasty, eh? If you must know, I was up in Yorkshire.'

Drake's heart skipped a beat. 'Whereabouts? Yorkshire is a big place, Michael.'

'Oakworth.'

'Oakworth? Where's that? What time?' Ellie asked, jumping ahead of Drake. He knew where Oakworth was, having spent time there as part of their family trip. Ellie had dropped her previous stern expression and was becoming a little too open and easy to read. She needed to calm down.

'It's a little place near Haworth, and all day,' Michael said with a shrug. 'I don't know the exact fucking time. I came back the following morning. Had a skinful, so didn't think driving was a good idea – don't want no points on my licence, close enough as it is.' The man smirked at Ellie, seemingly proud of his bad driving.

'Did you venture to Haworth at any point? That's what...' Drake totalled up the distance in his head, 'two miles away?'

'No.'

'No client in Haworth?'

'No.'

Drake pursed his lips. 'Anyone you were with in the evening that can vouch for your whereabouts?'

'No, as I already told you. I went back to my hotel after the meeting around four in the afternoon and stayed there. Drank the contents of the minibar and fell asleep. Check with the hotel.' He flung his hands up in exasperation. 'It was one of those independent cheap ones, the Marston. I wouldn't have wanted to sleep in their rooms sober, I can tell you...' he said, wiping his nose with the back of his hand.

'We will,' Ellie said, her gaze not leaving the man.

'So, what's this about, then?'

'There's been another series of murders like the ones I've spoken to you about in the past,' Drake said. He paused to let it sink in. 'You've just told me you were in the vicinity of the latest ones. Much like you were in the vicinity with the previous three of four sets of murders. Forgive me, but this has got me thinking it all seems a little... *suspicious*.'

'What! Fuck, no! I wasn't involved. Shit. It wasn't me!' He pounded the table with both hands. What little chatter there had been in the pub died down.

'Well, Mr Randall, you better start thinking fast about what you were doing and who can attest to your whereabouts,' Drake said calmly.

'Have you got any proof? Anything at all linking me to these things you're talking about?'

Ellie looked at Drake. He returned it. They knew they had nothing and wouldn't be able to pluck anything out of thin air in the next twenty-four hours if they took him in now. They needed to build the case, if there was anything to build.

'Are you going anywhere in the next few weeks, Mr Randall?' Ellie said, ignoring his question.

'No, I'm in Barndon for the foreseeable. My son, Paul, is

going to be helping me at the bar while he's off from teaching for half-term for a couple of weeks, so there's your fucking alibi if anything else happens.'

'Good, and your wife and daughter? If you go anywhere, you must notify us. This won't be just for our benefit but, trust me, it's for yours too,' Ellie stated, her lips forming a thin line while she waited on his answer. Drake noticed that, despite the earlier hiccup, she was, by and large, very good at not giving away her true feelings.

'My daughter Jessica's long gone, God knows where, like I give a shit about that whore. And Sarah's with her mum at the moment. She ain't doing too well.'

Drake winced at the man calling his daughter a 'whore.' He could never imagine calling his daughter such a word.

'Okay.'

'So... what? You're not arresting me or anything?'

'No, Mr Randall.'

'Well, if that's all ... then fuck off,' he said, leaning back against the padded backing of the bench seat and slinging an arm over the top in a mocking look of triumph.

'For now, yes,' Drake said, trying his best not to rise to the man's smug look of satisfaction. They stood up to leave.

Randall didn't make any move to stand, and his face didn't betray anything. They started towards the door.

Ellie stopped at the bar. 'If you, or your dad, remember *anything* that can back up your dad's story, please call this number.' She handed Paul a card with their contact details. He took them without a word and nodded, not making eye contact again. For a teacher, and someone of his build, he seemed spineless compared to his father.

'Good riddance,' Michael shouted as the door crept closed behind them.

'See what I mean?' Drake said, when they'd reached the car.

'Yeah, I suppose I do. Not just because of him, though. I'm used to his particular brand of bigotry, not that I should be – and thank you for not making a scene too. Normally I would have brought him in if it weren't for our case. But for a split second there, I felt we were close to something – some kind of actual development, you know? How do you cope with this lack of evidence? We can't back up *anything*! It must have been infuriating back then, let alone now.'

'That's the point. We need to build it, starting now. I'll get on the phone to Bradfield and get him to follow up on the hotel for us, and Randall's general movements. See if we can get any form of corroboration of his story. We've just got to be patient, Ellie – I find it incredible this man was near yet another murder, but he's had no involvement. What are the chances?'

Ellie shrugged. She opened the car door and got in, her face a picture of frustration.

Drake understood her feelings. He'd been there more times than he could count. But despite the discovery, he was struggling to get his enthusiasm up to quite the same level; he was nowhere near his old energetic self, the one who would've had a million thoughts and theories running through his mind straight off the bat. He felt devoid of *anything* when he pulled away from the pub, not taking in what Ellie continued to talk to him about while his ears rang.

Drake caught the man Randall watching them for a second as they drove past, his face strangely blank as the car crept from view.

37

The ringing in Drake's ears had dissipated a little, but the empty feeling was still there, burrowing itself ever deeper while they drove to their next interview.

Their destination, the Barrow estate, was a sprawling mass of fields and outbuildings spread over almost fifteen hundred acres. The Barrow family house proper was at the centre of this operational hub. The family used the multitude of surrounding outbuildings for storage, such as hay bales and silage. Others were for the various breeds of cows, pigs, sheep and horses that were scattered around the vast site in the summer months. He had never cared much for the farm; it stank of dodgy goings on as much as it did cow shit.

Ellie continued with her deluge of facts and statistics from the corporate website she'd been browsing during the drive.

The farm's agriculture produced a variety of different crops, such as winter barley, wheat, oilseed rape and beans. They'd since diversified into using some of their output in beer, biofuel and animal feed, in addition to opening the farm up to the public as the Barrow Family Farm Park. According to Ellie, they'd even started farming Wagyu beef cows, and that's where a lot of their money was now invested, being one of the sole suppliers of domestic Wagyu in the country.

Drake frowned while he digested all the information. Websites always seemed to be so full of it, and the Barrow Family Farm Park was no exception. It was a marketing dream. All smiling children, and small furry animals begging to be petted. It left a sour taste in his mouth.

This family, this farm, had come up in a few cases he'd dealt with in the past, enough to make him concerned. His colleagues had come to him with circumstantial evidence, detailing how on several occasions the Barrows had reportedly been involved with all manner of criminal activity, including blackmailing local officials, bent police and business owners. They'd even roughed up traders for better deals, or used scare tactics to ward off competition in the local area.

Their activities were mainly small-scale, not large enough or murderous enough for his team to get involved. But it didn't mean he had to enjoy coming to this neck of the woods and speaking to these people. They were all smiles and pleasantries to your face, but like snakes in the grass when your back was turned.

'When was the last time you spoke with the Barrows? Was it around the same time as our friend, Mr Randall?' Ellie asked, leaning against the armrest of the passenger door. Drake saw her wince when he turned down a country lane that seemed to leave nothing on either side of the car. It was a tight squeeze.

'No, it can't have been long after Stan turned the gun on himself. We met with them afterwards to ascertain their understanding of his whereabouts at the times of the killings. It all seemed to line up with the staff rota that they'd had in place. Now we knew who it was – or who we thought it had been, I should say now – it had all seemed to make sense.'

He stopped for a second and focused on reversing to a passing place they'd just driven by. The large red SUV coming from the other direction followed close to the bonnet, towering over their car. The driver continued to bully them back down the tracks. He didn't know what they'd do if another car came up behind them. Drake almost crashed the car in a ditch before the SUV squeezed past with a large, obnoxious revving of its engine. Country living at its finest.

'Arsehole,' Drake said, his face set in a grimace. 'Anyway, they – as in Samuel, Wendy, Samuel's mother, and Ann – were quite upset. Stan had worked with them since before Samuel was born. He was obviously around before Ann Barrow was even on the scene.'

'I see. I guess Wendy, in particular, had known him a long time.'

'Yes, they were a similar age,' he said, taking a right turn into yet another country lane.

'What happened to her?'

'Oh, she's long dead from what I understand. Cancer.'

'Shame. Perhaps she knew more than she was letting on,' Ellie said, reaching to yank down the sun visor to block the morning sun.

'Maybe, but we didn't have the time or the budget to go over things much past sewing it up with Stan Lawton as "The Man", and tying it all together with a neat little bow. Hindsight is a wonderful thing.'

'And what about Samuel's father, Alexander?'

'He'd died a few years prior, sometime around Samuel's thirtieth birthday. Didn't get a chance to speak to the man. He was the guy with all the money, though. Samuel, being an only child, was the sole heir to the Barrow estate. He and his mother ran it until her death, and now it's run solely on his and Ann's terms.

She's pretty timid compared to Wendy. That woman was a battle-axe.'

Ellie scribbled down some notes. 'Maybe we'll have some insights from these Barrows then. Have you given any thought about DNA testing them? Might help your colleagues in CID whilst we're here with a good excuse?' She pulled a set of DNA kits out of her bag and waved them in his periphery.

'I believe they are already in the system from the time of the original killings when we were still hoping the killer would slip up and leave trace evidence. The entire village is, basically. Don't worry, we had all bases covered ... even back in the dark ages, Ellie.'

'Hmm, really? There I was thinking technology could swoop in and save the day. You'd just got post-it notes and manilla folders back in 1998 though, right?'

'Oh, come on now, it wasn't that long ago. I'm not *that* old,' he said, leaning forward on the steering wheel. He *was* feeling it, though; the interview with Randall had just confirmed that. He simply wasn't feeling the same push he had back then. *You just need time. You'll get it together,* he thought.

'I think I was around thirteen years old then, if that puts it into perspective for you.'

He sighed loudly. 'Christ. Anyway, back on topic – you'll see soon enough, this family's a slippery one.'

'Didn't come up as potential suspects at the time?'

'Nope, we hadn't come up with anything. We'd only inter-viewed them as a matter of course, as the first murder was right here in Barndon and they were known to be... difficult. Then the other murders happened, in other towns and cities. It didn't go anywhere,' he went on, drumming the steering wheel in frustra-tion. 'You've seen the evidence from the previous cases – it could have been anyone. It was just blind luck Stan had done what he'd done. Now... now, I'm not so sure. And yes, I'm more than a little suspicious since our discovery of the earring. Hence our impending visit, eh?' He looked over at her.

'Fair enough. For me, coming at it as a newcomer, they're pretty high up my list. That list basically comprises Randall, the Barrows, and maybe Randall's son, now.'

'Hang on ... back up. What do you mean? Randall's son?'

'He had a similar build to the Man's description. Didn't you notice?'

'Well, yes, but ...' He paused for a moment, realising he hadn't given the man much thought. He was out of the question for the originals on age alone, but perhaps he'd heard things from his father. 'But I suppose you could be right. Keep him in mind, for the most recent one, at least.'

Drake looked over at her, but she continued to stare out the window. 'And regarding the Barrows, your ideas about Samuel sound plausible. But a lot of "probables" don't make a case. We'll have to see what they come up with when we get there, since it's now public knowledge that there's been another similar killing, thanks to the news. They could be aware and maybe have come up with a strong alibi or two,' he said, chewing on his lip while his mind drifted.

'Is there anyone else of note there?'

'Other than various staff members and seasonal staff, it's just their only child, Jonah. He was barely a teenager when the original murders happened. Seemed like an average teenager that had the misfortune of being born into that sort of family. If anything, he seemed weak compared to his father, who is a proper farming type. But, probably harsh judging a teenager.'

'Seems to be more often than not that farms find it difficult to keep to the generational thing these days. Children seem to want to fly free of the nest rather than keep it going for the next generation.'

'There's that old head on young shoulders again.' Drake glanced at her as he turned into another country lane. 'So, what about you, Ellie? Did you stick to the family trade by becoming a police officer?'

'No, I'm the black sheep of the family. My dad is a doctor and my mum works as an administrator. She was a housewife when I was growing up, so she was always around to pick me up off the floor when I got into mischief.' She smiled.

'I can imagine you being a bit of a tomboy, so picking you up and patching you up was probably a common thing?'

'Ha yes, you're right there. I was a little shit at times.'

'Wow, that surprises me,' he said, giving her a look from under his brow. 'But look at you now.'

'Yep, *look* at me now, working with big DCI Drake.' She laughed. 'What about you?'

'Oh, my old man was an accountant, and my mum died when I was young. She was attacked and never recovered. Never caught the person who attacked her, either.' He paused as the unwelcome memories came back to him. His father's way of dealing with his grief, his own pain and what occurred in the years that followed; those were things he kept buried.

He turned and gave Ellie a weak smile, the memories fading once more. 'Must have been part of what drove me to becoming a detective. Clichéd as that sounds.'

'Wow ... that's awful, Chief.'

'Yeah.'

They continued the journey in silence for a time, the grass verges a blur of green through his side window. 'Ancient history now, though,' he said, kicking the conversation back into gear. 'I don't believe it's what actively defines you, but it can shape you and push you in directions and ways you may not notice.'

'Yeah, I get that.'

'You'll be surprised to hear I was a bit of a maverick back when I started, too.' He waited for a reply, surprised when none came. 'So, no defining "I'm going to be a policewoman or detective" moment for you, then?' he asked.

'No, I just wanted to catch the bad guys and girls. These days there's just too much shit going down. I want to do some good, however small that might be.'

'True.' He nodded before indicating as the main entrance came into view. 'We're nearly there.'

They pulled into the estate. A large welcome sign with a colourful cartoon painting of an older looking Samuel and Ann greeted them, surrounded by wheat sheafs and cows.

Welcome to the Barrow Family Farm Park.

It made Drake feel sick.

38

White picket fences flanked Drake and Ellie on the long road up towards the family home. The various sheds they passed were nothing to marvel at; a shed was a shed, after all. However, there was the odd shining example of a barn where the livestock sheltered that showed money had been spent, and spent well. The newly tiled roofs and hoardings spoke to the obvious influx of cash.

A couple of bright green and yellow tractors hauling silage in large black plastic-wrapped bales passed them as they drove on. Drake was thankful the road was wide enough that they didn't have to make way for them. There would have been nowhere to go, and he couldn't imagine winning in a game of chicken. A bottle-green combine harvester was parked in another building, its work done for the year.

Those were expensive machines, he mused. *Must be making a fair whack if they weren't renting them.*

The family house came into view ahead of them.

It was a huge, whitewashed farmhouse. Long-established evergreen shrubs encased the frontage of the original portion of the house. The original site had seen a lot of extending and modernising over the years since he'd last been there.

The original farmhouse was now relegated to the left of the huge central hub extension, which displayed tall two-storey windows, stretching the full height of the building. The exposed interior looked bright, modern and minimalist, like some sort of Swedish showroom. It was a little ostentatious, to say the least, and it wasn't entirely in keeping with the character of the surroundings. A substantial, barn-style garage to the right of the new central building had also been built, complete with awnings for each bay.

'Right, let's see if we can nail this jelly to the wall,' Drake said, turning off the ignition and exhaling as he unbuckled his seatbelt.

'Confident then?' she said, glancing in his direction.

He winked. 'Always, Ellie. Always.'

* * *

They got out of the car and were greeted with the sounds of birdsong and a working farm. Cows could be heard in the distance, and a stable-hand was leading a beautiful chestnut shire-horse towards the stable yard. The clopping of its horseshoes resonated when they met the cobbled run.

'May I help you?' a quiet voice asked.

Drake turned to see an older woman approaching them. She looked to be in her early sixties, with a shock of white running through otherwise dark brown hair which extended down to the small of her back. She wore blue jeans, brown boots and a red chequered blouse. The woman had a pale complexion, which surprised Drake, considering the time she must have spent outside over the summer months.

'Yes, we're here to see Samuel and Ann Barrow. We have an appointment.'

'And you are?'

'This is Detective Chief Inspector Drake, and I'm Detective Sergeant Wilkinson,' Ellie replied.

'I see.' The woman looked them up and down, but obviously deemed them trustworthy enough to not ask for ID. Her face softened a little.

'Let me take you through to the main house, and I can rustle them up for you. As you've seen, it's quite a large estate we have, so it might be a few minutes if they've lost track of time.'

'No problem. Lead the way,' Drake said.

The woman led them into the house and into an expansive entrance hall, the large glass and steel-framed door shutting behind them with a sound like an airlock closing. It had a similar effect too, as it rendered the sounds from outside mute.

'If you'd like to wait here, I'll see about letting them know you've arrived.'

'Thank you,' Ellie said, taking a seat.

Drake preferred to stand. He didn't want to appear submissive to the Barrows when they deigned to make an appearance. The woman left, leaving Drake and Ellie alone in the strange silence.

The hallway was as minimalist as the interior he'd spied from the outside. A polished stone floor led to a large, ornate central staircase at the end of the hallway. The ceiling of the entrance hall was actually the roof, the second floor cut out to make way for a full extension into the next floor, which gave it a sense of space and light. The walls were whitewashed in similar fashion to the exterior, their décor sparse.

'They seem to be doing well for themselves,' Ellie noted, looking round. She seemed nervous, her hands clasped together.

'Yes, it's amazing what years of crossing the line can do for you,' Drake mused. He wandered over to a small abstract painting. It was like an angular Rorschach, all black splotches, and strong black lines. Drake thought he could make out some kind of caged animal. He was wondering what Samuel Barrow saw when the woman came back in and broke the silence.

'They'll be with you in just a moment. They're sorry to keep you waiting.'

'No problem,' Ellie said, looking up at her with a smile.

'I'll be going now. This farm doesn't run itself, sadly.'

'I bet,' Ellie remarked.

The woman nodded, walking past them and towards the door, her boots echoing in the hallway. The sound of the farm sneaked in as she opened the door, then silence descended again.

Soon after, Drake heard the distant echo of approaching footsteps. Samuel Barrow came into view on the central staircase. He took his time making his way down; the mezzanine floor first gave a view of his legs, his body, then finally, his face.

He'd aged considerably since Drake had last seen him; understandable, really. It had been twenty years, after all. But if Drake suspected him of foul play before, he was finding it hard to maintain that stance. He looked... he looked *respectable.* It threw Drake. Samuel was no longer the young man who seemed to have a chip on his shoulder; he was close to being considered an old man now, much like Drake was.

Samuel's eyes were the same deep-set, dark brown, but his now greying hair had been cut short and he was sporting a neat grey beard. He was looking better than Drake did, and Drake disliked him all the more for it. He'd taken on the appearance of a stereotypical farming type, just like the illustration on the entrance sign to the farm; all blue and white chequered shirts, beige chinos and brown suede boots. If it was the 1960s, he would have been leaning on a fence chewing on a wheat stalk, shooting the shit with the other farmers.

'Mr Drake, well, I'll be ... DS Drake, my apologies,' he said, smirking. 'It's been a long time. Forgive me for thinking we might never see each other again after our last encounter.'

The man made his way towards him and stretched out a hand. Drake shook it and came away feeling like he'd shaken the hand of a gorilla. The man's strength and old Oxfordshire accent hadn't abandoned him in the years since the original case.

'Yes, unfortunate times back then. It's Detective Chief Inspector Drake now.'

'Wow, they've done well by you over the years then, *DCI* Drake,' he drawled, taking a step back and giving him an animated once-over like a farmer measuring up a bull.

'And who is this lovely creature?'

'This *creature* is DS Wilkinson,' Ellie stated, not looking impressed. She didn't offer her hand, and Drake noticed, neither did Samuel.

'You training up the young ones now, Drake?'

'She's in my team, yes. I'd like it if you treated her with respect,' Drake said, his eyes narrowing for the second time that day. Still the same old snake after all these years.

'Oh, no offence meant on my part. Sorry there, little lady.' Samuel put his hands up in mock protest.

Ellie huffed and didn't answer.

Drake wasn't surprised; he wouldn't have either. But they had to keep it professional. He straightened up and sunk his hands in his coat pockets, gripping a ballpoint pen.

'Is there somewhere we could talk properly, Samuel? I don't want to stand in your hallway all day,' Drake said.

'Oh! Yes, where *are* my manners?' he said, piling on more mock surprise. Despite appearances, he hadn't seemed to have changed at all. 'Come on through, please, I insist.' He waved them through to the kitchen in the rear. It was a mixture of ultra-modern with a farmhouse twist. There was a dark blue Aga set into a chimney breast and a central farmhouse dining table occupying the centre, surrounded by off-black shaker cabinets and white marble worktops. It was immaculate.

'Do you actually use this kitchen, Mr Barrow? It's spotless.' Ellie ran her finger across the dining table.

'Why yes, Ann – my good wife – is never out of it. I say that, knowing she's not in the room right now.' He chuckled. 'She'll be with us in due course. She runs a tight ship, and so do I. Tidy house, tidy mind is what I say.' He cast a shit-eating grin at them both.

They were about to sit down when a voice came from the hallway.

'You talking about me again, Sam?' The voice was coming from the next room.

'Why yes, honey, suppose I was.'

Ann entered the room. Drake noted she'd not aged as well as her husband, appearing old and drawn. Dark bags rimmed her eyes, and her skin, though tanned, had a strange, grey pallor to it. Her hair was streaked with grey. What little brown hair that remained was struggling to be seen.

'And who are you two, please?'

'This is *DCI* Drake and DS Wilkington ...? Willington?'

Drake was getting annoyed; Samuel seemed to enjoy playing with them.

'DS Wilkinson,' Ellie said, leaning over the table to shake Ann's hand. A grimace flashed on Ann's face before she shook her hand and forced a grotesque smile.

'Pleasure to meet you both. Say, have we met before?' Ann queried, putting her hands on her hips and looking over at Drake.

'Yes, Ann, we have. I interviewed you and your husband regarding Stan Lawton and the Family Man murders. I'm surprised you don't remember me.'

'Well, shucks. That's been what? Twenty years? If I remembered everyone, I'd be designing rocket ships.'

'That wasn't a normal day though, was it?'

'I guess not. I'm sorry, DCI Drake,' she said, cocking her head at him. 'Would either of you care for a coffee, perhaps some tea?'

'Coffee for me, please.'

'Tea for me, thank you,' Ellie requested. Drake sensed she went for another type of drink to inconvenience the woman further.

'Coming right up,' Ann said, moving over to the kitchen cabinets. They sat in silence while she pottered around the kitchen. Samuel started whistling a listless tune and watched his wife work.

Ellie raised her eyebrows at Drake when they weren't looking. He shrugged and caught Ann looking at his reflection in the window. She immediately turned away.

'Right. Here we are.' Ann set down the mugs and teacups. She seemed overly pleased with herself. Drake peered into his coffee. It was very milky.

Ellie clasped her hands around her cup. 'Thank you, Mrs Barrow.'

They took a moment with their drinks before Samuel started.

'So, this obviously isn't some kind of social visit. What can we do you for?' he said, looking straight at Drake.

'Where were you last Wednesday evening? Both of you?' Drake returned Samuel's stare.

'Where were we? Why, we were right here on the farm. We were watching ... What was that film, honey?' Samuel said, cocking his head in her direction next to him.

'It was "The Shawshank Redemption" I think.'

'Yes ... "The Shawshank Redemption," yes, it was ... Prison film, it is. Bit talky for the likes of us, eh? You might not like it.'

'Have you got anyone who can corroborate that?'

'What? You mean apart from the honest woman sat next to me right now?' he said, with an amused smile.

'Yes.'

'Well, sure, my son Jonah, for a start. He came down and watched it with us. I can even tell you I went to Alan Jackson's shop around, I dunno... eight o'clock? We were out of the wine the wife likes, despite having a cellar full of other stuff.' He smiled at Drake before looking over at Ellie so she could get a face full of his grin.

Ellie made a note in her notebook before looking back at Ann and Samuel.

'Jonah, how old is he now?' she asked.

'He—' Samuel started.

'He's just gone thirty-three. They grow so fast, don't they? He's the apple of my eye.' Ann said with a proud smile. Samuel looked at her and frowned, as though she'd said something unusual.

'Yes, that's his age now,' Samuel finished.

'That's getting a little old to be still living at home. Did he not fancy living anywhere else?' Ellie queried.

'I don't know about *you*, Missy. But we're a close family. Jonah ain't got no business elsewhere. He works *with* us. He ain't got no reason to leave. His family is right here.'

'I see. Is he your only child?'

'Yes, yes, he is. What has that got to do with anything?'

'Just routine, that's all, Mr Barrow.'

'Right.' He looked at her, his eyes narrowing and full of suspicion.

'Is Jonah here? May we speak with him?'

'He's at work.'

'On the farm?'

'No, he does some technical work for local businesses on the side. IT, that sort of thing, ad hoc basis. I don't know the ins and outs of it. Me,' he said, pointing to himself. 'I wouldn't have a clue about the specifics of it all, so don't ask. But anyway, I haven't seen him today and I usually would have by now if he was on site. So, he's likely out doing that stuff.'

'Do you have a number we can contact him on?'

'Sure, but, hey, what's this about? We've been answering your questions, but are getting nothing back. What's going on?'

Drake rubbed his cheek, the stubble easing his aggravation somewhat. He didn't want to give too much away to them. But it *was* all over the news now.

'There's been another Family Man killing. Have you not seen anything about it?'

'What? How is that possible? Stan... Stan's dead!' His eyes were wide with shock. He stared at Ann with a look of confusion. To Drake's surprise, it actually looked genuine, and Ann's expression matched Barrow's.

Strange ... Figured they'd have been immediately on the defensive if they had something to hide.

'Yes, a new crime's been committed in Haworth, Yorkshire.'

'I'm sorry, officers. I'm having a hard time understanding how it can be that Stan has come back from the dead and done this.' He scratched his head, as though he had fleas. 'It must be a copycat,' he stated, volunteering the information as though it was something they wouldn't have considered already.

'I'm afraid to say it isn't looking that way. I can't say anything more than that at this stage.'

'Well, *damn,* Drake. That's just put a shitter on my morning,' he said, his elbow banging the table hard as he rested his head on a large. sausage-fingered hand. 'Was it a whole family again?'

'Yes, the wife's hospitalised. Traumatised, obviously.'

'The children?' Ann asked. There was a sad look in her eyes.

'Yes, the children were killed,' Drake stated.

She put a hand to her mouth. 'Those poor little things. How could anyone do this again?'

'Indeed,' Samuel muttered, a look of disgust on his face. The man sat fidgeting in silence for a time, taking his arms off the table and crossing them. He looked deep in thought while he gazed out the kitchen window. Seemingly having a *eureka* moment, he turned back, his eyes burning with sudden anger. 'Hang on. So, you're asking us where *we* were? Are you accusing *us* of being involved?'

'Calm down, Mr Barrow. We just know you were close to Stan. He worked here for all those years. We just wanted to tick a few boxes, see if you remembered anything about him. He had no family that we're aware of – has anyone come forward since then? A friend? A love child, even? Anything else that may have come to mind since then?'

'No, what is this? No. We have no part in this. We had *no involvement* twenty goddamn years ago and have had no involvement in this damn thing since, either,' he said, getting to his feet.

'Calm down please, Mr Barrow. This won't help us or you if you lose your temper,' Ellie said.

Drake smiled to himself. Even if he wasn't involved, he enjoyed getting him riled like this. The man was an arrogant prick.

'Okay, okay... I'm sorry. I just... It took me by surprise, is all. I don't enjoy thinking back to those times, to Stan. He betrayed me. Betrayed my trust and my family's,' Samuel said, slumping back down again.

Drake heard Ellie take a deep breath. It sounded like she was preparing for something.

'Do you have any clues?' Ann asked.

'Nothing we can discuss openly at this stage, I'm afraid.'

'Mr Barrow,' Ellie piped up. 'Forgive me, I wasn't around when the original case was on, so I have a question for you.'

'Yes?'

'Do you know Michael Randall?'

'Yes? Me and Mike go way back. Known him since I was a kid. Why?'

'Have you seen him recently? Have you noticed anything unusual about his behaviour?'

'Yes... and no. I mean, "no" as in I've not noticed anything. Why would I have?'

'We have a few lines of enquiry, that's all, so I was just—'

'Wait, hang on a darn second now, you know about his... peeping, right?' Ann said.

'His what?'

'You know, *peeping* and sorry, when I say "his" I mean Paul, Mike Randall's son, the PE teacher. People around the village have caught him looking into bedrooms before now, women's rooms. Damn near caught him trying to with me, one time. Dirty peeping tom.' She chuckled, sharp and dry. 'But I don't see why he needs to do that neither, good-looking boy that he is.'

What the hell? Drake thought. 'When was this?' he butted in. He didn't like being caught out in an interview by new information that *should* have been readily available to him.

Ellie pursed her lips at him jumping in on her line of enquiry, before taking a long drink of her tea from a comically dainty-looking cup.

'Oh, a few months back. Filthy bugger must have come up the drainpipe to our bedroom window. Samuel was off working somewhere else on the estate. It was when we had lighter evenings still, summertime.'

'You never fucking told me this, woman!' Samuel raged.

'Oh, hush now, Sam. I didn't want to cause a scene.' She tutted. 'I know how long you and his dad have been mates for, but then I was gossiping with some lady friends of mine and heard that they had caught him doing it elsewhere too.'

'Did he film it?'

'I don't know. I don't think so, not that I could see. Odd thing to do, what with him being a teacher and all – you'd think he'd have more sense.'

Drake needed to check the man's file. He could kick himself. He'd not thought to read up on the son; too focused on the damn father to think the boy could be just as messed up in other ways. It could be nothing, just a typical village pervert, particularly if there was no filming involved. It was a significant stretch to go from pervert to butchering a family in Yorkshire, but it would be worth checking on. Anything was at this point.

'Appreciate the heads up, Mrs Barrow. We will take that information on board.' Drake dismissed any further discussion on the matter, much to Ellie's chagrin, from the look she gave him.

Ann nodded, not looking impressed.

'So,' Drake said, 'has your family ever had any dealings with anything up in that neck of the woods? Up in Yorkshire?'

Ann smiled in his direction. 'Yes, detective, we've dealings with suppliers in most rural areas around the UK. We've established quite the business in the past twenty years. You may have seen that when you drove in, or if you'd read up on us,'

'Anything recent?'

'Not that I can remember, no. We have records if you need to look into it.'

'That won't be necessary right now. But a colleague of ours will probably be in touch.'

Drake knew they had nothing more they could ask at this stage. The fact that the Barrows had provided a concrete-sounding alibi it irritated him greatly. They'd need to check it out as soon as possible. The lack of evidence was grinding him down.

'Okay, I think that's all we need for now. We know where you are if we need you further.'

'That's all fine,' Samuel said, rising from the table. 'But I'm *not* sorry we couldn't be of more help, considering the implications, you understand.'

* * *

The Barrows stood at the entrance to their pseudo-manor house as Drake and Ellie departed, shrinking into the background of the rear-view mirror.

Ellie let out a loud sigh.

'Well, that was fun,' she said, with a tilt of her head and a smile. He wasn't sure if she was being sarcastic or not while he tried to pay attention to the road.

'Really?'

'No, of course not. *Man*, what a dodgy pair. They might as well have been wearing black-and-white striped tops, black masks and enormous bags that said "swag" on the side.' She laughed. 'I can see where you're coming from now.'

'Good.' He nodded. 'But what do you think? Could they be involved?'

'As you said on the way up, they seem the type to be involved in all sorts of shit. But murders of the kind we're investigating? Hmm, not so sure,' she said, taking up her now familiar position of leaning on the door with her elbow. 'That news about Paul

Randall, though, jeez. That could be nothing, right? But it could be *something* too. That's not normal behaviour, and certainly for not a teacher.'

'Yes, and not something I was expecting to be caught out on. I'll have to check in with Bradfield and the local police and see why it hadn't been brought to our attention. It's a bit of a red flag right now.'

'Ok, so, what's next? We getting down to the shop and verifying this alibi? Alan Jackson, wasn't it?'

'Indeed, on all counts. The man's a bit of a mess, I warn you.'

'How so?'

'Shifty, nervous – seems to be of a somewhat "sensitive" disposition, shall we say, and definitely on a different spectrum to our last two interviewees.'

'Well, not everyone can be big tough guys who never smile, eh, Chief?'

'Steady on,' Drake said, as they continued down the narrow lane back towards the centre of Barndon.

39

They soon pulled up, having agreed on their approach when interviewing Alan Jackson. Ellie walked ahead to the shop's entrance, with her boss following close behind.

She had been told by Drake about the original discussions he'd had with Alan. How the man had piqued his interest, if only a little, because Alan's build had fitted the description of the suspect and he hadn't got an alibi for the first two murders. Supposedly, he'd been out for a walk on both occasions.

Despite this, her boss hadn't taken him too seriously as a suspect, thinking it a bit of a stretch. Alan was a timid man, his manner and the way he carried himself making him appear smaller than his six foot of height. Drake said he certainly couldn't see him methodically and clinically planning and carrying out the Family Man killings; nor could he imagine Alan swatting a moth, let alone carrying out multiple murders. It intrigued Ellie all the same; she knew you couldn't discount people just based on their outward mannerisms.

The shop doorbell tinkled as she entered, her boss somehow

getting it to ring a second time on his entry, despite Ellie's hand on the door.

There appeared to be no one around until Alan Jackson peered round the corner of a shelf.

'Hello ... well, this is unexpected,' he said, catching Drake standing behind her. He didn't acknowledge Ellie, behaving as though she was invisible. 'DS Drake, long time no speak. I've not seen you around these parts for quite some time. I hope you're not here on official business?' The man seemed nervous as he finished putting away some soup cans on the shelves.

'Sadly, I am here in an official capacity once again, Mr Jackson. And it's DCI Drake now.'

Ellie suspected Drake was irritated at having to correct the assumption of his rank so often, but it seemed an efficient method of exerting new authority on old relationships, at least.

'Oh!' Alan said. He straightened up and went to stand behind the shop counter. He pressed on the surface with his palms and immediately looked more comfortable, having put space between himself and his visitors.

The man seemed to have finally noticed her. He stared at her, his face turning red.

'I hope it's not related to those awful crimes from before?'

'I can't comment,' Drake said. 'But I need to ask you a few questions, if that's all right?'

'Yes, I mean, I'm not sure what I can say or do that will help.' Alan scratched his head while turning an ever-deepening shade of red, and looked at the ceiling behind them. 'But, of course, I can answer any questions you might have for me.'

'Simple one – where were you last Wednesday evening?'

'I was here. My son, Adam, is back with us at the moment, but it was left to me to man the shop again. I had a few customers come in before closing at around nine p.m.' He smiled confidently, as though he'd beaten them at some kind of game.

'Anyone you can remember coming in, who can verify that?' Drake queried. He glanced over at her, and she returned his gaze from the magazine section near the counter, her attention on Alan.

'Yes, of course. Some didn't seem to be local, but you could check with Samuel. He came in that evening for some wine, if I remember rightly.'

Shit! She felt frustrated at yet another dead lead.

'Samuel Barrow?' She piped up, putting down a magazine.

'Yes, sorry, I'm used to people knowing most people in town. I guess you're not from around these parts,' he said with a cock of his head.

Ellie looked puzzled. 'What do you mean?'

'Oh... er...' he flapped. 'I didn't mean because of you... know... er. Sorry, your ski—I mean... I've not seen you before.'

'You mean my skin?' she said, unable to resist the urge to make him even more flustered. *This is priceless,* she thought, doing her best to stop herself from laughing.

Drake looked at her. She was smiling like a cat that had cornered a mouse.

'Yes, because you're colour—' He stopped himself. 'Sorry, I mean "black." There's not many *black* people round here.'

'I see. Well, Mr Jackson, I hope you remember me in future.' She locked eyes with him, her expression while doing her best impression of being deadly serious.

'I do ... er... I mean I *will*, sorry,' he said, averting his gaze. The man had started sweating, beads forming on his forehead. He looked like he was about to melt into the floor with embarrassment when Drake cleared his throat loudly.

'So, Alan, was Samuel with his wife?' Her boss asked, obviously wanting to change the subject, much to Ellie's disappointment.

'Oh... er, no, he wasn't. She might have been waiting in his car, though, for all I know. I didn't look to see.'

'Okay. I think that will be all. Thank you, Alan.'

'Oh, okay, that was, er... simple. Thank you, and good luck.'

* * *

Ellie heard Drake exhale loudly through his nose as they left the shop.

That's two people to cross off an already small list now. Overall, it was looking and feeling a little desperate again. She was beginning to understand how Drake must have felt all those years ago.

'Enjoy yourself?' Drake asked as they got back in his car.

'Yes, actually. Thought I'd press a few buttons and stop him looking so pleased with himself when he'd provided that alibi for Samuel Barrows.'

'That wasn't unexpected,' Drake said. He sounded as though he didn't want to dwell on Alan's awkwardness. 'But there's always some small glimmer of hope in the back of your mind. Sadly, just wasn't to be, not this time.'

'Maybe they did it together, went around killing people and providing alibis.' She let out a grim laugh.

'Yeah ... don't think so somehow, Ellie. Nice try, though.'

'Mmm.' Drake's phone started ringing as he was about to put his key in the ignition. He pulled his mobile from his pocket, and glanced down at the screen.

It was Miller.

* * *

They arrived at the London office a few hours later. The drive was a quiet one, the mood soured by the morning's events.

Ellie knew they needed a lucky break, and they needed it soon. Otherwise, there could be more deaths on their hands. How soon would that be, though, and where?

They exited the lift to the vibrant sound of the busy London office. Phones were ringing everywhere, and officers were scratching their heads, looks of frustration etched on their faces, or sitting deep in thought, nodding at a voice on the other end of a phone. Many were working at their laptops and computers, intent on their screens; it was business as usual for these teams. You wouldn't think that there was a mass murderer on the loose, Ellie thought. She was surprised how quickly her view had changed since joining the SMT. How small some of the other matters at hand seemed to her now.

Uniformed officers and plain clothes alike made way for them as they circled the office to Miller's corner. Drake finished a coffee before throwing the cup in a nearby bin with a little more force than necessary, and knocked on Miller's door. Ellie kept hold of hers.

'Enter.'

Drake held the door open for Ellie and followed her in.

Miller stood to greet them. 'Always the gentlemen, eh, Drake?'

'You know me, Boss,' he replied. Ellie found the familiarity comforting.

Miller didn't respond and sat down.

Ellie followed Drake's lead and sat. Their eyes level with her gaze.

'So, we've finally had the results back from the post-mortems. There had been some delay due to some nonsensical reason or another from pathology. Sorry about that, Drake. I know you'd wanted to be there and considering a case of this bloody magnitude, you'd think there'd be a degree of urgency.' She sighed, tapping a pen on her desk and looking over at Drake. 'Things aren't what they used to be, that's for sure. But, anyway, there are some interesting points to be noted.'

Ellie didn't think Miller appeared very enthused. She was hard to read, though.

'What did they find?'

'It appears the knife used in these killings bore the same characteristics as was used in the Family Man murders. Estimated length of eight inches, non-serrated edge. Complete overkill.'

Ellie watched as Drake's eyes squeezed shut in frustration.

'John, if we weren't sure it was the same killer as in '98, we have to start thinking that way now. It's all stacking up.' Miller stopped and waited for his response, her eyes fixed on him. Ellie felt like a bit part in the conversation.

'But what about the number of lacerations in the killings?' he mused. 'Not just on one victim, but all three. That must mean *something*, surely?'

Miller nodded. 'There were two less penetrative wounds before the final killing blow, in the father's case, and the eldest. The youngest had three.' She turned in her chair and put her arm on the desk. 'I know you're hanging on to this one, John, but the whole thing is still pointing to the original "Man" in terms of method and other things we have, such as the original items, the symbology—'

'Three on the youngest, then a little less thereafter? Would that not show some kind of hesitation, or lack of... I don't know? *Guts*?' Ellie blurted.

'It could do, but he still finished the job eventually. And I'd appreciate it if you didn't interrupt me, Sergeant,' Miller said, staring her down.

Ellie immediately regretted piping up; she didn't want to be judged so early on. Miller was a hard woman to please at the best of times, let alone with this case.

'I take it the results are back from the other items, such as the sheets used for the blindfolds, and the bindings?' Drake asked.

'Earlier today. They were conclusive in that there was nothing – no DNA, no hair, no fibres. The sheets hadn't even been washed. They were brand new, straight from the packet.'

'And finding where they came from would prove impossible, I assume?'

'Sadly,' Miller sighed. 'I don't see it leading us anywhere. The labels had been removed, so we don't even have a manufacturer to start with.'

'Fuck,' Drake growled. 'So, what do we do now?'

Ellie watched him stand up and pace the room, rubbing at his stubble and waving his hand in Miller's direction.

'We have no real leads, we have no witnesses apart from the wife. No DNA. No trace evidence of any kind. The kill site is clean. The original suspect, the one that had to have had at least *some* involvement, is dead. Honestly, I'm at a loss, Laura.'

'You and me both. I can't see us catching him before he kills again. And when he does, I'm sure it'll be the same story – the *same* situation. Our hands seem well and truly tied. We have *nothing* which links the families or forms a pattern to help us narrow down anything. We're next to helpless right now,' Miller said. She slumped back in her chair with an air of resignation.

'This can't be what we're left with.' Ellie's frustration was starting to bubble over. 'Surely, there's something we can do? We can't just sit back and wait, can we?' She stared at them both.

They returned her gaze but didn't answer.

40

Cari huffed as she leant on her elbow, her face half-stretched, half-covered by her hand. She must look like someone who'd had a botched face job, like the women that appeared on reality shows all the time these days. 'I wish I'd got the chance to see The Smiths live when they were still together. That would have been *so* cool. Morrissey is the *man*.'

'You think? He seems a little try-hard,' Eva said, seemingly amused. Cari found she always made comments like that, as though nothing was original anymore, or not what she saw as cool. She supposed Eva was right. Nothing really *was* that original anymore. But at least her new friend appreciated her music taste. Cari was jealous of Eva for that too; she envied her the experience of hearing the albums she recommended for the first time.

'Yeah, I can see what you're saying if you look at it now. But back then, he was sort of cutting edge, wasn't he?' Cari said, trying to not let it get to her.

I shouldn't really care, not really. Why try to convince her?

'I suppose,' Eva said, noncommittal.

Cari looked out across the school canteen; the place was

quietening down since the end of the lunch period was drawing near. The hatches for serving food had closed, so no one was going to get any more of the crap that was classed as food round here. Not that anyone would want it. It was pretty gross.

Her mind replayed the last few weeks while Eva messed around on her phone. It had been pretty cool since they'd met. She'd spent a lot more time with Eva than on the phone to her mates back in Leeds. She felt a little guilty about that. But what could she do?

Mum – when she was a little more lucid – was still keen that she had more friends, not focus all her attention on one person, but what did she know? She didn't *have* any friends. She never spoke of anyone up at the farm she worked at. And Dad, he spoke to anyone and everyone and was friendly enough, but no one had ever come round since they'd moved to Barndon. So, who were they to judge?

'Hey, I found this earlier. What do you make of it?' Eva said, pulling out a screwed up yellow post-it note from her bag. Black biro had been used to scrawl something on it. Cari couldn't quite make out what it said.

'Let's see.' She snapped the creased paper from Eva's fingers with a flourish.

TFMWFKYAYF.onion

Cari wasn't sure what she was looking at. It looked like a web address ending with the word 'onion', but that wasn't a normal thing like a .com, or co.uk.

Weird.

'No idea, sorry. Do you know what that means?' Cari said, frowning at the note some more before putting it on the table. She pointed at the "onion" part with a black varnished fingernail.

'That's like a domain or something, isn't it? Where did you find it? Have you tried entering it on your phone browser?'

'All right, all right, you sound like my dad with all the questions,' Eva said, poking her tongue out. 'Yeah, I've tried it. It doesn't lead anywhere, just brings up an error message.' She flapped the piece of paper like a fan. 'I found it on the floor after History this morning. I thought it was mine at first. It fell out of someone's bag or pocket, I think – no idea who, though.'

'Weird. How about Googling it?'

'Hadn't had a chance to do that yet. Let's give it a pop.'

Eva took out her phone from the back pocket of her school trousers and typed ".onion" into the search engine, her nails tapping on the surface of the smartphone.

'What the fuck...' she said, her face scrunching up. Cari wondered what that meant.

'What? What is it? Let me see.' She craned her neck to see over Eva's hands.

'Apparently it's some Dark Web thing,' she said, putting her phone down between them. A puzzled look spread across Eva's face as she glanced over at Cari.

'Dark Web? Sounds dodge.'

'You not heard of it before?' Eva said, starting up again before she could get a word in. 'It's like a really icky part of the internet. You can't access it normally, I think. I read something about it, but can't remember. I thought it was all to do with drugs and guns and nasty shit like that.'

'Oooh, maybe some kid is planning on a bank heist or something,' Cari said, the comment falling on deaf ears. Eva didn't react.

Though the comment wasn't that far-fetched anymore, was it? Things had happened in this school. Eva said some kids had knives confiscated from them in the past year. One even had a replica gun. It was worrying. Cari didn't like it, and it wasn't even a rough school.

Eva put her phone away while their German teacher, Mrs. Lens, walked past their table, giving them a thin smile. She was a stern woman, all pointy joints with a crow-like nose. She wouldn't be impressed if she'd caught what they were looking at. Eva didn't get her phone back out.

'You still okay for me coming round yours later? Maybe we could check it out,' she said, looking at Cari. Eva did that a lot when she questioned her; Cari always felt like she was being put on the spot. A little like Eva was playing detective, like her dad.

'Yeah, that'll be cool. Do you think we should look at this, though? Won't we get – I don't know – tracked by the police or something?'

Eva laughed. 'You worry too much. If they're anything like my dad, they won't even know what the Dark Web is, let alone track us!'

'But your dad is old,' Cari said with a smile. Eva was protective of her dad, DCI Drake. It *was* a cool title, like something from a television series or a film.

'Oi! My dad is the boss man round his place. He knows his shit. Just not technology so much,' she said, laughing again. 'I swear he barely knows how to use a printer, and who even uses those anymore!'

'Aww, poor guy. Least he has you for love and support, eh?' Cari said, digging a finger in her arm.

Eva squeaked and recoiled. 'Yeah.'

The bell rang, signalling the end of lunch. Eva picked up her bag and slung it over her shoulders, and they went their separate ways.

41

The study was silent, the forest beyond shrouded in darkness. Long shadows lay across Drake's face and the walls from the lamp on his desk, the weak halogen glow failing miserably to illuminate the gloom. The door stood closed to any of the other goings on in the Drake residence.

Creak. Drake repositioned himself in the old chair, leaning back while he examined the crime scene photos laid out on the desk. He'd had the full photographs printed out for him; not just those of the Cartwrights, but also the ones showing the fourth family, the Burgesses.

It made him uncomfortable to look at them and revisit those old memories. And so it should; before him was a shameful display of a cruel man's indifference to human life. And here he was, still bumbling along, allowing it to happen through his own apparent ineptitude. This "Man" still eluding him after twenty years.

He tired of scenes like this. He was coming to that realisation as the case rumbled on. It wasn't driving him like it once did all those years ago. He thought he'd have been going in, all guns blazing now that the case of his career had come back. But, in place of that, all he had was a feeling of drawn weariness. His bones *ached*. The familiar feeling of utter helplessness had begun to consume him once again, the same way it had done all those years ago.

All that time he'd sat in the office in London, staring at the walls of photos, demonstrating his inability to do what was required; underlining his failure to apprehend the Man. It had driven him as close to the edge as he'd ever been. He'd carried a heavy burden and now he was carrying it again, gradually being crushed under its weight.

He pinched his brow. He couldn't think straight. His brain felt submerged, slow and unfocused.

Drake shook his head, like an old drunk in the midst of a nightmare, in a feeble attempt to bring himself back to the present. He let out another sigh and blinked a few times, pushing himself to continue studying each photo once again. One after the other. Death after death.

What wasn't he *seeing*?

It has been weeks now since the killings, and nothing.

The younger Randall, Paul, had been harmless enough that there hadn't even been an official police report by all accounts, simply a local officer giving the teacher a friendly warning. Drake couldn't believe that someone caught doing something like that had been so utterly disregarded. Did no one understand that could be the start of something bigger, something more sinister?

It was well known that first offenders and even serial killers typically started with petty or small criminal activities, as Paul had done; perversions that graduated to stalking, then the need for greater gratification, the increase in confidence leading to abductions, assaults or murders. The escalation seemed inevitable to Drake. Perhaps his was a grim outlook, but the psychological evidence and a number of historical cases validated his concerns. Irrespective of whether Paul Randall was involved, it partly explained why nothing had been flagged to Drake or Ellie before their interviews, but it still beggared belief that the incident hadn't even been logged. But if there was no evidence tying the young man to the killings, what could he do? Drake chastised himself for feeling any hope. Hope did not rear its head often when the Family Man was involved.

To top it all, Michael Randall's luck had continued to ride high. The shitty hotel's CCTV for his stay had been "misplaced" somehow. So, even if it *had* been him creating that mess, they still didn't have any physical evidence to corroborate their suspicions, unless Michael Randall somehow incriminated himself, or they pulled a rabbit out of a hat.

Drake threw the photos back onto the desk in a fit of irritation, causing them to splay every which way.

He was disgusted with himself. The families deserved more.

Think.

He took a sip of his beer. The length of his wallowing had caused the condensation from the once chilled glass to dry, leaving a semi-opaque ring on the coaster.

A further growl of anger escaped him as he spiralled, the images of the crime scenes cycling through his thoughts. The image of Michael Randall, all in black, carrying out his work.

The phone rang, startling him out of his thoughts. He answered with his free hand, taking another sip of warm beer.

It was Miller.

'Laura? Please tell me you have good news for me.'

'I don't,' she said. 'There's been another one.'

42

Drake got out of his car. He knew he'd parked with little thought as to whether others might need access to the road, but he didn't care. He felt close to breaking point, and something had to give.

He looked towards the scene and spotted Ellie's car. *She must have really put her foot down to get here,* he thought.

She opened the driver's door and waved over to him. In grim silence, they joined up and walked towards the property together. Ellie looked dishevelled compared to her usual standards. She was in the same clothes as earlier in the day when they'd been reviewing her notes for the tenth time, and her hair was fluffed out of shape, as though she had been leaning on something or someone.

She still looked alert, though, which was more than could be said for him. Drake was battling his feelings of anger and despondency, coupled with the knowledge that he bore overall responsibility for what he had failed to stop once again, for the *sixth* time.

On hearing the news, he'd stomped down the stairs and slammed the door without explaining to Becca, other than to shout to her that he'd be back later.

The area had been cordoned off. White and blue tape with the words, *Police Line Do Not Cross,* in block capitals surrounded the entrances, using bollards and lampposts to form boxed-off areas.

Police lights flashed in silence. Ambulance services were tucked away to the side of the property. They sat unused now, the ambulance workers looking on helplessly. He didn't know why they stuck around; the wife would already have been taken away, and he didn't see the witness who discovered the scene anywhere.

A crew from the BBC had somehow arrived already, and were getting ready to report from the cordon. The anchor-woman stood focused on her microphone, a small notebook stashed under her arm. He was relieved she hadn't spotted him; it wouldn't have made for good television to have his face with its thunderous expression plastered over the screens.

They flashed their IDs upon being greeted by two uniformed response officers, who waved them on through the perimeter.

The back entrance looked difficult to access with the cars blocking the path, so Drake wound his way through to the front, Ellie following close behind. They made their way up the steps. The door was closed, but there was a light on inside.

He opened it to the familiar tinkle of a bell.

'Drake.' Miller greeted him. She was standing by the shop counter, just as Alan Jackson had a few weeks earlier. 'I'm glad you got down here so quickly. Seems you didn't beat the press, though – this will be all over the ten o'clock news, unfortunately.'

'I can't imagine why.'

'I know how you feel. This has surprised me as much as you. It's only been a few weeks, Drake. He's escalating.' She grimaced at the thought. The cheap fairy lights adorning the shelves behind the counter cast her face in a multitude of colours. Ellie wandered over to he post office area, leaving them to talk.

'What's it like up there?'

'Depressingly familiar.'

'Who discovered them?'

'It was a member of a family you interviewed recently, Jonah Barrow. That's their only son, isn't it?' she asked, though she already knew the answer.

'He'd called round to see Adam Jackson, and when he got to the house, he said he noticed the back door was ajar. Apparently, he knocked anyway and there was still no answer, so he guessed they'd left it off the latch by mistake. He went in, called for them again, and when he didn't get an answer, he went upstairs. Downstairs looked as though it had been used recently. The television was on. The lights were all on.' She stopped for a moment.

Her explanations were always so lengthy and exacting, Drake thought, like she was reading a mental notepad.

She raised her hand to stop someone coming in, indicating she'd be outside in a minute. 'When Jonah went upstairs, he said he found them in the dining room. Then he ran from the property towards the pub until he was at a safe distance, where he then called the police. Same situation as the Cartwright housekeeper – he assumed the wife was dead, so ran for it.'

'I see. I'm assuming they've taken her to the hospital already?' he said, receiving a nod in response. 'Did she say anything?'

'No, she was much the same as the other survivors.'

'Okay, I'll get Wilkinson on that tomorrow. And get uniform to take a witness statement from that Barrows kid, please.'

'You don't think you should see her too? And I've already got them on the case – Jonah was lucid enough to say he'd do the statement for us down at the station.'

'Good, we'll review it and speak with him. No, Ellie can talk to the wife this time, she'll tell me if there is anything pertinent. I trust her.'

He turned and saw Ellie's eyes light up. She was just in earshot. 'Well, I suppose I'd better see for myself,' he went on.

'Okay, I trust your judgement,' Miller said. 'If you need me, I'll be outside batting away questions from the press.' She moved to the front of the counter, nodded to Ellie and continued out of the shop.

'I'll be through in a moment. You go ahead,' Ellie said. 'Just need a minute.'

'Okay.' Drake nodded, stony-faced. He made his way past the shop's shelving and through to the living quarters.

The shop formed part of the Jackson's actual house. There was a back area for stock which led via a hallway to the family's lounge and living area, as well as the back entrance to the property. The kitchen, dining room and bedrooms were all above the shop itself.

Drake paused as he processed his thoughts. His overriding feeling was one of surprise; this was out of character. The Jacksons weren't a wealthy family. The Man hadn't killed families in modest surroundings such as these before, and their son was much older than the other victims; this was going against type. And why pick Barndon again? Was he really a local, or just trying to appear so? It was a question Drake had asked himself many times but, now it was becoming ever more urgent.

The sight of two officers ahead reminded him to slip a pair of gloves on. The smacking noise put his teeth on edge. He looked around for a set of overalls. One officer spotted him looking and came back with a set and a silent nod of the head.

Drake sighed. He felt as he couldn't see the woods for the trees, as though the Man was mocking him. He suited up awkwardly in the tight space and walked on through to the back.

All the lights were on in the lounge, giving the room a stark appearance. A SOCO was standing by the compact green fabric sofa in full garb, his mask pulled down under his chin so he could speak un-muffled on the phone. The television had been switched off. An officer stood guard by the back door, by the foot of the stairs. He moved at Drake's arrival, giving a slight nod as he allowed him access to the rooms above.

In the stairwell's turn, a photo of the family was hanging on the wall to his left. Adam Jackson, Alan and his wife, Ruth, all smiled back at him. Drake cast his eyes down, his mind turning over what she must be feeling as he climbed the steps. Sitting with your dead, mutilated family the entire time; it simply didn't bear thinking about.

The stairs protested as he navigated them. They were the steep, narrow kind found in old Victorian properties, the light blue carpet threadbare from the footfall. He imagined Adam Jackson as a child running up and down them, before pushing it from his mind.

Near the top, he saw the distinctive flashes and clicks of a SOCO's camera and the creaking of the stepping plates they'd used at the Haworth scene. Drake had never been upstairs in the house before; the questioning of Alan had always taken place at the local station or in situ at the shop, and he felt like an intruder.

Two SOCOs were having a discussion at the top of the landing, and moved to let him through. The space was tight, so he brushed them both as he squeezed through into the kitchen. A departing SOCO approached from the other direction, one who didn't look up in acknowledgement as they inched past each other.

The kitchen was of a functional galley styling; white cabinets lined both sides with a small gas hob and cooker in the middle, with an aluminium cooker hood above it. A sink was opposite, with a window above providing the Jacksons with a full view of the street. He could imagine Alan being a nosy neighbour, peering out at the goings on below. How the tables had turned.

At the end of the kitchen was the dining area. The dining table was just out of view, ensconced in the latter part of the right angle. A set of porthole windows beyond the table, coupled with the time of night, looked like a pair of dark eyes surveying the scene below. Drake was disappointed to see they weren't large enough to give a good view of the room from a neighbouring property or outside; it meant the Family Man had been free to carry out his attack without fear of being spotted, or the police being called. He sighed again at another closed avenue of investigation, and felt his guts churn.

Reluctantly, he stepped onto one of the first access plates and made his way to the head of the table, opposite the mother's end. It was a sight he'd hoped in vain never to see again. The Jackson males were in place at the dining table meant for four. They would not be removed just yet. The SOCO team would wait until the scene became less crowded; something which would be a long while, judging by the throng outside.

The wife's chair was upright at the head of the table. It had been moved from next to Alan, leaving a space on Alan's right side. His son was opposite, the empty chair next to him tucked into the table. Drake assumed the wife hadn't knocked herself over trying to get away once she'd been left alone, and an officer had freed her while still upright. An officer wouldn't have corrected it, as they'd be ensuring they preserved the scene. Standards were tighter these days, with procedures to be followed. Back in the long distant past – even the late nineties – you'd still have scene disturbance on the odd occasion, the older officers reverting to their heyday stereotypes, going in all guns blazing.

The table appeared to be one of the cheap flat-pack ones that had made their way over from Sweden and the chairs were similar, probably part of the same set. They weren't head height unlike the ones in Yorkshire, which meant the normal routine of restraining the child's head did not apply to Adam. Adam was slumped forward with his long ginger hair masking his features. Blood spray was evident from the dried strands stuck to his cheek, and where it had jetted across the table. There was no tablecloth present to absorb the flow of blood this time, either. The blood was thick across the surface, pooling on the floor and chair legs to a much greater extent than before.

Alan was in awful shape, his head cast back in death rather than forward, as in previous scenes. The position afforded a clear view of his spine through the neck wound and his mouth, gaping wide and ruinous. The man had been through hell. His hands and tongue lay amidst the congealed blood on the table. His eyes were open, staring blankly towards the ceiling in a permanent state of shock. His glasses lay bent and broken by the chair leg along with the expected collection of viscera in a mound at his feet.

Drake shook his head in grim resignation.

'Is it wrong that I'm getting used to this?' Ellie piped up, slightly muffled by her mask. He hadn't heard her come up behind him.

'Mmm,' he said noncommittally.

'That poor man – no one deserves this. No one, not even that Randall guy.' She made her way over to the son, and peered round to get a look at his face and neck.

'Chief?'

'What is it?'

'His wounds, they're ... "clean," so to speak. This was done with one cut rather than many, like the older scenes.'

'Let me see.'

He waited for Ellie to retrace her steps, her overalls swishing as she moved, so that he could get there via the floor plates. The room was cramped compared to the Cartwright residence.

Drake peered round to see the young man's face. Sure enough, it seemed only to have taken a single attempt to slice him open. Drake manoeuvred himself so he could lift the man's chin with a gloved hand to get a better view. It was a clean cut; no half-arsed superficial slashing, as though the killer had known how much pressure it would take this time round.

'You're right, Ellie. Clean cuts. It could just mean he's got back into the swing of it, though.'

'I guess so, but strikes me as strange that he wouldn't have done the same with the previous scene's remaining victims. You know... after practising on the youngest.'

'True. Something to think about for sure.'

'And what do you make of Alan? Seems a little frenzied in comparison. He cut him so many times. Is that ...?' She peered closer, her eyes widened in disgust. 'Fuck. He cut him so deep his damn *vertebrae* are visible? Jesus. Perhaps it was more personal – taking his frustration out on him?'

'Now you're just theorising, Ellie.'

'Just thinking out loud, that's all. And theorising is sort of in the job description.'

He ignored the comment. 'Anything else you've spotted?'

'Yep,' she said, pointing towards the window at the opposite end of the room. Carved just below the windowsill was his calling card. Only this time, there was a circle missing.

Indicating the one offspring instead of two, Drake presumed. He went over for a closer look, having to take an ungainly step for an ill-placed floor panel.

'There's no blood residue within this one. Perhaps he brought a different knife along for the job?' he mused, squinting at the carving.

'Drake.'

'What?'

'I think I've found something.'

He turned to see Ellie looking at Alan's hands on the table, and came back to see what she was pointing at. There was a ring poking out from under the base of Alan's right index finger. The Cartwright family's missing ring.

He scooped it up with a pen and kept it from rolling down the shaft with the tip of a gloved thumb. Bringing it up, he could see a tiny hair-thin carving of the Family Man's symbol on the outside.

43

The rain lashed down on the kitchen window as Cari put the dinner plates on the side for her dad to wash up, the noise making a steady thrumming sound as she returned to the dining room.

'Thanks for dinner, Mr Whitman. It was great.' Eva gave an innocent smile.

Don't fall for it, Dad. Don't.

'No problem, Eva. Happy to have you over to keep this one in line, she's a handful,' Ben said with a smile, nodding at Cari. She huffed in protest, disappointed that he'd fallen for Eva's charm hook, line and sinker.

'Dad, come on, not her, too. Can I not have one friend that you don't take the piss out of me in front of!' Cari said, looking in Eva's direction. 'That's basically why we had to move Eva, because of my dad.'

'Sorry honey, you know I can't resist. It's what dads do, right?'

'If you say so.'

'Ignore him, Cari, he's just being him,' her mother said irritably as she glanced up from her wineglass.

Cari had noticed she'd been quiet for most of the dinner. It was unlike her, and it set Cari on edge, particularly with Eva around. She didn't want her mother having one of her episodes and going off on one. She reminded herself that she was giving her mother one last chance before they'd stick to Eva's place if things got a little challenging.

But she just felt scared *for* her mother. Seeing her deteriorate during an episode without warning was horrible. Then later, she'd come back in the room like nothing had happened and she'd be "all there" again. It was why Cari hadn't pushed her dad much on getting her further help. She wasn't hurting anyone, and it was her mum, after all. Cari actually felt like *she* was being selfish. She didn't want her mother to go away, and she didn't know if she'd ever be let out if that happened. Or if her mother would ever forgive them for doing that to her.

'We'll be upstairs listening to music, unless you want to take the piss some more, Dad?'

'No, you go ahead. But don't have it too loud, please.'

'Okay.'

* * *

Cari closed the door behind them and put some music on at a normal volume.

'You got the note?' she asked, scratching her head nervously before moving to sit on her bed.

Eva pulled it out and waved it in Cari's direction. 'Yep.'

'Cool. Get my laptop too, would you? It's just over there.' Cari pointed to her desk. Eva grabbed it and sat on the edge of the bed, with the laptop resting on her knees. 'I googled it a bit more on the way to science class,' she said. 'Apparently you need a special internet browser to access it. Something called TOR.'

'Okay, cool. I've no idea what that is, but let's see if we can get that set up. I dunno if I can be bothered if it's too complicated,' Cari said, a little impatiently. She knew it wouldn't be anything exciting, just some shitty porn site or something. Nothing *that* interesting happened around Barndon, but with this ... the not knowing was weirdly compelling.

After a few minutes, Eva found a place that had the right files and downloaded the TOR software on to Cari's laptop. Going through the installation process, soon it was all set up. It seemed almost too straightforward.

'So, you're absolutely sure that this can't track us?' Cari asked. She was still a little dubious and felt a bit uneasy. Surely, they'd know *something*. Everyone knew the internet was a dodgy place, with identity theft and stuff. All you needed to do was choose an easy-to-guess password, or sign up to a site that sold on your information to third parties for you to have some sort of user history on the internet. Data – and particularly personal data – was money these days.

'I'm sure we'll be fine,' Eva told her. 'Like I said, I read up on it and apparently, it's *very* hard to trace you. That's the whole point – you don't have an IP address or anything, I think. So, there's no way of tracking you, and you need to know an address like the one I think we've got before you can even go anywhere. There's no dark web Google search engine equivalent to even find these addresses,' she said. She was spouting stuff Cari wasn't sure was right. But what did she know?

Eva continued arguing the case. 'Look ... if I'm not worried as a fecking policeman's daughter, then you shouldn't be worried either, okay?'

'Okay, fine, you've convinced me. But if it's anything properly dodgy, like guns or whatever, I'm out.'

'Yeah, all right, all right. Calm down.'

Cari put her hands up in a display of mock innocence. 'I'm calm!'

'Here we go then,' Eva started up the TOR browser before typing in the supposed address. 'TF...M...WFKY...AYF.onion.' She spoke out loud as she typed, pressing the final "n" with an unnecessary flourish.

The TOR browser looked like it was doing something, albeit at a snail's pace.

'This is slow,' Cari said. 'Guess it's not working.'

'Give it a sec.' Eva sounded excited, but Cari's negativity was starting to get to her.

The page loaded, and Cari frowned at what she was seeing.

A homepage with a solid black background and an enlarged folder icon with the label "*Fun for all the family*" typed beneath it in a crude font, and nothing else.

'This is weird. It doesn't feel right, does it?' Cari's heart beat faster. She felt unnerved by it all, as though someone or something was whispering into her ear to look further, but her heart was telling her otherwise.

Eva laughed and poked her. 'Don't be a wimp. I'm sure it's just drugs or something. You know what drugs are, right?'

'Yeah, shut up. Sure, I do,' Cari said, fending her off.

'Okay, let's see what we've got, then.' Eva clicked on the folder.

The website presented five video files in sequential boxes. There were no preview images, just five listings with a hyperlinked number under each, and what Cari guessed was a view count. There had been a few views, nothing over fifty, so the files weren't well circulated if the numbers were that low.

'Let's give 5 a go,' Cari said, steering the laptop mouse pointer to the '5' and clicking it.

'Oi!' Eva protested.

'Shh, it's started,' Cari hushed her friend.

The video showed a view of a large, Georgian-style house. It was dark, but the house had fancy spotlights cast up some walls between the windows, like posh houses tended to do. The camera started panning round the side, past some expensive-looking cars. Cari figured the camera must be attached to someone by the way it was moving and the level of it. Or maybe the person was just short.

'Weird. What is this? Are they filming a burglary or a surprise or something?' Eva said, pausing it. She sounded concerned, yet excited.

'Yeah, maybe it's that ... I feel weird about this. Do you think we should carry on watching it?' Cari said. Something didn't feel right. But her curiosity was getting the better of her.

'Let's keep going.'

'Okay.' Cari leant over again and pressed play.

The film resumed.

The crunch of gravel crackled out of the cheap speakers as whoever it was crept round the side of the property. Cari thought the person with the camera sounded like a man from the breathing; it was heavy and controlled, but he remained silent otherwise. The camera definitely seemed to be mounted to his chest, she was sure of it.

The man continued creeping past the cars, keeping his body crouched, before he paused by the trellis on the wall to the side of the house. The camera panned while he looked up and down. Cari and Eva could see a window. He took hold of the trellis and started climbing up with seemingly little effort.

'I don't like this,' Eva said, changing her tune.

'Me neither.'

Despite their growing unease, something made them keep watching.

The man continued scaling the wall before stopping next to an old-fashioned first-floor window. A black-gloved hand began fiddling with it, the only sounds his elevated breathing and the taps of his fingers as he worked the lock.

A grunt of satisfaction followed when he prised the lock open. The man pushed it open further. He leant in carefully, making more noise as he heaved a leg over the windowsill, bringing himself into the house. The camera lost focus for a second at the change in lighting, before adjusting and regaining the image.

The house's interior appeared to be as posh as the exterior, all sage green walls and white cornicing. The man's presence alerted no one. It was getting even creepier.

The man turned and pulled the window closed behind him before stepping swiftly into what looked like the master bedroom of the house. He seemed to assess the room, looking around for cover, before he settled upon a position which was upright behind the bedroom door. His breathing had already steadied after the climb.

'Cari ...' Eva said, her voice trembling slightly.

'Ssh!' Cari hissed; her heart in her mouth, she was transfixed by what was going on.

The camera picked up noise from off-screen. Cari's eyes widened, and the sounds repeated; it sounded like someone calling from somewhere else in the property. The words were hard to make out, but it sounded like a woman's voice. The noise of approaching footsteps sounded on the wooden flooring, slowly getting louder and louder.

Then, a woman entered the room. Her back was to the intruder with the camera. She was short compared to the man, pale and thin with blonde, shoulder-length hair.

Cari realised she had been holding her breath. She heard

nothing coming from Eva, either. Her heart felt it would explode out of her chest any moment.

The woman stood looking at her phone, oblivious to the intruder behind her.

Cari wanted to scream at her, to run, to turn around, to do *something. Anything.*

Move! Damn it! Move!

But it was too late. The man leapt at her.

The woman let out a startled noise as he grabbed her, muffling her cries with a cloth he held roughly against her face.

'Holy shit, Cari!' Eva leapt up from the bed, the laptop slipping from her lap and clunking on to a cushion on the floor.

Harrowing noises of the ongoing struggle emanated from the speakers while the video played on. Both of them were shaking. Eva felt violated, close to tears, but she couldn't muster up the words to speak. The sounds from the laptop seemed to get louder and louder as they sat in shock.

'Okay, I'm out. I'm out. I can't watch this,' Cari blurted. 'Seriously, Eva, I'm not doing this!'

Eva's eyes locked on Cari's, the tears streaming down her face. She started to say something, when Cari's mother came in, without knocking.

'Cari, do you want any dessert—' She stopped short at the sight of their tears, and looked down at the open laptop. 'Girls, what... *the hell*?'

44

'Andrea, we've got to call the police. This is seriously messed up.' Ben stared at her, the laptop still in his hands.

After hearing the commotion, he'd run upstairs to see what the hell was going on. He entered the room to find a video of what looked like a man restraining and dragging a woman on Cari's laptop, with Andrea and the girls in a state of shock next to it. The imagery looked *real*. He moved through and closed the laptop, stopping the recording.

The girls didn't know what to say at first. Andrea explained she'd come in to find them like that. Cari and Eva confessed with no arguments; about the dark web, about the note they'd found at school.

Despite his IT experience, he knew little about the dark web other than the basics like TOR, unusual URL addresses, drug marketplaces, Silk Road being the only authentic example that sprung to mind; contract killers he'd read about in the news, and other unsavoury uses. Just what two fourteen-year-old girls needed.

Jesus.

'Ben, you can't go calling the police because you've seen a suspicious video online. It could have been anything. It might be a scene from a film. You don't go calling them when you watch porn, do you?' she said. She sounded surprisingly calm and reasonable while they made their way downstairs with the laptop. He chose to ignore the porn comment.

'Come on, that didn't look normal, did it? It looked real.'

Her face was a picture of concern. 'Maybe we should watch some more, then decide?'

'I'm not sure I want to. Do you?'

'No, but we're being responsible parents, right? We could just skip through bits and see? Then we'll know if it's even real? It could be, I don't know ... roleplay or something?'

She could be right. It could just be a messed-up couple acting out some sort of fantasy. 'All right, let's look,' Ben relented grudgingly.

He set down the computer on his lap. Andrea joined him on the sofa, shimmying up next to him to get a better look.

He opened the laptop. The TOR browser was still open, and the clip had paused at the point the lid had shut, the shot frozen on an image of the woman being dragged backwards by her hair.

He skipped forwards thirty minutes.

The image reloaded, still paused, to a scene in a fancy-looking dining room. The cameraman stood at the head of the table, looking down at a blonde man and the woman from before, along with two blond-haired boys. They were all blindfolded, barring the woman, and seemed to be bound to the chairs.

'Andrea—'

'I don't like this any more than you do, but we've got to know what we're actually dealing with here. Just press play,' she said, squeezing his leg in a show of support.

He pressed play.

The man brought up a knife in front of the camera; a very

large knife, with a black handle. It disappeared from view, the sounds of distress from the man and woman intensifying when the cameraman brought out a butcher's cleaver. An amused grunt followed, like he was appreciating his knife selection.

'Ben, I don't like this—'

'That makes two of us.'

The man moved deftly over to the seated husband and untied an arm. The blonde man twisted and bounced in his seat, screaming through his gag and trying in vain to avoid his grasp. There was the heightened sound of pleading from the wife and terrified noises from the children in the background while the father struggled with what little movement was possible in his chair. The man paused, the fathers arm still held tight, for an agonising few seconds before, in one smooth motion, he struck the man's hand off.

'Whoa!' Ben and Andrea shouted in unison.

Ben jabbed the pause key and lowered the lid, the light still casting out where he'd not fully closed it in the commotion.

'No way! No chance – I'm not watching any more of that. Bloody hell!' Ben half-threw the laptop on to the coffee table, as though it was diseased. 'I'm sorry, Andrea, but that ... that's not right. That was *real!*'

Andrea face wore the same look of stunned shock that he'd seen up in the girl's bedroom. She tried to talk but Ben continued in sudden realisation, 'Andrea, hang on a second – hear me out. That must be that Family Man murderer that's been on the news! The one you and Cari were talking about a while ago. That was a family in a dining room, right? The guy must have filmed it and stuck it on that website. Holy *shit.*'

'Oh my God, yeah! Maybe you're right.' She looked like she was struggling to take it all in. He knew he was. 'Thinking about it, Eva's dad... he's a detective, isn't he? Let's get him over. They were due to come over soon for Eva anyway, weren't they?'

'Good idea,' he said, scrambling in his pocket for his mobile. 'I'll call now.'

Andrea grabbed his arm before he could move off the sofa. 'Wait, a second.'

'Andrea, can't it wait?'

'No, I mean, I don't think it can ...' She looked distressed and gripped his arm tighter. 'Ben, do you think it could be related to the sounds from the other night? I keep hearing noises. And I swear I saw something again the other night when I went to the bathroom, and when I was looking out the window, I could have *sworn* I saw something reflective.'

'What? Andrea, come on... No, of course not. You're being—'
Got to be careful here.

'—I think you're worrying about nothing,' he amended. 'There's not a Yorkshire murderer in our house. What you saw could be anything – the reflection of our lights on a foxes' eyes, or something.'

'Ben, honestly, I don't think so. This place has been giving me the creeps a lot, and I was reading about it. The original guy killed people in this area, in *Barndon*.'

She must be seeing things. But I shouldn't dismiss her so easily, either, should I? Perhaps I should check on her meds, just to be sure.

'Andrea, let's deal with this later. I need to make this call,' he said, trying to be as non-dismissive as he could before getting up and going into the hallway. He dialled the number Cari had given him when Eva had first come round.

'Ben, please! Listen to me!' Andrea pleaded from the living room, on the verge of sounding hysterical.

He was just going to go back to reassure her, when an agitated-sounding man answered: 'This is Drake.'

45

I watched Ben wander off into the hallway. He was talking to someone on his phone, his voice taking on a particular tone as he walked further and through to the dining room.

The half-open laptop was still showing that hideous paused image of a knife embedded in the man's hand. I pulled it towards me again and closed it. I didn't want to see that; even the thought of it made me feel sick.

I heard a murmur.

'Who's there?' My eyes were wide as they darted around the room. A familiar searing pain in my temple made itself known.

Look. My mother's voice was a whisper in my ear, her breath making my skin tingle.

'W—What?'

Take a look. She repeated, her voice coming from one direction, then another. *Go on.*

'No! Sh ... shut up!' I balled my fists against my temples. 'No! I'm not looking at that.'

Take. A. Look. Go on... just a peek, while he's not in the room.

'Mum—'

Do it!

I didn't want to get on her bad side; and it *was* a bad side, I knew that. So, I did what she asked. I opened it back up, the screen brightening once more. I grimaced at the images in front of me once again, the awful violence of it all.

'Please don't make me,' I begged. 'Mum, please ... no, n-no-no!' I held my hands over my ears and shook my head again, closing my eyes while I tried to stop her.

I concentrated on my breath, slow and deep, before taking one final one and holding it in. The seconds ticked by. I heard nothing. There was only silence in my breathless bubble.

She was gone.

I relaxed just a tiny bit, exhaling loudly as I moved to close the laptop lid.

Look at the address. Make a note of it. Now! Quickly!

'What? No! Why would I do that?'

Do it, or I'll be... displeased. You wouldn't want to disappoint me, would you?

'Okay ... okay, fine, please! I'm sorry, okay?'

I couldn't say no. It was too hard; she was always there. I wouldn't hear the end of it, and she could be so cruel. I didn't want her to hate me again, like before. Not her.

I took my phone out of my jeans pocket and made a note of the web address on Notepad.

'There. Happy?' I scrambled to shut the laptop again before Ben came back and I got in trouble.

Yes. Good girl.

Lid closed, I hugged myself. I felt dirty, and no amount of scrubbing would get the taint off of me.

I could feel her smiling.

46

'John, calm down! slow down,' Miller said.

'They've got the videos, Laura. They've got the damn videos!' Drake said, moving to get past her and out of Alan's shop. Drake opened the door, saw the torrential rain, and paused as Ellie came through from the living quarters. He needed to decide on their next steps before rushing off, but he had an overpowering feeling that this fresh evidence could evaporate at any second if he didn't get a move on.

'Fine. Miller, could you meet me at my house? Be there within the hour, if you can – you too, Ellie.'

'Oh no you don't! I'm coming with you,' Ellie told him.

Drake glared at her, but didn't protest.

'Okay. I'll be there within the hour. I'll wrap up here and delegate the rest,' Miller said. 'Are you sure about this?'

'These people have no reason to lie. The husband said he had seen footage of a family tied up in a dining room and a man getting his hand cut off – I can't think of many other situations like that recently, can you?'

Drake turned toward the entrance and set off into the downpour.

'This is huge' Ellie said, clambering into his car, her coat sodden.

Drake ignored her. He started the engine and slammed his foot down, peeling away from the crime scene. His eyes were glued to the road ahead, fixed with a look of single-minded determination, while the dregs of rainwater ran down his cheeks.

'Ellie, you know what this means, right? This could be *it*. This could be the break we need.'

He broke several speed limits while he barrelled over towards the Whitman's house on Reeds Lane.

'Are they far away?'

'Literally just round the corner now—'

'Oh, wow.' She gripped the arm-rest tightly as they shot round another corner and bumped over the centre of a mini-roundabout. 'Just don't get us killed on the way there, yeah?'

47

Ben ended the call to Drake. He felt an immediate wave of relief wash over him; the handing of responsibility to the authorities meant they could resolve this and move past it. It would soon be forgotten about. At least he hoped it would.

'Andrea, they're on their way,' he said, making his way back to the lounge. She didn't reply.

'Andrea?'

He came back into the room and found her sat bolt upright on the sofa.

Oh no, not again. His heart sank at the familiar pre-Barndon sight in front of him. *It must have been the stress of the situation. I should have seen it coming.*

Andrea was sitting like a statue on the sofa. She was staring straight ahead, her face blank and her eyes unblinking, the only movement that of her lips mouthing silent words.

Sitting next to her with care, he put his hand gently on her leg.

'Andrea ... It's me, it's Ben. Andrea, can you hear me?' he whispered in her ear.

Her eyelids fluttered in response, a sign that he was getting through. He pushed for a response again.

'Andrea, you're having an episode. Andrea, it'll be okay. Come back to me.'

No response again.

Damn it, if I could get my hands on whoever did those recordings.

Andrea took a sudden, sharp intake of breath, startling him.

'Ben, how was the phone call? Are they coming soon?' She looked calm, as though nothing had happened.

He forced a smile. 'Yes, they're on their way, hun. They should be here any minute.'

'Thank God, I don't want to watch any of that ever again. It's just so... so *wrong*.'

'Andrea ...' he started, but hesitated. Was it a good idea to tell her what happened?

'What? What is it? Did DCI Drake say something?' she said, looking at him, a worried look on her face.

I can't, I can't worry her with this. Not now.

'Oh, er ... nothing, it's nothing. Don't worry,' he said, rubbing her leg and smiling.

* * *

I loved that face. The love he had for me. I wish I didn't give him such cause for concern. Things would be better soon. I truly believed so. We'd move past all my 'issues,' I knew we would. Soon.

Ben, Cari ... Me.

I felt the familiar dull ache in my head.

48

'DCI Drake, thank you for—'

'Where is it? Show me, *now*,' Drake ignored Ben Whitman's outstretched hand and stormed into the hallway, his head snapping in every direction, his hair and coat dripping from the rain.

'It's in the lounge,' Ben said, guiding him through. Drake could see he'd set the man off-kilter with his aggressive entrance, a frown on his young-looking face as he ran his hand through his mop of brown hair. Ellie followed close behind.

Ben's wife looked up slowly from the sofa in greeting, like she'd just woken up.

'Is it still on the screen?'

'Yes,' she said. Her voice was alert and seemed at odds with her demeanour. 'But we closed the laptop. We couldn't watch anymore – it was horrific.'

She stood up and moved away from the sofa. The laptop she mentioned sat closed at the end of the coffee table.

'Right. DS Wilkinson, and I will need to view it. Please, if you could go upstairs and see to the girls,' he said, ushering them out of the room. 'I'll be taking Eva home with me, and we're going to have to take the laptop too, if it proves to be what I think it is.'

'Sure ... we'll do that right away. Whatever you need,' Ben said. He put an arm round his wife and guided her carefully out of the room, as though she were going to break at any second.

What was up with that? Drake wondered.

Ben stopped and turned back before saying, 'Oh, I didn't have time to mention it on the phone, but there was a note too. It had the web address for where these videos are on the dark web. I'll give it to you on the way out.'

'Thank you. Now, please – we'll need some time to review this.'

'Of course.'

The Whitmans left the room.

Drake waited until he heard them walking up the stairs before sitting down and picking up the laptop. Ellie moved behind the sofa and leaned over the top.

'Are you ready for this?' Ellie's apprehensive-sounding voice came from behind him.

'We need to be – if it's genuine, we're going to be in for a rough night.'

His nerves were jangling too; his heart felt like it would spring out of his chest at any moment. But he had to see. Had to see what this bastard had done. This man, this *thing* that had been a part of his life for so many years.

He lifted the laptop lid.

His eyes widened instantly. Ellie let out a gasp behind him at the image.

He pressed play, and the pained cries engulfed them.

* * *

Miller regrouped with Drake and Ellie at his house soon after their arrival. He brought them both up to his study in order to view the remaining footage undisturbed. He'd reasoned to himself that the station would have been too much of a circus with colleagues and the inevitable gossip.

He'd only managed a minute of the footage at the Whitman residence with Ellie. The father's mutilation proving tough to stomach, even for him, before deciding that it was real – the family, the house, the furniture. Everything was just as it had been at the Cartwright crime scene.

The Family Man had to have uploaded the footage to what Eva and Ellie called the "Dark Web" in order for it to be viewed by anyone who he had shared the address with. Miller was right; he was escalating, and escalating in a way where he wasn't satisfied to be just killing people, he seemed to need... to *desire,* an audience now of a different kind.

On the journey back to his house, Eva had told him about how they found the note, what they had done, and how they had accessed the footage. She was still shaken by what she'd seen.

Thank God she hadn't witnessed the actual violence, he thought.

He wouldn't be able to forgive the Man for that, for infecting his family. It was reprehensible.

'So, it's real?' Miller asked, her voice as expressionless as always. He couldn't imagine her staying that way for many more minutes, not with what they were going to be watching.

'It is, Laura. We both verified it as a match for the Cartwright crime scene. It's tough to watch, I warn you.'

'Unfortunately, we have to watch it. If there's something there that might lead us to catching him, we need to see it.'

'There's five of them,' Ellie said.

Miller gave her a look of disbelief. 'Five!'

'Yes, once we stopped the footage, I closed the video, and it returned to what must have been the main web page. There were five separate files. It looks as though he's filmed *all* the crime scenes.'

'We didn't have the sort of technology the Cartwright survivor described back in '98, though, did we?'

'Correct, but we've had home video cameras in various sizes since the late eighties. Not in such a small, wearable format I don't think, not commercially at least, but there are ways. And I guess we're going to see how soon enough,' Ellie explained.

The thought of what they would have to watch was hanging in the air. It reminded Drake of the feeling he got when he had to attend a victim identification in the mortuary; that horrible moment before a deceased loved one was revealed to a distraught relative.

'Shit,' Miller said, her lips forming a tight line.

'At least we can compare the latest Yorkshire scene versus the older killings, if that's what these other files turn out to be,' he said, trying to shine a positive light on what would undoubtedly be a very distressing few hours.

'Great,' she replied grimly.

Ellie sat down with a creak at Drake's desk. He had a slight moment of elation at the noise. It wasn't just him that made the damn thing creak after all.

She opened the laptop. A moment later, it displayed a directory screen with the numbered files.

'What're those numbers? Are those the number of *views*?' Miller asked in disbelief.

Drake nodded. 'Yes, I'm guessing there's been some way he has been distributing the link. My daughter and her friend found a screwed up post-it note at school with the web address on it – completely by chance. It must have fallen out of a bag or pocket.

A child at her school had already somehow got access to this. It's insane. We're going to need to get people down to the school as soon as possible and get the note checked for prints too. We need to know who wrote it. If that hadn't have happened, we'd still be none the wiser.' He paused, scratching his head in frustration. 'Who knows how many more there are, or how it got to be there in the first place. And God knows how many other children have watched it. It could spread around the normal web – even the *world* – if we don't get it down somehow. And until now, *no one* has reported it. I'm not sure what's more worrying.'

'Jesus.'

Ellie jumped in. 'And you can't just take down a dark web page. You need to know the server, and you need to initiate a cease-and-desist order, or similar, to the data centre that holds it for it to go offline. Identifying the server is quite difficult,' Ellie said, looking up at Miller, whose arm was resting on the back of the chair. 'We need to get in contact with the cyber-crime guys at NCA, GCHQ or NCSC – I forget which – as soon as possible, so we know what we're dealing with. If the Man's done his homework, he'll have ensured his IP information was encrypted and hidden at all points. And as the guy hasn't put any monetary transactional system in place, such as Bitcoin for example, or a password system, then nothing needs to happen first before watching the videos. The user just needs to know the address. That leaves less room for exposure and tracking him.'

'Shit,' Miller said, punching her palm in a rare outburst. 'Shit, shit … *shit.*'

'I know,' Drake said. 'He's still a tricky bastard. Even with this.'

'He wouldn't have done it if it was that easy to track him. He's been clever so far. But something will get the better of him soon. We just have to be patient,' Ellie said, and pursed her lips.

Miller paced the small room, deep in thought.

Drake watched her; the woman was on edge. She had to have distanced herself from the case, compartmentalised the killings somehow to keep herself mentally strong. But she seemed to have been caught out by this, just as much as they had been.

Miller appeared to steel herself. 'Right, let's get this over with.'

'Okay.' Ellie started the first film, the one with the most views. People naturally went sequentially through things, Drake supposed.

The playback started. The footage was low quality; visual static rolled slowly down the screen, reminding him of VHS analogue cassette tapes. The cameraman appeared to be in the midst of a storm, the torrential rain and wind buffeting him. Ahead lay a house, the windows shuttered or dark. It was hard to tell.

Drake felt a pang of familiarity upon seeing that first house. The one he'd attended all those years ago – the Taylor residence.

The sound quality wasn't up to much either, but a muffled voice came through the laptop speaker before the camera started moving, bobbing up and down while it advanced towards the property.

A man in a dark rain smock went ahead of the camera.

Drake gasped. 'Holy shit. There's *two* of them!'

Miller looked over at him, a stunned look on her face. 'This makes sense now,' she said. 'If he was filming the earlier ones and none of the victims knew about it, then the other suspect must have kept out of sight. Like some sick, perverted voyeur.'

This was the most animated he'd seen her in years.

The video continued to run.

The cameraman disengaged from what appeared to be the 'main' Family Man, and crept up to a window. There was some erratic movement as he looked up to check for signs of activity, before hefting the apparatus up and resting it on the windowsill.

Drake imagined one of the large cameras that TV cameramen held on their shoulders was the tool of choice here. That implied that the camera could have been old, even for 1998.

The man wiped the camera lens with a cloth before repositioning it on the windowsill. The focus seeming to shift in and out until it settled on a grainy image of a dark dining room. They waited in hushed silence until the light came on, a few agonising minutes later.

< < *Pause* > >

'Wait, do you see that?' Ellie said, excitement rippling through her. Her eyes looked like they'd pop out of her head at any moment.

'What? What is it?' Miller and Drake said, almost in unison.

'Look at the reflection in the window.'

Drake leant forwards, squinting to bring his eyes into focus on the still image. He could just about make out a figure reflected in the window. A man with a pronounced jaw, blonde hair and small eyes. He'd recognise the man anywhere, even with the poor-quality footage. It was Stan Lawton.

'This is all coming together now! It's why he knew details of what had gone on. He was the cameraman for the damn Family Man!'

'You're right. Holy shit, it's making sense. It's why he's been able to start up again. We never actually caught *Him*. We just caught his accomplice ... Jesus Christ,' Drake said, rubbing his stubble with a rasp. He was excited at the discovery, but agitated too, because his worst fears were all coming true. The Family Man had been free all this time, undetected, on his watch. And he was still out there. All these years, Drake had failed to catch him; what a fool he was.

'This bodes well for us finding out who the killer is,' Miller said, her eyes reflecting the scene on the laptop. 'Let's continue.'

They waited until the Family Man appeared, dressed head to toe in black with a large knife in hand. His mask showed only his eyes through primitive slits as he herded and threatened the terrified family into the dining room.

The Man looked to be around six feet tall and muscular, but not ungainly. He had a lithe quality about him, and he way he moved reminded Drake of a snake. He had a confidence about him that belied his inexperience, considering this was supposedly the first "official" crime they knew of.

The Man took out the bindings he would use from a bag he'd brought with him. He threw some to the wife, before tying up the father and forcing her to tie her children up; a little boy and girl, who struggled to get up to their seats. He then tied up the mother and checked on the children, before retying them himself.

The Man went out of shot and returned with towels from the house. He ripped them up and blindfolded the children. All the while, cameraman Stan was letting off an occasional approving huff or grunt.

The entire scene made for unsettling viewing, and the family hadn't even been hurt yet. Drake didn't know how he was going to make it through one of these, let alone five. He would just have to hope that he could use the old detective's technique of managing to distance himself from the on-screen events in some way; desensitise himself, depersonalise the victims somehow.

He noticed the Man never acknowledged the camera, or Stan; another way to ensure that the family wouldn't know what was going on beyond their kitchen. Who would ever have imagined that someone would film such a thing?

Now the violence began. The Man brought out a butcher's

cleaver and, with a clear glee, started on mutilating the father as naturally as if he was making himself a sandwich.

Four hours of hell followed. *Four hours.*

They had pushed on into the early hours of the morning by the time they reached the midpoint of the fifth film. Drake had forced a break on them after the first one, before they'd soldiered on with the next three. Their behaviour and comments had slowed to a halt. They'd become withdrawn, tired, but the necessity of continuing with what they were subjecting themselves to was written on all their faces.

Drake found the films all followed in a very similar format to the first. They were methodical, almost formulaic; by the fourth one, they felt like a production line of human pain and suffering. He hadn't needed to force himself to become desensitised to it. The desensitisation had occurred as naturally as the dispassion displayed by the Man in front of him.

But there had been some modifications to the style, with Stan opening the windows on every film from the second case onwards. It had the effect of enabling the camera to pick up more of the sound, and it was an addition that made Drake's heart sink.

There was never anything before or after each of the films to give away the Man's identity; each one only showed the lead up to the killings, and finished after the Man had carved his symbol and left the room, his work complete.

The newest one, the one that had been twenty years in the making, was where Drake saw a marked difference. The perspective was up close and very personal. There were no windows to keep the distance, to keep the dispassion, to allow them to view it as an almost unreal event. The new footage was in their faces; hot, heavy and lurid, displaying the pain, the anguish, the torment wrought from every member of the family.

The Man unclipped and positioned the camera at various

vantage points, moving it between the sideboard and the dining table as he meted out his unique brand of death. He seemed to revel in it even more this time after all these years.

Drake noted he hadn't seemed to have changed physically in twenty years. It was mystifying; perhaps he wasn't so surefooted or agile. But that could just be Drake's mind playing tricks on him after being subjected to so much these last few hours. He dreaded the thought that he might have to revisit them. The idea made him shudder, as though someone had walked on his grave.

Some of their theories regarding the latest scene had been confirmed; the Man *had* taken more effort to kill his victims. There had been some sort of subtle, momentary hesitation with the young boy, less so with the eldest and the father, but they had still been dealt several ugly slashes too before succeeding.

There was no sign of a cameraman or an accomplice. For obvious reasons, Stan wasn't there, and the Man must not have been able to find a willing alternative. Perhaps that's why he'd gone with the new method of filming. Or perhaps he'd just fancied trying his hand at it.

'Whoa, hang on for a second. Stop... stop!' Drake said, pointing at the screen. Ellie paused the footage and turned to look at Drake. 'Do you see what I see?'

'No? What is it?'

'The Family Man ... He's now left-handed.'

'What? You're kidding,' Miller said, peering in. Heavy bags had formed under her eyes and her breath was awful. 'Jesus, you're right. He's holding their heads with his right hand. The blade is in his left hand.'

Ellie said what they were thinking out loud: 'That means ... that means it's a different guy, surely?'

Drake nodded in agreement. 'Yes, I think it does.'

'But what does that mean for the original? Does that mean

there's been *three* of them? Stan, Man One and Man Two?' Miller theorised.

'I don't know. But there's a chance,' he said, his face grim. 'Let's carry on and see what else we can pick up. Maybe he's just playing up to the cameras, screwing with us. He could be ambidextrous for all we know.' He was weighing it up in his mind. It sounded like nonsense to him, but you could never be sure. If it was rubbish, and there was another, who was he, and how could he have had access to the other materials and the knowhow? Just when he felt they were getting closer, it was all pulling away from him again.

Drake averted his eyes as the eldest boy died in front of him.

49

Sat upstairs in his office, Ben couldn't stop running through the night's events. He was sitting in the room next to where his daughter had witnessed the brutal start to the Family Man footage.

It was just *wrong*. He couldn't bear the thought of what the family must have gone through. He kept thinking of Cari and Andrea, and how terrified they'd be – how terrified *he'd* be, knowing what he knew now of the killings.

His face was blank while he stared at the local news report, other tabs on the browser showing old news stories. There had literally just been another killing, this time in Barndon; his village. They didn't put names to the victims just yet, but they didn't need to. The picture of the cordoned off shop was all that was necessary. Alan and his son were dead. He'd only been in there a few days prior, not wanting to strike up a conversation with him yet again. He felt a pang of guilt, despite his feelings about the man.

Maybe I should take Andrea more seriously? He pondered.

Could it be this isn't just her illness making her imagine things? That she is seeing someone or something?

He closed the current browser tab, and focused on the CCTV shop page, deliberating the purchase for a moment.

I'll think about it.

He closed the laptop.

* * *

'Ben, are you sure you've checked all the doors?' Andrea said, staring at him with a slightly off-kilter intensity from their bed while he undressed.

'Yep, all locked, and all the windows are, too. Who'd have thought we'd be happy to have these ugly UPVC locking windows, eh?' he said, his voice muffled as he took his jumper off.

'Ben, please, you're still not taking me seriously – honestly, there's been a few times since the other night where I swear I'm being watched. The hairs on my neck and arms stand on end. It's not nice.'

Ben walked round to her side of the bed, sat down, and took her hands in his.

'Andrea, *please*, look at it from my point of view. You're basically saying that there's a serial killer or something staking out our house ... us, our child? He's only just killed some other poor family – you think he's going to pop round and do us in this evening with all the activity nearby? We're safer here than anywhere else right now because of that, surely? Anyway, we live in a pretty secluded spot. There are woods, there are animals, it won't ever be completely silent – if anything, that should be the scary thing.'

'No, I guess. But—'

Here goes. Ben cut her off.

'I know this is a sensitive subject, and please take this as it's meant to be.' He spoke carefully, choosing not to mention what he'd seen in the lounge earlier and take a softer approach. 'As something positive, and well-meaning ... I'm your husband and I love you dearly. But you've been on your current medication for a long time now. Perhaps it's starting to wear off and you're seeing or hearing things again, like the last few times the medication has become ineffective. Perhaps it needs reassessing?'

'No, Ben ... *please*. I think this could actually be happening. It's not my medication.'

'Okay.'

'What do you mean? "Okay"?' she asked, looking bewildered.

'I mean, "Okay, I'm taking your concerns seriously." I was looking just now at getting us some CCTV cameras installed, but it's expensive.' His eyes widened to emphasise the point. 'However, I want you to feel safe and what better for warding off any would-be serial killers and such? What do you say to that?'

'Thank you, Ben. That's all I'm asking ... that you believe me,' she said, leaning over and kissing his cheek.

'I do,' he stood up to continue getting undressed.

'I love you.'

'You too. Now, I'll have a look around one last time. That sound good to you?'

'You're a star! My hero!'

'Turn off the light when I leave the room, yeah?'

Ben ventured downstairs in the dark, trying his best to not wake Cari, who'd only just settled from the night's events. He felt his frustration burning inside. That girl didn't deserve to have any more shit thrown her way; it wasn't right. So soon after their move, too. It was supposed to be a fresh start.

Pacing around the house, it hadn't taken long for his eyes to acclimatise to the relative darkness. He'd double – triple –

checked all the locks downstairs on every window and door. Finally, he'd made his way to the window at the end of the hallway, pulling aside the new curtains for one last look outside.

All that met him was darkness, the outlines of shrubs and trees swaying beyond.

An animal yelped in the distance. Ben strained to see where it was, but who was he kidding? The sound had probably carried from miles away.

See, nothing to worry about, he thought, returning to their bedroom.

The figure stood up from its place beneath the window.

50

I'd waited patiently for Ben to drop off, just before midnight; from what I was hearing, Cari had finally got to sleep too. I could make out the gentle rise and fall of her breath as I leaned into the crack of her bedroom door. She'd always been a heavy sleeper. It had been a helpful trait over the years; she slept through nearly all my arguments with Ben when I'd "had my moments"; my *episodes*, as he insisted on calling them.

There'd been such a fuss when Mr Drake, sorry, *DCI* Drake, had come for the evidence. He looked like he'd seen some serious shit over the years. His eyes looked haunted and world-weary, but he was a good-looking man despite it.

Move. Her voice emanated from the door of Ben's office. The sound was nothing but a delicate whisper, a nudge. She repeated the request again, this time as if she was whispering in both my ears at once. The order resonated round my brain.

I liked it when she was gentle with me. It reminded me of when I was young and she wasn't so angry at me all the time, only ordering me around as she did back then. She used to cradle me in her lap, stroking my hair, just me and her against the cold, harsh world.

'Yes, Mum,' I whispered. My mind was ebbing and flowing as though I was in a dream.

I crept along the landing to Ben's study, my bare feet not making a sound. I braced the door, opening it as quietly as possible.

Good girl. We mustn't be disturbed.

The room stood pitch black before me, but for a crack of light at the corner of the window. Ben had installed blackout blinds, though obviously not well enough as usual. I refrained from putting any lights on, just in case. Not taking any chances, not tonight.

I gently pulled the door to behind us, closing it with a small, springy squeak of the handle. I groped around for my laptop, my heart in my mouth, nearly knocking over a pile of Ben's papers at the corner of the desk before I found it.

Shhhh, stupid girl! The dull ache in my head became more pronounced as she glared at me. A pair of eyes glistening in the dark, illuminated by that tiny sliver of light.

'I'm being as quiet as I can,' I whispered.

She remained silent, continuing to glare at me from her corner.

Lifting the lid on the laptop, I pressed the power button, and the machine whirred into life.

I recalled something Cari had said about needing software called TOR to access the videos and jumped on Google. I found the software and started installing it in a matter of minutes; easy-peasy.

It seemed to take an age, but finally it loaded up, and I could enter the address from my phone.

TFMWFKYAYF.onion

< < Enter > >

The website seemed to be doing something, albeit slowly. There was no black screen yet, only the sheer white of the laptop illuminating my face as it plugged away at loading the page.

I realised I hadn't connected any earphones and scoured the desk by the light of the laptop. Finally, having found a pair, I connected them and stuffed them in my ears.

'How're you going to hear, Mum?' I whispered.

The eyes settled next to my head. I could see her oval face now, the glow of the laptop giving it a shape and life in the shadows.

I can hear. Don't worry. She winked at me and bumped her head against mine.

I smiled at her touch. 'Okay.'

An image of a folder labelled *"Fun for all the family"* popped up on a black screen. This guy obviously thought he was hilarious. Admittedly, I did find it a little funny, despite myself.

I clicked on it. And finally, there were the films. All lined up for her ... for me.

My stomach suddenly roiled. My own voice popping into my head: *Should you be doing this? Watching this sort of thing?*

I felt a momentary pang of regret at what I was about to do. But I couldn't help it, she was *drawing* me to it. She had always been the curious one: all those nights sat watching true crime documentaries, horror films like *Dawn of the Dead*, *Last House on the Left*, even the original Dracula film, *Nosferatu*.

Now we got to see something real.

'It will be an honour,' she'd reasoned with me while I'd lain in bed.

I selected the first film and pressed play. A grainy woodland scene in the middle of a rainstorm playing out on the screen.

My mother sat next to me, smiling gleefully, while we took it all in.

51

Ben woke suddenly. The room was pitch black, and he couldn't feel or hear Andrea next to him. He reached out to prove he wasn't imagining things.

He wasn't. There was no one there. The bed and covers were completely cold on her side. He looked at the clock. It was just past half four in the morning.

Where could she be? Shit, she could have been gone for hours!

It stirred up the familiar feeling of panic in his stomach. He hoped she was still in the house; before, at their old place, she'd left a few times in the night. The thought of having to drive down the street and pick her up, finding her dressed solely in her bedclothes, made him anxious. They'd got some strange looks back in Leeds because of that, and it wouldn't be a great start with the new neighbours.

He got out of bed quietly, not wanting to startle her with any loud noises if she was nearby. He doubted he could get back to sleep again with everything that had happened last night.

He'd been relieved when Drake had taken Cari's laptop and

the note away from the house. He never wanted to see that again, if he had a choice in the matter. It was disgusting, malignant ... Downright *evil*.

For what felt like the hundredth time that night, Ben shook the thought of his family suffering such an attack from his mind, and quietly opened the bedroom door. He noticed the pale light almost immediately, frowning at the light coming out from under the study door. He couldn't recall having left his laptop on. He always made sure he turned it off; shut it down bang on time, not wanting to feel the urge to get back to work, to kick off yet another email trail. He'd never been one of those guys who lived by his work phone or laptop; come the end of the day, it was just that, no more work. The way it should be.

He crept up to the door and pressed his ear against it. He could sense someone in the room. It reminded him of the times when he'd caught Cari watching films on her laptop in her room late at night.

He winced at the feel of the door handle going down and craned his head round the door.

Andrea was sitting in front of her laptop.

He gasped and involuntarily shut his eyes when he caught a glimpse of what she was watching. His mind must be playing tricks on him. Perhaps he was still asleep, and this was all a dream? It couldn't be ...? She was watching the videos from the website.

What the hell was she doing, watching that? How did she even get a hold of it again?

'Andrea! What're you doing?' he whispered harshly, turning on the light.

No response came.

'Andrea!'

Silence.

He gripped her shoulder gently and rotated the office chair. The earphones popped out as she came full-circle.

She was catatonic again. Her eyes closed, but with the same activity as earlier beneath the lids, her mouth uttering silent words.

This is really worrying me now. Twice in one day... It had to be the shock of what they'd seen, of what she had brought up again on her laptop. It had to be!

He was terrified of the damage the images may have caused. And for her to have possibly rewatched it all, too. It had been *hours*.

'Andrea? Come back to me, love. It's me. It's Ben. Please,' he said, closing the laptop and gently cupping her cheek, stroking it with his thumb. She didn't respond.

'Please, just let me know you're okay,' he said, tenderly shaking her by the shoulder. She was still non-responsive. He tried again; still nothing. She was deep into it. Unlike her earlier episode, which could only have lasted a matter of minutes.

I'm going to have to leave her, like in the past, aren't I? I can't force her out of it, and even if I could, it might cause even more damage. We're going to have to talk about this after work when we're both back tomorrow, and figure out a plan. This isn't right.

He went to the airing cupboard, pulled out a blanket and wrapped her in it. He stayed with her for as long as he could, before tiredness overcame him.

Taking her laptop with him, he reluctantly turned off the light and closed the door before collapsing back into bed, leaving her shrouded in darkness.

* * *

Ben felt his wife enter the room a while later.

She climbed back in with a satisfied sigh. She sounded *content*.
Her icy fingers explored his body as she cuddled up to him.
He squeezed his eyes shut.

52

Ellie arrived home to the sounds of the bin men pulling out the grey wheelie bins for collection at the far end of her road. It looked like they'd emptied hers already, much to her relief. A screeching rubbish truck right outside her window was not what she needed right now.

The night had turned into morning, and she was longing for some modicum of sleep. She was thankful it was still dark; she might nod off before the sun came up, but if not, her years in Response had helped with her ability to force herself to sleep in the shortest of times – most times. And the blackout blinds, the blackout blinds helped too.

It's not cheating. She laughed weakly to herself.

She knew, even with her conditioning, it was going to be a pipe dream. Her daughter would be up soon, if she wasn't already, and Len usually stirred at her closing the front door to their house either way.

Ellie braced herself, entering the house with a muted clink of her keys. The stillness pleased her. Unless her daughter was a ninja, she thought she might actually be in luck after all.

Bella, her beautiful baby girl. She wasn't sure she could pick her up and look her in the eyes just yet. Ellie wasn't ready to see her cute brown eyes, and wide smile beaming back at her. Her little hands trying to play with her hair, and nuzzling into her neck.

She supposed it could be a comfort if she did look in on her daughter, but she didn't want to take that chance. She needed to sleep, be on her A-game for what was to come at midday with a few hours' rest in the bank.

The videos played on her mind still; horrific sounds bouncing around in her sleep-deprived brain. The first-person perspective of the final one had added another unwelcome dimension that she'd not been fully prepared for.

Could you ever prepare for something like that?

She hoped Miller and Drake hadn't seen her close her eyes at the split second of the child's passing. She didn't want to show them any form of weakness. It was necessary to be professional, to make the right impression, to show she was right for the job. Made of sterner stuff. Either way, it had been a baptism of fire though, that's for sure.

Ellie put her things down and crept up the narrow, steep Victorian staircase. A death trap for a small child, so they'd put gates in place at the top and bottom.

She wished she'd had that back when she was a little ball of energy herself. She still had the slight remnants of a scar at her hairline to show for it when she'd taken a tumble.

Ellie winced when she closed the plastic baby gate behind her with an abrupt plastic snap and stood sentinel-like for a moment, listening for her daughter.

Nothing, she thought uttering a *whew* under her breath.

'You okay?' Len whispered while she crept around their bedroom.

'Can I get back to you on that?'

'That bad, huh?'

'Yeah, that bad.'

Len couldn't see she was on the verge of tears in the dark of the room. She made sure he kept the lights off while she undressed.

'Come to bed,' he said in the fog of sleep, pulling back the duvet.

Her husband wrapped a comforting arm around her as she got in beside him. Ellie closed her eyes, allowing a solitary tear to escape and run down her cheek.

53

Drake was on his way to Barndon station, to reconvene with Ellie and Miller at midday. They'd still been up at five that morning with the videos and he felt like shit. He *looked* like shit too, this having been verified by the bathroom mirror just half an hour ago. But the last few hours of the night – that morning, in reality – had seen massive developments in the case. They were almost on the home stretch, surely?

Miller said she would liaise with the cyber-crime guys to see if they could pull down the website ASAP. They needed to do whatever was necessary to bring it down before it could spread any further. And if anyone could speed it up using the necessary clout, Miller could.

Before that, though, they needed copies of the videos as evidence. Ellie was adamant that bringing it down wouldn't be an easy task. It depended on the skills of the Family Man at masking all the ways of identifying the hosting locations, but they had to start somewhere. Drake was uneasy about it all; he didn't understand how they couldn't find someone from what they had already, but he bowed to the tech experts.

One of his most pressing tasks had been to speak with Reynolds and the forensic pathologist, find out who performed the Cartwright post-mortem and tear into them. How in God's name did they omit to tell him the suspect was left-handed?

It was fundamental.

He called from the relative privacy of his car in the carpark, the air turning blue as the conversation went on. It became apparent that the forensic pathologist, Charles Brand, who was supposed to have conducted the post-mortems personally, let Reynolds conduct elements as part of his pathology training. The missing details had somehow been left off the report to Miller and Drake, despite ol'Charlie boy having captured all the information on his main outputs. No doubt he had Reynolds to thank for that one too, Drake surmised, unless the pathologist was passing the buck.

Apparently Reynolds moonlighted as a SOCO as part of his development; he was working towards becoming a fully fledged forensic pathologist, and helped out because of the area's limited resources. Forensic pathologists were scarce, but the man was seemingly more of a hindrance than a help, in Drake's opinion. Even if he eventually qualified, Drake would have his doubts about the man. Either way, Drake would be giving serious consideration to making an official complaint and it made him wonder if they really had just missed the earring evidence that was left in the bowl in the dining room, after all.

He was still fuming when he entered the station.

'Drake?' He looked up, hearing a familiar voice. It sounded a little older than the phone call.

'Dave! Good to see you, mate,' he said, producing a genuinely warm smile. It had been a few days since their last meeting at a café for a debrief and a coffee.

DS David Bradfield was a short and chubby man – maybe

due to him being behind a desk for a few years, though maybe not. He was balding with a dark moustache, while what remained on top had greyed. Some would say he looked distinguished as a result, but for Drake, the sergeant reminded him of a member of the Old Bill. He could quite imagine him walking down the street, whistling a tune and twirling a truncheon. A timepiece hanging from his breast pocket.

'How are you? Seriously? I heard you and Miller and the new girl had a late night,' Bradfield said, stony-faced.

Drake reached behind his back to scratch an itch, grimacing as something clicked in his shoulder.

'Something like that – around five hours total of torture and child murder isn't what I'd wish on anyone. It was truly awful. I can't even put it into words.' He frowned, the images still fresh in his mind. His memory replayed the sounds of the later murders, making him wince.

'I can only begin to imagine, and that's more than enough for me,' Bradfield said. 'I don't want to take that into my retirement. Pictures I can deal with. Videos ... That's a whole other level of messed up, John.'

'I know.'

'FYI, I interviewed the Barrow lad, Jonah, in your absence, since I knew you wouldn't be in any fit state this morning. I went through his witness statement with him, standard stuff. He found the scene. Legged it, rang the police, nothing untoward there. He still seemed shaken by it when I spoke to him. I double-checked and phoned around a few local curtain twitchers I know of in the area, too. They can corroborate seeing him walk to the property and the aftermath of him shouting down the phone. He was in and out in a matter of minutes.'

'Thank you for doing that, Dave.'

'No problem.'

Drake knew him well enough to know that there was more to this than just an incidental chat. He could see that the man had something more interesting to say.

'But ...' he went on. 'I *may* have something for you. It might blow the case wide open for you, in fact, if it means what I think it means.'

'What? Tell me.'

'I'll tell you all together, if you don't mind. Save me having to do it two or three times.' He put his arms behind his back and motioned with his head for Drake to follow. Bradfield led him into a small side room used as a family room for breaking bad news or general questioning.

'Just a second, while I grab the others,' he said, disappearing from view.

The room was sparsely furnished with some low seating that brought Drake's knees up high, as though he was sitting in a child's seat. A small table was tucked into a corner. He wondered how many families had been told bad news in here. How many lives felt like they'd ended there and then?

A couple of minutes later, his boss and Ellie entered the room.

Miller looked like she hadn't slept at all as she took a position front and centre, while Ellie looked a little spaced out, leaning against the table. It was to be expected; what they had been subjected to was a mental battering he wouldn't have wished on anyone.

'Right, now I've got you all together,' Dave said, seeming a little too animated while he paced back and forth in front of them like an army major. He was just missing the baton.

'So, the good news ... the *interesting* news... I've received back the results of a DNA pass I requested the other week. I asked for it to see if there'd be any hits on any of the residents in Barndon, in particular. As you know, it's unusual that two – make that *three* – Family Man crimes have now been committed down here. The request was just standard procedure, of course. Speaking of which, I submitted it ages ago. Time really moves slowly around here,' he said drolly, his eyes flitting between them.

'Get to the point, please, Sergeant,' Miller said. She wasn't expecting anything exciting, judging from the tone of her voice.

'I got a match.'

'A match? A match for what? Spit it out, man!'

'Samuel Barrows is a match for ...' he said, doing an imaginary drumroll with his hands before hitting a cymbal. 'A certain individual by the name of Stanley – or Stan – Lawton, formerly known as The Family Man, now known as the Family Man's lackey. Or cameraman, if you prefer.'

Drake struggled to hide his surprise. 'Sorry, what?'

'Yes, you heard me right. As far as I can tell, he may well be Samuel's father.'

'You're kidding me,' Ellie said, an incredulous look on her face.

'Nope,' Dave said. 'The markers show he is almost certainly the man's father. We only got Samuel's DNA in the last few years, somehow. Maybe you could find out when you see him? Was he missed off the original submissions, or perhaps he avoided them?'

'Whoa! That may mean that Samuel Barrow has the potential to be the Family Man,' Ellie said. 'I've always suspected there was a chance. I mean, he now has a family link, he's a similar height, farming background – have we got an account of his whereabouts for the original murders?'

'Yes, he had his family as his alibi, and we had nothing to prove otherwise. Also, he was established as being in Barndon by three separate people for the Haworth crime, remember?'

'And therein lies the issue,' Dave said. 'I'm aware of all this, having been the man behind the scenes for the last few weeks. The Q to your Bond, if you will.'

'Well, what can we do?' Drake said.

'I don't have the faintest idea. As I said, I'm just Q. It's for you to do the work, Mr Bond ... Mrs Bond,' Dave said, looking over and nodding at Ellie.

'Right,' Miller said, looking between the pair of them. 'Drake, Wilkinson, you best get over there as soon as you can – even if he isn't accountable for the latest one, at the very least he's in the frame for families one through four.' She made a move for the exit.

Drake nodded. 'Sure, we're on it, Boss.'

'What should I do?' Dave asked.

'I don't know, Dave. You figure it out,' Drake said, not looking back as he hurried out of the room after Miller.

Ellie smiled and followed Drake, leaving the detective sergeant alone in the room, a befuddled look plastered on his face.

54

It was cold out. I suppose it would be in mid-November, but not this cold. It never felt quite *this* cold. I wrapped my arms tight around my chest and burrowed into my coat as much as I could. The wool felt cold to the touch, and I'd not brought my gloves.

The passing cars were getting too close for my liking. I had to climb up into the undergrowth in the country lane whenever one came hurtling by. They were too fast. My thoughts, too, were at a speed I was struggling with and there was always that damn *ache*. It was never-ending.

It hadn't helped that I'd woken up this morning feeling strung out, and I hadn't shaken the feeling since. I didn't understand it; we were in bed at a normal time last night. I thought I'd slept through. How can you sleep eight hours and still be tired? Maybe that awful video DCI Drake took away made me dream, but I can't recall dreaming at all.

Ben seemed weird in the morning too, come to think of it; almost distant. He spoke very little, and that was unusual for him. Perhaps I'd been fidgety and kept him awake? He's usually the one to make me feel livelier. The one to perk me up a little with his silly ways when I'm feeling down. Maybe he was freaked out by my blackout last night in the living room? He said nothing, but I can usually tell when they have happened by his reactions. That poor man, having to put up with me ... I missed him and I'd only been gone a few hours.

I'd felt so awful that I hadn't been able to stay at work, crying off to the lady I can't remember the name of. I knew Ben was working from home in the afternoon. Perhaps I could snuggle up to him for a bit and steal some of his warmth when I got home. Or maybe Cari, though she was probably off somewhere as it was half-term, wasn't it?

Anyway, all those hopes were for *if* I made it home, not when. I swear I was going to get hit one of these days.

'Jesus!' Another large car rounded the bend at speed; a gigantic black SUV of some description. I hopped up into the embankment just in time to avoid being run over. The near-death experience kicked my heartbeat up another notch, the pounding now in tandem with my head. The grass on the embankment had become so sodden from the recent rainfall that the damp started leeching up my jeans, slowly sticking to my skin and socks.

Great. Just ... great.

I flinched at the sound of another car approaching at speed. I'd not even moved off the damn verge yet. Patiently, I waited for it to pass. But it didn't. It slowed down. The car came to a stop as it drew level with me, and the window wound down with a faint electrical whir.

'Hey there, little lady,' Samuel said, leaning over and peering through the passenger window.

Oh, great. I rolled my mind's eye while outwardly putting on a polite smile.

'Hi, Samuel.'

Sorry, "Sam". He likes to be called Sam, doesn't he?

'Whatcha doing out here in the wet undergrowth like that? You'll catch a cold. You feeling all right?'

'I'm fine, thank you, Sam,' I said, squinting from the sunlight reflecting off the car.

'Say ...' he said, looking behind and in front of him. 'You want a lift? You look like you could do with a little help.'

I wasn't sure I could stomach a chat with him. Small talk just wasn't me. Never would be. But I *was* feeling shitty. At least, not "episode" shitty, just plain old shit. It would only be a few minutes' drive, hopefully.

'Sure ... okay. I owe you one,' I said.

I clambered down off the verge and tried the door, but it wouldn't open.

'Oh whoops, sorry about that. That's my fault, darling,' he said, turning and pressing a button. The door lock released, and I climbed up into the huge cabin before pulling the door in behind me. An awkward silence immediately descended.

'Lucky I was coming by, eh? A fine chance, indeed,' he said, the car pulling away.

'Yes, thanks again, Sam.'

'How has everything been since we last spoke? You settling in at your place, okay?'

'It's been great. My daughter is making friends at the local school. My husband, Ben, is getting on with work. We've even unpacked most of our stuff.'

'Well, ain't that just swell? That's just great. Good to hear.' He let out a gruff chuckle. Stilted silence followed for a few more minutes while he drove down the country lanes and returned to the normal roads back towards Barndon. The trees passing in a smear of red, yellow and brown.

I had to say something. It was becoming painful.

'Did you see the news about the killing in Barndon? That

poor man at the shop. His name was Alan, wasn't it? His poor family, too. His wife is still alive though, I read. How strange.'

'Yep, I heard about it. Small village like this, would be impossible not to. I've known him for years, many years. Awful ... Just awful.' He gripped the steering wheel, not taking his attention away from the road.

Something seemed a little off with him, as though something was making him tense.

'I'm sorry to hear that,' I said, trying my best to be sincere for the man I barely knew, who knew another man I also barely knew. His face was blank.

'That's life, darling. Shit comes up and kicks you in the face sometimes. And it also happened before too, long time back,' he said, while he approached the turn into my lane.

He pulled the car in halfway down to my house.

'Um ... Sam, why are we stopping here? My house is down near the end.'

This didn't feel right. What was he doing? My pulse quickened.

'I ... I wanted to ask you something before you go inside, that's all. While we have this opportunity.' He put the handbrake on and turned to look at me.

'Okay ... What? You're kind of weirding me out a little, Sam.'

'It's about your mother.' His face took on an intense stare.

'Huh? What about her? She's dead, Sam. I don't like to talk about it,' I said, averting my eyes from his stare.

My mother? What would he know about my mother?

'I know all that already,' he said dismissively. 'All about Miray ... Miray Arslan? Turkish woman? Spitting image of you?'

'Yes?' I said, confusion etched on my face, rightly too.

What the hell was this? How did he know my mother?

'Right ... Right ...' he said. He was gripping the steering wheel so tight the leather was making a cracking sound. 'And if you don't mind me asking, how old are you?'

'I'm thirty-five. Why?' My frown was set in stone at this point. This didn't feel right. He went back to being silent, as though he was contemplating something.

I gripped my knees and waited for his response, but all he did was breathe in and out heavily. You could cut the tension with a knife, and I felt I had to say something.

'Are you okay?'

He didn't respond. He continued to stare off into the distance, the man's hands still on the steering wheel.

'Well, *shit*, darling,' he said finally, making me flinch. He turned towards me. 'I ... Well ... I might just be your *daddy*.'

55

This couldn't be happening. This man ... my *father*. No, there had to be some sort of mistake.

How could he know that? He doesn't even know me.

I sat in stunned silence while he continued to stare at me. His deep brown eyes, *my eyes*, boring into me.

My head had resumed its pounding, the blood coursing and squeezing through the veins, straining and constricting as it pulsed. My vision clouded at the periphery, and I felt confined somehow, claustrophobic. A feeling of nausea rose from the pit of my stomach, threatening to overcome me. It was all too much. I didn't know what to do. I should open the door and run. Just run away and hide. But a strange thought about manners – of all things – came into my head.

It wouldn't be good *manners* to run away like that. It wouldn't be good *manners* to ignore him ... It would be good *manners* to stay and hear him out, despite every fibre of my being saying otherwise.

My head spun, despite everything feeling like it was moving in slow motion. I squeezed my eyes shut to block out the sickening feelings, but none of it worked.

'Andrea, are you ... What's wrong?' I heard his gruff voice.

I couldn't be dealing with this, not now. We'd moved to get away; to have a fresh start, so I could be closer to where my mother grew up. For happier times, not *this*. I remembered what Ben and I had said when we'd moved to Barndon. *This is a new beginning for all of us. New house, new town, new people.*

'New. Everything new ...' I murmured. An icy surge shot up my spine. The feeling becoming a strange feeling of déjà vu as the ice streamed through my veins. The suppressed memories were coming back to me so vividly, so *physically*, they seemed like an actual presence flooding into my mind.

My brain pulsed, the ache growing ever greater. I was having trouble processing everything I'd locked away. I remembered what my mother had finally opened up to me about regarding my father in the moments leading up to her death; all that I'd suppressed, all that I'd turned away from.

Incoherent flashes sparked and faded, as snippets of conversations formed and evaporated. I felt her presence. She was with me. A single word kept reverberating around my mind, the voice of my mother whispering it to me. It was joined by a cacophony of repeated voices, swirling round my skull, making me dizzy until finally aligning, sharpening into the letters of the harsh word.

They fell silent as I heard her crystal-clear in my ear, her breath warm.

She hissed the word: *Rapist.*

56

The repressed memories re-ran in my mind's eye like a small, stained screen in a seedy cinema, playing back the moment I'd found out my whole being was one born of violence.

It all made sense now; why she'd moved, and why she never spoke of her last few months in Barndon. My beautiful mother had once worked for a man, a man I now realised had to be Samuel. She'd been a cleaner, working nights for various places in and around Barndon. I vividly remembered her telling me that one evening, she'd been alone when he had come out of nowhere and overpowered her, assaulting her. She'd told me he'd been so brutal with her, so reprehensible. He said he'd kill her if she fought back any further. The feeling of helplessness had been overwhelming. She had been so frightened.

She'd told me through fits of tears that his parting shot had been the threat of reporting her to the police as an illegal. That she'd be sent back to *her* country. She then did the only thing she felt she could do. Once she was able, once she'd healed and once, she'd discovered my existence, she fled.

Now I was alone in a car with this man, with him knowing

where I lived. Thinking I'd come home to where my mother was happiest.

* * *

I stared into the footwell of the car, my awareness coming back to me. How long had I been silent for?

I turned to look at him, doing my best to smile.

The tears? Sam, those were tears of *shock*, maybe even of *excitement*. Yes, excitement, but shock too, must remember shock. Shock is believable as well, that'll do it.

'Andrea?'

'Mmm, yes, I'm sorry. I'm having a hard time processing this. It's all such a *shock*,' I said. I averted my eyes and rubbed my legs, plucking at the cuffs of my jumper stuffed in my coat.

"I'm sorry." I just said, "I'm sorry," to my mother's rapist... Can't think about that now. Got to get out of this car.

'I'm sorry ... I'm not upset. I've ... well, I've always wanted to meet my father. My mother never spoke about him.' I paused for a moment, then said, 'I'm sorry to ask. But are you sure it's you?'

'A fair question,' he said, nodding his head in thought. 'At first, I wasn't sure, darling, but after seeing you around. Why ... I was *convinced*. I genuinely thought Miray was back from the dead. I had to do a double take. It was a shock to me too, you know? Believe you me. But... *now*, I can see it. You have my eyes, but you have her beauty. Boy, she was a beaut,' he said, smiling at the memory, smiling at the memory of *raping* her.

I couldn't cope. This was too much.

'Your age, your likeness ... Your mother. It *must* be you,' he said, moving to put a hand on my shoulder.

I visibly flinched and backed away.

'Whoa!' he said, 'I'm sorry. I won't do that ... too early for familiarity. I get it.'

'She's dead. You know that, right?'

I couldn't bear to look at him, this *thing*. He made my skin crawl.

'Yes, I know, I said before. That's ... awful. I'm so sorry to hear that. Those few weeks we had, that fleeting romance, I remember it fondly ... she was a good woman.' He gripped the steering wheel with his right arm. I could have sworn I saw the faint glimmer of a smile, just for a second, a twitch. Then it was gone.

'I'm really sorry, Sam. Do you ... Do you mind if we speak about this another time? Soon? I'm really not feeling too well.'

'Oh ... er,' he said, looking uncomfortable, as though it was now *he* who was wondering what to do.

He was going to let me go, wasn't he? I would not be another victim of his hateful lust.

Who else had there been?

I tried for the door before he spoke further. It wouldn't open again. The central locking was still on. I panicked. Beads of sweat ran down my back. The feeling of nausea ever greater.

'Sam, could you unlock the door, please? I can walk the last distance. It's okay.' I was trying to remain outwardly calm, whilst inwardly screaming.

'Oh, er ... sorry, darling,' he murmured, as though he was remembering who he was supposed to be; happy-go-lucky farmer Barrow. 'Here you go.'

The door unlocked with a click, and I opened it immediately.

The air flooded in, the wind blowing my hair across my face. I gulped the cool air greedily, desperate to keep my composure. The rush of colours and sounds overwhelming.

'Can we speak soon, then? Please? We've got lots to talk

about, believe you me. Another Barrow in the family, who'd a thought it!' he said, a hint of excitement gilding his voice.

'Yes, of course, just not right now. I need to process things. I'm sorry. That's okay, right?' I said, getting out and looking back in the car, my hand ready to slam the door shut.

'That's fine, that's okay then, well ... I hope you feel better soon. I got me a daughter!' he said, in a grotesque display of whooping and cheering.

It was so bizarre. It was like he didn't remember what he'd done. How I'd been conceived.

I shut the door to the display, still hearing the muted celebrations he was making, and walked to the house as fast as I could. My arms were wrapped around me to stop the shivering, the grip physically keeping me together, if only for a few seconds more.

He beeped the car horn as he turned round.

Beep-beep.

When I reached the driveway, I ran.

57

I slammed the door behind me, my hands trembling as I fumbled the latch. My fingers refused to cooperate, the sound of my attempts echoing around the house until finally I worked the lock.

Silence.

Only the sound of my fear disturbed it now.

I was safe. He couldn't follow me in. Could he?

I leant back against the door, sliding down until I met the cold tile floor. I gripped my head in my hands and raked my scalp, hoping the pain would provide some sort of release.

It didn't.

Being out of sight, away from *him* in relative safety, I lost myself.

I let it all out, a fit of raging cries and screams.

My fingers gripped tighter as they dug deeper. I felt the warmth of my blood on my fingertips, sweat forming and beading, intermingling with my hot tears.

No one came to me. No one was there to help me. To look after me when I needed it most. The house was empty.

Ben wasn't there when I needed him, nor Cari. No one to take me back from the brink.

I pulled my knees towards me, covering myself with my arms and closed my eyes.

The silence of the house heightened, enveloping me as I held myself tightly. Breathing in deep, ragged breaths.

Alone.

* * *

He was why mother killed herself. It was *him*. It was him all along.

He'd found her, she'd said.

'He's found me, *he's found me,*' she'd muttered repeatedly, like a rhythmic incantation while she'd torn through the kitchen.

She hadn't responded to my questions, the tears pouring down her face in streams.

Instead, she'd pulled the knife from the knife block.

Her last words to me: 'I can't let him find you. I can't let him do to you what he did to me.'

Then all I knew was blood and darkness.

* * *

That man *had* found me, though; he was here, in Barndon. He knew where I lived. He'd finally found *me*.

But so had she. And she was here now.

I lifted my head.

She was by the stairs. Her face was a picture of concern at my pathetic vulnerability, all laid out for her to see in its rawest form.

But she had a lightness about her I'd not seen before. A shimmering glow while she smiled at me, bathing me in her radiance.

The darkness retreated to the edges of my mind, and I was caught in her rapture.

My darling ... Let me help you, let me help you forget. Her voice was barely a whisper, the words lapping at me like a gentle wave from a thousand directions. So calm, so serene, so... *ethereal.*

I was entranced.

'How?' I pleaded between sobs. I hadn't the strength to lift my head any longer.

'Please, just tell me how. I'm so scared,' I whimpered, looking at the floor, my nose bubbling as I wept. 'He's going to come back. He's going to find me. He's going to hurt me, like he hurt *you.*'

I could feel the fear building again. Threatening to overtake me.

Then let me help you, my daughter. Let me show you the way. Show you what you need to do. What we can do to protect you.

Her voice floated towards me like it was on the cusp of a wave, lapping around me more and more. I felt her touch, and the warmth surged through my body. She looked so radiant. So gentle. It was as if the angels had sent her down to rescue me, to save me from *him.*

To guide me. To protect me. To stop my pain. My love was overflowing for her. For my mother.

I took her hand.

58

'DS Bradfield.' The sergeant answered, Ellie having dialled him while Drake sped towards the Barrow estate.

Drake wasn't driving quite like the previous evening. There were more cars on the roads, more potential accidents waiting to happen. He was in full control of himself and focused on the job at hand. At least he hoped he was. He had some feeling of the old Drake back. He could feel a change in the atmosphere, a literal shift. They might just be getting somewhere, finally.

Ahead of them, a car edged out from a junction before seeing and reacting to their incoming car. The driver halted in time for Drake to slam on the brakes and sound the horn before it blocked the road. He veered round the panicked driver to the other side of the road before swerving back to the left-hand lane.

'Dave, it's Ellie. I've a quick request for you.'

'Are you guys okay there? Sounds like you've got a road rage incident going on.' Bradfield sounded amused, hearing the sounds of more drivers making their feelings known.

'Oh, it's fine. It's just Drake's driving skills,' Ellie said, grimacing. Her other hand gripped the armrest in a vice-like grip.

'I see. Please don't die. Anyway, what was the request?'

'Would you arrange for Paul Randall to come in for questioning today, please? I've a few things I want to check.'

'Uh, sure. Can I ask why?'

'No time. I need to run it by Drake, and we're almost at the Barrow estate.'

'Okay, I'll do that now. By the way, the initial report results from the note you handed over are in – there's a mess of prints, and no hits came back on the initial run on our system. I'd assume some prints are the girls from last night, and some are possibly from people at the school? We're working out way through them now to rule them out, it's slow going, but I can't see the person who made the note being stupid enough to leave a trace. You never know, though, eh? Oh, and obviously, we're going to be cross-referencing any handwriting that we have on record too.'

'Of course. Thanks for keeping me posted. You're a star. Fingers crossed, as you say.'

'Indeed,' he said, and hung up.

Ellie stuffed her phone in her pocket and turned to Drake.

'What was that stuff about Paul Randall?' he asked. 'I'd appreciate it if you'd run things by me first, you know.'

'Sorry, it kind of sprang into my head and I didn't want to wait. By the way, they're still working on the note forensics – they need to eliminate the ones from your daughter, her friend and so on, to isolate the person who uploaded the videos, if they left anything. Who knows, they could be another accomplice, or even the Man himself.'

'Of course. Hopefully Becca can arrange that with Dave and co. Now, Paul Randall?'

'Well, that note – they found it at the school, right? Who do we know that works at a school, and has a strange pastime?'

'Ellie, come on now, going from being a bog-standard pervert to watching and distributing Family Man killings, let alone carrying them out? And dropping web links at a school too, of all places?' he said, frowning.

Inside, though, Drake was kicking himself; Ellie had a point. They should check into it regardless, and him being dismissive wasn't the right approach.

'We have to check, to be sure.'

'Fair enough, your call. Good job.'

'I guess so,' she said, sighing at the sight of her favourite country lane. 'Please don't bomb it down this road, Drake. I don't want to die.'

'I'll be careful.' He smiled and sped up.

Drake took the turning for the farm entrance before blasting up the main road to the estate. Rumblings of thunder boomed in the background, providing an ominous backdrop. As though they needed more drama, he thought. He put on the headlights; now that it was November, the afternoons were drawing in earlier, but the weather meant the light was fading even faster today. Wind buffeted the car as Drake drove past stable-hands bringing in the horses before the storm truly kicked into gear.

Drake pulled up in front of the main house.

'Here we are,' he said, with a creak of the handbrake. 'That wasn't so bad now, was it? Ellie, I hope this interview goes some way to ending this. I don't want to go down another blind alley.'

'Have to stay positive, Chief. Could only be a matter of time before the cyber guys make a breakthrough, too,' she said, looking over at him with a smile.

'Maybe you're right. It just weighs heavy, you know?' he said, immediately regretting using those words, displaying a sign of weakness. His subconscious did the mental equivalent of covering his mouth with his hands. What was wrong with him? He'd never made comments like that to a colleague, particularly a younger one and of lower rank.

He sighed. 'Right, let's get on with it.'

He opened the door, the wind snatching it from him with such an immediacy that it almost rebounded back on him before he could react.

'Shit! You sure there's not a hurricane forecast?' Ellie leaned over the central column and peered out of the car.

Drake was half-convinced he'd be swept away any second now.

'Yeah,' he called through the wind. 'Come on out. Just don't think of tagging along with an umbrella. I don't want Mary Poppins for a DS.'

Ellie hurried out of the car, the door slamming with an almighty bang as the wind took hold. She pulled her coat around her. 'Let's get inside.'

They made their way up to the reception area. Drake didn't want to be there longer than necessary.

* * *

The woman who they had met previously, Diane Mersey, led them in and away from the squall outside. The airlock of a door sucked shut with a thump. It was just as eerie and sterile as before.

Diane left them to inform Samuel, who apparently was out on a trip to further afield for some supplies, though he was on his way back now.

Drake again turned his attention to the painting from before.

Despite fresh eyes, he still saw a caged animal. Ellie came over and looked, not taking her usual seat before stating: 'Why's he taken a shit on some paper and framed it?'

He sent an appreciative huff and nod of approval her way.

Sometime later, a large Land Rover sped up the driveway, the rain tearing down and the wipers doing their best to stave off what they could. The man pulled into the garage and entered via a side door.

Samuel looked distracted, Drake thought. He seemed to have lost his swagger, his grinning facade from their last meeting nowhere to be seen.

Perfect. Catching him when he's off-script might help us out a bit.

'DCI Drake... DS Wilkinson. *Another* visit... To what do I owe the pleasure? I'm honoured. Come, let's go through to the kitchen and go through the same old patter.' The statement dripped with sarcasm. Samuel continued on in the direction of the kitchen. There was no polite gesture for them to follow this time.

Ellie gave Drake a look and walked on through the echo chamber of a hallway and into the spartan kitchen.

'Is Ann going to be joining us?' Ellie asked.

'No darling, she's away on business in Yorkshire at the moment, funnily enough. Now, don't you go getting all twitchy,' he said, tapping his nose with a finger. 'She's aiming to be back later today, if all goes to plan. She's not fancying a murder just now.'

He sat down at the kitchen table, flexing his arms out and causing his sleeves to creep up a little. 'Please, take a seat. I can't imagine this taking too much of your time,' he said, leaning forward.

Drake and Ellie sat down, with Drake directly opposite.

'No tea or coffee for us today, then?' Drake noted.

'No, that's not my business. If you want that, you'll be waiting a good few hours, I'm afraid,' Samuel said, bringing his shoulders back.

'Why the hostility, Samuel? We've just got a few questions for you. Nothing major.'

'Oh, I'm sorry, fella. Have I got your back up? I *do* apologise,' he said with a smirk. He didn't flinch as he met Drake's eyes.

Drake allowed the man to posture for a moment, before continuing. 'So, Stanley Lawton. He's your dad.'

Samuel's face didn't change, his eyes betraying nothing. He looked over at Ellie, stony-faced, and took a deep breath, before exhaling obnoxiously through his nose.

'Heh ... I wondered how long it would be before that came up. Figured it was only a matter of time. Your woman here discovered that little detail, I take it?'

'So, you knew then?' Ellie said, not reacting to the 'your woman' comment.

'Course I knew. How could I not know? He told me as soon as I could stand on my own two feet. My fake daddy, the one my mother married, he was the one she wanted people to believe was my daddy,' he said, with a dismissive wave of his hand.

'Why didn't you tell us? Do you have something to hide, Samuel?' Drake said, his calm exterior at odds with his heart rate.

'Nothing to hide, just felt it wasn't pertinent.'

'It wasn't *pertinent*?' Drake felt his temper rising; this man knew how to push all his buttons. 'You thought it wasn't pertinent? The man who confessed to killing scores of people, and who we now know was your father "wasn't pertinent", really?'

'You heard me right, *DCI* Drake. What do you want me to do? Say it again for ya?' he said, tilting his head to one side.

'Did you know what he was doing? What he was involved in?'

'What do you think?'

'I think you did.'

'Well, I can see why you've not caught the actual Family Man all these years then.' Samuel laughed. 'You ain't got a damn clue, have you? He's still going around killing people, killing Alan and his son. That's on you, *Drake*.' He spat out the last few words, jabbing a finger in Drake's direction.

'Where were you on those nights twenty years ago?' Ellie's voice cut through the tension.

Samuel recomposed himself, his smile reappearing. 'Which one?'

'All of them. But let's start with the first one, Thursday, October 5th, 1998. Where were you between the hours of 19:00 and 08:00 the next morning?' she said, raising an eyebrow.

Drake knew the answer to this, having interviewed the Barrows at the time of the first murder. Samuel had said he'd been with his wife and son and she'd cooked for them. He'd even had a vivid mark on his hand from where he'd tried to help her and burned himself. It was nonsensical evidence, as though the man was taking the piss, but, yet again, there was no one who could prove to the contrary. It was his word against theirs.

Worth her trying it again though, Drake thought, *seeing if he said something contradictory, even incriminating.*

'You expect me to remember a specific day and time over twenty years ago?' He tossed his head back and started laughing again.

Ellie looked over at Drake. 'Well?'

'I have no idea, darling. And even if I did, how could you, or I, prove it now?' he folded his arms, looking as though he'd won. 'You ain't got nothing. Is this the quality of your police these days, Drake?'

Ellie looked like she'd explode at that last comment. But he was right, they hadn't.

'What about the videos?' Drake said. 'The five videos that we have showing the Family Man and your *father* doing what he does best?'

'The what, now?' A strange look flashed on Samuel's face, a mix of surprise and anger. He started tapping on the table.

'The videos, Samuel. Your father, your *real* father, he recorded the killings. Stood by and filmed them as they happened in front of him.'

'I don't know nothing about that, about *any* of it.'

'I think you're lying.'

'It's a free country. You can think what the fuck you like. But just because you *think* it doesn't make it true, now does it? I—.'

'Done much slaughtering at the farm in your time, Samuel?' Ellie's arm rested on the table, the other hand with a pen poised above her notepad.

'What's that got to do with anything? You sure ask some stupid questions for a detective,' Samuel tutted.

'Just answer the question, please.'

'Of course, back in the early days. We had to get our hands dirty, same as everyone else.'

'You still do it?'

'No. I pay people now to do that kinda work.'

'You right-handed, Mr Barrow?'

He gave her a hard stare. 'Yes, ma'am, that I am. What of it? Like most of the population – I ain't backwards.'

'No one is implying you are, sir,' she said, jotting down notes. From what Drake could make out, it mainly comprised *arsehole* and *dickhead*. Not particularly professional, but he couldn't blame her.

'Your dad, Stan, did he ever ... mistreat you when you were growing up?' Drake said. He knew fireworks were coming.

'Now you wait just a goddamn minute! If you're trying to say my daddy was a fucking kiddie fiddler, then you don't know shit. He was nothing but good to me, when he could be, when no outsiders were around,' he said, clasping the edge of the table. It looked like he was doing all he could to stop himself from leaping across the table and throttling Drake.

'Did he mistreat anyone else that you know of? Did he have any friends? Anything at all? You've been very helpful so far, Samuel. Anything more that you can give us? Anything you've withheld?' he said, a sardonic smile on his face.

'Don't you be a smart arse with me now, Drake. I told you; I know nothing about no killing.'

'Could we search your premises? Maybe look round your farm, see what tools you have here?'

'You what? Why? Jesus ... You think I did this, don't you?'

'No one's saying that.'

Like shit, they weren't. But they weren't getting anywhere with this. However, they *had* riled him. Perhaps enough to get him making mistakes when they'd left, or lead them in the right direction.

'I'm tiring of this. I've got places to be. Got a business meeting soon. Now, I think you both should leave. Get off my property,' Samuel said. He stood up abruptly, causing the chair to teeter before it righted itself with a clatter.

'Why Sam? Have we touched a nerve?' Drake smirked despite himself.

'Yes. Only in so far as that you're just wasting my damn time. That's how you've touched my damn nerve,' he said through clenched teeth. He balled his fists on the table.

'Okay, so you won't let us search your property?'

'Got a warrant?'

'No.'

'Then fuck off.' Samuel walked over to the kitchen counter, his back to them. 'We're done here. Come back here with a warrant, then you can do what the fuck you like.'

59

Ben pulled into the pub car park, having finished his half-day in the smaller local office. He wasn't strictly supposed to be going there; in fact, he was supposed to be at home unpacking the last remnants of their move. But why not stop off for a drink to build up some Dutch courage first? Then he'd be able to walk off the booze and surprise Andrea at work. A perfect plan, if he did say so himself.

And perhaps she could come back with him? It was a Friday afternoon and they could talk about what he'd seen, and her recent behaviour. They could work through it all together.

He put his hood up for the few steps between the car and the pub entrance. The weather wasn't letting up lately.

Inside, the pub didn't appear to be too busy just yet, which was an agreeable change of pace from the recent visit with Andrea and Cari.

'What do you want ...' The irritated voice paused, sounding like it was studying him. 'Ah, the Whitman lad. Ben Whitman, wasn't it?'

Ben pulled his hood back and saw who he now knew to be the

pub landlord, Michael Randall. He was not a pleasant-looking man.

'Yes, that's me. Still have to get used to people knowing who I am round these parts without having properly been introduced,' he said, trying to bring some cheer to the conversation.

'Yep,' Michael replied stony faced before going back to his newspaper on the bar.

Ben was almost done with his pint when Michael sat down at the table uninvited; he looked like he'd had a few too many since Ben had ordered earlier.

'Where's your woman?' he said, blunt as a hammer.

My woman? Who talks like this?

He didn't want to answer, but this was going to be his local, and he didn't want to get off to an inauspicious start.

'Oh, you mean Andrea? She's at work, I think.'

'I see. Why don't you get her home with you? Fine-looking woman like that, surprised you got time to be anywhere *but* with her. Her mother was much the same. Shame she ran away.'

Jesus Christ, he's a goddamn caveman.

'Wait, what? You knew Miray?'

'Course I did, we all did. She was the local beauty, yes, she was. Your woman is near identical to her,' Michael said, licking his lips, like he was recalling a memory Ben would rather not be privy to.

And, on that note, I think it's high-time I get out of here. I do not want this man talking to my wife about her deranged mother.

'Right, well, best be off. Things to do.'

He leered at Ben. 'Heh, I bet. Tell her she's always welcome here, eh? Me and her got lots to discuss.'

Ben didn't answer and got up to leave, not even wanting to down the last dregs of his drink. Perhaps they wouldn't be coming here too often after all.

'I didn't mean no offence, now,' Michael said, his face and voice stating otherwise.

'Okay,' Ben replied, slinging his coat on and avoiding eye contact with the man. He wanted to get out of there as soon as possible and avoid further scenes like whatever the hell that was.

Just when he was closing the door, he heard the man shout from the table. 'I'll see you and your *girl* later.'

60

'Hmmm. That went—'

'Badly?' Drake offered.

'I was going to say well, actually,' Ellie replied as they drove back towards the local station.

The rain had subsided to a gentle mizzle, but the wind was still blowing something fierce. Clouds continued brewing overhead, the thick canopy proving impenetrable. Once again, Drake had the headlights on, and it was only mid-afternoon.

'Oh? How so?' He felt like testing her, perhaps unnecessarily.

'We riled him, worked him up. He's bound to do something rash now, don't you think?'

'That's a positive mental attitude if ever I've seen it,' he said, smiling at her before turning his attention back to the road. 'But you're right – if he has anything to do with it, you can be sure as shit he's going to be running around right now, hiding anything he thinks can incriminate him.'

'We really going to get a warrant?'

'Yes, he's related to one of the key people in the case. We've probable cause, if only to find evidence for Stan, if it still exists.

I've had enough of his crap.' Drake turned out of the country lane. 'Did you make many notes?' he asked, still amused at what he'd seen of her supposed "notes".

'No, not this time round. Barring ones that can't go on record ... they're not very *complimentary* of our dear Mr Barrow,' she said with a mischievous wink.

They continued towards Barndon station. Few cars passed, but the last of the rain was clearing up the closer to town they drove.

Ellie looked deep in thought while the fields and autumnal trees whipped past.

He felt a sudden sharp grip on his arm. Looking over, Ellie appeared like she'd just had an epiphany.

'Drake ... Drake! I think I've got an idea.'

'What? What do you mean?' He looked over at her, his eyes flitting back and forth from the road.

'Hang on a second,' she said, putting a hand up and mumbling to herself.

Seconds turned into minutes.

'Pull over, would you? I need to talk it through.'

He continued on until he found a grass verge to pull on to. A car overtook them with an obnoxious beep as they came to a stop.

'Well? Don't keep me hanging.'

'This talk about notes, it got me thinking ... the note, the one that was left in the school. It was handwritten, right?'

'Yes.'

'The Barrow son, Jonah Barrow, he does odd jobs and works for "local businesses". That could include the school, right? In IT?'

'Yes, guess it could do.'

She was almost physically buzzing with excitement. 'Doesn't it seem weird that this guy, who *happens* to be related to Stan

Lawton, and *happens* to be at the scene of one of the crimes, also *happens* to do work for a school where a post-it note detailing where the videos are, *happens* to be dropped? I'd say it's not a stretch, wouldn't you?'

She sounded breathless. 'I think he wanted to get some sick kick out of spreading them online and spreading them at the school and God knows where else. I bet you that note will be a match to his handwriting once they're done analysing it all. Hell, he could even be the new Family Man, for all we know.'

'You what?' His heart skipped a beat. He was stunned. 'Come on now ... What makes you—'

'I guarantee you, as well as the handwriting matching, I bet my life *and* my family's life that he's left-handed,' she stated.

'He could have just found the videos online though, and spread them himself, even if your hunch was correct.'

'Just trust me on this. Let's look at the evidence – he's from a farming background, and he knew Stan. He's intelligent by the sounds of it. If not the Family Man, then he must have at least some links to this, like Stan did. There's *history* here, Drake,' she said. He had to admire her determination in wanting to see her hunch through.

They sat in silence while Drake tried to process what it could mean.

Jonah Barrow, Samuel Barrow's son, involved somehow, perhaps even in the killings; it sounded strange, outlandish even, but that's what this case had been from the start.

Had he learned from the original videos, or just later uploaded them?

It seemed far-fetched. But it wasn't out of the question. Nothing could be out of the question, and he was at the scene for one of the murders too, as Ellie rightly pointed out. It *was* quite coincidental.

But he would have been a young teenager for the original killings. He couldn't be responsible for those, could he? But then, how did he get the original items? Had Stan left them with him – or perhaps it really had been his father, Samuel, all along?

Jonah could be their way of getting proof. He could be the key to *everything*.

'And what about Paul Randall? It could be him, too. He works at the school? He has a sick bastard for a dad. Why not him?'

Ellie looked deflated at his question.

'He was supposed to be working at the pub, wasn't he? He could have been there for the entire Alan Jackson murder, right?' she said, looking hopeful once more. 'I mean, we've got him coming in for questioning anyway, so we can check his handwriting too, see what the deal is with him.'

'I don't see why not,' Drake said. He was kicking himself again for not seeing *something*. Not even contemplating the angle that his old self would have been all over like a rash. It wasn't acceptable.

'Hmmm, we best get Jonah in for questioning and a handwriting sample as well, then.'

'We don't need to, at least not for this check,' Ellie said with a knowing smile. 'He submitted a handwritten witness statement to Dave, didn't he?'

* * *

They flew into the police station, making a beeline for Dave's desk. Entering the office area, Drake saw him sitting with his back to them. Papers occupied any and all available space around his small computer monitor and laptop. There was barely any sign of the desk surface poking through.

His headphones blared out something Drake couldn't quite decipher. It sounded jazzy, whatever it was.

Ellie grabbed his shoulder and Drake could've sworn he almost struck the ceiling in shock, his arm slamming into the desk as he leapt out of his chair. Drake put out a hand to stop an in-tray before it slid off onto the floor.

'Jesus, don't do that to me, Ellie! You could've given me a heart attack at my age,' he said, puffing and propping himself up with a hand on his knee. The headphones hung disjointed from his neck.

'Sorry, couldn't resist,' Ellie said with a laugh.

'Heartfelt, truly. I felt that deep in my core, though that may be just my heart giving out,' he said, clutching his chest and pointing at Drake. 'Did he put you up to this?'

'No, of course not,' she said. Drake put his hands up, protesting his innocence. 'Dave, do you have access to the note that was found at the school?'

'Yes, I've got a photo on this computer here. I could get the original soon too, if you need it.'

'Fantastic! Bring up the photo for now, please. And, Dave, can you pull out Jonah Barrow's statement whilst you're at it?'

The man paused for a moment, putting his thoughts together and understanding what she was getting at. Drake watched on in amusement.

'You want to compare his handwriting against the note, is that it? That was next on my list. It's been a pretty busy day, you understand.' He stroked a moustache tip. 'Anyway, I'm no writing expert, so we'd need to get someone in if there were obvious similarities, either way.'

'Got it in one, Dave. You're good at this.'

'Sheesh, where do they get you young people these days? No

respect,' he said with an exaggerated shake of his head. 'Just give me a moment.'

Ellie smiled. 'Thanks. We know you're doing your best. It's only been what, twelve hours?'

His fingers worked over the keyboard, bringing up the picture of the scrawled, messy note. He then retrieved the witness statement for the Jackson murder scene from his desk drawer.

Drake snatched it from him and bent down, holding it up against the screen. As far as he could see, Ellie's thought process was right. It appeared to be a match on first inspection.

Ellie obviously agreed, judging by her expression.

'Jesus! We got him. We might actually have got him, or at least one of them. He has to have some kind of involvement.' Ellie clapped, unable to hide her excitement. 'What do we do now?'

'Let's get him in on the pretext of needing some clarifications,' Drake said.

'On it,' Dave said, tapping in Jonah's number.

'Hang on, Dave, just a second.' Drake held a hand up in his direction. 'Did you get a hold of Paul Randall?'

'Yes and no. Well, actually it was his dad, Michael.'

'And?'

'He said that Paul would be here shortly. Also, Michael wanted me to give you a message... It's not pleasant,' he said, wincing.

'What was it?'

'He said, and this is verbatim by the way, "*...tell that Drake bastard and his whore that they shouldn't think that they can get to me through my son. I'm warning you, Drake, I could make this turn nasty for you, mark my words.*" I told you it wasn't pleasant – sorry, Ellie.'

Ellie didn't answer, and looked at Drake. It was water off a duck's back. It was all empty threats, nothing that he hadn't heard before.

'What? So, he's basically incriminating himself by threatening a police officer and on tape, right? That man...' Drake shook his head, looking bewildered.

'Yes, exactly.'

'Ellie, I think we're going to have to pay that man another visit after this. He's not doing himself any favours. Perhaps we've riled him enough that he'll make mistakes as well.'

'Chief, at this rate, we'll have pissed off every dodgy man in Barndon by this time next week,' she said. 'So, back to Jonah – when he was with you, did you notice what hand he was using?'

Dave pondered for a moment. It was as though you could see the cogs whirring in his mind. Drake found it unbearable.

'Well, spit it out, man!'

'I'm sorry, guys. I can't say with any certainty, unfortunately. It's not something I was really looking out for.'

Drake struggled to hide his disappointment. 'No problem.'

'Dave, get in touch with Jonah. Make it as routine-sounding as possible, fingerprints required to discount him, all that stuff,' Ellie requested.

'Roger,' Dave said, putting the phone back to his ear.

61

'Andrea, you home?' Ben called, closing the front door. He needed to talk to her.

The house was quiet and dark downstairs, and the door to the lounge was closed.

He frowned and turned on the hallway lights.

That's unusual. We've never closed that door before.

He put down his laptop bag along with the food he'd had to buy from the nearby petrol station, courtesy of the understandable closing of the shop. He took off his coat and shoes and crept towards the entrance to the lounge, cupping his ear to the door. Something that was becoming much too frequent for his liking.

He frowned again at the silence. *She must be asleep.*

The downstairs internal doors didn't have locks on them, so they would never have to break down such thick doors if Andrea had locked herself in. That experience had been common in their old home when they were in an experimental period with her medication.

Ben opened the door a crack before it came up against something blocking it.

He looked down through the crack in the door to see his wife curled up against the wall and the source of the obstruction, a coffee table, up against the door. He held back a gasp at the state of the room. Her laptop lay smashed among shards of broken glass. Dark stains and marks littered the walls, and all the chairs and cushions were overturned and splayed on the floor.

'Andrea!'

He pushed the door harder, and the coffee table gave way enough to let him through. He clambered in and rushed to his wife's side, his movements not rousing her.

'Andrea, are you okay? Please be okay,' he said, hands squeezing her shoulders.

She shrieked at his touch and bounded away from him, scrambling along the wall as though a cattle prod had shocked her.

'Get away from me!' she cried. 'Get away from me!'

Her eyes were wild as she continued to push herself further away from him. Her hair drenched with sweat, the strands plastered to her face.

'Andrea, it's me. It's Ben. Calm down – you're safe now. What happened? Are you hurt? Everything's going to be okay,' he said, taking a cautious step towards her with outstretched hands.

'No... no, it's not. No... no-no-no, don't you understand?' she hissed, her eyes unblinking.

He tried his best to remain calm, for himself as much as her. 'Andrea, you're not well. You're having an episode. Calm down.'

'Shut up, Ben, shut up, shut up, shut up! Can't you hear it? Can't you hear *her*?'

'Her ... what? Who do you mean? Andrea, no ... Please, snap out of it, focus on me. There are no voices, just me. Just Ben.' His arms were still outstretched, eyes pleading.

'She's telling me not to listen to you. Not to listen to your *lies!'* she cried, crouched down and looking beyond him, as though there was someone or something standing behind him.

'Andrea?'

She cowered further, making herself even smaller while she gripped her head and talked to the wall. 'Yes, Mother. I will, I won't listen. I won't listen, I promise, I won't.' She jittered and scratched at herself as she went on: 'I know, and I will. It won't be long now. I promise. It won't be long. Soon... Don't say that. No. I can't do that. I won't. Anything but that. N-n-n-no!'

Ben stared on in disbelief at his wife. How could he have got it so wrong? How could he not have seen? Last night, it had to have broken something in her – he should have acted sooner. Damn fool!

'Andrea, please.' He stepped cautiously towards her, trying his best not to make any sudden movements, even though it was tearing at every fibre of his being, seeing her like this. He wanted to hold her and soothe her and make it all go away.

'Listen to me. It's going to be okay. We'll be okay, all right? Everything will be fine. You've just got to calm down ... just breathe, okay? Will you do that for me?'

'No! You'll hurt me. Just like that man, Samuel, hurt my mother!'

'What? What do you mean?' he said, feeling more confused. 'Samuel? What's he got to do with this?'

'He raped her, Ben! Okay? I'm his *daughter!*' she blurted out.

'What! But how did you find this out?'

'He told me today.'

'That he raped her?' he said, incredulous.

'No ... no, my mother told me that.' She buried her head in her hands, her hair knotting between her fingers.

'Andrea, come on, you're not making any sense. Miray is dead. You know this isn't true.' His face was a picture of disbelief.

'That's not true. She's with me, always. She protects me! She can't be dead. She's over there! Can't you see?'

Ben looked over his shoulder to where she was pointing amidst the debris. There was only a floor-standing lamp. Nothing more.

This is all too much. Rape? Samuel? Her mother is alive? He put his head in his hands. *This could finally be it. The day I've been dreading all these years has finally come. How could I have been so ignorant? So stupid.*

'Andrea, please, you've got to calm down. You're hysterical.'

Ben knelt in silence before her, letting her slow down. Not stimulating her with questions.

'Okay ... I will, Mother. I will, I promise ...' he heard her whisper before turning to him, suddenly looking lucid. 'B-Ben...? What's going on?'

'Andrea, it's okay, you're going to be okay. Just focus on me.'

He crept closer. He was within arm's reach of her now.

'Stay back!' she said again, tears running down her face. Her eyes boggling at him. 'He won't stay away, Mother! Help me! He won't leave me alone!'

He'd not seen this with her before, not to this degree, and not with her supposed mother being the focus. The person who had made her life a misery solely lived in her dreams before now. This was new, and it was frightening. He needed to get close to her, to reassure her, to reassure himself.

He lunged for her and took his wife in his arms. 'Andrea, come back to me. To Cari, your daughter – please!'

Ben looked her in the eyes, the woman before him shrieking again and trying to twist out of his grip. She was stronger than he thought. He fought against her struggles, trying not to use his full strength for fear of hurting her, before she somehow broke free and slapped him.

Reacting, he pushed her harder than he intended. The back of her head hit the wall with a horrible thud, the impact causing her to stumble forwards.

Oh God, no!

'Andrea! I'm sorry, I'm so sorry!' he said, shocked by his actions. He held his arms out to her, but she recoiled away, her sweat-drenched hair covering her face.

He went to steady her again, to make it right, but she stumbled backwards and onto the floor.

'Andrea!' he cried out, rushing to her side. She didn't respond as he attempted to bring her head up, brushing her hair from her face.

'It's been here. It's been *in this room*,' she shrieked at him, recoiling. She broke down again, covering her face while her chest and shoulders heaved with each sob.

Ben closed the gap, putting his arms around her.

'Hun, it's going to be okay.'

She didn't flinch. Allowing physical touch. That was progress. She had to be back with him now. The change could be like flicking a switch. It was terrifying. Once more, he had to remain calm for her sake, but he was anything but calm.

'Andrea, please tell me – what's going on? What do you mean, it's been here?' He stroked her head, trying to bring her down. *What else could there be?*

'The thing that's been watching our house, I saw it. I saw *it, I saw it!*' she jabbered between sobs. She raised her head and looked into his eyes, her face red and puffy. She looked so helpless.

'Andrea, where did you see it?'

'Upstairs, in the corridor at the window. *It was staring at me!*'

'Okay. What did it look like?'

She averted her eyes. 'I … I don't know.'

She nestled back down into her arms, loud sniffs punctuating the ragged sobs.

'Andrea, I think we have bigger problems than the house here. Along with all that you've said, I've just been at the farm. I bumped into Samuel Barrow as he was leaving and asked where you were. If I could see you to surprise you. That I'd only be a minute.'

Ben stroked her arm. 'He ... well, he looked *confused*. Like I was talking rubbish. He told me ... Andrea, he told me you don't work for him. That you *never have*. He said he never heard back from you about the job and assumed you weren't interested.'

She twitched.

'He said his only interaction before giving you a lift today was at the pub a few weeks back. Today, he saw you and was worried you'd get hurt. He gave me a lift to the petrol station just now so I could grab us some food, laughing that he was turning into our taxi man, for Christ's sake.'

'What? No, that's not true. Ben, please believe me – it's not *true. It's not true, he's lying! He's a fucking rapist!*' she said between sobs. Andrea raised her head and looked into his eyes, her face red and puffy. She looked so helpless.

'Andrea. I'm sorry, but it *is* true. A colleague today said his other half has seen you walking around every few days past their house near the park that overlooks the village. I thought little of it. You're normally quite distracted, and perhaps they were mistaken. But then going to the farm—'

'I've been at work. I've ... I've been at the farm.'

'Andrea, are you sure? What do you do there? What were you doing there this morning?'

'I... I don't know,' she said, averting her eyes again.

'What were you doing there yesterday?'

'I... Ben, I don't *know*. Please. Stop it! Stop asking me!'

'It's just... you've been sort of blacking out lately, and Andrea...' He hesitated. 'I caught you watching those videos last night as well. Have you been doing that again, too?' he said, pointing at her laptop amidst the debris.

'What? No! Stop it, Ben, why are you saying these things? *Why are you lying to me?* I would never do that. How would I have found them? I wouldn't do that! *Stop! Please! Mother, help me! Help me make it stop!*'

She screamed into her arms, loud sniffs punctuating the harsh cries.

This wasn't doing her any good. He'd have to put it to one side for now; he could see she hadn't fully regained her sense of self yet. Why did he have to mention the farm, the videos? Why couldn't he have kept his mouth shut? It made him wonder whether it was *him* that was the problem, saying shit like that.

There's a time and a place, for God's sake, you damn idiot.

They sat in silence while he continued to hold her to his chest. Over time, Andrea's breathing steadied. He turned in front of her, his arms outstretched, while he finally had a chance to check her over.

She hasn't hurt herself, that's a relief. Just some scrapes and marks on her face, and her head isn't bleeding from the knock.

A few moments later, her breathing normalised. The spark seemed to come back to her eyes, and she blinked animatedly as though she'd just woken up.

'Ben ... Ben! Oh ...! What have I been doing? Why's the room like this?' she said between sobs, her face blotchy and streaked with subtle and not-so-subtle nail marks from where she'd scratched herself before he arrived.

'You've had an episode, Andrea; A big one.'

'Oh no,' she wailed. 'But I was doing so well. I had to have blacked out or something. Why don't I remember!'

'Andrea, I think we might need to get you to the hospital.' He continued to keep his voice calm, despite his inner turmoil. 'Your episode was severe. I think this is too much for me, and for Cari – we need them to help you.'

'No!' She looked up at him, her face crumpling. 'No, Ben ... no-no!' she pleaded. 'Please, they'll put me away. It would kill me! Don't do it, Ben. Please, Ben. Don't do it, I beg you.' She sounded terrified.

'It won't be forever – we'll have you back in no time, maybe even this evening or tomorrow. I think it might be the only way we can help you,' he said, close to tears again. 'Cari and I, we thought you'd turned a corner. But today, with your behaviour, what you say you've been seeing and hearing ... it's all got to you, hasn't it?'

'I ... don't know. I just don't know anymore,' she said, confusion etched on her face. She sat and contemplated, the moments turning into minutes.

He broke the silence. 'Are you okay on your own for a moment? Let me get you a glass of water and your meds.'

'Yes, I would like that,' she said, her voice weak.

'One moment, stay right there.' He got up and walked out of the room, pouring a glass of water at the sink and opening the cupboard for her medication.

What had happened to her? Was he really that bad a husband that he couldn't have seen what was happening before his very eyes?

I ignored her concerns and look at what's happened. I hope to God this is just one of those one-off moments. This is all my fault. I don't want to lose her.

A wave of guilt washed over him. Things will be different in Barndon, she'd said. Shit, it was the worst it had ever been.

Opening the prescription box, he couldn't see any blister

packs, half-empty or otherwise. In a panic, he scoured the other cupboards to see if they had been misplaced, but there was nothing there.

So, on top of everything else, she potentially hadn't been taking her medication for today, or however long since he'd last checked. He tried to think of when he last looked, summing it up in his head.

Holy shit, I don't even know. It could be weeks, he realised, stunned and distraught at the dereliction of one simple task.

He was at a loss for words, but he couldn't bring it up now. She was balanced on a knife edge as it was, and the sooner they got her to the hospital, the better.

Ben took a moment to compose himself at the sink, his hands gripping the edge tightly, before returning to the room and bending down to hand her the drink.

She took a few mouthfuls, her colour returning slightly.

'Andrea, do you remember what happened? Anything at all that might have triggered this?' he asked, biting his tongue about the medication.

His wife looked like she was trying to delve into her memories and produce something, but was finding it challenging.

'I ... I was upstairs and closing the window since it had got dark out, thinking bugs might be attracted to the house lights, you know ... I thought I saw something outside, then the next thing I know, I'm down here and you're holding me in your arms. Ben ... I'm scared. I still feel *off*, like there's something in the back of my skull.'

Her eyes skittered around the room while she spoke, genuinely fearful. 'Could you check upstairs? Make sure I've not done something up there before Cari gets home? She's back soon, isn't she? I don't want to scare her if I've made a mess upstairs, too.'

'Okay. I'll do it now. I guess she could be back any minute. Then we'll take you to the hospital and get this all sorted out and have you checked over? Just as a precaution ... sound okay to you?'

'Yes, okay.' Her voice was little more than a whisper. She put the glass on the floor and bunched her knees to her chest. 'I love you, Ben. You know that, don't you?'

'Hey, don't be silly. I love you, too. Cari loves you. Everything will be okay, I promise.'

Ben walked quietly from the room and went upstairs. The landing lights were still on, and the window she'd spoken of appeared firmly latched. There didn't appear to be anything out of the ordinary. Andrea wouldn't have to worry about Cari seeing anything.

'Andrea?' he called back down to her. 'Nothing to worry about, everything's fine up here—'

An arm wrapped round his neck and something slammed into the back of his knees, forcing him down to the floor and knocking the breath from his lungs. He thrashed violently, flinging his legs out as he choked against the rigid arm. It tightened further as he gasped for air, his arms flailing helplessly. He scratched and scraped at the chokehold until he let out one last gasp and his body went limp.

62

Paul Randall appeared at the station sergeant's desk not long after Drake had listened to his father's threats on tape for his own amusement. Ellie, meanwhile, had stationed herself in the interview room.

The Randall man wore the same clothes as when he'd last seen him in the pub, a dark t-shirt and jeans, despite the inclement weather. The t-shirt was much too tight for his powerful-looking frame.

'Paul,' he said in greeting, 'thank you for coming in at such short notice.'

'What's this all about? Why do you want to see me? I thought it was only my father you were harassing.' His eyes flitted around the room and down at Drake's shoes, betraying his nerves.

'If you call following up lines of enquiry with suspects who have no evidence as to their whereabouts harassment, then I apologise,' Drake said. He felt agitated, and he wasn't even in the interview room yet.

'All right, fine, you've got me there. But he did nothing

wrong. I know he's ... well, he can be an *arsehole*, but he's innocent.'

'You may be right,' Drake said, non-committal. 'Is he at the pub, do you know? We may come to see him after this.'

'Yes, he is – as he said he would be when you saw him last, remember? No trips planned for a while now. He's been in a foul mood ever since you spoke with him,' Paul said, frowning.

'Okay, thanks. If you'd follow me, please.'

They made their way past the front desk and down a drab corridor to the interview room. Ellie didn't stand to greet him, instead gesturing for him to sit.

The interview room lights gave off a pitiful glow. It was a little more foreboding than intended for an informal chat. A CCTV camera was tucked away in the corner of the ceiling, while a table and four chairs were all that furnished it, along with a recorder and the related paraphernalia. Drake leant against a wall; he didn't fancy sitting for this.

Ellie started the recorder. 'How are you, Paul?' Ellie asked.

Paul glanced at the equipment. 'I thought this was just a chat?'

'Don't worry, just standard procedure. You're not in any trouble.'

'Okay.' Paul frowned slightly. 'In answer to your question, I'm good. Though when you saw me working at the pub during my time off, I still had to prepare for next term, so it isn't exactly what you'd call relaxing, but I do what I can to help. And now this term's been bloody busy, but you caught me on a rare off day.'

'Relaxing? Does relaxing for you include looking through women's windows and such like?' she asked, point-blank.

Drake winced to himself; she really was going for it from the off.

'Hey now, that's uncalled for. I'm here of my own free will, and I *don't* do that anymore,' he said, immediately on the defensive. For a man his size, he seemed to have shrunk a few inches under Ellie's accusatory gaze.

'You don't? Okay.' Her voice dripped with disbelief. 'Mr Randall, would you be so kind as to take this pen and paper and write a brief statement regarding your whereabouts yesterday evening?'

Paul looked puzzled. 'Write it? Why can't I just tell you?'

'Are you refusing?' Drake said, sitting down and meeting his gaze.

'I just ...' he looked as though he was trying to choose his words carefully, 'I just don't understand this. I'm not a veteran of these sorts of things, but I don't think that's normal procedure, is it?'

'Please. Entertain us, just this once,' Ellie said, not breaking eye contact with him, tilting her head to one side. He looked down.

'Erm ... what if I say no?'

'Then things might have to become official. Perhaps your previous misdemeanour, the one that was so handily brushed under the carpet, may have to become a public record. Perhaps the school will find out what you've been up to,' Drake said, clasping his hands together on the table.

'Whoa, okay, there's no need for that. Okay. Okay. I'll write it for you, okay? Whatever you need,' he said, what little confidence remaining, having drained out of him at Drake's words.

'Before you do, would you know if Jonah Barrow has ever worked at the school?' Ellie said, twiddling her thumbs on the table.

'Jonah? Yeah, he's been there on and off these last few weeks. Why?'

'Do you do any ...' She paused for a moment; Drake could see where this was going. 'IT tasks and such like for the school, Paul?'

'Me? No.' He laughed nervously. 'I'm awful with computers. Why do you think I'm a PE teacher? We wouldn't need Jonah otherwise, would we?'

'Okay. Please make the statement.'

Drake noted her voice had tightened at the discovery about Jonah. She was excited that her theory was being confirmed. He had to admit, he had a feeling in the pit of his stomach too, but they needed to play this out further.

Paul took the pen in his left hand, Ellie's eyes sparking as he did so, and he dictated while he wrote, 'I was working at the pub until five. The regulars will be able to corrob ... corroborate? *Corroborate.* I then went for a walk. I had nothing to do with the murder at the local shop.'

'This is what you're getting at, right? The murder?' he said, looking up at Ellie before gazing at Drake next. They both looked at Paul without replying.

'You went for a *walk*. Can't you be more specific than that, Mr Randall?'

'No. I went for a walk. I can show you the route.' He sighed while he finished his neat, joined up lowercase statement with an unnecessarily elaborate signature. He sat back in his chair and started playing with his fingernails.

Drake frowned; this wasn't what they'd expected. This certainly wasn't what Ellie had been hoping for. Perhaps it wasn't going to be as clear cut as she'd anticipated.

Ellie shifted in her seat before continuing. 'Paul, where were you when your dad was in Yorkshire?'

'I was up there too. He'd given me a lift while I visited friends.'

'Friends? But weren't you working? Wasn't it school term time?'

'No, some building work had been going on at the school, which affected my lesson structure in the school hall. It meant they cancelled the lessons for my pupils from Wednesday onwards.'

Ellie and Drake frowned in unison.

'Why didn't your dad mention any of this?' Drake asked.

'I guess he didn't feel it was necessary,' Paul said. 'Perhaps he didn't want you questioning me like you are now.'

Drake didn't respond; instead, he scratched at his stubble. He knew what Ellie's next question would be.

'Paul, do your friends live in Haworth?'

'No.'

'Are you sure?'

'Yes, of course I'm sure. Come on, what is this? I've already shown you I can't be a suspect in the murder at the shop. If you're going to keep on with me like this, I'm going to need like a solicitor or something, aren't I?'

Drake jumped in; he could see it could get messier than need be at this stage if they weren't careful.

'That won't be necessary, Paul. I think we're done for now. I take it you'll be at the pub, should we need anything further?'

'Yes, of course.'

'Then you're free to leave,' he said, and stopped the recording.

* * *

Ellie looked at Drake with a look of sheer frustration when he re-entered the room after escorting Paul to the front desk.

'What the hell was that ... *sir*?'

'Ellie, I shouldn't need to explain myself to you. He was going to shut down. If I didn't step in then, it would have got a lot messier and he would have become more closed to our lines of questioning than need be.'

'But he's left-handed, works at the school *and* was up in Yorkshire!'

'That's not enough. You saw his handwriting.'

'That doesn't mean anything. He could have made it neater on purpose.'

'Then we'll get the writing analysed. Even if it's neater, it will still have the telltale signs.'

'Hmmm, okay, sir,' she said, looking put out at his handling of the situation.

He had trampled on her good work, he knew that. But they were only halfway through, and Paul wasn't going anywhere.

'We must be patient, Ellie. We're getting closer to the truth now, I can feel it. Let's see what happens with Jonah. You heard Paul, he's been at the school too these past few weeks, though I wouldn't believe his bullshit about being incapable with computers either.'

Ellie remained silent.

Drake pursed his lips. 'Just trust me on this, you'll see. We'll get our man.'

63

Drake had sat in an uneasy silence with Ellie while she'd stewed on the outcome with Paul Randall. He was pleased it was only a minute or two before they received notification from the desk sergeant that Jonah Barrow had turned up. He wasn't one for awkward silences, even with a relative junior.

Not long after, the sergeant was guiding Jonah into their interview room.

As they stood, Jonah Barrow appeared, wearing an assured smile. There didn't appear to be any nervousness in his body language from being in a police station. It struck Drake immediately how different Paul's and Jonah's behaviour were. Drake found this peculiar, and he needed to understand why.

The deep-set brown eyes of Jonah's father looked back at them. The man was strikingly similar in terms of height and build to his dad, and he'd shaved his head since Drake had last seen him as a teenager. He could almost have been Sam or the Family Man twenty years back.

The similarities between Sam and Jonah ended at physical features, however.

The man dressed young for his age; his clothing that of someone in his thirties trying to look like he was in his early twenties still. He wore a black hoodie, near skin-tight grey jeans and trainers with a black and white checkerboard pattern. All he needed was a skateboard and baseball cap to complete the look.

Drake couldn't believe that he hadn't seen him before now. In his mind, he was kicking himself. He had to be involved. There was no question. He had to be. This apparent witness interview would go some way to proving that; he could feel it.

They all sat down. Ellie took two tapes and inserted them into the machine before starting the recording moments later.

Drake reeled off the formalities, and started: 'Thank you for coming down to the station so quickly and at such short notice, Jonah. You mind if I call you Jonah?' Drake said, sitting back in his chair.

'Not at all,' Jonah replied with a thin smile, his timbre sounding effeminate by Samuel's standards. 'Anything I can do to help Adam and his family.'

'That was awful what happened. I'm so sorry you had to go through that, Jonah,' Ellie said, her voice not belying her true feelings. She was doing a good impression of sounding compassionate.

'Yes, it wasn't great. I'd rather not talk about it again, unless you need me to, that is,' he said, a look of regret on his face.

'Of course. We wouldn't dream of doing such a thing,' she replied.

The room went quiet. Jonah didn't offer any reply.

'How was the film you watched with your parents on Wednesday, October 24th?' Drake asked.

'Film? What film?' He fidgeted. His eyes shifting to Ellie before studying the table. He wouldn't be getting any moral support from her.

'The film you watched with your parents that evening? I'd like to see it, but can't remember what it was called for the life of me. I'm getting old. What was it called again?' he said, looking at Ellie in faux amusement.

'Oh! Sorry, yes, I must have misunderstood. It was called "The Shawshank Redemption". We had some wine while watching it. You're a fan of films then, Mr Drake?'

'I am now.'

Little shit, he wasn't around then.

Perhaps his parents were covering for him. Their only child; a potential murderer.

'Anyway, we digress. That wasn't why we asked you to come in for us. We would like to speak to you about something else.'

'Oh?'

'Yes, you see, we want to clear something up, something that's been bothering us.' He produced the witness statement with a flourish, half-slamming it on the table in front of Jonah.

'What? Did I miss out something from my statement? Or was it hard to read my handwriting? Sorry, I was in shock still, I suppose. It's messy sometimes. I always write with a computer these days, so get little practice,' he said, pulling on one of his hoodie's cuffs.

'Well, funny you should mention handwriting, Jonah. Very funny, actually.' He produced the school note in its plastic evidence bag before tossing it in front of him.

'Could you explain this to us?' he said, leaning back in his chair. He crossed his arms and tried to stop himself from looking too satisfied.

Jonah's eyes narrowed for a split second before he caught his breath and coughed dramatically, like he was buying himself time.

'Where... erm, where did you get this?' Jonah said, his voice catching again while he shuffled in his seat.

'We found it at the school. You work there sometimes, don't you, Jonah?'

'Yes, I do. Just help them with standard IT support stuff, nothing major. I do it for lots of places.'

Ellie looked over at Drake. The man had just confirmed her theory to him. He ignored her while he continued with his line of questioning.

'I see. Well, this note – do you know how it came to be at the school?'

'No, sorry. I've never seen it before.'

'You've never seen it before? Interesting, because it looks *exactly* like your writing, Jonah. Don't you think?' Ellie said, a curious look on her face.

'Just a coincidence, I'm sure,' he mumbled.

'Speak up for the recording, Jonah.'

Jonah repeated it louder, but he sounded less confident than before.

Drake decided to go in heavy. 'What were you doing uploading the videos on the Dark Web, Jonah?'

'What videos? Dark Web? What?'

'You know what we're talking about. Don't give us that – we mean the five videos depicting the first five Family Man killings. You uploaded them, didn't you? There's no use lying to us, Jonah.'

'What? The Family Man? No ... I didn't, that wasn't me, that's crazy,' he said, shifting in his chair.

'Funny, we have evidence to show that you did.' Ellie crossed her arms. 'Our cyber-crime division has proof that it came from you, from your house.'

'What ... how?'

She pursed her lips, letting him stew for a second. 'They have a team of ethical hackers. Seems you were sloppy, Jonah.

They traced you after hacking into the servers you'd hosted them on.'

The statement surprised even Drake. She hadn't mentioned hacking to him. Certainly not 'ethical hacking', whatever the hell that was. She had to be bluffing.

'I ... I...' Jonah's face was turning red now. He started fidgeting again and refused to meet their gaze.

'Jonah, we've caught you out. Why don't you admit what you've done? There's no use pretending with us,' Ellie stated.

His face had graduated to a puce colour, his eyes looking like they'd pop out of his head at any moment.

The time ticked by while Jonah tried to dig himself out of his hole. They let him stew, the implication hanging in the air. The man still wouldn't look either of them in the eye. The silence was deafening.

Drake was just about to press him further when Jonah uttered one word. 'Okay.'

'What do you mean "okay"?' Drake leant in, his hands resting on the table, preparing himself for whatever was coming next.

'It was me. I did it.'

'Did what, Jonah?'

'I ...'

'Jonah?'

'It was me,' he said, verging on a whisper. 'I was in Yorkshire; I killed that family ... did those videos too. My grandad, Stan ... He ... well, he showed me his trinkets. He showed the videos to me when I was a kid. I uploaded them. I did it. It was me.'

Drake's mind reeled at the confession. That one statement changed everything, turning his world upside down in an instant. Jonah, this mundane man, had just gone one step further and admitted to the killings *too*, not just the videos. Could it be that simple? But it all made sense now. The new camera style, the different blindfolds and bindings. The several attempts with the knife with a different hand. It was because it *was* a different person. It was Jonah. The Family Man copycat was *him*.

Drake didn't know which way was up. He looked over at Ellie, who looked like she was trying her best to rein herself in. Her leg bounced furiously under the table.

But before either of them could get another word out in response, Jonah's disposition seemed to change. He'd stopped his nervous fidgeting, straightening up in his seat. His face unreadable, bordering on blank.

He started laughing.

'What's so funny, Jonah?' Ellie said, tilting her head to one side. 'You've just admitted to an awful number of murders and could be looking at some very serious jail time.'

'It's the look on your faces.' He continued laughing. 'You lot thinking I was some pathetic little boy when it's been me all along. You people ... I'm sorry, you're a joke. I'd kill them all again in a heartbeat. It was *amazing*. Man, I even watched you two idiots come and go from the crime scene. You didn't even see me.' He drummed a rhythm on the table while he struggled to contain his obvious amusement.

'Why did you do it, Jonah?' Drake said, crossing his arms. His brow furrowed. The man's behaviour had taken an unusual turn at this stage, even in Drake's experience.

Jonah shrugged. 'Because.'

'That's not an answer, is it?'

'Because I wanted to see how it felt, all right? The videos ... I've watched them so many times. It was like an obsession. They blew my mind.'

He sounded as though he was talking about something normal, like a film or a piece of art, not slaughtering families. *Children*. 'But they could be better. Let's say, they were "of their time", eh? That Dark Web business, well, I wanted to show them off. To fuck with people, and what better place than a school? It seemed such a waste to keep them to myself,' he chuckled. 'Hell, maybe a few of the kids at the school might even grow up to become like me ... a killer. I couldn't just stick them up on a normal website and have it linked back to me, could I?'

'Like you?' Drake scoffed. 'I think you failed there, Jonah. We've seen the originals. You're an amateur by comparison. I don't think anyone would want to be like you.'

'What? What do you mean?'

'Look, Jonah,' he said, changing the subject. Knowing that comment would stick with the bastard now. He knew the type: narcissists, perfectionists, murderers. 'You've just admitted to a very serious crime. And who knows what else you've done—'

'That's all I've done. I swear it. The Jackson one. That wasn't me. God's honest truth,' he said, putting his hand on his heart with a smirk. 'Adam was my friend.'

'Then who was it?'

'I don't know.'

'You don't know? Come on, Jonah. We're not buying that. You just happened to have carried out a near identical set of murders in Yorkshire, and you just *happened* across another scene, really? And what about the ring from Yorkshire ending up in Barndon?'

'Pfft, you want that, then you get me a solicitor. Then maybe I'll talk. You're not getting another peep out of me.' He smirked and broke into laughter again.

'Was it your dad? Was it Samuel?'

'My *dad?* You guys are just so completely clueless, aren't you? Oh my God, you're funny. You're so far off the mark.'

Drake sighed to himself. The man knew he had their attention. He was going to do everything he could to toy with them now.

Jonah continued laughing as Drake finally decided to read him his rights and his right to legal representation seeing as he wouldn't get any more from him. The man was becoming increasingly shrill as the seconds rolled by. Ellie tried talking to him but was getting nothing back. The man wouldn't stop. It was getting to the point of hysteria.

Drake continued his line of thought internally. *But who killed the Jacksons? They'd only potentially solved one case out of six with Jonah's confession. If what he was saying was even true? He could still have been solely responsible for uploading the tapes, nothing more.*

Despite the enormity of what had just unfolded before him, Drake felt unsatisfied. The sickening feeling of despair returned; they were so close, yet something wasn't right.

He ended the interview in disgust, sitting back while the laughter from the other side of the table washed over him. The man continued his hysterics while they waited for the station's desk sergeant to take him away to one of the holding cells.

A struggle followed until Jonah was eventually forcibly removed by three officers to be processed and printed and finally placed in a cell.

64

Drake puffed out his cheeks and ran his hands over his face. 'That was... bizarre.'

Ellie looked up from the table. 'I don't know, Boss. I've not had much experience with murderers.'

'He's not in his right mind. The gloating ... He was like a child, desperate for attention. As though he was trying to show off or impress us somehow. There was a strange naivety about him. It doesn't sit right with me.' He heaved a sigh of disgust and crossed his arms. 'And he'll have a solicitor present next time we speak with him. So, it may take a different turn in the future.'

He raised an eyebrow in her direction. 'Was that true? About the cyber-crime task force? You know, GCHQ and all that?'

She shrugged. 'Not entirely. I thought I'd try it. If it didn't work, he could have shot me down. Doesn't look like he'd done his homework. He had the opportunity to drag it out and deny it. But like you say, he appears to be that much of a narcissist that he jumped on the opportunity. He *really is* that gullible and naïve, it seems. I thought he might have just said he found the site by accident,' she said, shrugging again. 'But you need to know the address, and the likelihood of him finding it, then dropping the address somewhere as well ...' She rolled her eyes and smiled. 'He really went for it hook, line and sinker, didn't he? The cyber specialists *will* attempt to hack into it though – it wasn't a lie, just a bending of the truth and timescales. They *will* find it leads to him.'

'You're not kidding. The guy has a screw loose. He was revelling in it. A sociopath like that. It's amazing he didn't go out and do it sooner.' Drake grimaced. 'You *would* have to be insane to do what he's done. I need to understand whether he had any involvement in the shop killings. Despite his protests, him just finding them like that. Something doesn't sit right. He must have done it, or been involved somehow—' he stopped, feeling a vibration in his pocket.

He pulled out his phone. It was Becca.

'John.'

'Becca, what's up?' Drake frowned. 'You okay? You sound upset.'

'I am. It's Eva. She's found something else related to your case. She... we need you home. It's really disturbing.'

He scratched his chin. 'Becca, I'm in the middle of something. Is it urgent?'

'I wouldn't call you at work if it wasn't,' she said.

He knew not to argue. He hoped it wasn't another video. Eva knew of the Jacksons and had been in their shop before. He hoped curiosity hadn't got the better of her. The video might already be up.

'Okay... I'm on my way. I'll be home soon.'

'Good, love you,' she said and hung up.

He stuffed his phone back into his pocket and stood up to make a move for the exit.

'Drake? Everything okay?'

'Becca's saying she needs me home – Eva's found something else related to the case.'

'Do you want me along?'

'No, it's okay. You see if you can get something more out of Jonah once he's calmed down,' he said. 'And get Dave working on that warrant for the Barrows. We can flush them out, once and for all.'

'And what about Paul Randall?'

'Let's see how Jonah plays out for now. I don't think Paul should be entirely out of the picture until everything checks out. Come by the house if I'm not back soon and you find out more. We may need to go straight to the farm together.'

'Sure thing, Chief.'

Drake went to the exit and turned back as if he'd forgotten something.

'And Ellie?'

'Yes, Drake?'

'You did good today. Well done.'

The clouds loomed over the house and the surrounding countryside, giving the scene the same foreboding, oppressive atmosphere from earlier in the day. He liked the autumnal weather when he was home. Not when he was out in it. But, despite the malaise of the past few weeks, and the dark turns of the last few hours, he was feeling positive. There had been progress now, and the case was actually moving in a favourable direction. Maybe things were changing for the better? He felt genuine optimism for the first time since the case reopened. He just hoped Eva would not be traumatised by what she'd found.

Pulling up to the house, he could see the usual lights were on, the silhouette of the maple tree skeletal before the light.

He got out. Bunching his shoulders, he made a hasty move for the door, the wind billowing the bottom of his coat.

'Becca, Eva. I'm home. What is it? What's so urgent?' He closed the door behind him, the sounds of the elements dulled to a low ebb.

Drake chucked his keys on the side table with a *clang* and wandered on towards the kitchen, past the lounge. It was quiet, the ticking of his father's clock the only noise punctuating the silence.

He frowned and peered into the lounge.

By the time he was aware of a presence behind him, it was too late. The intruder grabbed him from behind, thrusting a cloth to his face. The sweet chemical smell overwhelming him as he struggled weakly. Drake could only muster a few seconds of fight before his eyes rolled back in his head and he fell silent.

65

Drake snapped back to consciousness with a sharp intake of breath. Now awake, an intense feeling of dislocation descended upon him. His throat and chest were tight, making his breathing short and panicked, and worst of all, he couldn't *see*.

He attempted to blink his eyes for a few seconds and force them open, but he was met with pain and hot, stinging tears. And it wasn't just his eyes that didn't feel right, his body felt restricted, somehow. His head and heart pounding painfully as his thoughts evaded him. He couldn't make sense of his situation. He felt high, and hot; oh, so hot.

What the hell was going on?

There was a sound, a muffled noise, somewhere in the distance. He tried to speak; to call out, but couldn't. He still couldn't breathe properly. Suddenly feeling like he was suffocating, he became aware of something in his mouth.

A curious noise sounded again in the distance, a voice piercing through the fog in his brain.

He focused on the sound; trying to pinpoint its origin was

enabling his senses to begin a slow recovery, as though he was tuning an old analogue radio.

Then something blunt struck the back of his head. The strike brought his senses back into sharp focus with a snap. The strike and resulting head-rush caused a wave of nausea to flow over him. It was all he could do to stop himself from being sick.

It was clear to him now; he couldn't see because he was blindfolded. He couldn't speak because he was gagged. He couldn't move because he was tied up. His body sat bolt upright; tied to a chair.

Oh, shit.

A sharp object dug into his chin, lifting his head up a notch. Then without warning, light flooded his eyes. His captor had ripped the blindfold off. Bright light dazzled him, his eyes stuttering and gluey; faint shapes slowly came into focus, illuminated by the lights of the kitchen.

Becca! Eva! No!

Eva sat to his left and Becca on his right, with him at the head of the table, the end furthest from the doorways leading to the hallway and garden. Both women were bound and gagged, but Eva had also been blindfolded.

He realised now it had been them; they had been trying to wake him. Desperate for him to do something.

Oh my God, he's got my family. He's got me.

Drake's mind raced.

Come on, man, got to remain calm. Got to get you out of this. Got to get them out before it's too late.

Tears ran down Eva's cheeks beneath her saturated blindfold. Becca, by comparison, was stoic, sitting straight like a statue. Trying her best not to panic in front of their daughter, even though she couldn't see.

'Drake, you there? John? John Drake? *DCI* Drake? Hello?'
Drake heard another muffled voice speaking in the distance.

He looked straight ahead; the grogginess returning slightly after the initial hit of adrenaline.

It was then a figure stepped into view in front of him.

Jesus Christ, it's Him.

The Man was clad head to toe in black, an ugly knife in one hand. He was playing with it, gleefully juggling it from one palm to the other. A camera attached off-centre to his chest.

'Good to see you awake now, Drake. Nothing more annoying than having to wait for you to wake up, spoiling my fun. You were out like a light,' he said, cackling at his own comments.

That voice.

That gravelly voice. He couldn't believe it. His instincts had been right all along. That voice... it was *Samuel.*

He shouted at Samuel in retort, but it was muffled and nonsensical beneath the gag.

'Speak up, *DCI* Drake. I can't hear you,' he said, sounding like he was smiling under the mask. He moved over to Drake in one swift movement and pulled down the gag, causing him to cough and splutter.

'Let my family go,' he blurted, taking in gulps of clean air. 'Whatever you're going to do, they don't need to be a part of this.'

'I'm afraid that's not going to happen, Drake. You know what I do. Why would I let go of your family?' Samuel chuckled at his own words.

He had to think of a way out of this mess. Try a different tack. But, what? He was dealing with a madman. A madman with over twenty years of experience.

'I can't believe it. It was you? All along it's been *you?* Honestly, I have to say – I'm actually disappointed,' Drake said, disbelief tinging his voice.

Samuel's temper burned bright. 'You what? What did you say!'

'You heard me, you fucking inbred,' he shouted, wrestling against the restraints.

He wanted him angry. He might become irrational and make a mistake, maybe give him an opening. But he was going to be on thin ice. More than he already was.

'Me? An inbred? I'm a Barrow. I'm pure. We're originators. You? What are you by comparison? Fucking nothing,' he said, spitting out the last few words.

Drake laughed at that. 'Get a grip. You're the son of a farm-hand. Nothing but a dirty secret. An *accident*. Your mother hadn't planned for you when she was having her fun. You're nothing but a mistake. A sad, pitiful one,' he retorted, sneering at him.

Samuel pulled off his mask in response to Drake's barbs.

Their eyes met. He glared at him. Samuel's face full of fury, his eyes ablaze.

'You better watch what you say, *Drake*. It's *you* that's in the precarious position here. You...' He pointed the knife at him before turning it on Becca and Eva in turn, '... and your pretty little family.'

He moved over to Eva and grabbed her chin, cupping it and squeezing her cheeks hard. She cried out beneath her gag. 'Eva here. She's a teen. Don't get many of those. Well, not until the other day with Alan's boy, at least, heh! She's going to squeal a good'un when I cut her throat, choking on her own blood in front of her *daddy*. Oh yes, indeed,' he said, licking his lips.

'Don't you touch her!' Drake shouted. Panic was getting the better of him, despite his best efforts. The situation was on a knife's edge.

'Why not? I can do whatever I want. Hmmm. Maybe I'll start

on your wife instead. Never had me a real woman before when doing this. They're all usually so much younger, their lives ahead of them ... now's as good a time as any to try it out, right?' he hissed, moving behind Drake and to the other side of the table where Becca sat. He pulled her head back by her hair.

'I always had a thing for the wives, didn't I, Drake? That's what you and your psychologists think, am I right? I think this time will be different, though. Maybe I'll leave *you* alive. Purify *you*, make you the target of my Purpose.'

'No, don't!' he pleaded in desperation.

Purify? Purpose? What was he talking about?

Drake hopped and wriggled in the chair. He was disgusted at himself; for being so foolish, for being disarmed so utterly in front of them. But what could he do? Samuel was right. He had him where he wanted him. He was at his mercy. Samuel had blindsided him. He regretted his words earlier.

He pushed the thought from his mind. *Hindsight, always with the damn hindsight.*

'But you know what I find funniest of all? You actually think that I *hate* the wives.' He laughed, rubbing his chin with the butt of his knife. 'You do, don't you? But you couldn't be further from the truth. No sir, heh-heh.'

'I don't understand. What do you mean? What "Purpose"? You kill their entire family in front of them. That can't be anything but hatred, you sick bastard.'

'Oh, so you want me to go into the details eh, *Drake?*' he drawled, an ugly smirk forming. He pulled on Becca's hair again and ran the knife along her throat. Just enough pressure not to draw blood.

Drake's heart was in his mouth.

'Why then?' he asked, realising his only option was to keep him talking. Something would happen, someone would come along and interrupt him; someone *had* to, otherwise they were all dead.

'Always the detective, eh? Professional curiosity, is it? Well, okay then, from one professional to another ...' Samuel paused, relishing every moment.

Drake looked at the soulless lens of the camera. If they weren't to survive this, they'd soon be part of his collection for eternity.

Samuel continued. 'You see, I don't hate women – far from it. I *love* women. I want the best for them, for their future. You don't see things the way I do, Drake. The way things should be. Women wasting their lives with degenerates. Men that don't deserve them. I *free* them from those shackles, those bonds... When I watch their houses, night after night, I see what no one else does – the suffering in some cases, the sadness in others. So, I do what I do. I go in, and I kill, purging them of their old lives, leaving them free to try again.'

'Mother always taught me to strive for bigger and better,' he said, tipping his head. 'She did the same when she renounced Stan. He wasn't good for her, even I could see that. And it worked – you saw what I've built up there because of her. So, I followed her advice, in in my own way. I *reset* them, reset their *lives,* I enable their *rebirth* into their new world—'

'Jesus, Samuel, listen to yourself. You're insane. You kill people. Their *children.* You can't rationalise that.' Drake couldn't believe what he was hearing. Samuel thought he was *saving* these women?

'Drake, Drake, Drake ... Don't you go saying that. Don't you fucking lecture me,' he said, folding his arms and tutting. 'I've been watching you for a long time. Such a long time. I've seen how happy you and your family are, or should I say, *were.*' He laughed. 'You don't deserve yours either, and you know it. Deep down ... I think you know it.'

'But why torture the husbands to such lengths? What's with the hands? Why kill the children? They're bloody innocent, regardless of what you think of the men!'

'Come now, DCI Drake. You can't let me have a *little* fun now, is that it?' He sighed and started stroking Becca's hair. 'Fine ... I torture them, because *I can*. You've seen my operation up at the farm. Stan taught me to how to handle a knife and kill since I was what, six? Granted, it was just chickens, cats, dogs, you name it. But soon I was professional, working on the farm, slaughtering the cattle. But that's not enough. It never is. I wanted to see what it was like gutting a man, severing his *parts*, making him *powerless*. It's *all* about the power and the control that I have over them, Drake. Over you and your little operation now, too. You should try it.' He crowed. 'Whew! It's really somethin', I can tell ya!'

'Samuel, if you care so much for them, why put the wives through all this agony? Why not just kidnap the father and leave the children and wives alone?' Drake said, reaching for his bindings at his wrists, his fingers barely able to brush the fabric.

Shit! He needed to do something, and he needed to do it soon. Drake's mind raced, his panic escalating. *There's only so long I can keep Samuel and his ego talking.*

'Do I have to spell it out? For the love of God, Drake!' Samuel slammed the table with a gloved fist. 'The pain and the suffering ... it's to *purify* them for their new lives, free of their wretched offspring, *his* seed. You're obviously not a reader of the good book, so I'm not surprised you don't understand. Damn reprobate,' Samuel said, rolling his eyes. 'I put them through the wringer so that they can start anew, to do *better*. Killing those kiddies, it's such an absolute. The look in their mother's eyes – it cleanses them. It cleanses *me*.' Samuel paused, looking like his mind was elsewhere for a moment. His eyes filled with a look of love, as though he was reliving happy memories from his childhood.

'Samuel?'

Drake worked at his bonds further while Samuel was distracted. He only managed a second or two before Samuel became present once more. He turned, thrusting his knife in Drake's direction.

'But why blindfold the children? If it's that *cleansing* for you,' he said, his disgust loud and clear, the knife less an inch from his eyeball.

'Come on, Drake. I'm a "Family Man" at the end of the day.' He cackled at his own joke and slammed the knife into the table, lodging it in place. 'I don't want to see that. Can't say I take outright pleasure in killing them little ones, but they serve the ultimate Purpose. *My* Purpose.'

'Jesus Christ, Samuel. They're just children.'

'Now, now Drake – don't you go taking the good lord's name in vain,' he said, hooting with laughter.

'What about your dad, then? I don't understand why Stan killed himself. We had nothing at that point. I bet you knew that.'

'I did. My dad, though, he was getting worked up about it all. Fretting, worrying ... he wasn't sleeping. *You* Drake, you drove him to it,' he said, pulling the knife out of the table and pointing it at him once again. 'With your appeals and all that shit. Coming to our house, even in the beginning, it made him anxious. Truth be told, I think he was getting cold feet. But it was as much a surprise to me as it was to you. It devastated me.' He sat down on the chair next to Becca, looking like he was about to well up.

Drake wanted to kill him. To end it all, as a father and a husband.

'He did the right thing. You should do the same. End this. No good will come of killing us now. This is over,' he said, looking over at Eva once more.

'Hoo-hoo, Drake, you *are* a funny one. Don't ever try to become a negotiator, or a psychologist, or some shit. It ain't working, no way ... not on me. There's no way you're getting out of this. Why would anyone come here now? You're just another family to add to my collection. But anyway ... What's say we get this party started, eh? What say you? I ain't never killed a woman like this, instead. This should be my first time, if memory serves ... Boy, oh boy, she sure is pretty,' he said, standing and grabbing at Becca's hair once again. He bunched it and pulled her head back before pointing the knife in Drake's direction. Trying to goad him into action.

'No! Don't!' Drake cried out. Samuel stopped just after he drew the knife a touch across her throat. The point drawing a small trickle of blood that slowly petered down her neck. She cried out beneath her gag.

She looked back over at Drake again, taking her eyes off Eva.

Her eyes pleading with him.

'Any last words, Drake?'

'Jonah!' he blurted out. 'What about Jonah! He's ... he's in custody. Surely you want to see him again?'

'That little shit? Fuck him. He's the one that's screwed this up, releasing those videos. *My* videos. Going off and killing that family up north. I was so angry with him. You wouldn't believe. Having to cover for that little runt,' he said, before shouting in exasperation. 'That ... that was humiliating, knowing he'd *copied* me behind my back!'

He seethed, his lips pursed and spiteful. 'But least he tipped me off he was going down to the station – though it interrupted my other bit of fun and games a little. But soon as I heard and, after your little warrant threat at my place, I *had* to come here,

Drake. Taking my son, regardless of what he did, that was the last straw. I'd left you alone. Spared you. But now I've *had it with you!*' His face was a ball of rage, his eyes small, angry flints. His hands flexed, one around the knife, the other still gripping Becca's hair.

'He actually thought I'd be pleased? Sick cunt. I'd always had my doubts about letting him in on things. Seeing what his daddy got up to ... The family business. Now I know I should have trusted my gut.' He sighed. 'If you hadn't caught him, I was planning on dealing with him myself eventually, you know? Despite everything, family ... I can't have no loose cannons in this business. You understand that, don't you, Drake?' He yanked on Becca's hair again. She yelled out, her eyes bulging with fear.

'Aren't you worried he'll give you up before then?' Drake said. Sweat was soaking his clothes and stinging his eyes.

'Nope, that's one thing I did right. He would never do that to us. He loves Ann and me.'

'Do you really believe that? He's already admitted to the videos and the Cartwright murders.'

'Guess I'll have to trust my gut this time. And to be fair to the little shit, he was useful, for one thing at least.' Samuel nodded at the camera on his chest with a smirk. 'And besides, I've got me a daughter now. Long-lost, but soon back in the fold. It's where I was when I got the news about Jonah and I'll be back there soon, yes, sir.'

'Wait ... your daughter? You have a daughter?'

'Yeeep,' he said, smiling at the thought, and pointing the knife at Drake. 'And that's where my new hope lies, not Jonah. But in that little beauty. She's got my eyes, Drake. Have you seen her?'

'No, I don't know who you're talking about.'

'Andrea, of course, the new girl in town. We're going to have so much fun, me and her. She looked so happy when I told her.

Just like her mum and me – oh, yes. I'll train her up good, just you wait,' he said, a rictus grin across his face. 'Now, let's get this show—'

Andrea? Does he mean Andrea Whitman? Shit, I need to keep him talking.

'Alan! What about Alan?' Drake gasped for air, trying to fight his panic. His heart felt as though it was going to jump out of his chest. He was all out of ideas now; there was nothing left in the tank.

'Alan? You're just about to watch your family die, and you want to talk about that pissant shopkeeper?' he said, smiling at the thought. 'He was a long-time target. I'd not killed like that for so long, and Jonah's cock-up ... well, let's say that reawakened something of that desire. It had been so *long*, Drake, you wouldn't believe. I'd kept my head down for so long, after you got my father killed. Alan's family would have been next if Stan didn't do what he did. His wife was a *beaut* back in the day, and she was wasted on him and that little ginger shit of a son.' He scrunched his nose up in disgust. 'But finally, I saw an opportunity, and I seized it with both hands. Twenty years... Twenty *damn* years I've had to make do with temporary workers, farmhands, vermin, the sort no one would miss. Hone my craft. It wasn't the same, a little less *showy* shall we say, but boy... you should see my work room, Drake. Hoo! It's beautiful.'

Samuel started laughing again.

'Shit, Drake. I've loved toying with you. Who in their right mind would kill their alibi and his family too?' he said, through continual fits of laughter. 'It was literally a free kill to me, and Jonah, well, he'd given me the opening I wanted. I *needed*.'

Samuel wrenched again on Becca's hair. She looked down at him again, her neck taut. A tear ran down her cheek. Her eyes pleading with him.

'Right! Time's a'ticking... Say goodbye, John boy,' he said, followed by a final grotesque cackle.

'Wait! No! You can't do this!' He shouted. 'Becca, I love you!'

Eva screamed through her gag at the realisation of what was about to happen, fighting against her restraints.

What followed next seemed to occur in slow motion as Samuel drew the knife across his wife's throat.

'No!' Drake's anguish howled out of him.

His wife's accusatory eyes flickered between him and Eva while she struggled for what seemed like an eternity, until, finally, the light in her eyes went out.

She was gone.

Samuel took a deep breath through his nostrils and let go of her hair, her head slumping to her chest as he leered at Drake, his face a grotesque mask of satisfaction.

Drake squeezed his eyes shut, desperate to shut out the pain. A piece of his soul forever shattered as his daughter's screams enveloped him.

66

Drake continued to struggle against his bonds, despite his disbelief at what had just occurred. He felt numb, the absolute shock of what happened hitting him like a sledgehammer. But he had to block it out for as long as he could. He couldn't give up on Eva, not now. He couldn't let despair cloud his judgement. He'd sacrifice himself before he'd let anything happen to her; and the position he was in, that was looking more and more the likely outcome.

'Drake ... you there, Drake? Hello? I really hope that was as good for you as it was for me,' he said, sneering at him.

'You son of a bitch! How could you? How could you do that in front of my daughter!' he spat.

'You. That's why, Drake. *You*. It makes everything worthwhile. All these years, and then you pop up again. I tell you what, Drake, it makes a change doing the mother instead. Hoo-wee! Maybe I'll do that in future,' He stood pondering in an exaggerated pose, the point of the knife under his chin, Becca's blood staining his skin.

'Hmmm ... I wouldn't worry for long about your daughter if I were you. You know what happens next. I should probably head back over to Andrea's after this... after *you*. What do you think?' Samuel said, a barely contained grin on his face while he wiped the knife on his wife's jumper.

'Don't you dare!' Drake strained against the chair and his bindings. He could have sworn he felt them give a little.

The development took his attention off Samuel for a moment.

'Drake... Hello? You're not paying attention, Drake. I get angry when people don't pay attention. You don't want me to take it out on little Eva now, do you?' He grinned. 'This effect you have on me, Drake, it's got to stop. You've already got me doing things different. Making me take my attention away from the Whitman's like that ... most unlike me, most unlike me *indeed*. I've been watching them for weeks,' he said, walking round to Eva's side of the table.

'No! Don't touch her!'

'What? Like this, you mean?' Samuel sniffed at her, running his nose up her cheek. She squealed beneath the gag and continued sobbing, her body shaking.

'What do you want, Samuel? What do you want? Name it.'

'What do I want, Drake? Why? I want nothing, not from—'

A sound came from the front door. A knock, then another.

Samuel ducked down low before moving to the kitchen door and out of sight. Eva squealed, but Drake knew better than to shout. He knew what would happen if he alerted whoever it was to their plight.

At the lack of answer, the knocking became more persistent. They must have spotted Drake's car outside.

'Hello? Drake? You there? It's Ellie.' Her voice muffled; she knocked again.

His eyes widened at the sound of his partner.

Ellie ... Shit, she must have wanted to follow up. I don't want her getting hurt.

Samuel crept over to Drake.

'Don't you make another sound, or I will gut your daughter without a second thought,' he hissed, yanking the gag back into Drake's mouth. Samuel made his way over to Eva, whispering similar threats to her, which caused her to instantly stop battling her restraints.

Drake saw the top of Ellie's head move past the kitchen window in the moonlight while Samuel continued to threaten Eva. It looked like she was checking out the perimeter of the house.

She must sense something isn't right, Drake thought. *She must.*

He realised that if Ellie were to look through the kitchen door leading to the garden, she could spot him and raise the alarm; the kitchen diner would be well illuminated in the darkness. He had to distract Samuel, raise enough of a scene for her to spot them.

Drake started squirming and rocking in his chair, causing Samuel to turn and hot foot it toward him, his knife stowed at his side. His face was one of contempt.

'What did I fucking say to you, Drake? What ... did ... I ... fuck-ing ... *say,*' he growled.

Drake shook his head in reply and grunted an appeasement. Samuel returned to Eva, who had started making a lot of noise again.

Out of the corner of his eye, he caught Ellie peering through the kitchen door. Their eyes locked for a split-second. She appeared stunned by what she saw, then vanished a split second later.

Thank God. I just need to distract him more now. But how?

Without giving it any more thought, Drake lunged with his

body weight away from Samuel and Eva, the chair teetering on two legs for a second that seemed to last forever. The next thing he knew, he was falling to the ground. A flash of pain shot through his arm and shoulder as he struck the floor.

He heard Samuel curse through gritted teeth before he turned back to him. Samuel put his hand over Drake's mouth and before Drake could react, the knife came down, stabbing his bound but splayed hand. It went straight through his palm, the point pinging off the tiled floor as the metal pierced flesh and bone.

Drake's eyes widened with shock as he bit down on his gag, the pain coursing up his arm. His vision seared white, and he cried out.

'I warned you, Drake. I warned you ... your daughter's next!' Samuel spat, eyes narrowed. 'Don't you be doing that again, you hear?'

He turned and crept around the side of the table towards Eva. She was still crying beneath her bindings. He stood and pulled back her head by her hair, exposing her neck to his knife.

At the same moment, the kitchen door burst open, the sound of splintering wood and glass ringing out as it exploded against the kitchen counter.

'Don't move! Drop the knife!' Ellie shouted at Samuel.

Samuel didn't move. He held his position, knife poised, Eva's neck exposed.

He laughed at her, an ugly grin on his face. 'Or what, Detective *Wilkinson*? What're you going to do? You don't even have a gun.'

'No, but an entire squad of armed police is on their way. I can assure you that won't end well for you,' she said, as though it was a normal conversation. She didn't flinch. 'It's up to you how you want to be leaving this house, Samuel.'

With Samuel distracted, Drake had worked his way along the

floor, so he was in line with Samuel's legs. He kicked out hard, attempting to trip him with all his strength. Samuel staggered for a second, but he didn't fall.

Amid the distraction, Ellie stormed toward him, seizing what little opportunity Drake had given her. Diving into Eva and Samuel, she drove them all to the ground in a mass of limbs.

Samuel maintained his grip on the knife, despite the fall, but had lost his grip on Eva.

Slashing wildly, he caught Drake's arm, slicing it to the bone. Drake cried out, but the adrenaline numbed some of the pain. He tried to dive on Samuel from the floor with his arms still bound behind him, a vain attempt at knocking the knife out of Samuel's hand. He only succeeded in jarring him, but it gave Ellie enough time to grab at Samuel's knife.

She missed, and he sliced her outreached hand. Ellie yelped in pain, the knife drawing blood from her palm. Amidst the melee, Eva had scrabbled away as best she could, still blindfolded and bound to her chair.

The struggle went on in a tangle of limbs. Once again, Ellie tried for the knife, this time managing to slap it from Samuel's hand. It slid away into the corner of the kitchen as Drake, bleeding profusely, made one more attempt to leap on top of him. Slamming down on Samuel with all his might, he knocked the wind out of Samuel with a pained grunt.

Drake's attack gave Ellie another opening. She scrambled over Samuel towards the knife. He grabbed desperately at her legs before getting a grip on her ankle. The resulting yank slammed her head on to the tiled floor with a teeth-rattling crack. She stopped, stunned for a moment, before continuing to struggle towards the abandoned knife.

Samuel snarled and pulled on her leg, working his way up to her waist as they thrashed. His hand grabbed at her shoulder, gaining some purchase. He used it to anchor himself again and inched himself closer. He was an arm's length from the knife, Ellie a hand's length.

She cried out in one last effort, surging for the knife and grabbing the hilt with her hand. Samuel's hand slapped feebly at her wrist before she turned and, in one sharp motion, slammed the knife down into his shoulder blade. A sickening thud sounded from the force of the knife driving in between Samuel's shoulder and ribs.

Samuel howled in pain, his back arching and spasming before he scrabbled away, the knife's hilt protruding from his back.

'You goddamn bitch!' He used the wall to pull himself upright, blood smearing on the wall. Stooped, out of breath and sweating, his skin pallid, he tried to nurse his shoulder with his hand.

Ellie scrambled to her feet on the opposite side of the kitchen, next to a countertop. Blood spattered the ground as she cradled her hand. Drake was on the floor, in a growing mass of blood from his own similar wound, his arm numb. He could hear Eva crying, still devoid of her senses, trying to make herself as small as possible on the floor.

His partner breathed heavily, taking in large gulps of air. 'You've got nowhere to go, Samuel. It's over.'

'Oh, that's nothing. I ain't going down without a fight,' he snarled, sweat pouring off him, his skin growing pale from the shock of the stabbing.

'Yes, Samuel, you are,' Miller stated, standing at the kitchen door.

She stood to one side and a swarm of armed police stormed into the room, all semi-automatics and body armour.

Samuel's eyes bulged with surprise before he made a desperate attempt to run for the door to the hallway. Drake flailed with his legs one final time, catching Samuel as he scrambled past.

Losing his footing, Samuel crashed headfirst into a kitchen counter, meeting the corner with a sickening crunch. His body went slack amidst a blooming pool of blood on the floor.

67

Ben watched Andrea head towards the horizon. She was running, hand in hand with her daughter, both in fits of laughter. They looked so happy, so at peace.

Cari waved back at him, looking radiant in the sun's warmth.

But Ben didn't feel happy. He felt something was wrong, something desperately wrong.

They were running towards a cliff edge, the sun turning blood-red on the horizon.

The clouds were blackening and swirling in a sea of violence above his family as they reached the precipice.

He screamed.

They fell.

68

Ellie stopped in front of the driveway, wincing as she pulled on the handbrake. The injury to her hand was making its presence felt. The bandage the paramedic had wrapped around her hand was tight, too tight. She couldn't help but study the injury as a patch of blood began blooming outwards on the gauze.

Shit. At this rate, I'm going to need to reapply the bandage.

Ellie tried her best to keep the memory of what had happened out of her mind. She needed to suppress it, if only for a few more minutes.

It had barely been an hour since the encounter with the Family Man. An hour since Drake's wife had been murdered in cold blood. But she felt as though she couldn't stop until she'd followed up the last strand in the damned case. And who else was going to do it? Drake was in no fit state. That poor man and his daughter were completely traumatised, but he had still insisted the Whitmans needed to be checked out. To make sure they were safe.

Ellie was convinced they were, but she still felt she needed to prove herself; she felt she'd let Drake down. She should have been with him, should have insisted she'd accompany him to his house when he got that damn call. If she'd done that, Drake's wife might still be alive.

The others were only a matter of minutes away, but Ellie decided against waiting and got out of the car. The wind was getting on her nerves, blasting her face and pulling at her coat as she walked up the path.

The Whitman house, cloaked in darkness, looked more than a little ominous.

I really hope this doesn't take long.

She knocked on the door. Not getting any response, she tried again after a few moments, then gave the handle a try.

The door opened with no resistance.

Curious.

'Hello? Your door's unlocked,' Ellie called out through the crack.

There was no answer.

'Hello?' she called once again. Still no answer.

'We're in here! Please!' A woman. The voice sounded vaguely familiar; it had to be Andrea Whitman. 'We're in the dining room!'

'Okay. I'm coming in,' she replied, opening the door into the hallway. It was dark. Why was it so dark, if there were people in the house?

She scoured the entry way walls for a light switch before finally finding one which lit the hallway. The light dispelled a little of the strange, thick atmosphere in the house, but the ominous feeling in Ellie's gut remained. Something didn't feel right. It was too quiet. Where was Andrea?

She scanned the entrance. An elaborate staircase led up into darkness, a door ajar to her left. The hairs on her arms prickled as she crept forward.

I wish I had a gun right now, she thought, an irrational feeling of exposure washing over her. But this wasn't America.

'In here!'

The call came from the right-hand side of the property.

Turning towards the doorway to the dining room, Ellie could make out three shapes sat at a table in the darkness.

Oh, my God.

Her heart pounded as she hurried to the room. It was immediately obvious, particularly from what she'd seen in the past few weeks, that the husband and daughter were no longer alive. The daughter was gagged and bound to her chair. The dad was strapped at the chest, his wounds and the surrounding area matching the Family Man's usual horrifying MO.

It really doesn't get any easier seeing this, does it?

The calls she'd heard had been coming from Andrea. She was at the head of the table, her head slumped, a mass of blood and sweat-soaked hair shrouding her face.

'Andrea, talk to me. Wake up,' Ellie said, as calmly as she could. She checked her surroundings carefully before deeming it safe to move over to her. She resisted the urge to shake her awake. The poor woman had been through enough. But Ellie wanted desperately to get a response, if only so that she wasn't alone amidst the death.

Gently, she lifted Andrea's head with her good hand. The woman's eyes remained shut, but seemed weirdly *active* beneath her eyelids. Andrea murmured to herself, but Ellie couldn't make out any of what she was saying. She didn't understand how she'd been calling out, completely lucid, but was then so completely out of it.

'Andrea ... Andrea Whitman, can you hear me?'

Ellie carefully brushed the woman's hair back from her face.

Andrea was still limp when, out of nowhere, she let out a blood-curdling scream.

Ellie jumped back, her heart leaping out of her chest. 'Holy—'

Andrea stopped screaming just as suddenly, returning to her previous state as if it had never happened.

What the actual hell was that?

'Andrea? Can you hear me?' She braced herself for another scream, but there was nothing. The woman was totally unresponsive once more.

Ellie sighed, crushed by her discovery. There would be no one else to find. The Family Man and his depraved son were in custody, having carried out one last kill. She phoned in to Miller and monitored Andrea from the doorway, deeming her in no fit state to be moved on her own. It wouldn't be long now. Police sirens were already blaring in the distance.

* * *

The arriving forces and emergency services must have come straight from Drake's house; Ellie recognised the woman who had bandaged her hand, and another ambulance crew she hadn't seen earlier.

Miller was first on the scene. Ellie left her to survey the carnage while she kept her distance in the hallway.

The wife had been unsteady on her feet as the ambulance crew led her out to the waiting van to be checked out and taken to hospital. She didn't scream again, thankfully. That was not a sound Ellie wanted to hear again in her lifetime; a mother's scream for her murdered child, her dead husband.

Ellie took a moment on the staircase to gather herself while the wind continued unabated outside, making the scene even more bleak. She felt an overwhelming feeling of dejection after the earlier elation of catching the Family Man. Yet another family had been torn apart on her watch, and they'd been so close to stopping it from happening. It could only have been a matter of hours.

She watched while the ambulance crews took the bodies out past her and into the ambulances. That poor young girl: she'd had her whole life ahead of her, and now it was gone, taken by those monsters. She'd seemed like a good kid from the little Ellie seen of her, and Ben, a caring husband and father. Andrea would have to live with what she'd seen and the deaths of her family for the rest of her life, and Drake... he'd just lost his damn *wife*. His daughter had lost her mother and now her friend, too.

The thoughts were becoming too much, images of Bella and Len bubbling up to the surface. She shook them from her mind, making her way outside. She rubbed at her face in a vain attempt to somehow scrub away the evil of the day; the taint of death was going to stay with her for a long time, that much she did know. An ambulance shot off with its lights and sirens blaring, startling her.

She heaved a sigh. Drake was right. This sort of work really *did* take its toll.

69

Drake sat on the bench in his back garden and looked out into the distance, the trees of Barndon Forest swaying in the late autumnal wind beyond. He felt as though he was hovering just above the ground, as though the previous day had been some sort of dream, and he was in the midst of some sort of lucid continuation. He was certain what had happened was all nonsense. It had to be. His wife would come out to see if he wanted a cup of tea. She'd ask how he was, and what he'd been working on, her bare feet amidst the wet autumn leaves and grass. Drake would warn her she'd catch a cold if she stayed outside too long. That she wouldn't want to be subjected to his awful attempts at cooking while she got better.

He smiled to himself at the thought.

An image of Becca's face flashed into his mind's eye, staring back at him, blood pouring from the laceration to her neck.

He shut his eyes, but it wouldn't go away.

Her eyes stared at him in perpetuity, accusing him. Burning into his mind.

You did this. It was you. I would be alive; our daughter would still have a mother if it wasn't for you. If you'd just stayed away. Left us alone.

Drake shook his head in disbelief. The hot tears trickled down his face.

He realised now what he'd done, how he'd brought about his wife's death. He hated himself for it. It was all his fault.

He broke down and sobbed, his grief absolute.

70

'Aren't you cold? Don't you want to come inside?' Ellie asked, sitting down next to him on the garden bench.

He didn't respond, letting the questions hang in the air as they looked out towards the forest.

Drake thought she looked tired, as though she'd tossed and turned all night with little in the way of actual sleep. Her bandaged hand looked out of place for a woman who was usually so stylish, the white gauze bandages a stark contrast to her dark skin.

He had gone to the bathroom and splashed his face with water when he'd known she was on her way to see him, ensuring the tears were washed away, the redness banished. But he couldn't hide that his features were even more haggard than usual, his eyes lost and distant.

Drake's hand pinged with pain, reminding him it wasn't just his partner who was injured. His hand pulsed beneath the bandage, as did the arm in a sling beneath his coat, one sleeve hanging empty to his side. The knife wound had been close to severing a tendon, according to the doctor.

He didn't care.

'How're you holding up?' he asked, his throat feeling tight.

'How am *I* holding up? What the hell, Chief? How are *you* holding up, more like? How is Eva? Should you really be staying here, all things considered?'

'She's as you'd expect. Bereft, distraught, angry – with me, mainly.'

'With you? What? Why?'

'Yes, with me... if it wasn't for *me*, Samuel would never have had a reason to be here. To do what he did. She's holding me responsible,' he said, looking out over the desolate fields opposite his house. 'If I'm being honest, I hold *me* responsible too. I should never have taken this case again. I should have listened to Becca, heeded her concerns. But no, she could see that I wanted this, and she gave me one last chance. She let me do it *for me*. And for what? She's paid for it with her life. I'll never forgive myself. *Never*,' he said, his voice catching.

'And do you know the worst thing? My heart hasn't even been in it, either. Since we went to Yorkshire, I've not felt the same – haven't been driving myself the way I once did. So, my beautiful wife gave her life for my half-hearted attempt at reconciling an old case. A case I didn't even truly want.'

Drake no longer cared what he said in front of her. She'd saved his and Eva's life. What was opening up to her going to do? Nothing would embarrass him, not now. He was too far gone to care about it, about *any* of it.

She took his hand and gave it a squeeze. 'Drake, you can't think like that. *None* of this is your doing. You didn't do those things in there. *He* did. He chose to do what he did, not you.'

'I'll agree to disagree. But thank you, Ellie.' He looked out once again at the trees, the wind catching the crumpled leaves at their feet.

Drake rubbed at his stubble before gripping his brow between his thumb and forefinger as he put forth his theory as to how it had all happened.

'Ellie, with Jonah Barrow doing what he did, then Samuel killing Alan and his son, and us closing in on him ... I think it kicked up his bloodlust. It made him reckless. We drove him into lashing out. It's my fault he came here, my fault he—'

Killed my wife.

He grimaced and swallowed hard, doing his best to keep his emotions at bay for just a little longer.

'Boss, don't think like that. You were just doing your job. What any of us would do.'

Drake didn't respond. He *couldn't* respond. Everything was becoming too much, but he needed to know. He had to ask, just this once.

'Is he alive?' Images and sounds slammed into his mind of Samuel cackling at him.

'Drake, do you really want to be talking about this?'

'Yes, I do.'

'Okay. Yes, sorry to say, he is. He's alive.' Her face scrunched up in anger. 'He had a nasty knock to the head, and I fucked up his shoulder good and proper, so he might not have use of it again – but yes, he's somehow still with us.'

'And the wife, Ann?'

'We took control of the estate soon after we got Samuel. It looks like she was in on it, too. She had a key to a ... a secret "room" of sorts.' She paused, looking like she was trying to find the right words for what she was about to describe.

'Chief, it was some sort of murder room, like a literal slaughterhouse for people. I don't even want to begin to imagine. Drake, he's been at this for years, *decades*. It looks like he simply changed his MO once Stan died, moved on from such public kills. It's sickening. There are photos, belongings from previous scenes, more videos, all catalogued ... He had small cages, chains—a damn *drain*, for God's sake.'

'Yes, he told me at the... in the...' He stumbled over his words, once again finding it hard to conjure up the previous day. 'In the kitchen, that he'd just taken to killing differently, that he'd adapted. I'd hoped it was just him exaggerating and showing off.'

'I'm sorry, Drake. It doesn't look that way. Judging by what we've found, it looks like it could be years of work, putting faces to names, contacting families ... you name it. Also, a partial print *was* found on the note from the school. It was Jonah,' she said with a shake of her head. 'He either subconsciously wanted to be caught, or he really was just a naïve little shit behind all that bravado and narcissism. That was why I came to your house – so I could tell you. I tried calling, but there was no answer.'

Drake didn't react. It was all words to him now; Samuel had ruined him. But he had to press on, if only for a while longer.

'What happened at the Whitman's? Miller's clearly hiding the details from me, sheltering me from it all as if I'm a child. Tell me.'

'Okay.' She hesitated.

It must be bad, he thought.

She sat, looking conflicted for a moment or two longer. 'I went round as soon as I could after getting my hand patched up.' She took a deep breath, as though she was weighing her words carefully, then her shoulders slumped. 'I was too late. He'd beaten us to it.'

'What? They were *dead?*'

'The father and daughter were dead from what I could see, but I found Andrea at the head of the table as the mothers always are ... *were.*' She grimaced. 'She wasn't in a fit state to talk.'

'Strange,' he said, frowning.

'Why, Boss? That's pretty standard for this case. Plus, it turned out I was wrong about her—'

'Samuel had talked as though he hadn't done that yet, as though it was something he was going to do once he... once he'd killed my family and me.'

She shrugged. 'Maybe he got confused in the heat of the moment.'

Drake shook his head. 'I don't think so. He was revelling in it, teasing me with it. Trying to show he was in control. He said he was going to get her to join him, basically. The ramblings of a madman.' He frowned and scratched at the sling on his shoulder. 'What was the scene like? Did you have to untie her? Get her up off the floor?'

'No, I didn't.'

'What do you mean? Was she still in situ?'

'She wasn't tied up. She wasn't even gagged. There was nothing to suggest she had been. No wrist marks, nothing ...' She trailed off, her mouth moving but no words coming out as a terrible realisation dawned on her.

Ellie's mouth dropped open. 'No... Drake! She couldn't have? No, it's not possible!'

'Where is she right now? We can figure this out,' Drake said firmly.

'She's at the hospital. They took her there for observation.'

'Call them. Now!'

'Okay, okay,' Ellie said, taking out her phone and dialling the number for the Oxford hospital. She got through to the staff nurse.

Drake's mind raced at the implications. Andrea couldn't have done it. Could she? How would she know how to? And why? It didn't make any sense. Eva had mentioned she had mental health issues. Could seeing that recording have triggered her, somehow? Or maybe Samuel's revelation tipped her over?

Ellie listened intently before hanging up curtly. 'Drake—'

'What? Is she okay?'

Ellie's face was slack with shock as she relayed the news. 'They just checked for me. John, she's *gone*. She's left the hospital. She didn't take her phone or any of her belongings.'

Drake's heart sank. This couldn't be happening. It wasn't possible.

He called Miller to explain the situation, pursing his lips while he waited for her to answer.

After he'd laid out his theory to his appalled boss, Miller remained silent for so long that he thought she'd hung up. When she spoke, it was to assure him she'd get in contact with the hospital and Barndon station immediately, to check for any sightings via CCTV or otherwise. He insisted she let him know as soon as she had more information; it was still his case, in spite of everything.

Following a tense wait, Drake received the update he'd been dreading. There were no sightings of Andrea after she left the hospital. The CCTV trail had gone cold. There was no trace of her. Nothing.

Andrea was gone.

THE TIES THAT BIND
DCI JOHN DRAKE BOOK 2

Available now at Amazon!

Kindle | Kindle Unlimited | Paperback

The smallest decisions can have the deadliest consequences...

His life in tatters, DCI John Drake is struggling to move past the events of *The Family Man*. But when a brutal new serial killer surfaces, he seizes the opportunity to pull himself back from the brink.

Despite her public commendation, DS Ellie Wilkinson has been sidelined into a support role. Still dealing with what she witnessed at the Whitman's house, she's determined to work with Drake again. But as their new team begins to delve deeper into this latest case, dark secrets are uncovered. And what they reveal raises the stakes for everyone involved...

Can they stop this vicious new killer? And will Drake finally confront his demons - or be consumed by them?

ALSO BY M. R. ARMITAGE
DRAKE

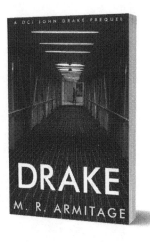

Sign up to my newsletter at www.mrarmitage.com for your free copy!

A killer has been prowling London's airports, leaving a grim trail of victims. The police are confident they've identified the culprit, but a young Detective Sergeant John Drake is adamant they've got the wrong man.

Set against the backdrop of October 1998, Drake grapples with what could be his final case with CID. Caught between orders and an unwavering need for justice, he struggles to make his theory heard. As time slips away, Drake must either unveil the true killer or more lives will be lost.

Can Drake overcome the odds and find the real killer, or will he have to stand by as more people die?

ACKNOWLEDGMENTS

I underestimated how difficult these things are to write, but I'll try my best.

Thank you, Mum and Dad. Your ongoing support has been brilliant throughout this process. Though, I have to say; I felt for the two of you, having listened to me waffle on about it whenever I came round for dinner. Your comments of 'Where the hell did that come from?' when finishing that rather nasty first draft will stay with me for a very long time!

Thank you to my draft readers who I took by surprise with my writing. The relief in all your voices after reporting back that 'it wasn't so bad after all' was encouraging, so thank you to JB, Andrew, Naz, Kit and Jon.

Margaret, your editing, dry humour and limitless patience have left me a much more confident writer.

And, finally, Rhett, thank you for your awesome designs and almost saintly patience. We got there in the end!

ABOUT THE AUTHOR

M. R. Armitage is an author hailing from Reading, England.
Surrounded by a distressing number of unread books, he hopes
one day to read them all rather than just buying more.

Visit my website:

www.mrarmitage.com

And keep in touch on Facebook:

facebook.com/MRArmitageAuthor